"RUN! LAUREL, GET OUT OF THERE!"

Laurel looked up in time to see Darren charging down the bank. What was his problem? The first trickles of cool water touched her feet.

Suddenly the water was calf deep, swirling and tugging hard at her ankles. Now she did run, splashing toward Darren. In seconds the water was knee deep. A chunk of driftwood hit her, and she went down into the water.

Taking great leaps through thigh-deep water, Darren was beside her. She grabbed his outstretched hand. The river dragged at her, and their hands began to slip.

His arm came around her waist, lifting and carrying her to shore. At the top of the bank, Darren stopped. "Are you all right?"

"Yes." Her voice was less steady than she would have liked.

Darren's arms tightened, and his mouth came down on hers. It was not a gentle kiss, but full of anger and passion. Abruptly he broke off and put her on her feet.

"Next time I tell you to move, you move!"

Laurel twisted away. "Excuse me. I would have been just fine!"

He crossed his arms and glared at her. "Just fine? I saw you go under twice."

She glared back at him until she noticed blood running down his neck.

"You're hurt!"

He reached up and touched the back of his head, looked at the blood, and shrugged. "I'm fine."

"Stop with the macho 'I'm fine' thing. Let me see."

He grinned. "By all means, ma'am." Then he got on

one knee and bowed his head. "At your service."

Laurel hissed between her teeth, partly out of irritation and partly at the gut-twisting sight of Darren's blood. She touched his head, lifting his hair. He was cut because of her.

"You've got a half-inch gash here. You need stitches."

His eyes met hers, and the look in them accomplished what even the raging river had not: Her knees went weak.

A sardonic smile tipped his lips. "I'd rather have a scar to remember you by."

PRAISE FOR KAREN RISPIN'S...

African Skies

"Karen Rispin took me to Africa with vivid description, rich dialogue, laughter, and an incredible romance. I cared. I didn't want the story to end. Watch out—this is a book that goes straight to your heart."

DEE HENDERSON, AWARD-WINNING AUTHOR

Summit

"Filled with the thrill of the outdoors, this exciting romance is one that adventure lovers won't want to miss."

ROMANTIC TIMES MAGAZINE

Rustlers

"Horse lovers will enjoy this book and its characters who have experienced some very difficult life situations. Karen Rispin flavors her story with a ranching atmosphere, and effectively builds suspense with an interesting twist."

ROMANTIC TIMES MAGAZINE

PALISADES IS A DIVISION OF MULTNOMAH PUBLISHERS, INC.

AFRICAN

SKIES

KAREN RISPIN

Multnomah®Publishers *Sisters, Oregon*

This is a work of fiction. The characters, incidents, and dialogues are products of the author's imagination and are not to be construed as real. Any resemblance to actual events or persons, living or dead, is entirely coincidental.

AFRICAN SKIES
published by Palisades,
a division of Multnomah Publishers, Inc.

© 2000 by Karen Rispin
International Standard Book Number: 1-57673-626-1

Cover illustration by Aleta Jenks
Background cover image by Tony Stone Images

Scripture quotations are from:
The Holy Bible, New International Version (NIV) © 1973, 1984 by International Bible Society, used by permission of Zondervan Publishing House
The Holy Bible, King James Version (KJV)

Palisades is a trademark of Multnomah Publishers, Inc., and is registered in the U.S. Patent and Trademark Office.

Printed in the United States of America

Library of Congress Cataloging-in-Publication Data:
Rispin, Karen, 1955-
African skies/by Karen Rispin.   p. cm.—(Palisades pure romance)
ISBN 1-57673-626-1 (pbk.)   1. African—Fiction. I. Title. II. Series.
PR9199.3.R5237 A68 2000   813'.54—dc21   00-009546

00 01 02 03 04 05—10 9 8 7 6 5 4 3 2 1 0

"If I rise on the wings of the dawn,

if I settle on the far side of the sea,

even there your hand will guide me,

your right hand will hold me fast."

PSALM 139:9–10

CURRY, CINNAMON, UNWASHED BODIES, DIESEL EXHAUST—THE rich stew of scents made Laurel's nose tingle. Sunlight poured down at double strength, flowing over her body like warm honey and flashing painfully into her eyes off the vehicles in the street. Laurel glanced at the man striding along next to her. Like everything else in this place, Darren Grant hit her senses at maximum intensity. More than six feet tall, he walked with the grace of an athlete. Wide shoulders, narrow hips, muscles moving under darkly tanned skin, he was worth a long look. If she were in the market to look.

Which she wasn't.

He turned his head and caught her studying him. His eyes were dark but gold streaked, like his hair—and the wry humor that sparked in them, as though he'd caught her doing something not quite kosher, brought heat to Laurel's face.

She nearly walked into a solid phalanx of turbaned Sikhs. Both parties dodged at the last minute, and Laurel's hip bumped a roadside stand. Two wooden carvings hit the sidewalk with a clatter, and she fell to one knee. The heat of embarrassment stung her cheeks as she bent to pick up the carvings.

Her friend, Julie, had seen her off at the airport in Calgary only yesterday, but already that seemed a lifetime ago. Julie must have sensed some of the nervousness underlying her excitement because she'd hugged her hard. "You're going to be just fine there. I wouldn't be into watching baboons all day, but if they are as much like people as you say, it should be interesting. Especially for someone who loves animals as much as you do."

"I can't believe I'm actually going!"

"God has good things for you. I know it. Look what He did for David and me. He's got somebody for you too."

Laurel had shaken her head. "It's great you and David are together, but I'm not looking for anyone; I just want peace of mind and a better idea of how God wants me to serve Him." Besides, she had yet to find a man with whom she could serve God and who shared her love of nature.

Julie had laughed and given her one last hug. "I'll be praying for you. Have fun."

Fun! So far, Kenya was more than a bit overwhelming.

"Pole, pole!" The black man keeping the stand had her by the elbow. He bent and dusted off her knee talking fast in what must have been Swahili.

"I-It's okay, r-really." Laurel backed up. What was the man saying? She looked around for help and met Darren's grin. Somehow the asymmetry of a nose that had obviously been broken only made his face more attractive. Deep dimples creased his lean cheeks, and his eyes twinkled with mischief.

Laurel couldn't help laughing with him, but then she had to jump aside to dodge the ministrations of the man from the booth. "Will you tell this man to stop dusting my knee?"

Before Darren could say anything, the man stopped. Laurel blushed when she realized the man must have understood her. With a sardonic glance at Laurel, Darren said something to the booth man in his own language. The man turned to Laurel, took her arm, and pulled her eagerly toward his wares. "Come, come! I show you excellent carvings. Most beautiful."

Laurel looked back at Darren. "What did you tell him?"

"That you'd be happy to buy one of his carvings as you are an animal lover." There was an intensity in Darren's eyes, and Laurel had the odd sense that there was something deeper—some hidden meaning perhaps—in his comment.

Before she could question Darren, though, the man from the booth was pressing a carving of a lion into her hands. As she took it, the breath caught in her throat. *I'm really in Africa. I'll be seeing real lions!* Her hands quivered on the cool, heavy hardwood. Suddenly she longed to be out of the city, out where the animals weren't made of wood but were wild and alive, out where she could watch them and learn to know them.

Darren said more incomprehensible words to the booth man, who took the lion from her and pushed an even bigger carving of a rhinoceros into her hands. Laurel blinked at the price he listed. Darren laughed, and the man quickly cut the price in half. Laurel focused on the man's threadbare clothing. He could obviously use the money. Quickly she paid up. He took her American dollars with effusive thanks.

"At least your love of animals has done one person some good." Darren reached to carry the rhinoceros for her. The thing must have weighed ten pounds.

"What is that supposed to mean?"

Darren shrugged as he tucked the carving under his elbow, as though it were a football. "You've got a lot to learn about Africa."

"I can hardly wait to get out and start." She gave a little involuntary skip, then reached for her carving. "I'll carry my own rhinoceros, thank you."

He dipped his head. "Are you sure? It's not often I get to carry a rhinoceros for a beautiful woman."

Beautiful woman? Laurel knew perfectly well that she didn't have the tall, lithe form that was in vogue. No matter how fit she was, she would always have more curves than she wanted. More than likely, the man beside her had made the comment without even thinking about it. With his looks, he'd probably had ample experience with casual flirtations. She cast a sideways glance at him and caught his quick grimace of chagrin...he almost looked startled by his own words. But he didn't turn away—instead, he kept his eyes on hers for a long, confusing moment.

Suddenly her stomach felt very odd—like she was on one of those carnival rides where the bottom drops out...

Snap out of it, Laurel. This is ridiculous. You don't even know the man, and yet you're letting him get you all flustered. She tore her eyes from his, lifted her chin, and held out her hands. Best to show him right from the start that she was impervious to his attempts at charm. "The rhinoceros, please."

He blinked and started to say something, then clamped his mouth shut and handed her the carving. With a quick movement he brushed by her and strode ahead. Laurel hesitated...had she somehow offended him? The African man laughed and made some comment from behind her. She turned to give him a silencing stare and noticed a badly overloaded minivan careen past them, people all but streaming out of the windows and hanging off the outside.

The sight jolted her—as had so many sights in the last hour—with the awareness that she was clearly out of her element. All the more reason to keep her so-called escort in her line of sight.

Her hands tightening on the wood carving, she hurried after Darren Grant.

He had picked her up at the Nairobi airport only an hour ago. Joan Doyle had hired him, or so he'd said. First he'd take Laurel to have a quick look at the city of Nairobi as he had some things to pick up. Then he'd be flying her out to the remote Ndovu Ranch where she'd be joining Doyle's ongoing scientific study of a troop of olive baboons.

Now she followed Darren into a store. As she stood waiting, she listened and watched, trying to get a feel for the city. Before now, she'd avoided travel, mostly because her mother had pushed her in that direction. But this was fun. Of course her mother would be pleased.

She shook the thought away. Pleasing Lilith had nothing to do with it. Laurel had stopped caring what her mother thought when she was about ten years old, almost fifteen years ago.

All of Laurel's life, Lilith Weaver had embarrassed her with strange clothing and an earth mother facade. She'd never been permitted to call her "Mom," only Lilith. It was against her mother's wishes that Laurel had become a Christian. Lilith had also reacted against

Laurel's drive for academic excellence, not wanting her daughter to be, as she put it, enslaved to the corrupt establishment.

Laurel's father was only a little better. She went to him in the summer, but he didn't seem to want her in the house with his new wife and smaller children. A churchgoer, he sent her to Christian camps for most of the summer. It was there she'd made her commitment to Christ, where she'd learned to find consolation and feel God's love in nature and in His creatures. A month ago when Laurel had told her mother she was going to Kenya, Lilith had stood, sweeping back the cape she often wore. "Good, maybe there's a chance that you'll get in touch with your inner self. But studying monkeys! Whatever made you choose that?"

Laurel held out her hands. "I feel God's love when I study any of His animals."

"Your God! I meant real spirituality, not some paternalistic, suppressive, male-dominant deity. Besides, baboons are disgusting!"

"They're like people, Lilith. I read about Joan Doyle's troop, and the animals are fascinating; their dramas and interactions are like a soap opera. I've always loved animals and plan to spend my life working with them. You know that! When I got a chance to go to Africa and study primates with someone of Joan Doyle's standing, it was just too good to pass up. Besides, there are more people working for the environment in Africa. Maybe I'll be able to make a real difference. I still can't believe I'm actually going. It's surprising that Joan would have accepted me on such short notice, a real privilege."

Lilith turned to pace, her cape swirling dramatically

over her long skirt. "You and your animals! Don't tell me you're serving God by caring for His creation. I don't want to hear it again. First university, and now your career, all focused on animals. At least you're traveling. How could I have spawned such a straight-laced child? It must be your father's fault. I should've never let you see him after I left him. To truly travel you have to go with the flow, live in the minute, be one with all things."

Laurel's shoulders sagged as she resigned herself to another dramatic oration. Independently wealthy, Lilith put on a show of being against materialism. Even her name was something she'd chosen for herself. At the end of the speech, Lilith spread her arms. "Go and see the world, my child. Whatever the reason, the travel can only have good results. You have my blessing." Stepping forward, Lilith had swept her into an embrace heavy with the sweet smell of marijuana.

Even that was only window dressing. Lilith rarely used the drug but had found a perfume that smelled of it. Everything with her was for effect. Sadly, Laurel had hugged her back, feeling the thin bones under the cape. Here in Kenya, across the ocean from Lilith, she couldn't be farther away from her mother than she had felt at that moment.

"Daydreaming?" Darren's voice came from right beside her. "You must be exhausted. Let's find you something to eat; maybe that will help a bit." He eyed her carefully. "We'd better go to an upscale restaurant where you'll get food you recognize."

"Instead of what?"

"Chicken tika and potato bhagia from Ahmed's place down the street."

Laurel tossed her head. "I'll take Ahmad's place."

"Good for you! Let's go."

Half an hour later they were sitting at a tiny, greasy table with exotic food before them. Laurel said a quick prayer of thanks, keeping her eyes firmly away from the roaches running along the bases of the walls. She took a determined bite of the delicately spiced chicken; it was fantastic. Suddenly she realized just how hungry she was.

"Mmm, this is good. What did you say it was?"

"Chicken tika."

She took another bite and chewed slowly, savoring the unusual flavors. She was planning to be in Kenya for six months, and she couldn't go that long without Christian fellowship. Maybe Darren could help her. It wasn't likely she'd find much fellowship out at the study site, but Joan Doyle had said they'd be going into Nairobi periodically.

"Do you know where I can find an evangelical church to attend in Nairobi?"

Darren's eyebrows shot up. "You're a Christian and working with Joan Doyle?"

"Aren't you working for her, too? You said she hired you to fly me there."

"Working for her, not with her; there is a difference. Forget I said anything. About churches, there are lots in Nairobi, but Nairobi Baptist Church is an excellent one. You'll find a lot of non-Kenyans there, people from all over the world."

Was this man a Christian? It didn't sound like he went to the church he'd just told her about. Still, it would be good to know one other child of God in this strange continent. Never one to beat around the bush, Laurel said, "So are you a Christian, too?"

Darren's eyes were sober but full of a kind of light as he nodded. "I am."

Laurel waited, watching his face. *You can't just say that much and stop.* Finally she asked, "I know you're a pilot. Are you with one of those missionary flying outfits I've heard about?"

"No." He didn't add any more.

It turned out that they were flying out of Wilson Airport, not the same airport she'd flown into earlier. Darren's plane was something called a Cessna 210. A big-bellied man was on the ramp doing something to the plane next to Darren's, but Laurel stared at the 210. With the pod underneath the fuselage it looked vaguely like a pregnant guppy. Compared to the big jets, it didn't look much bigger than a guppy either. She'd always thought she'd like to fly in a small plane, but...

"This is it?" Her voice came out higher than she intended. "I mean, it's not really all that little." She pointed at another plane parked not far off. "That one is smaller, isn't it?"

Darren was methodically weighing each box in a heap of supplies and then loading them onto the plane. He glanced in the direction she'd pointed, then back down at the boxes. The muscles in his arms bulged as he picked up a heavy crate. He moved with easy grace. A hot wind blew off the runway, lifting her hair. Laurel's question hung in the air.

Darren finished loading the gear, then circled the

plane. His lean hands touched the machine with a kind of reverence. After he'd peered at each part of the aircraft, he looked at her as if no time had passed at all. "Yeah, my 210 is bigger. The one you pointed to is a two-place 150. This one can do some real work. I gather you haven't flown in a small plane before?"

"I've wanted to, but it's so expensive, and somehow I never—" A loud sound brought her head around in time to see a plane slightly bigger than Darren's buzz down the runway and lift off. A little shiver went through her. She was in Africa, and she'd be flying in African skies. All this was actually happening to Laurel Binet.

She looked back at Darren and caught him eyeing her from head to toe, seemingly taking in every curve. The heat of a blush rushed into her cheeks. *The man's nerve!*

Seeing the look on her face, he laughed. "I was only trying to figure out how much you weigh. Not that I didn't enjoy the view. You weigh…about 120 pounds?"

"What?" Laurel's voice came out in a squeak. "You are the strangest person I have ever met."

"That may be, but I have to know your weight to load the airplane safely."

For a second Laurel wanted to hit him, and then she was laughing with him.

"Well?"

"You were almost right. I actually weigh 125 pounds. Do pilots develop an eye for a person's weight, kind of like auctioneers at a cattle market can tell the weight of an animal?"

A bray of laughter from behind her made Laurel

jump nearly out of her skin. She spun to face a large man whose racial background Laurel couldn't place. He was an even coffee and cream color all over—hair and skin matching exactly—but his eyes were gray. He slapped his thigh. "Cattle! Passengers as cattle! Darren is especially good at assessing the weight of the pretty young heifers like you."

"Thorvald." Darren's voice held a definite warning.

The man only grinned at him. "You haven't been reformed long enough to fool me. Remember, I've known you since you were a sapling, flying that saint of a father of yours from place to place. His religion sure didn't take with you for a long time." He tipped his big head to one side. "You figure it will last now that it has?"

Darren gave the man a straight look. "Yes, Thor, it will last." He turned to her. "Laurel, I'd like you to meet Thorvald Singh, an old friend of mine."

Thor stuck out a plate-sized hand and engulfed hers. "Glad to meet you. Don't mind me. Darren is quite nice once you get used to him. Good pilot, too. You're in very practiced hands."

"Thank you."

What had the man meant when he'd said Darren's father was a saint? Or that the religion didn't "take" with Darren until recently? As for that practiced hand crack, it was pretty clear that Thor had been talking about Darren's piloting skills. Just who was Darren Grant anyway?

LAUREL GOT INTO THE SEAT AND BUCKLED HERSELF IN. DARREN
handed her a bulky headset. The whole plane felt less
solid than her old Honda Civic. There was a set of controls in front of her. Fascinated, she stared at them—but
was jolted from her study when, moments later, the aircraft accelerated down the runway.

Her hands were clenched so tightly her nails dug
into her palms. This was taking much longer than in a
big jet. She glanced at Darren, but he looked relaxed, even
happy, and very much in control. Her stomach jiggled and
her ears buzzed with the vibration. Suddenly it lessened
and they were in the air.

The shadow of the plane raced alongside getting
gradually smaller along with everything else on the
ground. A road with a wide, dusty berm full of pedestri-
ans and bicycles swept under the wing. Corrugated iron
roofs winked in the sun. To one side she could see the
tall buildings of the downtown core.

Her hands, which had begun to relax, tensed again
as the plane tipped into a turn. The horizon swung, and
she laughed like a kid, surprised to find herself enjoying
a carnival ride. Darren's voice spoke in her headset,
"Great, isn't it?"

"I love it!"

Darren's eyes twinkled as he shared her excitement.
Then he turned back to the controls and pushed one of
the knobs on the panel with deliberate attention. The
engine tone changed.

She gestured out the window. "Do you ever get tired of it?"

After another second of focused attention on the panel, he looked at her. "Of the African landscape or of flying?"

"I was thinking about flying, but do you get tired of either one?"

"Nope. Africa is where I belong. So far, flying is what I do. I'm definitely tired of some other stuff, but of Africa or flying, no."

She shifted in her seat, fighting the strong urge to ask him what stuff he was talking about. She wanted to know. But that fact alone kept her silent. She wasn't here to find out about Darren Grant. And the sooner she got that into her crazy head, the better off she'd be.

Laurel wrinkled her nose and turned her attention back to the instruments in front of her.

"Why don't you try it?" Darren took his hands off the controls.

Laurel's mouth fell open. "You want me to fly this plane?"

He motioned to the controls in front of her. "Take the yoke."

"But I don't know how! You fly it."

He just shook his head and gestured again for her to take the yoke.

Her stomach tightened. This was crazy. What if she made them crash? "No. I can't."

A smile twitched at his lips. "*Someone* better fly the plane."

She reached out, then pulled her hands back, glancing at Darren. Surely he wouldn't let them crash! *Of course he won't,* an inner voice chided. *He's just giving you a chance to experience something new. Why not give it a try?* She chewed her lip. She *had* always wanted to fly a plane...

Taking a deep breath, Laurel put both hands firmly on the yoke.

Darren nodded, clearly approving. "Put your feet on the rudder pedals. The first thing I want you to do is nothing at all. Just feel how she flies herself."

"You mean it didn't matter that you let go? You scared me half to death for nothing, you turkey!"

He threw back his head and laughed, and as the joyful sound rolled around her in the small cockpit, Laurel was captivated. Darren Grant seemed more alive than anyone she'd ever met before.

Laurel couldn't hold back a smile, so contagious was his exuberance. "Okay, you got me. So are you going to teach me a little bit about flying or not?"

His smiling eyes came to rest on her. "I wouldn't keep anyone from flying who wanted to try."

She focused on his explanation of the different instruments and how the controls worked. "So, I pull back on the yoke if I want to go up. To turn, I move the yoke and push on the rudder pedal on the same side?"

He nodded. "Close enough for now. Let's see you turn to the right."

Laurel's shoulders tensed as she moved her hands. The Cessna responded. Excitement coursed through her like electricity. She was flying a plane!

"You're doing great. Straighten her up. Watch the turn and bank indicator."

The little plane tipped gracefully and came around gently. "It worked!"

"You really like this?"

She looked over to meet his eyes. The answering elation she found in his gaze surprised her, and a link, a current of what felt like intimate understanding, flashed between them. She must have shifted her hands because the plane tipped to the right. Overcorrecting, she made it dip to the left.

"Take it easy. She'll settle if you're gentle with her, firm but gentle." Darren had made no move to take over. Instead, his warm voice coached her as she began to learn to keep the Cessna flying straight and level. He let her keep on flying. With a kind of inner exultation, Laurel concentrated fiercely on staying on the right altitude and heading. Except for a strange enhancement of her senses, a kind of inner distance, fatigue from the long trip from Canada, seemed to evaporate.

Peripherally, she was aware that they were flying over dramatic terrain. There was a mountain ahead and to the left, but she was concentrating too hard to really look. Light turbulence shook the plane. The gentle buffeting made for more corrections. The back of Laurel's neck started to ache. She kept overcorrecting so the plane wandered.

"I've got the plane." Darren had been silent for so long that Laurel jumped at the sound of his voice. "Lean back and take a look around."

The controls steadied under her hands. She had a powerful impression of strength and stability, like Darren was touching her through the plane...

She started at the thought. What was *wrong* with her? She didn't know this man, wasn't all that sure she liked what she did know. Why on earth was she reacting this way to him?

Because there's something about him...something that stirs you deep inside.

She shook the suggestion away. It didn't matter. Darren Grant didn't matter. She was here to do a job.

"You did great."

"I actually flew a plane!" She turned to look out the window. "Wow." Her voice was just a breath.

"One of the most beautiful places on earth."

The intensity of his voice caught her attention. His eyes were on the mountain. His face was softer, more open than she'd ever seen it. *He shines with the way he loves this place.* She stilled an impulse to touch him. *Laurel, that's crazy!* She flushed and looked outside. Every sense she owned was wide open and the glory of the mountain poured in.

"What's it called?" The question came out hushed, almost reverent.

"Mount Kenya. The tribes who live here used to say god lived there. Want to take a closer look?"

Laurel nodded mutely. Black, jagged peaks rose out of a gleaming snowpack. The top was higher than the plane, though it was some distance away. The mountain wore a cloud like an ermine collar, soft and gleaming white at the top where it hugged the cliffs, dove gray farther down as it snuggled against deep green forest. Unlike the mountains where she'd worked in Alberta, this mountain was individual. It stood alone, its peak upthrust into the African sky—old, dark, and laden with meaning.

"God lives there." Laurel repeated Darren's phrase in a whisper. "What kind of god?"

"They would say, one that steals the breath and

freezes the very bones of anyone who comes too close. A cruel god who throws death at random and can never be completely placated. That was what god seemed to them from their experience with his mountain and from the suffering in their own lives."

Laurel shivered as she looked at the dark teeth of the two tallest peaks. *Darkest Africa.* An image of death and hopelessness in an old and alien continent suddenly filled her mind. "No! God isn't like that. It was only cold and thin air that stole their breath and froze them."

"Look at it from their point of view." The shadow of the cloud around the mountain fell across the plane. "They knew nothing of freezing temperatures or high altitude." No gold showed in his eyes. "What would you think if you saw most of your children die of famine and disease? If a woman had to birth ten children to raise three?"

Turbulence jerked the plane, shoving Laurel against her seat belt. Her mouth tightened. Darren was right. Under those circumstances God would seem random, even evil. "Is it still like that here, seven children dead out of ten?"

The plane was shuddering steadily, like a car on a washboard. Wisps of clouds whipped past. The forest looked very dark below them. "Kids still die, just not quite as many. Of course, now we've got wars, overpopulation, and AIDS. Africa is a continent of refugees, and you came to study animals."

Laurel's eyebrows shot up at the bitter edge to his comment. She shifted uneasily. "If it's so bad here, why do you stay?"

"Mostly because I was born here."

"Is that all there is to it?"

"Do you really want to know?" His eyes searched hers.

Laurel blinked. There was a vulnerability to that look that she hadn't expected. "If you want to tell me, I'd be honored."

"You heard Thor. It hasn't been this way long, but I've found God's grace again, the hope He gives in spite of all the pain. I want to spread it around a little in this beautiful mess of a continent. Nothing else, no matter how appealing, is worth the powder to blow it to you know where." As he spoke, the plane came into a shaft of sunlight, lighting the gold streaks in his hair and his intense eyes.

"Look." Darren's finger jabbed the windscreen, pointing.

Laurel turned her head to see an eagle flash past just off the left wingtip. She had a vivid impression of its fierce glance, and then it was gone. "What kind was it? It was huge!"

His smile was white against his tan face. "A crowned eagle. Did you see the crest? That's a treat. They're not common."

She stared at him, brows raised. "You make no sense at all, Darren. You talk as though it's wrong to care about animals; then you get all excited about an eagle. You even knew what kind it was."

His expression was unreadable. "I care about animals. There are choices to make, that's all. Things that are more worth doing." He glanced out the window. "Now that we're past the mountain, do you want to fly again for a bit?"

Choices to be made? What did he mean? She half opened her mouth to ask but stopped. It was none of her business. Besides, once he dropped her off, she'd probably never see the man again. Which was just fine with her.

Liar. She clenched her teeth against the inner mockery.

Darren raised an eyebrow and gestured at the yoke. "No?"

She shifted in her seat. "Yes, thank you." At least flying would change the uncomfortable direction her thoughts had been going.

Darren coached her, occasionally talking on the radio to Nairobi as he'd been doing all along. The land was changing, turning from green to reddish buff, drier, and spotted with odd flat-topped trees. Once, as she flew onward, Darren's hand came over hers as he showed her how to reduce power with the throttle.

She did her best to concentrate on what he was saying, but the feel of his warm, callused hand on hers was making it hard to breathe for some reason. Their eyes met, and Darren hesitated, startled awareness sparking in the depths of his eyes.

Laurel snatched back her hand and grabbed the yoke hard. The plane pitched upward. She swallowed and brought the nose down again. The sensation of his hand over hers stayed with her, a ghost of steady strength. She resisted an urge to rub off the feeling. *Get a grip, Laurel!*

What was it Julie had said to her that time? "If you do exactly the opposite of what someone is pushing you to do, it's still a kind of slavery." Julie had been the only friend Laurel had ever talked with about the ways Lilith had pushed her toward sex. Julie's statement had shocked her at the time. But she was right, and Laurel was reacting to Darren with the same old knee-jerk withdrawal.

Julie's words came back to her. "Even your relationship with Ian was more just an idea, wasn't it? A cold man, married to his work. You picked a safe one there." Laurel had squirmed but had to admit Julie was right about that too.

Even if I'm not looking for someone to get involved with, I shouldn't be so bound by old fears. Silently she prayed for help and wisdom.

"I'll take it now." An odd edge to Darren's voice brought Laurel abruptly back into the present. He was focused intently on something on the dash. He tapped one of the gauges, tapped it again, then looked at her.

"I'm going to land and check this out."

"Check what out?" Laurel's last word came out in a squeak as the plane suddenly nosed over into a steep decent.

"Oil pressure." He glanced at her. "Hey, don't worry. We're right over Benson James's camp." His hands and feet moved, and the plane crabbed sideways and dropped even faster. He made some quick motions, doing something to the throttle and another knob, then the engine spluttered and quit.

The silence beat at her ears. Laurel grabbed her seat belt with both hands, gripping so tightly the nylon dug into her palms. She searched Darren's face. His eyes were narrowed, intent, and focused. She clenched her teeth against the questions she wanted to blurt out. *He doesn't need distractions now!* Air poured in the vent, caressing her tense jaw.

The plane leveled out, then tipped into a turn causing Laurel's fists to close even tighter. Seconds later the wheels touched ground, and they were bumping down a dirt strip. The plane stopped, still intact.

"Thank you, Lord!"

Darren looked over and grinned. "Amen to that, always."

Quick motions outside the plane caught her eye. There were goats and a boy staring at them from under brushy brown trees. Suddenly the child turned and ran, tattered shirt flying in the breeze. Laurel unclenched her hands and rubbed one sore palm with the other thumb. Darren opened his door, and she could hear the goats bleating.

"Are you okay?"

She managed a shaky smile. "I guess I wouldn't want my first day in Africa to be boring. What made the engine quit?"

"I did. The head temperature started to climb. I wasn't going to risk an engine fire."

Engine fire! Laurel's stomach suddenly felt weak. Thank God for Darren's competence.

"I'm really sorry about this. It shouldn't have happened. Thor said he'd checked the plane over. He's an excellent mechanic." Darren glared at the oil pressure gauge.

"Hey, I'm just glad to be alive."

The sound of a vehicle engine made both of them turn. A battered khaki Land Rover pulled up beside them sending a swirl of dust over the plane. Sunlight poured through the plane's windshield. Laurel could feel a trickle of sweat starting along the edge of her hair. A pencil thin man in the same faded khaki as his Land Rover's paint leaped out, then stopped in his tracks. "Darren Grant! You! Here?"

Darren jumped down from the plane. The thin man grabbed his hand and pumped it, slapping Darren on the back. "You've come! The boy told me a plane had landed, but I didn't believe him, didn't hear you at all. Why didn't you buzz the camp, man?"

"Couldn't. We landed dead stick. Benson, this is Laurel Binet. Laurel, Benson James. His current project is studying spring hares."

Benson reached into the plane to shake her hand, but his attention stayed on Darren. "Dead stick? No engine? Good thing the strip was here then."

"Yes." Was Darren's voice wary or was she imagining things?

Laurel had gotten free of her seat belt, but opening the door was awkward with the handle almost behind her. Darren circled the plane and opened it for her. "There's a lever under the seat to move it back." He reached to do it for her.

She climbed out. Compared to the inside of the plane, the air outside felt deliciously cool as it wicked the sweat off her skin. She took a deep breath. The air smelled almost spicy, and it sang with insect voices. *Africa.*

She stepped away from the plane and stumbled on unexpectedly shaking knees. Darren reached to steady her.

"I'm okay, really."

Darren looked into her eyes, as if for confirmation. His touch and his gaze made her mouth go dry. The moment lengthened like a cat stretching. Benson cleared his throat. Laurel jumped and Darren dropped his hand.

"Can I offer either of you a ride into camp, a cold beer, or the use of my shortwave radio?"

"Thanks. I've got to find the problem first, but I'm sure Laurel could use a cool place to wait. Laurel?"

If I say I want to stay near Darren, I'll sound like an idiot. "Thank you. Is there a way to tell Joan Doyle I'll be late?"

"Joan Doyle?" Benson's arched brows spoke volumes.

"She'll be working with Joan." Darren's voice was flat.

Benson slapped his leg and guffawed. Laurel stared at him. What on earth was wrong with Joan Doyle that Darren and this man should react as they had to the news? He caught her gaze and shook his head still chuckling. "Don't worry, nothing to do with you or Joan. She's a great old girl."

If not me or Joan, Darren then? Before she could ask Benson, though, he turned to Darren, suddenly business-like.

The men talked about radios and who they could contact with a cell phone to call Joan's cell. As she listened, a sudden wave of fatigue assaulted Laurel, nearly bringing her to her knees. She climbed into the Land Rover and leaned her head back. *It's just jet lag and the comedown from adrenaline.* But still, it pulled her under like a heavy drug. Maybe there hadn't really been any tension between these men after all. She was probably just so tired she was imagining things.

Benson got in a few seconds later.

"Darren said you just got in from Canada. Come and have a cool drink. It'll make you feel better. What is it, 4 A.M. or some such back there?"

She looked at her watch. "Five in the morning. I've been up for twenty-three hours."

"You didn't realize that until just this minute?"

"I guess with all the excitement, a new city, flying a small plane, dealing with Darren—" She tried to stop them, but the words were already out.

Benson raised an eyebrow, but other than that, didn't react to her comment. She folded her hands tightly and looked out the window. Thorns, sky, golden dusty ground flickered past in a blur.

In camp, Laurel's eyes kept going out of focus as she tried to drink the sticky sweet orange stuff Benson had offered when she'd refused beer. Squash, he'd called it. Her ears seemed to be full of clay. Benson was saying something. With a great effort she focused on his words.

"Would you like somewhere to have a little lie down? You're swaying in your chair."

"I'm sorry, but yes, please."

He showed her to a tent, apologizing for the clutter. All that she could see was the camp cot. A flat place to lie down.

"I'll just go and see how Darren is doing." He chuckled. "Maybe having you around will take a little of the starch out of his stiff neck."

Laurel sank onto the cot. Benson had gone. *Stiff neck?* What was he talking about? She stared blearily around the unfamiliar space. Sleep pulled on her, weighing her eyelids down. *God, I'm way out of my depth. Hold me*. It was all the prayer she could manage.

As she fell toward sleep, images of Darren's eyes, sunlit and then shadowed, the feel of his hand—flowed though her. She turned uneasily, but the dreams dragged her in as though she were drowning.

Darren looked past the open cowling to see the Land Rover coming back onto the airstrip. He took a deep breath, then stood wiping his hands on a bit of rag. Once Benson James had been a good friend, but now...

The man climbed out of the vehicle alone. Darren stopped wiping his hands. "Where's Laurel?"

Benson grunted, his arms crossed. "She's out cold. Was half asleep on her feet by the time I got her to camp. Sleeping like a baby on the spare camp cot. Did you find the problem yet?"

His hands moved again inside the engine. "A hose cracked."

"That what this mess is from?" Benson ran a stiff finger through the greasy streaks behind the cowling. "You have to radio for parts?"

Darren shook his head. "Should be able to jury-rig it to get me back. I've got oil."

"And Laurel?" Benson paced stiffly, like a dog with its hackles up.

"We're only a twenty-minute hop from Ndovu. I'll drop her off." *Maybe if I go back to work, he'll calm down.* Darren turned back to the engine and contorted himself to get at the far end of the hose with a wrench. He'd have to take it out so he could get it clean and try to make a temporary patch.

Benson stopped just behind him. "So how's the religion coming?"

Darren turned the wrench and spoke without looking up. "I don't want to fight with you, Benson. Last time I came, you told me to stay away until I'd changed my mind. I'm not going to do that. This stop wasn't planned."

He could hear Benson taking quick, agitated steps, his boots crunching in the sand. "Not so long ago, whenever you weren't flying, you were in the bush, working with me, with other animal behaviorists, or just walking alone through the wild land. You know the land as well as anyone alive. How can you walk away like this?"

"I still spend time in the bush."

"Yes, but it's people, people, people all the time. Famine relief, schools, but mostly church garbage. What is it? Nature poison to you all of a sudden?"

Darren twisted the wrench, banged his knuckles, and just managed to bite off a foul word. He straightened. "I'm not out to offend you."

"I just don't get it."

"Do you really want to listen to an explanation now?"

Benson took two steps, stopped, and turned. "Last time, I thought you'd be back in no time, that nature would draw you back."

"I wanted something I could give myself to, something that was worth living for. But nature wasn't it."

"It is worth living for!" Benson crossed his arms, glaring.

"For me it was a trap, a distraction from what's really important. If people are hurting, I can't, and should not, spend my energy on animals."

"Listen, man, you've got to lighten up. So you tried to make nature replace this God of yours. Get over it. Can't you still help out with the conservation stuff and just enjoy life? I know you love the bush."

"I do, and that's exactly the problem. I can't let it lure me away from the important things God's called me to do."

Benson snorted. "Huh! Important things. We have to talk about that."

"I'll listen, but you're not going to change my mind." Darren turned still holding the wrench. "Don't you have work to do? How about we talk later."

"Right. It's close to evening. You've got to finish this in the light, and I'll be out doing data collection. Studying nocturnal animals messes up one's sleep patterns. If you're willing to put up with talking around two in the morning, I'll listen. Anything that can keep you away from wildlife has to be powerful."

"I'll be there."

Benson hesitated, halfway into the Land Rover, and looked at Darren over his shoulder. "I saw the way you and this Laurel bird were looking at each other. Maybe she'll soften you up a bit."

Darren shook his head, but Benson only laughed, slammed the door, and was gone.

3

LAUREL OPENED HER EYES TO FIRELIGHT FLICKERING ON CANVAS walls. Her belt had twisted and was digging into her hip. *I've been sleeping in my clothes? Right. I'm in Africa, and the plane broke down.* She could hear Darren's voice. She looked at her watch in the dim light. Twenty after two? *No, that's the time at home.* Her head hurt and her throat ached, dry with thirst. *Two in the afternoon at home. Go east, so add what, ten hours?* It had to be after midnight here, but the men were still up talking.

She sat up…and groaned. She was stiff, and her mouth tasted as if the Russian army had marched through in bare feet. She touched her head. Her short, dark hair was sticking up in every direction. *And my brush is in the plane.*

Fragments of conversation drifted to her. "It's a choice of who eats. Look, if a sick animal and a sick child were in your care, and you could only save one of them, which would you choose?"

Laurel stopped moving. That had been Darren's voice. There was a long pause. *The child, of course.* Laurel mouthed the words silently. Thank God, she'd never been in that situation.

Benson's voice echoed her answer. "The child, but the issue is rarely so clear cut. Especially when you look at it on a large scale. Things aren't so black and white."

"Aren't they?" Darren sounded so sad.

Laurel ducked through the tent door. Both men looked in her direction. Darren got to his feet. Firelight played over the strong planes of his face. "Feeling better?" He had on a battered bush hat that threw his eyes into shadow. The beautifully molded line of his top lip caught the light as it curved into a warm smile.

And I look like something the cat dragged in. Laurel checked the impulse to back into the shadow. Instead she lifted her chin. "I'd feel a lot better after a big drink of water, a shower, and some clean clothes, but I slept well." She turned to Benson. "Hope I didn't keep you up."

"Darren and I had some things to discuss."

Darren turned his head sharply toward Benson.

Benson's left eyebrow went up, and he grinned at Darren, flashing teeth in the dim light. "I can even offer her a shower if she doesn't mind lukewarm water."

Laurel shook her head. "I know it's the middle of the night here and—"

"No problem."

"You might want to see the shower first, if it's what I think it is," Darren cut in.

"At this point I don't care. I'd cut a hole in the ice to get clean."

Darren laughed and held out his hand to Benson. "If you'll give me your keys, I'll go bring Laurel's bags from the plane."

"Just the backpack," Laurel called after him. What had she gotten herself into now?

He was back in minutes, putting her pack into the tent. Laurel dug out the things she needed and came back to the men. "Okay, where do I find this shower?"

"You show her, Darren. It's down that path." Benson grinned and tipped his chin toward a gap in the bush.

Darren picked up a flashlight and something else and headed away from the fire. Laurel followed. "There." He shone the light on a dark canvas water bag hung in a tree with a showerhead attached at the bottom. It was completely out in the open.

"That's it?"

He tipped his head, smiling. "Look, you don't have to do this."

"You guys will stay by the fire, right?"

"Will do. I'll leave you the flashlight, but I wouldn't use it while you're showering."

She laughed as she suddenly realized how visible that would make her, a wet and shining white beacon in the night. "Right."

"Here, you might want these." He dropped some huge black sandals on the ground. "They'll keep your feet out of the sand. Have fun." His teeth flashed in the dim light and he was gone.

Alone, she was suddenly aware of the night around her. *Snakes? Scorpions? What else moves in the night?* She shivered, then touched her dirty hair and set her jaw. Carefully she laid out her clean clothes on a handy thorn branch. Towel, shampoo, brush. She shone the light on the showerhead. *Okay, I just pull that little lever down....* She turned off the flashlight.

A half-moon painted the sand pale silver. Black, jagged shadows mottled the ground. She could hear the men talking in the distance. An animal called out, a deep eerie whoop. Laurel froze with her half-unbuttoned shirt clutched to her. *A hyena, you've heard them on videos. They're not generally dangerous to people.* She swallowed hard. *Okay, God, help me with this. You brought me to Africa*

*and gave me a chance to come and work where Your creation
is under a lot of stress. Help me to learn fast and make a real
difference for You here.*

As she prayed for help, the verse from Philippians
came to her. "Whatever is beautiful…think on those
things." She stood still and looked at the moon, and
gradually her fear faded. This, too, was God's work. She
stepped out of her clothes and stood under the African
sky. Little eddies in the air played over her body.

This is weird. She pulled the lever and cool water
sluiced over her skin. It was one of the fastest showers
she'd ever taken. She hit a hitch when she tried to dress.
Her feet were caked with sand. *I forgot the sandals!*
Balancing on one foot then the other, she managed to get
most of it off, but she still had some up the inside of the
jeans she pulled on.

With the security of clothing on her body, she stood
and looked around. She shook her head hard to make
her hair fall in place, then stretched. The stars looked
close enough to touch. She took a slow, deep breath.
Even the air smelled wild. Laurel held her hands out
wide, palms up to the star-studded sky. *I'm in Africa!* The
animals were here waiting for her…God's beautiful
earth…His creatures. *Let me learn to serve You with joy in
this place.*

A hyena whooped again. This time she only jumped
a little. *It isn't dangerous.* Still, she hurried to pick up her
things. Until she knew more, she'd definitely feel better
appreciating the hyena's song in the firelight with people.
With Darren.

For once she didn't resist the thought. It was true,
she felt safer when he was around. "Nothing wrong with

that," she muttered as she headed back to the fire. "It's not like I'm looking for any kind of romantic involvement. He's becoming a friend. Nothing more."

Benson was not in sight, but Darren was there. Laurel's tension eased at the sight of his solid profile. He sat with his back firmly facing the shower. He must have heard her, but he didn't turn around. "All okay?"

"Just great. I've never had a shower quite like it."

"I bet." He did turn now. "Benson has gone to get some of his stuff out of the tent. He and I will doss down out here."

"Hey, you guys can have the tent. I had a good sleep already."

Benson stuck his head out of the tent. "You sure about that, lady?"

She glanced at her watch. "It's three in the afternoon at home, and I just slept almost eight hours. I don't mind some time to sit by the fire."

"I'll hit the sack then. Darren, there's an extra bedroll here. I'm putting it over by the door."

"Thanks. I'll be there in a bit."

Benson laughed. "Take your time, mate."

Laurel shifted on the hard log, uncomfortable with the innuendo. "You don't have to stay up to keep me company. Just show me where to find drinking water and I'll be fine."

Darren got up and poured her a glass of water. "It's been boiled and filtered, but you'll find it has a bit of a taste to it. I can put squash in it."

"That sticky orange stuff? I'll risk the water."

He smiled, a flash of eyes and white teeth, and handed her the glass. She felt his nearness in more than the physical sense; it was as though the essence of the man reached out to her, comforted her. She smiled at him. "Thanks."

He nodded, then sat down. "Most women wouldn't want to be alone in the night here."

"I guess I'm not most women." She paused. "Actually, I did hurry a bit when that hyena howled. It was a hyena, wasn't it?"

Laughter sparkled in his eyes as he nodded and leaned back, stretching his long legs toward the fire, his hat moving down over his eyes. The wood flamed red and orange. Laurel sipped the water and wrinkled her nose at the sulphur taste, then slowly finished it. A log popped, then hissed, shooting out a blue tongue of flame. She could see Darren's shirt move when he breathed. *I could ask him about the plane, but it's too peaceful to talk.* She leaned back and watched the sparks rise until they joined the stars. Looping toward the firelight, a moth just missed immolation.

Laurel picked up a stick and lazily stirred the fire. She glanced at Darren. Was he asleep? His eyes were completely hidden by the hat brim now. Flickering firelight moved over the corded muscles of his forearms where they crossed over his chest. Something not far away coughed, making a two-tone whistle. Laurel tensed. *Leopards cough!*

"Zebra. Down by the water," Darren spoke the reassurance without moving.

He has a lovely voice, warm, kind of a melodic baritone, and his accent isn't quite plain American; there's something else mixed in. Laurel sighed and stretched out one leg.

Darren turned his head and smiled. "If you ever

camp out here, stay back from open water. That is, if you don't want a parade through your bedroom. Benson has it about right. Water is close enough to fetch quickly in the Land Rover, yet far enough to avoid warthogs in the tent ropes, and we're off the game trails."

"I'll remember that." There was a repeat of the noise and little thuds in that direction. *Do I really want to sit here without Darren to interpret the noises?*

"Listen, Laurel, you should probably try to sleep now whether you feel like it or not. It's five hours till dawn."

"You go ahead. Besides, Benson is sleeping. I'll be fine." *I hope.*

Darren stood and went into the tent. Laurel crossed her arms, suddenly feeling cold. He hadn't even said good-night. The tent door moved, and he came out carrying what looked like a roll of canvas with metal sticks poking out the end. This he put by the fire. *He's going to sleep here?* But he was walking to the Land Rover. He pulled out another similar roll and dumped it on the other side of the fire. "This is mine from the plane. That's Benson's."

The knot in her chest relaxed. She wouldn't be alone. *He really is sweet.*

Darren had unrolled the one from the tent and was inserting the legs. He flipped it upright and stuck his fist though a tear in the canvas. "I'll use this one."

"No, you're the one that has to fly."

He looked up with a quick grin. "Want to fight for it?"

That grin! Did he have any idea the devastating way it worked on her? She sincerely hoped not. "No, you'd win. And I think you win at too many things already. At least I can put the other one together." She wrestled with it. "Camping back home, I just used a thermarest."

"More cold, fewer creepy crawlies." He knelt beside her. "Here, I'll show you." His shoulder was close beside her as he put the thing together in seconds. "You should really have a mosquito net."

"We have mosquitoes at home, too, far more than are here tonight. I haven't died of them yet." He was way too close. Firelight touched the angle of his cheek.

He looked at her. "Right, but here you just might."

"What?"

"You are on malaria medicine?"

"Oh, that. Yes. Then a net shouldn't matter."

"Look, if Jane Doyle offers you one, use it, okay? There's increasingly resistant malaria around. For now, cover up completely with the blanket I'll give you." She could feel the warmth of his body through the small space between them. He touched her gently on the tip of the nose and stood. "I'll just get the blanket."

"Right, thanks." Her voice sounded odd even to her. Almost hypnotized, she took a deep breath. *Julie's maxim or not, enough is enough.*

Darren tossed a light wool blanket to her. "G'night."

"Good night."

He lay down and efficiently rolled himself into another blanket, head and all. With the curve of his back toward her, he seemed instantly asleep. No mosquito was going to get into that roll.

Laurel held the blanket up to her face. *Yep, you can breathe through it.* She jerked it away from her face. It smelled disturbingly of Darren. She looked at him again. He looked like a mummy, a very nicely made mummy.

Obviously he was an old hand at this. *Well if that's the way it's done.* She tried to do as he had, but rolling up into a blanket obviously took practice. She almost fell off the cot twice before she gave up and simply covered herself. A second later she pulled the blanket off her face. Hours of smelling Darren's warm scent was worse torture than any mosquito could offer, malarial or not.

For a long time she lay listening to the fire crackle. She heard the zebra again and the hyena. Once there was a snort and thump very close. She stiffened, but the sound was not repeated and Darren's steady breathing didn't change.

Laurel watched the stars move slowly overhead. The earth pressed upward, holding her, a tiny speck on its broad, rolling surface. "God, creator God, can You hear me?" The whisper floated into the night and was gone. "I'm here, in Kenya, on the east side of Africa." Something flickered across the stars. A moth? A bat? "Show me what to do here. How to live in this place." Laurel bit her lip. "Also with," she'd almost said Darren Grant, but she hesitated and changed it to "men." *Being a nun would be so much easier, just God and me.*

The moon slid behind the horizon. Only a dull red light came from the embers of the fire now. She thought about getting up to throw more wood on the fire. *What if there is a scorpion or something I can't see?* Laurel stayed put and focused again on Darren's steady breathing.

Clear, bubbling bird song woke her. She opened her eyes to the light of early dawn. Turning she looked across the fire, gray embers now. Darren was still wrapped up in his cocoon. Laurel shivered, sat up, and shoved her feet into her hiking boots, then moved to the fire. Africa was supposed to be hot, but the dry predawn air made her wish for a jacket. She poked around for coals hot enough to start a flame. Full light came so fast that she was reminded of seeing the old Disney classic, *Babes in the Woods*. The backdrop had switched from night to day like pulling a window blind.

Forgetting the fire, Laurel stood to greet the sun. As it flushed the sand and thorn brush from gray to red gold, she smiled and opened her arms.

"Beautiful morning, isn't it?"

She dropped her arms and spun around. "You're awake. I didn't..."

He sat up, smiling. "Actually, dawn is my favorite time of day. I can sure see why the ancients used to worship the sun." His expression clouded. "It's so easy to get distracted from God."

Laurel frowned. "Not by something like this." She made a wide sweep with her arm. The east had already flushed from pearl pink to clear blue. "This just shows God's glory."

She expected him to say something, to explain his odd comment, but he didn't. He just shrugged. "Listen, since you're up, do you mind having breakfast at Ndovu?"

"You got the plane fixed then?"

"Patched good enough to get you to Ndovu and me back to Nairobi. But I would like to get going so I can get it fixed. I've got a charter booked for this afternoon."

"It's fine with me."

"Thanks." Darren stood and stretched. "Excuse me a minute." He headed off in the direction of the facilities, such as they were.

She turned to try to take her bed apart. It seemed like he'd been saying the sunrise distracted him from God. *I must have misunderstood.* She shrugged, rolled up the blanket, and put it in the Land Rover.

Benson showed no signs of emerging as they cleaned up.

"D'you mind walking to the plane? It's not far. That way we won't have to bother him."

"I'd enjoy it."

"I'll just leave Benson a note." He pulled a sheet of paper out of a battered notebook.

"Say thanks for me too."

"Will do." He propped the note where it would be seen.

Laurel watched him move, graceful and efficient. *Should I ask about that comment on the sunrise?* He picked up his cot and blankets, once again in a compact roll, and reached for her pack.

She dodged his assistance and slung it over her own shoulders. "Thanks for the thought, but I'm pretty used to carrying my own pack."

He smiled. "I can tell."

She watched as he did a quick once-over of the area where they'd slept. "You camp a lot, don't you?"

"Used to." He set out down the path.

"Your plane used to break down more?" She picked her way through the brush as she followed him.

He glanced at her and flashed a grin. "Actually, it's since I got this plane that I quit camping so much."

Laurel shook her head. If there was one thing Darren Grant seemed to excel at, it was confusing her. "I'm sorry; that doesn't make sense."

"Actually, not camping as much makes a lot of sense to me."

She halted at that, arms crossed in front of her. "What *are* you talking about?"

He didn't answer for several strides, then turned and stopped. "I've changed gods. Gone from Gaea to Yahweh." Her complete confusion must have been evident on her features because he came back toward her a couple of steps. "It's really not that hard to understand, Laurel. I just needed to focus on God's priorities, not my own. And I figure healing hurting people is more important to God than camping and soaking up nature. How's that?" His tone was teasing, but his eyes were sober.

She raised an eyebrow. "Not much better."

"If you're interested enough, work it out." He started to turn to go but stopped again to face her. "You know, you confuse me too. It's like you're paying lip service to God while still serving at the mother's table."

"At the...what?"

"Mmm." In spite of the sun, his eyes seemed shadowed, sad. He turned abruptly and walked onward.

Laurel stared at his back as she tried to work out what he'd meant. *Gaea?* She'd heard of the Gaea theory, that the earth itself was an organism. As a scientific theory it was interesting. The earth did cycle nutrients, carbon, water, and energy. Damage in any one spot affected the rest. But that couldn't be it.

The mother's table...wait a minute!

Her eyebrows shot up. Gaea was the name of a pagan goddess, Mother Earth. Alarm swept through her. Was Darren saying he'd worshiped the earth and nature *instead* of God? And that because she was studying animals, she…

Outrage swept through her that he would think such a thing. Laurel shifted her pack and hurried after him. By the time she caught up, he was at the plane, walking around it in that same methodical way he had back in Nairobi.

Nairobi. Was it only a day ago that she'd been there? It seemed half a lifetime ago. Laurel stood and watched Darren. It wasn't hard to see that he didn't want to be interrupted, but still, what he'd said irked her.

So what? So what if he thinks that of you? You don't have to defend yourself to this man.

True enough. And yet…

It bothered her. She was honest enough to admit that. She didn't like the idea that he thought she worshiped anything but the Father.

Darren opened the cowling and spent a long time checking inside. Finally he nodded to her, picked up her pack, stowed it, and then opened her door. As he helped her in, she thought he was going to say something. He hesitated, then shook his head and strode to his side of the plane.

Once in the plane, all thoughts of Gaea and Darren's opinion of her fled. *Just let the plane run safely, please, Lord.* Darren was totally focused, tipping his head to listen to the engine sound. Takeoff was quick, and then he was talking on the radio. Laurel found that she'd clenched her hands together tightly.

It seemed only minutes later that the plane started down again. *More engine trouble?* Eyes wide, Laurel searched Darren's face. He caught her look. "We're approaching Ndovu."

Her breath came out in a gasp of relief.

Ahead, a strip of bare dirt appeared at the end of a track. Darren brought the Cessna down gently. He switched off the engine and looked at her. The sudden silence was broken only by clicking sounds as the engine cooled.

They sat there, both of them, in stilled silence. Laurel had the feeling they were waiting for something...but what?

Just as she decided to break the moment and open her door, Darren slanted a look at her. "Listen, I probably shouldn't have said what I did about you and Gaea." His warm, brown eyes held hers.

"What I do, I do to serve God, Darren."

"Mmm." He pulled off his headset.

When she held her silence, he shrugged slightly. "Maybe it's just that you haven't seen."

Seen what? Was there something here that could shake her whole system of beliefs?

"Here comes Ibrahim now. He must have heard us land. He'll take you up to Joan's compound." An old, beat-up Jeep had just come onto the far end of the runway. Darren put his hand on hers. "I have to go, but if you get lonely, ask Ibrahim to get you into contact with Jede and Isaac. They're good people, believers. I think he'd do that, unless things are worse than they were."

What things? Suddenly she didn't want him to go. The night had seemed so much safer with him nearby, and he was a Christian. She bit her lip. At least there would be the animals. She'd come to find a way to serve God here, and she'd better get started. A few minutes later, Laurel stared after Darren's plane as it receded into the deep blue sky.

"Memsahib Binet?"

She turned to meet Ibrahim. His handshake had been an education in itself. The man's hand was as hard as iron, but the contact had been gentle, his movements so graceful as to seem almost effeminate. Now he was gesturing toward the battered Land Rover with the same grace.

"Darren Grant will return at the correct time, but we must go to Joan now." Ibrahim's English was clear but stilted. She had an urge to repeat the words to try to capture his delightful accent. He'd spoken Joan's name with a significant emphasis that gave her great importance, as if the woman were the end of a pilgrimage. Laurel smiled; certainly she had come on a pilgrimage halfway around the world.

I'm going to see, learn, and work with a whole new part of God's creation.

She climbed into the Jeep.

As they drove off the runway and onto a rough track, Laurel looked over her shoulder at the white speck that was Darren's plane. "Ibrahim, you said that Darren would return at the correct time. What did you mean?"

"He is the one which brings food and such."

"How often?"

Ibrahim glanced at her, frowning. "As I have said. He arrives at the proper time."

Whatever that means. Working here was going to be interesting if she couldn't understand people even when they spoke English. She settled into her seat, staring ahead of her, doing her best to still the apprehension that fought to come to the surface.

She was here for a reason. If she was to be of any use, she'd better start learning. Given the way Darren Grant thought about nature, he wasn't going to be of any help, no matter how often he turned up. She glanced up at the sky again, then crossed her arms and focused on her surroundings.

4

"So how was the pretty little heifer? Did she feel as sleek as she looked?"

Darren eyed Thorvald Singh's grin as he got out of his plane. "Stuff it, Thor."

Thor shrugged. "Okay, okay. So why else did you come back in the early morning instead of last night?"

"A hose cracked. Had to jury-rig it. Have you got one I can buy?"

"Got something that will work anyway. It went after you left the girl then?"

"No."

"Aaah, then I was right." Thor chuckled deep in his throat. "She was sleek as a little impala doe, that one. Enough to lure any man off the wagon."

"You were not right." Darren pulled the wheel chocks out of the cockpit. "We landed at Benson James's camp and spent a perfectly innocent night."

Thor frowned and looked hard at Darren. "You're telling the truth?"

Darren stood from placing the chocks. "Yep."

"Darren Grant, the godly monk." Thor shook his head. "Who would have believed it? Or maybe you'll marry and become the papa with a beard and a Bible."

Darren grinned at the image. "I doubt it. If I ever do get serious about a woman, it will be with someone who can work with me here, and I don't mean with animals." He tied down one wing of the 210 with quick, impatient movements as if he could tie down his own mind in the same way.

Thor gave a belly laugh. "Grant and Grant Charter Company, a true African mom-and-pop outfit." The big man put down his screwdriver, turned, and crossed his arms. "You and me are misfits, Grant. Belonging nowhere. We were born here. We're even citizens, and don't wish to be anywhere else. But we're the wrong color and have none of the political ties that come with being tribe, clan, and kin, to people in power. In short, we're not all that welcome. To stay in Africa, we need to dance with the devil, and I think you have forgotten how to dance."

Darren shoved a rope through the loop under the plane's other wing, threaded it through the tie-down anchor, and yanked hard.

"Careful, you'll break the rope. Yanking on the plane isn't going to fix anything. Spiro called, says he has a job for you. He says this one is clean enough for any saint."

"Would you believe him?" Darren walked back to the cockpit.

Thor followed him. "Not if he wanted something from me. But what's the difference? He will pay you well. Look, boy, for years you flew anything anywhere for anyone who would hire you—munitions, contraband, famine supplies. You partied like a man with something to prove and flew the same way." He tipped his head. "You are how old now, twenty-seven, twenty-six? It is good that you calm down a little, but this religious pose, it is ridiculous."

Darren hauled his battered backpack out of the plane. "I was running, Thor."

"And now God has caught you? So what will He do with you? Make you starve trying to find work for this little thing?" Thor banged the side of the 210 with his fist. "You could be making real money flying multiengine aircraft."

Darren swung the pack over one shoulder. *Money? What was that compared to trying to make a difference for God? Not that he'd made any huge impact yet. But at least he wasn't wasting his time enjoying himself watching animals in the bush, or just flying for the sake of flying.* "Look, Thor, I want there to be more to life for me than making money or a name for myself. You have the name and the money when you want it. Is your life full?"

"I am an artist!" Thor pointed the screwdriver in his hand at Darren emphasizing his words with quick jabs. "My medium is aircraft repair, and I am known all over Africa. I work where I want, not for money, but because I choose."

"I know, and is that enough?"

"I helped you, got you work when you had nothing, and you give me this lip?" Thor's gray eyes narrowed.

Darren stood his ground. "You did help me, and I thank you. I value your friendship, so I'm asking you. Not to belittle you, but to offer you something of great value."

Thor let the hand with the screwdriver fall. "I'll go and get you that hose."

Darren watched him go and said a silent prayer for his friend. He turned to open the cowling. *Maybe Thor's right. What if I can't survive as a businessman here if I don't dance with the devil?* Heat off the hot metal made the air quiver. The engine was too hot to work on yet. Darren folded his arms. *What I'm doing now just doesn't cut it, financially or spiritually. Flying small charter for people like Joan Doyle.* He snorted and went to get his tools.

I'm a sanctimonious fool. What's the difference between working for Doyle or with her? He set his jaw. Still, he wasn't about to waste his life with that kind of thing all the time. Not like Laurel.

The image of her face floated in his mind's eye, and he saw again the way her eyes sparked with excitement as she took in this new world around her. She was so full of determination, so full of passion...so sure she was serving God in what she did.

Are you so sure she's not?

He shook his head at the inner question. Of course he was. Laurel's ideals were pie in the sky. How could she spend all that time, that energy, on animals when there were so many people hurting...sick...dying. *Maybe she's never seen real human suffering.*

Well, she'd see it now. It was pretty obvious around Ndovu.

He hesitated, then silently prayed for her and for Jede and Isaac. Those two were right in the thick of it, bringing God's hope to people who needed it badly. At least he could pray for them and help when he got the chance.

At that moment, Laurel was bouncing through the bush on Ndovu Ranch in Joan Doyle's Jeep. Dry grass crunched under the tires, and the air was full of the dusty scent of the savanna. Laurel closed her eyes, savoring the smell. It was almost spicy. She wished she had more time to absorb it all, but Joan had made it abundantly clear they were in a hurry.

The woman had barely let Laurel put her suitcases in the small, round, mud-brick cabin where she was to stay before they'd headed out in the Jeep with Ibrahim driving.

"Thomson's gazelles." Joan gestured toward some animals.

Laurel caught her breath. Little golden gazelles with neat black bands on their sides bounded off the track.

Scanning the grass, Laurel saw dark bushes in the middle distance, then one raised a long, snakelike neck. *Ostriches!* She was still staring at them when Joan grunted. "That old bull giraffe is looking better."

"Where?" Laurel spun around. The animal was on the opposite side of the track, not twenty yards from the Jeep. "Ohhhh, he's floating."

Joan laughed. "Their gait does look like that." She said something sharp to Ibrahim. He stopped the Jeep, sending dust swirling over them.

"We walk from here." Joan reached for a knapsack. "Ibrahim will pick us up when I radio at dusk." Almost a full head taller than Laurel, the older woman's lean frame looked as hard as driftwood as she strode ahead. A fly landed on Laurel's face. She swatted at it. Others buzzed around her ears. Flapping her hands, Laurel hurried after Joan, who didn't even seem to notice the bugs hovering around her.

How can she let them just land on her?

A vivid flash of bird wings, iridescent blue and purple, jerked Laurel to a stop. "Wow, what was that?"

"A roller. They can be quite startlingly beautiful, but

we aren't here to watch birds." Joan motioned impatiently for Laurel to keep walking. "Working here you'll have to make a deliberate effort to keep your mind on the Kopje troop. There is always other wildlife around, and it's very easy to get distracted."

Joan strode on still talking. "This area has lost most of the larger predators, though there are leopards around. It's an impoverished sample of African savanna and under tremendous pressure."

"But it's still beautiful."

"Yes, of course."

Laurel couldn't help but wonder if the woman was as brusque as her words. She almost sounded angry...as though Laurel's observation had irritated her.

Joan went on. "I'll introduce you to the troop. Your first job is to recognize each of the animals and gain acceptance. I'm rather in a hurry for you to start observing in the next couple of days."

Laurel's mouth fell open. The woman had to be kidding. From what she'd read in Joan's published research, there were almost fifty animals in the baboon troop. How could she learn to recognize so many animals so fast? "Won't I be working with other graduate assistants?"

"No. Due to unfortunate circumstances, you are my only academically qualified assistant at the moment." Joan stopped and the look she directed at Laurel seemed to hold some kind of challenge, as though she were daring Laurel to argue with her. Joan's face could have been beautiful—she had the kind of bone structure models dreamed of. But there was something pinched about her, something hard and sharp that overpowered any real beauty.

Laurel merely nodded. From the look on Joan's face this was not the right time for probing questions. What on earth had happened to the others? Joan had taught at UCLA for part of the year and should have had several graduate students.

The woman had started talking again. "I'm going to try for the first time to carry the study right through the rains. Until now, I've left because the area becomes completely inaccessible and because I had teaching responsibilities. You do know how to ride a horse, don't you?"

Laurel blinked. This woman's conversations took more sudden twists and turns than the primitive mountain roads she'd seen from Darren's plane. "Did you say ride a horse?"

"Are you deaf? Ibrahim has agreed to bring in some Somali ponies for us to use when the rains make driving impossible. Can you ride?" Joan waited for an answer with narrowed eyes.

"I've ridden before."

"Good." Joan spun on her heel and walked on. "Ibrahim's nephew Farah is watching the troop now. The boy knows more than you'll ever learn about the baboons. He's the youngest of many whom I've trained myself to do observation. Most have moved on. Besides my own people, I need a few with formal training in animal behavior to help me with specific research facets. I hope you'll do, but you do look soft."

"I've worked with black bears in Canada." *Just because I'm not built like I'm made of planks does not mean I'm soft.*

Joan whistled loudly and was answered from a spot several hundred yards off. "I want you to stay well back.

The baboons are habituated to Farah and me, but they'll have to get used to you."

Laurel fought back a frustrated response. This was hardly the first time she'd studied animals in the wild, for heaven's sake! *Lord, give me patience with this woman...* Shaking her head, Laurel looked up to see a slim boy appear on the ridge and beckon.

Excitement filled her then. She was going to see the animals! They were why God had brought her here, and she was finally going to see them in person. She followed the boy, and as they neared the crest of the ridge, Laurel jerked to a halt, staring in wonder.

There, below them, clumped in twos and threes, fifty olive baboons were scattered across a bare patch of dirt. Most were grooming each other quietly. Small ones dodged through the group, playing what looked like a game of tag. Two tumbled like wrestling children.

Her eyes on the animals, Laurel started walking again...and nearly ran right into Joan when the older woman stopped and turned to speak. "See the big males? There's one at the far end of the troop."

Laurel nodded, looking at a larger animal that had a thick mantle of hair, really a mane, around his heavy shoulders. She scanned the group. There were six other big males.

"Be especially careful not to make direct eye contact with them. They could take it as a threat." Joan's voice was emphatic.

Just as Laurel focused on him through her binoculars, one of the males yawned, showing gleaming canine teeth almost two inches long. "I'll be careful." She would too, but those teeth hadn't dampened her enthusiasm one bit. *He's well armed, but then so were my bears, and they were bigger.*

Eagerly she tried to find differences, recognizable characteristics. Nothing was instantly apparent. *I'll figure it out. I will, and getting to know each of these characters should be even more fun than it was with the bears. The bears weren't anywhere near this social...*

"Laurel, this is Farah."

She looked up to find herself facing a thin boy of about fifteen. His movements were more diffident than Ibrahim's, but he had the same grace as he reached to shake her hand. As she shook it, he flashed her a shy smile.

Joan pulled a clipboard out of her pack and began taking notes while she questioned Farah. Laurel turned to watch the baboons.

The little group closest to her looked serene and graceful. A tiny black baby was huddled close to its mother, while behind her one of the big males was carefully grooming her hair. Both adults had dark skin and fur tipped with tan and silver. The baby's black hair stuck out like a tousled crew cut, showing pink skin underneath. It let go of its mother and stood on little pink feet. Wobbly but determined, it imitated the big male in grooming its mother. Laurel found herself smiling.

"That's Fupi and her baby, Jeepu."

"Jeepu?"

Joan laughed. "He's fine now, but he must have hurt his left eye soon after he was born. At the time the Jeep was missing its left headlight. Voilà, Jeepu. The male with them is their friend Leo." She started to point out other animals and name them. Igor, Drea, Argus, Gilbert, Cleo;

the names circled in Laurel's mind.

"See the male over there that has an infant following him?"

Laurel nodded. "I wondered about that. Males aren't usually caregivers, are they?"

"You've obviously done some reading. Good. But Gremlin, the little one, lost his mother to a predator a month ago. If he were any smaller, he would have died. That male was her friend, and he's adopted Gremlin. With the big male's friendship, Gremlin seems to be just managing."

Joan handed her a black binder. "This should help you get to know the animals. Farah will help you with recognizing individuals. I'm going to do some observing." She moved off quietly to stand closer to the baboons. Farah stood waiting. With his slim dignity and air of readiness, he reminded Laurel of a page waiting on a knight.

Laurel opened the binder to find photographs; each animal seemed to have its own page of three or four pictures. Carefully she looked at the first page: a rather moth-eaten looking female. She scanned the animals again for the female in the picture. Finally she pointed at random. "Susan?"

Farah shook his head. "No, she is there." He tipped his chin up and thrust his jaw out.

"Where?"

"Just there!" Farah repeated the odd motion more emphatically, this time extending his lower lip as well. Laurel blinked. What was the boy doing? She lifted her hand and pointed at the baboon Farah seemed to be looking at.

"That one?"

Joan left the animals and came over. "Don't do that."

Laurel started at the harsh tone of her voice. "What?"

"Point like that. It's rude. Crass. Much too intrusive. Only we boorish whites point that way. Watch Farah's eyes and the tip of his chin."

Rude? Boorish? Laurel could see that if one were pointing at a person, but at a baboon? She had to bite the inside of her cheek to hold back an irritated retort. No point in alienating Joan right off the bat, but really! Did she have to be so abrasive? *If anyone's being rude here, Lord, it's her.*

But she managed to deliver a fairly calm "thanks" as she turned to study Farah again.

Joan nodded and moved away.

Tentatively Laurel tried it, pushing her chin in the direction of the female. Farah turned his head away, struggling against laughter. She grinned. "Okay, you teach me how."

Farah sobered enough to try. She imitated, and both dissolved into giggles.

The baboons were moving now. Tiny babies clung under their mother's bellies while older ones rode like jockeys. Joan walked along, almost among the animals. Laurel had to hang back. *Soon that will be me; surely it won't take long, not if I'm quiet.* Farah stayed with her. Laurel caught small, dark eyes stealing glances in her direction.

"Who is that one?" She pointed with her chin, trying to indicate the big male with the baby tagging along. "He stays back like he's new, but he's adopted Gremlin."

"Yes. It is that he is new. Gremlin's mother was his only friend because he had arrived only a short time. Joan has called him Chewbacca."

Laurel laughed. The animal did have something of the *Star Wars* character's look.

As the sun dropped lower in the sky, Laurel found it hard to concentrate. Fatigue dragged at her, as if she were wearing weighted shoes. She stumbled over a twisted stick that lay in the short grass.

Farah caught her arm. "Sorry, sorry. We are going just there, to that place. The time will be short."

The boy's perception startled her and nearly brought tears. *I really must be tired.* "Thank you, Farah." She looked in the direction he had indicated. She was getting better at understanding chin pointing, in any case. A big hump looked like a huge pile of boulders stacked in clif-flike formations.

"That is the place of sleep for this animals."

Something was moving behind the rocks, kicking up dust that glowed in the low sunshine.

"*Mbuzi*, memsahib!" Farah called, and Joan swore loudly. Leaving the baboons, she strode ahead toward the rocks. Farah trotted after her, then looked back at Laurel. "Come quickly. It is the goats of the infidels. Joan will drive them away."

The goats of the infidels? That sounded like something from an alternative reality. Laurel shook her head and hurried after the others. She came around the rocks to find Joan screaming at several small, ragged boys who were already trying their hardest to drive off a big herd of goats. The boys were yelling in high voices and throwing dirt clods at the animals. As the children and goats moved off, Joan followed, making what appeared to be an angry speech. One of the smallest boys started crying. A bigger one turned, glared at Joan, then hiked the little fellow onto his back piggyback style.

After a few minutes, Joan came back. Her face was pale and set. As she passed Laurel, she suddenly turned. "They're a plague, stripping the land, breeding like rats!"

"The goats?"

"The people—the foolish, out-of-control, suffering, overbreeding people!"

Joan turned and strode toward the baboon troop. Laurel stared at the woman with her mouth open. She had sounded so angry...no, more than that. She'd sounded almost unbalanced.

Darren's objections about her working for Joan came to mind again, and she hugged herself. *Have I gotten myself into more than I bargained for, Father?* What if what was going on here was more than studies for the purposes of conservation? Joan's attitudes and comments made Laurel wonder if the woman hadn't gone over the edge from conservationist to antihuman radical.

She's just passionate about her work, like Darren is passionate about what he thinks is important. He's not a radical, is he?

The thought of Darren gave her a sudden longing for his presence, for the strength and stability she'd felt in him. Laurel shook her head and followed Joan and Farah toward the baboons.

Lord, help! I've known the man for less than a day and I can't get him out of my mind. If anyone has gone over the edge, it's me!

As unnerving as that thought was, it was nothing

compared to the fact that, deep inside, for all of her moaning and protestations to the contrary, she didn't really seem to mind it.

Not one little bit.

5

FOR LAUREL, THE NEXT COUPLE OF DAYS WENT PAST IN A
multicolored blur of sunstruck days and disturbed
nights as her body clock tried to adjust to an African
rhythm. On the fourth night, she finally slept deeply.

The cool air caressed her cheeks as she stepped outside. There was no sign of dawn in the east. Everything
touched her newly wide awake senses with a kind of
vivid joy. Stars glittered in a black velvet sky undimmed
by artificial light sources. Soft voices came from the
direction of the kitchen where African workers were
preparing breakfast. A hyena called—a wild, whooping
cry—and she smiled. Even the lizards on the walls of the
outhouse hadn't bothered her this morning. She lifted
her arms to the African sky and praised God silently
with her whole soul.

Someone lit the pressure lantern, bringing her back
to the present. It broke the peace with a hissing noise
and a wide strip of light across the ground. Instantly
moths were looping through the light, making patterns
like abstract drawings.

Darren had called this place Joan Doyle's camp.
Laurel hesitated. So much for not thinking of him. And
yet…like everything that had happened in the last couple
of days, Darren seemed part of an odd dream—one she
couldn't quite shake any more than she could forget the
feel of his warm, callused hand over hers. *And he stayed
with me that night.*

I was buzzed from jet lag, every sense wide open, that's

all it was. She sighed, then forced her attention back to her surroundings. When Darren had called this place a camp, Laurel had pictured tents, but she and Joan each had their own round, thatched cabin. Everyone called the little cabins *bandas*. Laurel's had empty bunks, and two of the simple, one-room cabins stood empty. The Africans, most of whom seemed to be related to Ibrahim, stayed in another group of bandas some distance off. She'd been told they were of the Somali people. She and Joan ate in a dining room banda served by Ambaro, one of Ibrahim's daughters-in-law.

Walking toward the light, Laurel wrinkled her nose. Whites live here, blacks live there. But Joan seemed to take it completely for granted. *And for some reason, she treats me like some kind of lackey. Or enemy. I don't get it.*

Seeing Joan walking toward her, Laurel waited, straightening her shoulders, readying herself for the encounter.

"I'm going to leave you to observe without me this morning," Joan said as she got nearer to Laurel. "I'll be there in the afternoon."

Oddly, apprehension shivered up Laurel's back. "Will Farah be with me?"

"Do you think I would trust you with identification by yourself?" Joan lifted her eyebrows. "You'll be observing the troop in a fifteen-minute rotation, watching each animal in turn as usual. Is that clear?" The woman swept past her. Silently Laurel prayed for patience.

In the dining banda, Laurel sat down, and Ambaro put a slice of pawpaw in front of her. "Thank you, Ambaro." The first few times, she had seemed startled that Laurel thanked her, and she still was very reserved.

This morning Laurel was rewarded by a shy smile.

On her own, Laurel arrived at the Jeep before the Somalis. She leaned against the cool metal and listened to the dawn chorus of birds. A cough made her turn her head to see Farah and Ibrahim waiting at a little distance.

"Sorry, I didn't hear you coming."

Ibrahim just nodded with great dignity, but Farah said, "No matter. We had just been finishing our prayers."

Prayers? Oh, that's right; they're Muslim. She felt a moment of loneliness for another Christian. *But Darren told me some names.* Laurel frowned. Isaac and Judy. No, not Judy, but something like it.

"Ibrahim, do you know anyone named Isaac? Darren Grant said he lives nearby, and I should ask to meet him."

Ibrahim looked at Farah. Both said nothing.

"Do you know him?"

"There is no one among us called Isaac." Ibrahim turned to look ahead, mouth turned down. Farah wouldn't meet her eyes. Laurel turned away, frustrated. They were hiding something, that much was clear. But she was certain it would do her no good to push. She would just have to find out what she wanted to know another way.

Throughout the day, Laurel continued to feel as if all her senses had been newly washed. She was very aware of the heat of sunlight on her skin, the smell of dust, the pattern the flat-topped acacia trees made against the sky. Farah's skin gleamed with copper and red highlights. The big male baboons' shoulder mantles shimmered when they moved. This had to be one of the most amazing and beautiful places on earth. There were hyenas in the night, poison snakes in the rocks, and leopards in the river bush, but who wanted a safe wilderness? The danger that lurked under every surface only gave the beauty a sharper edge.

Laurel stood well back from the troop, watching Fupi through her binoculars. The female moved toward her. Others followed. Soon there were four baboons within meters of her. A thrill shot up her back. *They're accepting me!* She held perfectly still. The animals flowed around her, sun glinting in their eyes as they glanced at her. Laurel couldn't keep a smile off her face.

She and Farah worked hard. Watching Chewbacca and little Gremlin was especially interesting. Laurel had read that the males moved between troops while females stayed put. Chewbacca still didn't have many friends yet. He tended to be aggressive except with Gremlin. The little guy looked ridiculously small beside the big male.

At noon, when the baboons settled to groom and rest, Farah came over. "Why do we watch this animals?"

Laurel sat back on her heels. "You never asked Joan?"

Farah made a graceful movement with one hand. "She is not..."

"Not easy to talk to?"

Farah nodded eagerly. "I have asked my father and Ibrahim. Both have said I should be silent. Joan offers good pay, and I am a foolish child." He shrugged expressively. "Perhaps it is that they do not know. So I ask you. This baboons are useless. I cannot eat them. But we follow all day, writing down each affair, which female is mate, which child shall play. Cattle or camels, even the goats, to know them would perhaps bring wealth, but baboons?"

Laurel pulled off her hat and ran her hand through her hair. *Farah, too! I've tried so many times to answer this for people.* Her mouth tightened remembering. It was so discouraging when even some Christians seemed only to see animals as just a source of wealth or companionship and don't realize our responsibility for God's creatures.

Can I tell Farah my real reasons? That I feel caring for creation is something God wants done and is important to Him? No, her reasons wouldn't resemble Joan's, and he'd asked about hers as well. She tried the more conventional gambit. "Many scientists say that the baboons are like people. We can learn more about people by studying them. The more we learn about animals, the better our ability will be to help them."

Farah spat on the ground. "There is no God but Allah, and he has made us. I am no monkey!" The boy's thin body quivered with indignation. "I will not watch for this reason!"

Laurel sat abruptly on a twisted dry log. She was going to be in big trouble if Farah quit because of her. She held out her hands. "I don't know what Joan thinks, but I agree with you that God has made us. Maybe He made us a little like the baboons for a reason. He put us in charge of the animals, and it's easier to care for something you understand. Maybe He meant us to learn from the other animals."

Farah sank down onto his haunches. He looked away from her toward the troop, his face intent. "Perhaps you are right. The ones who come, the Meru people, indeed they are like baboons."

"The who?"

"The Meru people, the infidels which Joan also

hates. Those which have invaded the Wilson ranch." He pointed with his chin to the west, explaining patiently. "They are eaters of unclean meat."

Laurel blinked. He sounded like some Old Testament prophet. "Do the Meru own the goats that Joan was so angry about?" Laurel had tried to ask Joan about that episode but had met a stone wall of hostility.

Farah nodded. "The Meru are crowding into Somali land! Indeed you are right; they are like baboons. I shall tell my father this reason. Perhaps knowing this baboons will help us to defeat our enemy."

"That's not what I meant." Laurel felt like holding her head together with both hands. This was getting more and more bizarre. Studying baboons to win some kind of civil war?

"The Meru are human, aren't they?"

"Perhaps." The boy lifted his chin and stared into the distance.

"Then they are no more baboonlike than you or I."

"Chewbacca is grooming the small one, Gremlin. I will write it." He turned and stalked off, obviously unconvinced.

Laurel sighed and turned back to watch the troop. Chewbacca started to move, with Gremlin not far behind. She watched the big male pick something up in his sensitive fingers, sniff it, then taste it. Gremlin came over, stood on his hind legs to grab the big male's hand, and sniffed too. Laurel smiled. *Lord, it gives me joy to watch them. I can feel Your love.* Why did so many people miss the centrality of creation in God's plan for people and miss the joy too? Caring for creation was hard, complicated, and sad sometimes, but she loved it!

The bulk of the troop was moving now. She frowned; they hadn't rested long. A few minutes later Farah froze, head up, listening intently. Nervously, Laurel followed suit. Several of the baboons had paused as well.

"They come." Farah sank down onto his haunches.

"I don't hear anything." As she spoke the radio crackled to life. It was Joan wanting to know where exactly they were. Since Laurel couldn't tell her, she handed it to Farah who switched to Swahili. A few seconds later he handed it back.

"They are there." He tipped his chin. "Did you not hear the car? Joan will walk to this place."

Chewbacca, about ten yards from Laurel, grabbed a grasshopper, put it in his mouth, and looked nervously into the bush. He moved off a bit farther, still foraging, but glancing often into the bush. A few seconds later, Laurel too could hear Joan coming.

"They're up and moving early," Joan said as she walked up. "Did they settle for noon rest sooner or not rest as long?"

"Not as long." Laurel held out her observation sheet, pointing at the times.

Joan gave a disgusted grunt. "Those despicable goats."

She turned to Farah. "Take her out to the Jeep."

Farah nodded and beckoned Laurel to follow.

She shook her head. "I'd rather stay."

"That's a laudable sentiment, but I need you in camp. Take my laptop into the dining banda. I want you to get familiar with the data entry program and enter your observations from this morning. Besides, Dr. Kimathi is flying in from the Primate Research Center in

Nairobi, and someone should be there to meet him. Farah will take you to Ibrahim at the Jeep." Joan turned to walk away.

Flying? Does that mean Darren is coming? Suddenly the day seemed brighter. She turned to follow Farah, then hesitated. "If I'm to meet this Dr. Kimathi, could you tell me something about him?"

Joan stopped midstride. "It's the government body that oversees this project and a couple of other primate projects. Kimathi's the director. There's a booklet in the desk somewhere." She waved her hand as if shooing flies and walked quietly into the troop. Laurel pressed her lips together, fighting back her frustration. Joan made her feel like a schoolkid.

"Let us go." Farah beckoned again. As they got nearer the Jeep, Farah turned and looked at her. "This man Kimathi, he is Wakikuyu," Farah said the last word as if it were a noxious disease. "She has spoken against the Meru; the Meru are the brothers of the Kikuyu, yet she works with Kimathi." He grinned. "Lately things do not go well between them."

"Dr. Kimathi is angry with Joan?"

Farah shrugged. "Perhaps it is that not only Kimathi is angry. Why is it that the graduate assistants have not come? Here is the car." Farah pointed through the trees. He inclined his head gently, turned on his heel, and walked off.

Back in camp, Laurel thought about asking Dr. Kimathi why Joan had no graduate assistants. *It's none of my business anyway.* She made a face and went to get the laptop computer.

As the afternoon dragged on, she kept listening for

the sound of an airplane engine. Under the strong sun, the corrugated iron roof of the dining room banda pinged and clicked as the metal expanded. Sweat trickled down Laurel's spine.

This is ridiculous! No one should bake under a tin roof on a day like this. She put the laptop on a chair, cleared the notes off the table, turned it on its side, and hauled it out the door and into the shade of a tree. A few minutes later she was back at work.

Outdoors the air was hot and still, but nothing like the oven indoors. Flies kept landing on the back of her hands and on her face. She grabbed a paper and flapped it wildly at the flies.

A burst of soft giggles made her look up. Four of the Somali children were watching her. They stood several yards away, liquid eyes in slim, dark faces regarding her solemnly. Laurel carefully said the Swahili greeting she'd learned. This time she got a shy response from the biggest child. The rest simply stared. Feeling like something on the far side of a set of zoo bars, Laurel tried to get back to work.

Darren was right. I might as well be from another planet.

She finished entering data, then started to go back through the information already entered. Soon she was reading with fascination the history of each of the baboons in the troop. She didn't even notice when the children left. Hours later, a slant of sunshine across the table made it hard to read the screen. She looked up.

It's late! She moved in her chair. *Ow, I'm stiff.* She stood, rolled her shoulders, then reached for the sky, every muscle stretching ecstatically.

She hesitated midmovement. Where was Dr. Kimathi? *Did Darren crash?* Laurel's mouth twisted and she shook her head. *Get a grip.* Frowning, she sank back into her chair and tried to get back into the data. She couldn't stop glancing at her watch. It was almost five-thirty. The abrupt tropical night would come in less than an hour.

If he's coming, he'll be here soon. Laurel headed for her banda and slipped out of her dusty shorts into a clean sundress. She ran a brush through her hair and went back outside. She was hauling the table back inside when the sound of a plane came through the still air. Minutes later she was bouncing along in the Jeep as Ibrahim drove furiously toward the landing strip. They pulled up beside the plane. A dignified black man emerged from the plane. He wasn't much taller than Laurel and had a round face and an even more rounded middle.

Laurel looked past him into the cockpit. *No one! So who was flying?*

"I assume Joan was not able to meet me. I trust she is not ill." Laurel blinked at Dr. Kimathi's words. He didn't sound pleased.

"No, she's fine and should be in camp any minute. I'm Laurel Binet. I work with her."

Kimathi's handshake was limp. Laurel kept looking past him. There was a shadow on the far side of the plane. The person who owned it was coming around.... Laurel felt her heart jerk. Darren!

He looked up and smiled at her—and Laurel felt a jolt of awareness that, if anything, her memory had underplayed Darren Grant.

6

DARREN LOADED THE JEEP WITH SURPRISING EASE. THOUGH the boxes looked heavy to Laurel, he barely seemed to notice their weight as he lifted them onto the vehicle.

She might as well admit it: Just watching the man made her happy. He gave her such a sense of...what? safety? security? Whatever it was, she couldn't escape it. No matter how much she might want to.

"Want a hand up?" Darren was smiling at her. Dr. Kimathi sat very straight in the front seat, apparently not at all bothered that there was no cover on the vehicle to protect them from the sun or wind. Laurel eyed the setup, noting that the back was full of boxes. There was nothing to do but climb onto the top of the boxes or walk.

"No, thanks." She scrambled up, and Darren joined her with one long-legged step.

"You're already getting a nice tan. Almost look like you belong around here."

"Almost?"

He tipped his head. "I'd say you have a ways to go yet."

She held out one arm. "I bet I'm as dark as you are."

His muscular forearm joined hers, and the touch of his skin made her insides jump. The Jeep started with a jerk. Distracted by Darren, Laurel almost did a back flip over the boxes. His arm caught her in the nick of time.

"Thanks."

His arm was solid behind her as he set her right again. "Anytime." Their eyes met, and he smiled. "What do you think of Kenya so far?"

"So far?" A jolt threw her into the air, and she scrambled to get a grip of her own before she knocked them both out of the Jeep. "Bumpy at the moment." *And not just the Jeep ride.*

"That's all? Nothing else?"

"Well, giraffes have the most amazing purple tongues. The flies are a pain. Bottle birds actually sound like someone dumping a wine bottle and…" She let go for a precarious moment to wave an arm at the golden orb sinking through a deep red band on the horizon. "Look at the colors. The whole place is…is…" Words spun through her head: wild, strong, rough, old, awesome, harsh, gorgeous. "I don't know, but today I was thinking that I could stay here the rest of my life."

Darren had turned to look at the sunset. He twisted back to her face with a startled intensity. "You want to stay in Africa?"

"It was just a thought. The place is magnificent, and there is so much to learn."

"The animals."

Laurel nodded. "Yes, but that's not all. Remind me to ask you about the goats of the infidels."

"Goats of the infidels?" He laughed. They were already driving into the compound. "Look, I've got things to do now, but I'd love to talk later. Deal?"

"Deal."

He nodded once looking into her eyes, then jumped down. Darren shook hands with both Ibrahim and Dr. Kimathi. There was a gracious formality to his movements as he did that.

Kind of foreign, but nice.

With Darren gone, the wait for Joan to come back into camp seemed interminable. Dr. Kimathi was reserved, pompous, and very dignified. She sat with him trying to make polite conversation next to a hot, hissing pressure lamp. Ambaro brought the strong, sweet, milky tea that Laurel had already learned to call *chai*.

Finally, Joan came back, and supper was served. Dr. Kimathi and Joan talked formally about recent developments within the troop of baboons. The tension in the air was suffocating. *Darren was smart to disappear.* Where had he gone anyway?

Dr. Kimathi wiped his mouth, put down his napkin, and leaned forward. "How can you continue here without the support of UCLA? You no longer have the money or connections that are needed."

Laurel stopped chewing. *Without the support of UCLA? That was why there were no graduate students!* Joan Doyle was well known around the world. What on earth had she done to lose her support?

Joan's chin went up, and she gave him a look that could have fried eggs. "I intend to stay and continue, Samuel. You know perfectly well that I usually accomplish the things I set out to do. I have a new source of funding. It is adequate. Perhaps even enough to keep the squatters off Ndovu Ranch."

"Be careful, Joan!" Samuel Kimathi was nearly growling.

Joan threw out her hands. "Help me, then. Don't you have any influential family members? Isn't your uncle a minister in the cabinet? We cannot lose this project. We're learning too much, and we've followed this troop for so long."

Dr. Kimathi frowned and changed the subject. "Come and show me your research records. Ms. Binet—" he nodded in her direction—"was saying that some interesting things are being learned concerning the role of the males in the troop. If the work is significant, perhaps the Primate Center will speak for you."

Joan had started to rise, then froze when Kimathi said "perhaps." She shut her eyes, the battle of emotions playing across her features. With a sigh, she stood and led the way to the office.

Laurel got up, not sure whether to follow or not. Neither of them looked back. Watching them walk away from her, she felt her stomach knot. *What kind of tangle have I landed in?*

She sank back into her chair to think. Obviously, Joan had accepted her because the graduate students from UCLA weren't coming. When Laurel applied, Joan had asked for references and for her parents' addresses.

Laurel frowned. *Joan said she had a new source of funding.* Laurel had received a fund-raising plea a couple of weeks after she sent in the application. Would her mother have received one, too? Lilith wouldn't have paid attention to that, would she? Is that why she'd gotten the job, because Lilith had sent a big donation?

Laurel paced across the little room. *She wanted me to travel. Is she doing it again? Using her money to make sure I do what she wants? But she doesn't really like me working with animals. She wouldn't!* Laurel headed for the door. Remembering how Lilith had used money to manipulate made her stomach hurt. She had to get out in the air, away from people and their stuff.

Thud! Impact with something warm and resilient

knocked her back. "Darren!"

He laughed and steadied her. "Why the hurry?"

Looking up at him, her thoughts scattered like chickens in front of a car. " Um, I was heading out where I can breathe."

"Where you can breathe?"

She shook her head, half laughing. "I don't have asthma or anything. I guess I mean be calm, collect myself, feel God with me. I don't know. All my life, I've done that best away from people, outdoors. You're here now. It can wait."

"You sure?" His dark eyebrow tipped up slightly.

I'm not sure about anything. Especially about being so close to you. She took a deep breath trying to clear her head. "We had a deal. It would be silly of me to back out. Besides, maybe you can explain some things."

He sat, straddling a chair backwards. "Goats of the infidels?"

"Right." She couldn't help smiling when he grinned at her like that.

"I've been thinking about that. Farah's words, right?"

"How did you know?"

"Elementary, my dear Watson. I know a little of the situation here through Jede and Isaac. Any of the Somalis are likely to think of the people on the Wilson as infidels, but I figure Farah and Ibrahim are the only ones who know enough English to talk to you. Ibrahim is pretty cagey about what he says. Voilà, Farah." He flung out his hand, bowing.

Laurel laughed. "Sherlock Holmes himself, but I don't get the bit about the people on the Wilson being infidels. Is that where the Isaac you mentioned is? I asked Ibrahim about Isaac and…what was the name?"

"Jede."

"Okay, Jede. I only asked about Isaac because I couldn't remember the other name, and he said there was no Isaac here. Actually, he said, 'there is no one of that name among us.'"

"There isn't. Isaac and Jede are with the Meru."

"The baboon people!"

"What?"

Laurel shook her head, half laughing at the look on his face. "Just something Farah said. He'd asked me why we were studying baboons. I wasn't sure about telling him my reasons, so I told him so we could understand people better. He was indignant at first, then suddenly said perhaps the Meru are like baboons." She sobered. "Darren, what's going on here? He called the Meru enemies. Does that have anything to do with Joan Doyle losing her support from UCLA?"

He stood, nearly knocking over his chair, and took two strides over to her. "You're sure she's lost UCLA's support?"

"She and Dr. Kimathi were talking about it. Kimathi seemed edgy, almost like he's afraid to associate with her."

"I don't like it. It's only going to increase the tension, and it's bad enough already." He paced across the room and back, then sat down facing her. "Enough of that. I want to know about something else you said. Why didn't you want to tell Farah your reasons for being involved in this study?"

"Well, he'd kind of asked in general why this study was happening, and I doubt if my reasons are the same as Joan's. It's really her study. Darren, what is going on here?"

He ignored her last question. "What *are* your reasons for working here?" His eyes were so intent they made her nervous.

Here we go again. She searched through the words she'd said to others. For Darren, she wanted the heart of it. "I guess I want to do the first job God ever gave people, caring for creation. It really matters to me. Also, it's where I've felt His love. God's strength, beauty, attention to detail is so obvious in creation. It's like comforting, powerful music around me." She shook her head. "I'd practically have to tell you my life story."

"Come with me. I want to show you something. It will begin to answer your questions about what's going on, and it might let you in on something you seem to have missed so far in your life."

Missed so far? He was already heading for the door.

"You want me to come now?"

"Kimathi will be here until I fly him out tomorrow. Joan isn't likely to leave. Come on."

With Darren, alone in the night! She wasn't sure if the thought pleased or terrified her, but at this point it didn't matter. *I have to know what's going on here.* "I'm coming." She nearly had to trot to keep up with his purposeful strides as he headed for the area of the compound where the Somalis lived.

"*Jambo* Ibrahim!" he called out as they approached.

Ibrahim answered from beside a fire in front of one of the bandas. Both men strode toward each other, shaking hands with real enthusiasm and talking quickly. Laurel saw Farah crouched on his heels with several other men and boys. Their eyes gleamed in the firelight, obviously listening with interest. Darren and Ibrahim came to some kind of agreement, then Ibrahim handed Darren keys that glinted in the dim light. There were a few more words that sounded like friendly good-byes, and Darren turned away.

"Remember, the Meru are like baboons!" Farah called out. Ibrahim said something that Laurel guessed was a translation. There was a wave of laughter, including women's laughter from inside the nearest banda.

In the red flickering light, Laurel saw Darren grimace. "That we could do without." He was heading for the Jeep. "I have Joan's permission to use this when she and Ibrahim don't need it."

She gripped the door frame as they jounced to the airstrip. Warm and cooler patches of air swirled past. She shut her eyes. *Lord, keep me steady. It's hard to think.* Wind lifted her hair like a gentle benediction, and Laurel took a long, slow, deep breath.

The flat, smooth stretch of the strip ended abruptly. A pothole nearly threw her out of her seat. They'd turned on to what was obviously a wide footpath. The headlights glanced off thorn brush and dust. Darren's big hands on the wheel moved easily as the Jeep lurched through what looked to be impassable hummocks. There was less and less grass. A catlike animal showed in the lights for a flash before it ran, its long-ringed tail trailing.

"Genet cat. He's probably getting fat off someone's chickens."

On remote ranch land? That's where Joan's baboons lived. But there were those goats, and she was talking about squatters. Something caught her eye. A spot of dim yellow-orange light shone through the bush, then another one. The Land Rover was bouncing too much for her to get a good look. The track was almost nonexistent now and the Jeep was climbing steeply. Suddenly Darren wrenched the wheel to one side and pulled on the emergency brake. A wash of dust came forward over them and made a reddish haze in the headlights as he turned off the engine.

"Look."

As the dust cleared, Laurel could see that they were on one side of a long dip in the land. Many specks and smudges of flickering firelight speckled the far hillside a couple of miles away.

"Campfires?"

"These people are not camping. These are little farms; each fire's a family's outdoor kitchen." He had crossed his arms on the wheel and leaned forward, looking into the darkness.

"Joan's squatters?" In the moonlight she could see faint outlines of what looked like tiny fields or gardens.

"Squatters, but semilegal. Mostly they're on the neighboring ranch, which used to belong to a family called Wilson. The border is the bottom of the ravine."

"People on the Wilson..." Laurel frowned. "Then these are the Meru. I still don't get it. The stuff I read about Joan's study said the Ndovu was remote ranch land with very little human pressure."

"It used to be. When Ndovu and the Wilson were settled in the thirties by English families, the land was almost empty. It was full of wildlife and used only occasionally by the Somali for seasonal grazing."

"But the stuff I read was recent."

"The Wilson changed hands three years ago. Now it belongs to a Kikuyu politician. He's quite happy to take money from the squatters to let them stay."

"And Farah despises them because they're on traditionally Somali land?"

"Yes, but it's older and more complicated than that. The Somali are nomadic Muslims, of the same Semitic language group as the Jews and Arabs. They're fierce, proud, independent people. You've probably seen those traits in Farah."

Laurel nodded.

"These people on the Wilson are Meru people from the Bantu language group, agrarian people. Historically animists, they're now mostly nominal Christians, infidels as far as Farah is concerned. They are as different from him racially and culturally as you are to an East Indian. Since independence, Bantu tribes, who have no love for the Somali, have dominated Kenya's government. Farah has some reason to feel a grievance."

"All the people who work with Joan are Somali." Laurel said slowly as she tried to work out the implications in her head. She frowned. "This is crazy. The land is too dry to farm. It's got to be. Why would they want to come anyway?"

"Have you seen the population growth curves for Kenya?"

"Yes, I did. Even on land this dry then... But how could they survive at all, even for one season?"

"More and more people have been moving in each year. Joan has had enough influence to keep Ndovu Ranch from being overrun, but that may be changing.

We've had three good years in a row."

"This is good?" She gestured at the dusty ground.

He laughed. "I guess you've never lived in really arid country. This is what it's always like in dry season. They've gotten a meager harvest off, enough to survive on since the rains didn't fall."

"How often do they fall?"

"About four years in ten, up here. That's why the Somali are nomadic."

Laurel felt sick. "Those little boys with the goats…"

"Yes." He was looking at her, his gaze expectant, as though he wanted some specific response.

"Isn't there some other way?"

"Not unless you expect them to sit at home and starve. There are too many mouths for the farmland to feed, so the people spread out, move into untilled land. It's a choice of who survives—the people or the wildlife."

"Or neither." Sorrow washed over her at the hopelessness of the situation. "Darren, there has to be a better way."

"If you find it let me know." For all that his voice was flat, there was a gentle tone to it as well—as though he really did hope she would find a way.

He turned away from her and started the engine. The Jeep bumped downhill. Laurel's eyes stayed focused on those golden specks of warmth, spreading like a sparkling blanket, devouring the wild land. The delicate winged shape of a bat flashed through the headlights. Something bounded across the track that looked like a foot-high jerboa. Light licked across the feathered tail, tiny paws, and huge eyes.

"Spring hare, Benson's beastie," Darren's voice was still tight.

Benson! This was what Darren had talked about that night with Benson. What had he said? *"If you had a hurt animal and a hurt child and could only save one, which would you choose?"* But it wasn't that simple. It couldn't be. Her head hurt. Before that tide of humanity, how could any wild thing survive for long? Tears made cool tracks down her cheeks in the darkness.

Darren brought the Jeep to a halt near her banda. He looked at her, the contours of his face gilded by moonlight. She could hear his sudden intake of breath and was startled when his hand came out to cup her chin. "Laurel, I didn't mean to make you cry."

"How could I *not* cry?" She pulled away from his warm hand. "You told me that the wild land won't last long. You think that Chewbacca, Fupi, little Gremlin…that all the baboons, the giraffe, leopards—" she made a wild expansive gesture with her arm—*"all* of the animals and the beautiful, wild land here are doomed." She shook her head. "Do you really think I shouldn't care?"

"I don't know if it's doomed." He clenched both hands on the wheel. "Joan has had the clout to keep most of the squatters out of her area. She's fighting to keep favor with politicians. Maybe she can pull it off."

"But what about the people? If they farm land this dry, won't they strip it, make it barren, and end up hungry anyway? I've read about desertification." Laurel's voice quivered. "The little boys I saw. What will happen to them?"

"I don't have any easy answers. I wish I did. Besides, you can't care about those children and the baboons."

"But I do, Darren."

He shook his head. "You've got a lot to learn."

"I'm not the only one."

His gaze narrowed at the challenge in her tone, but she didn't back down. "Throwing out God's creation can't be right. He created this world for us to enjoy. He shows Himself to us in its beauty. It says so in the Bible."

He opened his mouth, as though to argue, then clamped his lips together and turned away. Laurel rubbed her temples, tired to the bone. "Why does everything have to suffer? I hate it!"

At her impassioned cry, he looked at her. For a moment they held each other's gaze.

"I hate it too." The anguish in his deep voice tore at her, unleashing another wave of tears. He reached out and smoothed the hair back from her forehead. "There is so much pain."

Almost involuntarily, she leaned into his hand.

Darren groaned and pulled her into his arms. A tight knot deep in her chest loosened under the strength of his embrace. She gave a shaky gasp and lifted her face, caught between protest and surrender. His warm lips moved over her face, closing her eyes, touching her tears...

She was falling, spinning, being pulled inexorably by a deep current, but to what? She wasn't certain. All she knew at that moment was that Darren Grant filled her senses more completely than she'd ever dreamed possible.

The sound of a child's giggle right beside them made them both jump. Laurel tried to throttle the dizzying current of emotions racing through her. She met Darren's eyes and saw he wasn't doing much better.

His steady gaze bore into her, but his breath was shallow, erratic…as though he'd just run up a steep incline—or fallen down one.

Laurel pressed trembling fingers to her mouth, where his lips had been a second before. More giggles made them both turn their heads. The same two who'd watched her earlier spun and ran, still giggling.

"Kids! You can never get away from them in Kenya." His voice was ragged. "It's better that I go now." She had the distinct impression that he hadn't planned that kiss and was as shocked as she was.

"Me too." She sounded shaky even to her own ears. She swallowed hard and climbed out of the Jeep. "Thanks for showing me those people, Darren. I do want to understand."

He stood and looked at her, his lithe form silvered by moonlight. "You're serious?"

"Yes, I am."

"Come with me to church tomorrow then."

"If I can." She watched him stride off into the night, melding into the African darkness without a ripple.

7

AT BREAKFAST THE NEXT MORNING, JOAN AND DR. KIMATHI got into an intent discussion that excluded Laurel, leaving her to her own thoughts. She ate her porridge and wondered if she should go to church after all.

That kiss! It was like I was drowning. Avoiding a knee-jerk reaction was one thing, but this was more like getting sucked in by a whirlpool. She toyed with her spoon. Lilith always listened to her body, her feelings. Laurel made a face remembering the parade of men she'd shared breakfast with. Men that inevitably walked away from her mother. *That's how she ended up with Dad too, and there were never any two people less suited.*

Julie had insisted that not all men were like that. *Her David doesn't seem to be.* Laurel sighed.

You know what this is, Laurel: a classic approach-avoidance conflict. She frowned, thinking of the pigeon she'd seen in one experiment. Food was put in a place where the bird had earlier received an electric shock. The poor thing stood there paralyzed, unable to go up to the food and unable to leave.

Thank God I'm not a pigeon. I can think this through. This was church he'd asked her to come to, not a date. And she really wanted to go to church; it'd been too long. Silently she asked God for wisdom. She patted the porridge with her spoon.

It was true, she didn't know a lot about Darren, but then she wasn't going to learn much if she avoided him. Certainly going to church together was a good way of getting to know each other better…of finding out if they wanted to pursue a friendship.

Or something deeper, she thought as the memory of their kiss washed over her again.

Deeper! The very idea of being in a deeper relationship with Darren Grant made her feel warm all over. She took another bite of porridge. Ugh, it was completely cold.

"These animals must not be lost." Joan's fist hit the table. Laurel turned, startled. *What are they talking about?*

"Perhaps you could move them. It has been done before." Dr. Kimathi was looking at the wall, not at Joan.

"Not with my troop, it hasn't. The national parks have already refused me, and there is nowhere to go that is not being overgrazed. I've been on Ndovu Ranch since the Hales owned it. There is nothing wrong with Ndovu if we can keep the squatters off and their goats away. There is no reason the baboons shouldn't be fine here with proper protection."

Kimathi stood. "Perhaps we can continue this fascinating conversation later. Shall we go out to observe the animals?"

Joan's lips were compressed into a tight line. "Yes, we should." She nodded in Laurel's direction. "I want you to work on records. You do know where everything is that you'll need?"

"I'd like to go to church this morning."

Joan rocked back on her heels. "To church? Where?"

"Darren Grant invited me to come with him to a local church."

"Handsome pilot meets beautiful woman?" Joan threw back her head and guffawed, her sinewy neck showing in the lamplight. "By all means, go with Darren, but I want you back here by two o'clock for a shift at observation." She sobered and her eyes got hard. "Any local church has got to be Meru. If you must go fraternize with the Meru, tell the old men that I want their people and their filthy goats off Ndovu land."

It seemed ages before Darren turned up. Laurel had put on a dress and sandals, then gone to work on the computer. Outside under the trees, it was cool and pleasant early in the day. She kept glancing up, looking for Darren to arrive. Her mind slid to the feel of his warm lips on her cheeks and eyes. She swallowed hard and forced herself to concentrate on the data in front of her.

As she entered data, Laurel pictured each of the animals. *They're in trouble. Serious trouble.* Back in Canada, Laurel had seen some of her bears killed by greedy poachers, and now these baboons and all the rest of the wild creatures on Ndovu were in danger. The people on the Wilson were hurting badly too. *Lord, whatever else happens here, please help me be a force for healing, not hurting. Make some way to help both people and creation, please!*

A trickle of sweat ran down her spine. The coolness of the morning was gone. It was getting late. Where was Darren? Another half hour crawled by. Laurel stopped typing and clenched her hands in her lap. It was going to be embarrassing to tell Joan she hadn't gone to church. She could already hear the woman's laughter.

When she glanced up and found Darren's long frame leaning against a tree trunk only feet away, she was ready to spit nails. "So you decided to come after all?"

Darren's eyebrows arched. "After all?"

"We must be late."

He let out his breath in what sounded like an amused grunt.

"Don't laugh at me!" She stood abruptly, her fists planted on her hips.

"Who said I was laughing?" He levered his shoulder off the tree, his hands out in appeal. "You said you wanted to learn. You might as well start with African time. Things happen when they happen, then they go on until they're finished and stop."

Laurel narrowed her eyes. "I don't buy it, Darren. You're a pilot. You must be able to schedule a day of flying."

He grinned. "You know, you even look good mad?"

She nearly threw a binder at him.

"Hey, take it easy. I'm sorry you thought I wasn't coming. Somehow I forgot how new you are here."

She lowered the binder. "I suppose that's a kind of compliment."

"It is, truly." He lifted his hands, palms up. "Forgiven?"

She laughed. "I do want to go to church."

His expressive face flashed into a smile. "Ibrahim has the Jeep, so we'll have to walk. If you find me too irritating, you could follow behind me, as a polite African woman should."

"In your dreams!"

"Actually, my dreams were quite different." His eyes were on hers.

Heat, swift and unsettling, swept her face, and she changed the subject. "You keep talking about Jede and Isaac."

The crinkle of amusement in the corners of his eyes told her he hadn't missed the diversion, but, much to her relief, he played along all the same. "You'll meet them this morning. I told them you'd probably be at church, and they're looking forward to it, especially Jede."

"But who are they?"

"They're a young married couple, really neat people. Some of the Meru elders who've moved onto the Wilson asked AIC, one of the big denominations in Kenya, for a church. Jede and Isaac came in response. Isaac was one of Dad's students; he's a couple of years older than me. Jede, well, you'll have to meet Jede to appreciate her."

As she walked beside him down the dusty path, their shadows like black butterflies stretched and moved underfoot.

Darren looked down at her. "On the ride up in the plane, you asked if I'm ever tired of flying."

Laurel nodded. "You said not of flying, but I had the impression you were tired of something."

"I wish there were some way I could keep flying and still be a part of a group that's making a difference for God—the way Jede and Isaac have. You'll see what I mean if you get to know them. Right now, most of my flying jobs aren't too different from driving a delivery truck or a taxi."

"So why don't you join a mission flying group? There are quite a few of them."

He shrugged. "They offer what is still essentially a flying taxi service. I'd have no steady contact with one group and even less contact than I have now with people who don't know God."

"Don't you think the mission aviation groups are useful?"

"Mission flying is essential to a lot of people who *are* committed to one group. The hospital Mom worked at when I was a kid couldn't have functioned without the mission planes and pilots."

"Your mom is a missionary nurse?"

"Mom's a doctor, not a nurse." He looked away. "I didn't see much of her when I was a kid."

"But now you want to do something like she does? Touch people directly?"

Surprise lit his eyes. "I never thought of it that way." He hesitated. "I guess you're right, in some aspects anyway. She touched individuals, not a whole group. No, that's not exactly true either.... She had a real impact on the student nurses, the hospital staff." Darren turned, astonished understanding filling his features. "You're right." He shook his head, looking at Laurel as though she were a wonder. "How could you know that? I didn't even realize it...but it's true. I want to reach people like Mom does, and like Dad." He shook his head. "I'll have to be careful not to repeat their mistakes."

A laugh escaped Laurel at that. "That I can relate to, but I can't say I want to be like my mother. Or my father, for that matter."

"No?"

"No." She brushed the comment aside. "You were saying you wanted to make a difference with a group of people but still fly."

His eyes told her he'd noted her avoidance of the subject of her parents, but he just nodded. "Right now it seems Thor, and people like him, are my...my mission, if you will. But I don't have steady contact with him, so it's frustrating." He shrugged. "Enough of this. You want to know what's going on around Ndovu."

But I want to know about you too.

A little group of children suddenly surrounded them; they followed, whispering to each other. Darren bantered with them in Swahili, provoking choruses of giggles.

Laurel smiled, warmed at the adoration she saw on the small faces. Clearly Darren knew how to win children's trust. "We should invite them to come to chur—"

Darren's quick shake of his head cut her off. "Didn't you listen last night? These are Somali kids. They'd be whipped within an inch of their lives if they ventured near a church, Laurel. Not that they'd want to go there. Did Farah sound like he'd spend much time with the Meru?"

"No, but…well, aren't there any Somali Christians?"

"A few, and those usually move away, into cities. They're seen as traitors, defectors to the infidels." He ran his hand through his hair. "Haashi, a Somali Christian and one of the bravest men I ever met, actually traveled to Somalia itself, northeast of here. I heard that he has a tiny church, but they live under terrific persecution."

Warm dust sprinkled Laurel's sandals as she walked. The kids from the compound ran off calling good-byes. Ahead she could see where the tiny, dry gardens began. A rich smell of smoke and domestic animals overlaid the wild scents now. There were more of the pesky flies. Suddenly other children, darker and stockier than the golden brown Somali children, came in two and fours until Laurel and Darren were surrounded by a kind of entourage.

"What is your name?" One called out in heavily accented English.

"Where are you going?" They egged each other on in boldness, calling out the questions almost in unison and giving no time for a reply.

"Give me a money!"

Darren laughed and said something that Laurel couldn't understand. The kids dissolved into giggles and pulled back a bit.

"They were just practicing their school English." Darren's eyes were sunlit.

"Give me a money?" Laurel mimicked, trying to get the accent right. A chorus of giggles greeted her attempt. "They learn that in school?"

"Hey, not a bad accent. They figure we're rich, so it's worth a try, isn't it?"

The kids had quit calling out and simply walked with them, staring steadily. Several were packing smaller children, almost babies, on their hips or backs. Laurel found herself looking right into the huge, luminous eyes of one of the tiny ones. Those eyes widened, and the little one wailed with fright. The whole circle giggled and comments flew as the little boy holding the baby jounced him up and down to try to comfort him.

"Didn't know you were so scary, did you?" Darren said.

"I just smiled at him!" The baby was still watching her with wide, frightened eyes. "I feel like a sideshow."

His cheeks creased in a grin. "Pretty nice one at that. Seriously, we do tend to stand out. I used to feel stupid when we went somewhere that I didn't know the local language. If you know the language, it's easier."

"But this is a different language again, isn't it? I mean, I've been trying to learn some Swahili from Farah, and he taught me Somali greetings, but—"

Darren's eyes crinkled in real pleasure. "That's great! Let's hear it. Greet the kids in Swahili."

She tried, and in chorus they answered, eyes and teeth flashing into smiles. Laurel looked back at Darren. "How many languages do they know?"

"Two, three, maybe more."

"Boy, does that make me look dumb."

"But you're learning. Keep at it. You might get as smart as one of these kids yet." He was laughing at her, but with so much warmth in his eyes, she couldn't help smiling back.

The whole pack of kids followed them to church. Not that it looked like anything Laurel would have called a church. It was simply a corrugated iron roof on poles. There were no walls. The seats were homemade wooden benches. A child ran to bang on what looked like a piece of a truck spring hanging from one of the poles.

"He's rung the church bell. The congregation will be here shortly." Darren grinned at her startled face.

"The bell rings, so it's church time?"

"Right, and here come Jede and Isaac."

She's beautiful! Laurel suddenly felt short, pale, and dowdy near Jede's willowy height and rich, golden brown skin. Isaac seemed earnest and dignified, but Jede's smile made Laurel instantly feel at home.

"I'm so glad you've come! Darren told us you might." Laurel was charmed by the woman's British accent. "Come and sit down with me. Isaac wants

Darren to do part of the sermon, so they've got to talk."
She guided Laurel to one of the front benches. "So tell
me, are you enjoying Kenya?"

The bench wobbled as Laurel sat down. "It's a little
confusing, but so far I love it. I'm learning so much. I
hardly know anything yet. Even the little kids know
more than I do."

Jede laughed. "I've felt like that before."

A child ran up and touched Jede's arm, then stood
straight and said something in her ear. Jede answered
and turned to Laurel. "Excuse me. You will be all right
here?"

"Of course."

Jede touched her arm and went with the child. For
the first time since they'd arrived, Laurel had time to
look around. *Wow, this really is a different church.*

Because the church had no walls, she could see the
people walking toward them down several paths. All the
women, including Jede, had scarves tied on their heads.
Laurel was suddenly aware of her bare head. She shifted
uncomfortably on the hard, wobbly bench. The women
wore bright cloths over print dresses or blouses. Other
cloths held babies tied to their backs. Some of the men's
shirts were torn. It wasn't hard to tell that life wasn't easy
for these people.

As they came to sit down, each adult came to shake
her hand.

Awkwardly she tried her Swahili greeting on one
older woman. Her wrinkled face creased into a huge
smile and the work-hardened hand tightened on
Laurel's. "Eeeeh, jambo! Jambo sana!" A burst of other
words followed. When Laurel mutely shook her head,

the woman gave her hand one more good shake, smiled, and sat beside her. Another joined her and another, and Laurel realized that women sat separately from the men.

The smile on Laurel's face felt pasted there. She could feel eyes on the back of her neck. The roof pinged in the heat, and a line of sweat trickled down her stomach. People kept coming, crowding in beside her, each one simply squishing themselves onto the end of a bench. Everyone else seemed perfectly comfortable with the contact.

Jede came back, gave Laurel a smile, and squished onto the end of the bench behind her. *I feel like a pink sardine in a can of dark ones.* Only the front of the building had a wall. Darren and Isaac walked from behind the wall to sit in two rickety, wooden chairs. A knot in her chest seemed to loosen slightly. *One other white sardine.*

Crowded as they were, they stood and began to sing the first song. Energetic voices belted out the tune. She knew that tune! She joined in, singing in English. Suddenly a great warmth and joy swept through her. The women beside her didn't seem like strangers anymore. They were sisters in Christ.

She blinked when Darren stood and went forward to say a few words. He seemed almost a different person, much more like the dignified Isaac in demeanor. *He's obviously not only switched languages but cultures as well. I'm the only white sardine, after all.* But it didn't seem to matter anymore. *We're all God's children, these Meru and I.*

The sense of connection with the people around her carried her through Isaac's long sermon. Afterward most of the people came to shake her hand again before they left, but this time Laurel felt none of the strangeness.

Amid much laughter, she even learned the Meru greeting, or one of them. There seemed to be different ones for different situations.

Jede came to stand beside her. "You're doing wonderfully!"

"Thanks. But it is so good to have you talk to me in English. I feel overwhelmed."

"I know what you mean. When we first moved here I was so lonely. I know the Meru language now, but I'm still often lonely."

"Where are you from?"

Jede laughed. "I'm a city girl from Nairobi. My friends thought I was crazy to come here." She looked over at Isaac. "They didn't think I should marry Isaac either, but what can you do when you love a man and want to serve God with him?"

Serve God with him. That sounded so good. Would she ever find a man to tend creation with her for God? Darren Grant? Not likely, given his attitude. She shook off that thought and focused on Jede.

"So Isaac is from here?"

"No, he's Kamba, and I'm of the Masai people." She laughed. "No one wanted me to marry a man from a different tribe. Some of my uncles have hardly spoken to me since we married. Isaac's relatives didn't like it either. They talk a lot about serving God, but actually putting God first before family tradition, well, that's a different thing. We decided to be Africa Inland Church missionaries and AIC asked us to come here." She shook her head. "My family couldn't believe it. My father was so angry. 'I didn't educate you to go live like a bush rat!'" She shrugged as if to dismiss the pain and looked at

Laurel apologetically. "I must be boring you. We just met each other, and here I am blurting out my life story."

"No, it's fascinating." *Like seeing into a different world.* "I've felt isolated, too, especially from other Christians."

"You and Darren are coming to dinner at our place, aren't you?"

"I'd love to!"

Darren came over shaking his head. "I'm sorry, Jede, but we can't. I'm booked to fly Samuel Kimathi out at two, and that's in less than half an hour."

"It is?" Laurel couldn't keep the surprise out of her voice.

Darren laughed. "We'll have you on African time yet."

Jede grabbed her hand. "You will come and visit, won't you? Could I come and visit you?"

Laurel's hand closed over the slim brown one. "I will, and you're welcome to come any evening."

Even the insect chorus was silent in the still, hot air as they walked back. The children didn't reappear. Darren was very silent.

"Is something wrong?"

He nodded slowly. "Isaac told me that most of the people are already low on food. Unless the rains come early, things are going to get rough. Welcome to the real Africa." His voice was slightly ironic and his eyes sad.

"Is there anything I can do?"

"Did you bring a magic wand with you?" The tease was back in his voice, but no twinkle showed in those gold-streaked eyes. Laurel didn't answer. What was there to say?

"Isaac said there's a persistent rumor that by bribing

some government official, Joan stopped the drilling of more boreholes on the Wilson."

"Is that terrible?"

"It's complicated. More water means less death during the dry season for people and domestic animals, but it also means the land would be stripped bare near the wells. Boreholes speed up desertification and make things worse in the long term. They've only got one reliable well at the moment." He stuck his hands in his pockets. "Nobody knows where Joan Doyle got the money for that kind of bribe."

Again Laurel thought of Lilith's money. She shook her head, pushing away that fear. "How far do the people have to go for water?"

"Some of the women walk ten miles a day. If they're lucky, they have a donkey. If not, they carry it themselves."

"Ten miles!"

Darren laughed at her tone. "Oh yes. A strong, hardworking woman is worth many cows." He looked her up and down. "You're a little small but built well, perhaps fifteen cows."

"Darren Grant!"

His eyes twinkled at her indignant response.

"Do they really buy and sell women?"

"Once again it isn't that simple. A dowry isn't exactly a purchase price. More a recognition of a woman's worth. The church is divided on the subject." They were walking onto the airstrip now. "I'll stay here. Dr. Kimathi should be here soon, and I've got to do the preflight check." He faced her. "Now that you've seen a bit of what's at stake, maybe you can understand my reaction to Joan Doyle better."

"I'm beginning to. You think it's a clear-cut choice—people or animals, black or white."

"Isn't it?"

"I don't think so. Look, twice in the last couple of minutes you've told me things aren't simple. I don't think this is so simple either."

He lifted an eyebrow and started to speak, then shook his head. "I don't want to argue with you, Laurel. Thanks for coming to church with me."

"Thanks for taking me. It was amazing. I learned a lot, and I'm really glad I met Isaac and especially Jede."

He took her hands. "Keep on learning. You have a good heart."

That heart seemed to have stopped entirely at the touch of his hands. She took a deep breath and looked into his eyes. "Darren, if I learn, it doesn't mean I'll come to agree with you. I can see that things are difficult here, but they weren't always easy at home either. There has to be a better way than a black and white choice."

He looked down but didn't drop her hands. He took a slow breath and his fingers pressed hers. "We obviously have our differences, but I don't want you hurt. I don't like the tensions building around Ndovu Ranch. You be careful."

"I'll try."

He nodded, touched her gently on the nose, and turned to go.

"Darren, would you do something for me?"

He turned back, eyebrows arched.

"Come and spend a day with the animals. Try to see things from my point of view."

"I've seen baboons before. It won't change anything."

"Since you've come back to God?"

He frowned and said nothing.

"Will you come?" She could hear the Jeep approaching.

"I shouldn't, but I'll think about it. Meanwhile, you be careful!"

The Jeep drove up, and they turned to see Joan and the others. Before long, Laurel was watching Darren's plane recede into the blazing blue sky. Sadness rested on her heart, weighing it down.

We see things too differently. How could we ever belong together? Tears stung her eyes, and she brushed them away.

8

"SO HOW ARE ISAAC AND JEDE?" DARREN'S FATHER HAD PICKED him up at the strip by Kijabi Station. Tall, wild olive trees leaned over their vehicle as they drove toward the house.

As usual, his father seemed more concerned for those Darren worked with than he did for Darren himself. With a weary sigh, he pushed away the old resentment. "Isaac and Jede are fine, Dad." He rubbed his hand across his face. "Actually, I think Jede especially has been having a hard time."

"I wondered. There can't be many women there with whom she has much in common."

"Laurel Binet, the grad student I flew up to Ndovu Ranch, came to church with me Sunday. I think she and Jede might spend some time together."

His father pulled the car into the driveway and turned to Darren with raised eyebrows. "You invited one of Joan Doyle's graduate students to church?"

Darren nodded but said nothing more. Both men got out of the car. This wasn't the house that he'd grown up in, but most of the furnishings were the same. It had the feel of home. His father's tall, slightly stooped figure preceded him into the living room.

"Your mother is at the hospital. She intended to be home, but things got busy. She said to give you her love."

Darren barely suppressed a smile. "Not much has changed has it?"

His father laughed. "She did *intend* to be here, really." He sank down onto the couch and motioned to a chair. "Sit down and tell me about this Laurel."

Darren slowly folded his long frame, forcing the tension from his muscles. His first response was to tell as little as possible, guarding something he cared about. *Cared about? Does Laurel mean that much to me?* She'd better not. Their priorities were way too different.

"Laurel is probably a little younger than I am. Like I said, she's working with Joan Doyle."

"You said she was a grad student."

Darren frowned. "Come to think of it, I don't think she is exactly. She said she had the opportunity to come study animals in Africa and jumped at it." He leaned forward. "She's in way over her head up there and hasn't got a clue. It's all, 'I want to take care of the nice animals; God made them, too.' And she's in a minefield, blindfolded with all the good intentions in the world."

"You mean the trouble between Joan Doyle and the local district commissioner?"

"That, and I flew Kimathi in a couple of days ago. He's definitely cold toward Joan, and that's new. There's trouble between Doyle and her university as well, and now she's flush with a new source of money. Isaac told me there's the threat of fighting between the Somali and Meru. I wish Laurel wasn't anywhere near that place."

"Then you wouldn't have met her." His father's eyes were laughing.

Darren crossed his arms. "Maybe that would have been better."

His father's expression grew somber. "I was just kidding, Darren. She's really something, eh, this woman? Should your mother and I come up and meet her?"

Darren stifled a flash of irritation. Not at his father's

probing, but at the idea of them coming up to Ndovu. It was unlikely that his father would do so, even if Darren did ask. Over and over when he was little, his father had talked about coming to watch Darren participate in sports or coming up to boarding school on his birthday. His father had never come. Again Darren dropped the old reactions and focused on his father's question.

"Yes, Laurel is something. Different. Beautiful, but not in a conventional, Barbie doll sort of way. Thor said she was sleek as a gazelle, but it's more than that. She...shines. From the inside. Like she's filled with light and grace."

His father laughed. "You really do have it bad. You'll be writing poetry in a minute."

Darren frowned. "I was just trying to describe her. But for all of that, we have almost nothing in common except our commitment to Christ."

"After the rough years, it's good to hear you say that. So Laurel is a Christian? That's interesting." His father leaned back, smiling. "You know, the Nairobi Baptist Church has got that trip to the coast planned. If she's in as rough a situation as you think, she could probably use a break from Ndovu. Why don't you ask her?"

Darren shook his head. "I don't think so. Christ isn't all she's committed to. She wants me to come and watch her baboons with her for a day."

"You used to spend hours watching the wild animals out in the bush. If I remember right, didn't you get suspended from boarding school once for taking off and hitchhiking down to one of the parks—Tsavo, wasn't it? It should be right up your alley."

Darren stood and paced across the room. "That was

a long time ago." *And you let the school find me and bring me back; never even came to see if I was okay.* He hadn't been okay. Not really. Somehow that trip, hitchhiking on his own and doing just fine, had been the final turning point in his rejection of his parents' values. Out in the wild land, he'd turned from God to the beauty around him for solace. He'd ended up at the camp of an Australian pilot who was working with some British woman studying elephants. Every day for a week he'd flown with Ian Toms, and by the last day, he'd landed the plane himself.

Darren's stomach ached. *I can't go back to that...back to the things that pulled me away from God. Not even for Laurel.*

"Well?" His father was watching him.

Darren looked away. "I said I'd think about it, but I doubt I'll go."

"It's not like you to avoid an interesting experience." When Darren didn't answer, his father stood and walked into the kitchen. "Come on, let's find something to eat. While we're eating, you can tell me how business is going."

Darren's jaw tightened. He wasn't about to tell his dad things weren't going great. "I'm surviving. I've had a few new contracts recently."

"I still don't see why you don't just quit and join the mission. We could use your skills."

Darren shook his head. "How are things going with your pastoral class at Bible school?"

His father laughed. "Nice change of subject. Actually, I'm a bit frustrated. The idea of a leader as a godly servant is so hard to get across."

Darren began building sandwiches for both of them as his father talked about his class. *At least I didn't argue with him this time.* He handed his father one sandwich and sat down to listen.

Laurel is right—what I want to do isn't so different than what he and Mom are doing. He watched his father gesture excitedly with the sandwich as he explained a point. *He still doesn't have a clue what he and Mom put me through.* At least he was forewarned; if he ever married and had children, he'd be more careful. Automatically, he thought of Laurel. He shook his head. Not a chance.

A couple of weeks later on another blazing hot day, Laurel looked over the baboon troop again. "Are you sure? He could be behind some of that scrub thorn-bush."

"No, he has left. Chewbacca is not there." Farah waved his hand gracefully, including the entire troop of baboons.

Laurel shook her head and looked again. "He must be. He was with them last night."

"It is of no account. The males do not stay. Perhaps he has found a more beautiful mate."

"What about Gremlin? He wouldn't leave Gremlin, would he?"

Farah shrugged. "Perhaps it is the will of Allah that Gremlin will die. How can one resist such things? It cannot be done."

Laurel clenched her teeth. *What can I say to that kind of fatalism?*

The ground was very dry, almost bare. Laurel was as

fit as she'd ever been because the troop traveled farther each day, not resting long anywhere. Today, she kept up with them, watching sadly. *Even the babies aren't playing anymore.* A mother and baby paced by, the little one riding like a tired jockey. The gritty dust stung Laurel's eyes.

Gremlin, with no mother to ride and no Chewbacca to keep him company, wandered forlornly. He tried to come close to Leo and groom him, but the big male walked away. His older sister Cleo stayed with him for a while. Could she manage to help him? Laurel shook her head; Cleo was so young herself. Farah was probably right about Gremlin.

A light touch on the back of her leg made her look around. Gremlin was there, gently "grooming" her, asking her for help as if she were one of the bunch. With her heart aching, she turned away.

She knew all the reasons she couldn't get involved—every scientist did—she wasn't a baboon. She couldn't be Gremlin's protector in the group and get involved in the continuous maneuvering for status, safety, and food.

But it hurt her terribly to turn away.

God, thanks so much that he wanted to be my friend. If it can be Your good will, please bring this little animal through to adulthood. I know You find pleasure in his life.

By the end of the day, Cleo was spending more and more time with Gremlin. *Maybe she can actually keep him alive.* In spite of her doubts, Laurel felt a little lift of hope.

She took a deep breath and looked up. Farah was staring to the east, his face set. She followed his gaze. The horizon was smudged with dust. *The goats of the infidels.* She half smiled. Some of those infidels had become good friends. Then she looked back at Gremlin and her stomach tightened. *If it weren't for the goats… They do more damage than a thousand gazelles.* She shook her head. There were children with those goats, one or two she knew by name. *But the kids won't be much better off when Ndovu is barren dust as well.* So what were the options, could she do anything but watch and grieve?

Darren would see it as black and white—the welfare of the children herding the goats or the lives of a baboon troop. Her mouth twisted, and she walked quickly after the troop. She hadn't seen Darren for weeks. He'd brought supplies several times, but only in midday when she was out observing. In fact, she'd heard the plane the day before. *He's avoiding me. There's no way he's going to come watch the troop with me.* Resolutely, she pushed away the ache inside. *It's a good thing he isn't around!*

Farah spat on the ground in the direction of the goats. "May Allah judge!"

Jerked back into the present, Laurel protested, "Farah! God loves them too."

"But they are infidels!"

"Don't Muslims honor Abraham and Jesus as well? Jesus said that God is not willing that anyone should be lost. He loves everyone, including you."

He gave her a stunned look, as if that was an idea he'd never considered before. "We must watch the animals," he said and turned away seemingly lost in thought.

By the time she came into the compound, Laurel was exhausted. The baboons had traveled even farther than usual. After supper, she walked slowly back to her banda.

"Laurel! Jambo."

"Oh, I'm so glad you made it. I missed you last night."

Jede took her hand. "It's good to see you too. Today was bad?"

"Just dry and hot and very long. I wish the rains would come."

Jede nodded. "Now you sound like a true African. I think I would have gone crazy by now if you weren't here to talk to."

Laurel smiled. "I don't think so. You and Isaac would have managed with God's help."

"Who can know. Still, I am glad you're here. The time helping you with Swahili and just talking is like a holiday."

"Exactly."

"Hey, Mbaika, the older Meru woman who's kind of taken me on as a project, came over again today. That reminds me, I haven't taught you to weed properly yet." Jede was laughing.

"Weed?"

"Eeeeh," Jede agreed using an African form of agreement. "Mbaika says, every good wife needs to know how to weed. Not Masai, but Meru, Kamba, Kikuyu." Jede listed some Bantu tribes.

"And Mbaika taught you?"

"Tried to, last rains. I don't think I'll ever get it quite right. Darren is enough of an African; you'd better learn to weed too. Here, let me show you." Jede snatched up a stick, bent over at the waist with her legs straight, and started to dig energetically at the ground. She glanced over her shoulder. "Get to it. We've got to build up your stamina."

Laurel laughed, then sobered. "Why'd you say that about Darren?"

"He was here yesterday, brought supplies in. He came over and I talked to him for a long time. He kept asking about you."

"So why didn't he come and see me then?" She shook her head, appalled that her throat was suddenly tight.

Jede put a hand on her arm. "Maybe Darren is afraid you'll distract him from what God has for him to do."

"I'm some kind of evil temptress? That's crazy." Her chest hurt.

"Isaac has known Darren and his family for years. When Darren went away from God, when he wasn't flying or partying, he was always out with animals, out in the bush. He told Isaac that the bush was kind of his place of rest then."

Serving Gaea. Laurel frowned. "So he's afraid to get near the animals. Are you sure?"

Jede shrugged. "No, it was just an impression. As far as being concerned about animals when people are hurting, Isaac agrees with him there, and I…" Jede sighed. "I don't know. You confuse me, but that's not what we were talking about. Darren cares about you."

Laurel crossed her arms. "We're just too different in the way we see things."

"No! I've told Isaac that it would be so good if you and he got married."

"Jede, you're crazy."

"I don't know. Listening to you these weeks, I'm beginning to think that there is something to what you believe. You keep talking about people and animals living in peace, making a pattern like Eden. Isaac thinks it's foolish to dream of that, but I am not so sure. If it could be like that, even a little…" She shook her head. "Also, if Darren was comforted by the animals, maybe it was really God he saw there all the time."

"But he doesn't think so?"

Again Jede shrugged. "Maybe if we could do something somehow, something to actually show Isaac and Darren that it's not a foolish dream, this idea of living at peace, caring for creation."

Laurel looked at her with sudden hope, then shook her head. "People don't hear if they don't want to listen. Darren is so sure he's right. He kept saying that I'd learn and change."

Jede laughed. "Are you both waiting for the other one to change?"

Am I? Hoping? "Look, doing something constructive with the mess we're in here can only be right. Can you think of anything we can do? I don't mean to convince Darren, but just because it should be done. I've been trying to think; some places have found better ways to do dryland farming."

"I've read of that, but who would teach us? It cannot support as many as the traditional way." Jede held out her hands. "Then, if the rains fail, the traditional way will support no one at all."

"If we could find some other way to make some income, supplement the subsistence farming…"

"Out here?"

There was a long pause between them. A cicada started its rhythmic buzzing and then another.

Jede bowed her head and rubbed her fingers together. "The idea that we're supposed to care for creation scares me a little. Since we talked about this the first time, I've been reading Genesis and some of those other passages. If God did plan for people to take care of the rest of creation for Him, won't He judge—"

"I like that idea!" Joan had walked over silently in the dark. Laurel jumped at the sudden interruption, but Joan wasn't finished. "I don't have much time for God, or gods, for that matter, but if any one of them would do something for nature, I'm all for it." Joan looked at Jede. "No offense, but I wish you'd take your congregation elsewhere."

"Isaac and I didn't choose this place." Jede's eyes were steady.

"No, I suppose you didn't. You were pretty full of high-flown rhetoric a few minutes ago. 'God planned for people to take care of the rest of creation for Him.' Ha! I don't see much evidence of that among people who call themselves Christian, either here or anywhere else."

"Why do you think I'm here?" Laurel cut in. She couldn't let Joan get away with that statement.

Joan tipped her head. "I suppose there's always a first, but I didn't come here to talk philosophy, Laurel. I'll be gone tomorrow, a meeting in Nairobi. I'm counting on you to carry on. If I can't get all the things done, banking and so on, I may stay another day."

Joan gave precise instructions for the next couple of days and told Laurel firmly that Ibrahim was in charge in her absence. The two friends watched Joan stride off into the night.

"She's quite the woman," Laurel said. "I've never met anyone like her. Believe me, God has used her to teach me many things." Like patience. And loving the unlovely.

"But Laurel, she is right. I don't ever remember hearing Bible teaching on man's responsibility to care for creation."

Laurel sighed. "It's hard in some places at home, too, because some environmentalists are openly pagan and negative about Christianity. It's hard to share some goals with people like that."

Jede shifted in her chair. "Here it's a little more direct and less abstract. The baboons raid gardens and steal desperately needed food."

Laurel swung around. "Are they?"

"Not so much now, and I don't think it's your baboons. Mbaika was telling me that the first year was really bad, but now there are more people on the Wilson, and I think the baboons that used to live there are mostly hunted out. Still, children have to guard the gardens all the time. The gazelle, warthogs, baboons, birds—everything wants our food."

Laurel felt sick. "Isn't there any way? Does everything have to be destroyed?"

Jede put a hand on Laurel's arm. "Maybe God will open a way. He is not helpless! But I'm worried for the children especially. They have stuff in their bellies, but not the protein and vitamins they need. So many of the little ones are dull eyed and listless."

Again they sat silently listening to the night sounds. *Jede is right. God isn't helpless.* She lifted her head. "At least we can pray."

They did so, sitting facing each other holding hands. Laurel's heart eased as one by one, they laid in front of God each thing that had been worrying them.

They prayed for Isaac, for individuals in the church,

for peace between the Meru community and the Somali, that wise heads would prevail over the young men who would choose to fight. They prayed for Joan Doyle and for Farah and for the wild creatures as the drought worsened. They prayed for Darren and for wisdom for Laurel.

Gradually the silences grew longer, and the peace deepened as they searched their hearts for things that needed to be laid before the Father of all.

After a long silence, Laurel said, "We lay all these things before you in the name of Your Son, Jesus Christ, Amen."

Laurel stretched her arms over her head and winced. Her body ached from sitting so long and after her long day, she was about ready to drop, yet she had rarely felt such peace and joy. Jede squeezed her hands. "Oh, that was good. I'd better go. Isaac will be home soon."

Laurel looked after her. She couldn't imagine dealing with all that Jede and Isaac had to face. No vehicle, no way of getting to help if one of them got sick. *Maybe it's easier if you take the risk with someone.* Jede and Isaac had differences and difficulties, but they were so obviously of one mind.

Before she could halt it, the image of Darren came into her mind—and with it, the sharp longing to see him, to hear his voice, feel his hand on her face....

She shook her head. No, it wouldn't work. It couldn't. Their differences were too deep to overcome. It was better if he stayed away.

Because if he came back, Laurel knew, deep inside, that her heart would be lost. Forever.

9

JOAN WAS GONE FOR TWO DAYS. AGAIN DARREN CAME TO PICK her up when Laurel was out observing—as she was when he dropped her off that afternoon. *Hey, I could ask him for flying lessons!* That thought jumped into her mind so abruptly it made her laugh. Obviously some part of her subconscious hadn't given up on Darren Grant. Laurel tried to tell herself it was best that she'd been gone when Darren was around, but her heart just wouldn't agree. It was filled with disappointment.

She shook her head. Had she really thought it would be so easy to stop thinking about him? Obviously, she'd underestimated his impact—and her own stubborn heart. She gave a short laugh.

Farah heard her laugh and turned to her. "What is funny, memsahib?"

"Nothing, Farah. Only a thought."

"It is good to have a thought that makes laughter." He replied solemnly, nodding his head like a wise old man.

Maybe so, but these thoughts were making more frustration than laughter now. *Why can't I get him out of my mind? Just because he's kind, wants to serve God, and is the most awesome man I've ever met*—She sighed. Thoughts like that were making it worse, not better. *Use a little discipline, Laurel. Just shut your heart and mind to the man!*

Farah pointed with his chin at Cleo and Gremlin. "Joan will be glad that Gremlin has found a friend.

Perhaps he will live if the rains come soon."

Small and smaller, the two animals sat close together. Cleo was grooming Gremlin. All day Laurel and Farah had stayed close to Cleo, moving with her through the troop. She'd done nothing to respond to the two of them, but they seemed to have attached themselves to her in any case.

"I wonder where Chewbacca is."

"Only Allah truly knows the ways of wild things."

"You're right, of course, but we're working at learning a few of the secrets." She focused back on Susan and watched as the matriarch sided with her smallest son who was squabbling with another daughter about Cleo's age.

The day rolled on, hot and dusty. She didn't hear the plane leave. Ibrahim came to pick them up. In spite of herself, as soon as she'd greeted him she asked, "Is Darren Grant in camp?"

"No, *memsabu.*"

Her heart sank, and she found both Ibrahim and Farah looking at her with far too much speculation. *Did I miss hearing the plane leave somehow?* No, she'd been listening with more attention than she cared to admit. Had another pilot flown Joan back? *No, that was Darren's plane I saw. I know it. So where is he?*

As she got out of the Jeep, the first thing Laurel heard was Joan yelling. *She's chasing that woman and child away!* Joan was waving both arms at them, as if they were chickens she was shooing out of the compound. The two came toward Laurel, looking back over their shoulders.

As the woman came abreast of Laurel, she turned and saw her.

Her eyes are so desperate. Laurel flinched as the woman clutched her arm with powerful hands, crying out something that was obviously a plea for help. She repeated Jede's name several times. Laurel stood rooted in place. *What am I supposed to do?*

The woman suddenly dragged the child, a tiny girl of about five, forward. She jerked the girl's arm upward into sight. Laurel nearly gagged. The child's arm was swollen and scored by a long, pussy burn. Her face was a mask of stoic pain. Laurel tore her eyes away from the child's arm to see Joan striding toward them, still yelling in Swahili, making violent shooing motions.

"Wait!" Laurel stepped in front of Joan. "The little girl needs medical attention."

"That's not my problem." Joan's eyes were narrowed. "There's a well of human misery in Africa that can drown you if you let it. I have no intention of drowning. You and I are here to study animals. This is none of our business. You're green here, but you'll just have to get over it. "

"Isn't there a clinic, some sort of medical facility?"

"Not within walking distance. I'm not about to run a free ambulance service to ailing Meru squatters. She can pay and go by *matatu* like anyone else."

"Matatu?"

"One of those covered pickups or minivans that are on the road everywhere. Haven't you learned anything?" Joan raised her voice. "Ibrahim! Why is this woman here?"

"Because she needs help!" Laurel cut in. "Are you blind?"

Ibrahim ignored Laurel, speaking only to Joan. "She must have come in without being seen by my people. I will drive her away now." He turned on the woman and started haranguing her.

The woman clung to Laurel's arm. Laurel lifted her chin. "Leave her alone! If you won't do it, I'll drive them to the clinic, wherever it is."

"Not in my Jeep you won't! They'd be after us for rides to market, for rides to catch a bus. It's like opening a small hole in a dam. We'd be swallowed up! You can't help every sick child in the district."

"No, but maybe I can help this one." Laurel could feel Ibrahim's eyes on her. Tall and stiff as a poker, he stood beside Joan radiating disapproval of Laurel and the woman. Farah looked confused. Joan stared at her with tired and cynical eyes, then turned and walked away with Ibrahim striding behind her. Farah hovered for a second, and then followed the others.

Laurel found she was shaking. The woman's fingers bit into her forearm. Gently Laurel tried to pry them off. Her mind darted like a trapped rabbit. *If I could get the keys and take the Jeep...* But even if she did, she didn't know the way to the nearest medical facility. Joan certainly wasn't going to tell her. She'd have to try and help the woman and child herself. Laurel swallowed convulsively and motioned for the woman and child to follow her to her banda.

Like anyone with a little sense who worked in the remote regions of Kenya, Laurel had come equipped with a comprehensive first-aid kit, even some medical supplies including antibiotics and large dressings. But her stomach wouldn't stop shivering. Just because she had stuff that might help, didn't mean she knew how to use it. Laurel motioned for them to sit on her bed and went to get hot water.

The two were waiting in exactly the same place when she returned. Ambaro hadn't wanted to give her hot water. Back in her banda, Laurel tried again to communicate, but it was no use. They shared no language. The little girl turned her head aside and stoically put up with Laurel's attempts to clean the wound. Only the short gasps of breath, like small, silent sobs, showed her fear and pain.

"Hello, Laurel?" A male voice called from outside her banda.

Laurel's head jerked up as a warm flush of recognition shot through her. *Darren was here! But Ibrahim said—* It didn't matter why he was here. "Come in. Hurry! Thank God you're here. I can't tell what these people are saying. Joan was trying to chase them away, but—"

"You wouldn't let her. Farah told me as soon as I walked into the compound." He bent over the little girl's arm.

"She should see a doctor. I don't know how to do this." Laurel's voice was close to panic.

"It looks like you've made a good start." He turned to the woman and spoke. She answered eagerly. Darren listened, then turned to Laurel. "She says that Meli fell into the fire a week ago. Her father-in-law wouldn't allow her husband to give her the money for a matatu, and now the wound is getting worse."

The woman burst into speech again, and Darren translated quickly. "Her mother-in-law had heard Jede speak of you. Desperate for any help, she risked coming here." His eyebrows went up. "Going into Somali territory couldn't have been easy."

"But now what? Are you sure we can't take her to the clinic? You said you have permission to use the Jeep."

Darren looked up from sorting through her first-aid material. "You've got what we need here. The clinic would mean an exhausting all-day wait for these two."

The woman must have understood some English because she nodded emphatically and said a phrase that included the word *slim*.

Laurel looked at Darren. "Slim?"

"That's what they call AIDS here. Hospitals and clinics are rife with it. They say that one person in six in Kenya is infected. I've lost friends. The child's wound will need more than one dressing. It's up to you."

"Slim." Laurel said it again with a shudder. It seemed like a black joke about dieting. "Can you show me how to help them?"

He smiled. "That I can do." His big hands were incredibly gentle as he treated and bandaged the ugly wound. "You're going to have to do this every day. You've got antibiotics here. Give her one pill yourself each day, or her mother may be pressured to sell it."

"Sell it?"

"The little one is only a girl, and antibiotics are worth money—money that could buy food for the whole family." He held the antibiotic capsule gently to Meli's mouth, speaking to her. She stared at him with huge, frightened eyes, and then opened her mouth like a little bird.

"I'll do my best." She watched as he explained things to the woman, who nodded then shook Laurel's hand over and over. *"Asante! Asante sana!"* The woman then grabbed Darren's hand and shook it, holding it with both of hers. He put both his hands on hers, almost bowing and answering gently, then turned to take the little girl's uninjured hand; his tall, strong body gracefully folded to the child's level.

As the two left, Laurel stood by Darren in the doorway, waving. She looked up at him. "Thank you. When you turned up, I was never so glad to see anyone in my life."

He grinned. "You did look a little flustered."

"A little! That's an understatement." Having him this close was putting her off balance. She walked out into the open and sat on one of the chairs in front of her banda, the ones she and Jede often used. "How did you turn up at my door exactly when—"

"When you needed me?" He reversed the other chair around and sat on it, arms folded on the backrest. "That, I think, was God's timing. I was down visiting with Jede and Isaac. She's been at me to come and see you, talk to you. She thinks I might learn something from you. Me, I'm not so sure, but…" He shrugged.

Jede, what have you done? Laurel bit her lip. "You've been avoiding me."

"Avoid a beautiful woman? Why on earth would I do that?"

Despite the teasing tone of the words, she saw something deeper in his eyes. She was right, and he knew it…he just didn't want to admit it.

"I can think of one reason."

Some of his easy playfulness faded, but he still kept his tone light. "Oh?"

"Sure. You'd keep your distance from someone if you felt it wasn't wise to get to know them too well…as a precaution against coming to…to care for them too much." She didn't turn from the considering gaze he focused on her. Instead, she held his eyes.

The silence around them was thick, heavy…as though something of great import rested on his reply and they both knew it. After a moment, he inclined his head. "Dangerous," he agreed, "and definitely unwise."

She looked away. "Darren, I'm not going to quit caring about nature."

"But you care about people too."

"Of course I do." She hugged herself, not sure if the cold she felt was physical or emotional. "But, as you're so fond of saying, it's just not that simple and easy here."

"Oh?"

"Of course, *nothing* about this place is simple; fascinating, beautiful, compelling, but not simple."

"And?" He scooted his chair forward slightly, his eyes intent on hers.

"Before I came here, I thought I could look out for nature—for the land, the animals—and leave people to someone else. I don't mean friends or people I meet, but sort of on a bigger scale, like you were saying."

"Make a difference to a group of people for God?"

"That's right. Now I'd like to find a way to do both."

His whole posture sagged. "I don't think that's possible, not here."

That sounds like rational thought, not fear. She sighed. "So why did you come over? Jede must have told you some of this."

"I don't know." He stood and turned his back, head bowed. "Actually, that's not true. I just couldn't get you out of my mind. If there's a chance that Jede is right and we can see things the same way…"

Laurel's heart seemed to stick in her throat. *See things the same way. I wouldn't have any logical reason to run.* She got to her feet as if to get ready to run, but the fear was mixed with an agonizing hope. "Darren, I don't think—"

He spun around and put a finger on her lips. She felt the shock of the contact right to her toes. "Don't say no yet. I've got to fly out before the light goes, but can we try to get to know each other a little better, do some talking?"

She hesitated, chewing her lip.

"I'll even come watch your animals with you if that's what it takes." He reached for her hands.

She looked down at the strong fingers over hers. *If I could help him get a little more balanced view of nature… Father, help us. We both want to do what's right in Your eyes. Help us see what that means…and how we can do it together.*

One dark eyebrow went up quizzically. "Please."

Unable to speak, she simply nodded. He bent and warm lips touched her forehead lightly; then he was gone. For a long time she stood there, her body humming from head to foot, her mind in turmoil. *Watch it, Laurel. He's a great guy, but if he doesn't change his mind about nature he's not for you. Even if he does…* She bit her lip. Running away from emotional involvement was so much simpler. *Why did I ever listen to Julie?*

Slowly Laurel went back into her banda and knelt at her bed. "Dear Lord, I'm not sure I should have agreed. Help me keep my head around Darren and not get swept away. He's strong medicine, and it's hard to keep my mind clear."

She lifted her head and stared at the wall. *Maybe it would be better if I just left this place. How can I work with a woman who'd drive an injured child away? And then I wouldn't have to deal with Darren.* She laid her hot forehead on her hands for a long moment before she stood and went out to get some supper.

The next evening, the woman and child didn't return.

Jede came looking for her at dusk. "Can we go somewhere and talk?"

Laurel drew Jede into her banda. "What is it? Are you okay?"

Jede wrapped her arms around herself as if she were cold. "Njeri, the woman who came here last night, visited me. She's afraid to come back here into Somali territory. She thinks the Somali would drive her away, especially now that they know she's coming."

"Would they?"

"I don't know. Muslims believe in helping people in trouble. But, as you know, the Somali people don't think much of us."

Laurel clenched her hands together. "There's something else we need to talk about. All day long I've been thinking. I'm not sure I can work for a woman who'd try to drive a hurt child away."

Jede grabbed her hands. "You can't go! I need you here, and maybe God put you here for other reasons, too."

Laurel's jaw tensed and her throat hurt. "What reasons?"

"You've helped me, and there's Darren."

"That's part of the trouble."

"Njeri is waiting at my house. There's she and her

daughter, and what about the baboons? If you left, you'd never know what happened to Gremlin."

"But can I stay? Is it ethical?"

Jede took her hands. "Has Joan made you do anything that you felt was wrong?"

"Not so far."

"Maybe you can make a difference in Joan's attitude."

"Me?" Laurel laughed. "She's about as malleable as dried oak. I still don't know what I should do, but I'll come with you now. Let me just get the bandages and things."

Jede and Isaac's house was made of uneven brick that looked exactly the color of the ground in the flashlight beam. Not much bigger than Laurel's banda, it had two tiny rooms inside. A kerosene lamp glowed on a rough, wooden table. The first time she'd gone there, she felt a bit awkward, very aware of the difference between this house and the houses she'd been used to. After a couple of visits, the awkwardness had faded so that this was simply her friends' house.

As Laurel walked in, Njeri rushed to greet her. Meli stayed against the wall, watching with huge eyes. Still and wooden, the tiny girl endured the bandaging, then opened her mouth for the antibiotic. Her eyes were dry, but there were tears in Laurel's by the time she finished. Njeri then pulled out a little cloth and untied it to reveal three pieces of egg-shaped fruit that Laurel didn't recognize. She pressed them into Laurel's hands, and the woman and child left.

Laurel turned to find Jede watching her thoughtfully. "Will you run away?"

"I don't want to. I don't know." Laurel sat on the edge of a wooden chair and stared at the fruit without really seeing it.

"Please stay. Sometimes things seem so hopeless. The whole place is on edge now, people running short of food, tension with the Somali. Old men playing political games, and Isaac and I are caught right in the middle." Suddenly Jede was fighting tears. "At least they respect Isaac, but me—half of the people hate me because I'm Masai, and the other half because I've been to university."

Laurel dropped the fruit on the table and put her arms around her friend.

Jede's words came out between gulps. "It seems like people only come when they want something from me. The girls chase me and imitate me, trying to be sophisticated city girls. They only come to study the Bible with me to look at how I dress." She gave a hiccupy, half-hysterical giggle. "I think if I stuck a plastic spaghetti scoop in my hair, they'd all find one at market and do the same. Laurel, when God sent you, it was like reassurance that He still cares."

"He does, and so do I." *Thank You for letting me encourage Jede, Lord. At least I'm doing one thing right.*

"There is something else. I heard today that a baboon had been killed raiding gardens across the ravine. They're saying this is one from Ndovu." Jede hid her face in her hands.

A shaft of cold apprehension shot through Laurel. *Chewbacca!* If the troop started raiding gardens, how could anyone stop them? *They'll all be killed.* She swallowed hard. "It doesn't change our friendship. No matter what happens."

Jede took a long, shaky breath, turned to face Laurel, and took her hands. "Thank you. This is going to make things more complicated, though."

"Maybe the animal wasn't even from Ndovu. Is there any way we could get the carcass? That way we could see if it was one of the Kopje troop."

"I already asked Isaac." Jede stood up and paced across the floor. "He was angry with me. He said if I asked for the dead one, then it would be bad for our ministry. Like I told you, already some people mistrust me because I am Masai. The Masai used to raid the Meru, stealing cattle. They would think that I'm siding with the Somali against them because Joan Doyle is for the Somali."

What can I say? Laurel's chest felt tight and her throat hurt.

"I showed him what we were talking about in Genesis 1 and 2 and Psalm 104—how God made places that are for the wild animals—and I said that His pattern was for man to live in peace, tending His creation. You know, the ideas we were talking about? I told him that, yes, it is difficult, but we shouldn't throw away God's pattern."

"You told Isaac that?"

"Yes, and he left."

"Jede!"

She laughed. "Don't worry. He does that to walk and think things through. He'll be back. I'm going to make us both some chai. I know I could use some."

The hot, sweet beverage warmed Laurel inside and out.

There was the sound of footsteps outside, and Isaac

came in. He stopped abruptly. "Laurel, you are here?" He reached to shake her hand.

Jede was already pouring chai for Isaac. He took a long swallow. "I went to talk to old Kamau. It's his nephew who was said to have killed the baboon."

"Isaac!"

Isaac made a shushing movement at Jede with his hand. "Kamau says the carcass is still there, and they will bring it to demand compensation." He reached out to lay a hand on Laurel's arm. "It is perhaps good that you are with Joan Doyle. Maybe you can speak for the people, open a way so that an agreement can be made. It is said that Joan Doyle has received much money. Perhaps it can be used to make peace."

Laurel opened her mouth to protest, but shut it again. *Me influence Joan? That will definitely take a miracle.* "Will you pray for me?" She asked finally.

"We will." Jede's smile gleamed in the dim lamplight. "And God will answer. You will see!"

Laurel hoped so. She really hoped so. Because if He didn't, they would all suffer.

10

THE NEXT MORNING WHEN LAUREL WOKE, THE JOY SHE SO often felt at seeing God's beauty around her had fled. In its place was a heavy load of apprehension.

Can I do this? Talk to Joan in a way that will make a difference? She didn't seem to be able to get a full breath of air. Laurel slid out of bed onto her knees. "Lord, whether what I say makes a difference or not, I know I have to try. I need Your help."

When Laurel walked into the dining banda, Joan had finished eating. "Hurry up, get some food into yourself. We have work to do."

Laurel stood facing her. "Joan, there's something I need to tell you."

"Later." She gestured dismissively and headed out the door.

"Please listen." Laurel followed her out to the Jeep. "I found out last night that a baboon had been killed raiding someone's garden."

Joan's breath came through her teeth like a hiss. She whirled to face Laurel, her face a mask of angry pain. "When?"

"The day before yesterday. Look, Jede says that the baboons that used to live at the Wilson are mostly gone now. This was a big male, and I wondered—"

"If it was Chewbacca?" Joan grimaced. "It might be. The Wilson used to have two troops, and he was born to one of them. So far, the Kopje troop hasn't traveled to raid gardens, but each time a new male comes in, I live in dread that he'll teach them. Luckily the older females are the ones that do the leading." Her voice rose. "The baboons *belong* here. Subsistence farms do not!"

Laurel held out her hands. "Don't make these people hate us and the baboons more than they already do. Isn't there some way we could compensate them for the crop they're losing?"

"You're out of your mind. The farmers don't belong here! This year has been barely below average for rainfall, and already the land is stripped. Children go hungry and baboons are abandoning infants. I will not support such nonsense in any way. What we need is—" She clamped her lips shut abuptly and turned her head away.

Joan stayed in that position, her straight body bent, almost hunched over the fender of the Jeep…as though she had twisted herself over to protect a wound. A sudden, shocking thought jolted through Laurel. Was Joan crying?

Farah's eyes gleamed in the reflection from the headlights as he looked at Laurel. Ibrahim stared resolutely at the horizon.

The seconds stretched out. Tentatively Laurel reached out toward the older woman. "Joan? What is it?"

Shrugging Laurel's hand off, Joan spun to face her. "What *is* it? What is it! Africa is becoming a barren cesspool of human misery. My baboons are being killed. And I can say nothing! Not without losing funding and support."

"Losing funding?" Laurel struggled to make sense of Joan's words.

"Yes, losing funding! I asked UCLA to use their influence to stop this flood of people. I talked to the National

Wildlife Federation and the UN and anyone I could think of, then some bleeding liberal at UCLA called and told me to tone it down. I lost my temper and my funding and my job there." Her voice became sugar sweet. "A radical position is not in the university's best interest."

She spat on the ground.

"If you cannot speak against those Meru with words, we can speak with spears!" Ibrahim said suddenly, his fist making a thrusting motion.

"Don't be foolish. What would that accomplish besides to bring the Kenyan army down on you? I don't want my people killed as Shifta bandits."

"The cause is just," Ibrahim insisted.

"And you think that would stop the army if there were killings here?" Joan's voice was bitter.

"No, but if Allah wills, it is not a bad thing to die for justice." Ibrahim's fine-featured face was tipped back arrogantly.

Laurel stared at him with a mixture of horror and admiration. *Die for justice?* She suddenly thought of the children that had followed Darren and her to church. "Wait! Isn't there some way to work this out? You have funding, Joan. You said you have a new source of funding. Couldn't we compensate people to move farther from Ndovu? Jede and Isaac went out on a limb for me. They talked the people into coming to you. Please?"

"And talked you into pleading for them?" Joan's eyes were shrewd. "I've lived here twenty-five years. Let me handle this."

She climbed out of the Jeep. "I'll wait here for the delegation. UCLA didn't stop me. Neither will a few subsistence farmers. The work *will* go on! Now you get out there and continue watching our troop. Let me know how Gremlin is doing without Chewbacca around." She turned and strode off into the darkness.

Laurel moved to go after Joan, but Farah put a hand on her arm. "It is better that we go watch the animals." Still she hesitated, but Farah went on. "You have spoken as your friend has asked you to do. For now, what is there to do but leave it in the hands of Allah?"

In the hands of God. Farah didn't see things like she did, but his words were a good reminder of what she already knew—the Lord was in control. She bowed her head. As the sun came over the horizon, painting the dry bushland with golden light, Laurel prayed. God was big enough to make this glorious sun rise; big enough to make the ostriches they passed backlit and haloed by the dawn light; big enough for anything.

All morning her eyes kept glancing back in the direction of the compound. What was happening there? What would Joan do? Jede and Isaac were sure to be disappointed with her. Her stomach hurt. To make things worse, Gremlin was not doing well. He was more listless and searched for food with less energy. Cleo and Gremlin again stayed close to her.

Laurel found that she could walk close to a larger feeding animal and it would move off, allowing Cleo and Gremlin access to the food because they would stay closer to her. Laurel knew this was bad science. She was tipping the scale in Gremlin's favor. She told herself that she'd only do it once more so that Gremlin had a full belly at least one morning, and then she'd quit.

Susan had found an area thick in dry acacia pods. Argus chased her off. Laurel walked over, sure Argus would move, but he didn't. He spun and openly threatened her, hair on end and dagger-sharp teeth showing. Farah called out a sharp warning. Laurel backed off quickly. Her heart was pounding wildly.

Farah came over, eyes anxious. "You must watch where you go. Joan would be most angry! She said that—" he paused midphrase and looked up—"*Ndege!* The airplane, it comes."

Laurel followed his eyes to see a distant white speck. Rapidly it got closer; the sound of the engine grew, and the blue and white shape of Darren's 210 swept low across the bushland.

An hour rolled by slowly, and she never heard the plane leave, but Darren didn't come out to the troop either. What was he doing? Speculation about what might be happening back at the compound wouldn't leave her alone. The sun poured down on her head like a heavy, oppressive hand.

Argus had come over and was sitting close to Susan now. She moved away, but he approached again. The third time she stayed put and allowed him to groom her. Laurel reached for her pad. That was new. Those two had never had anything to do with each other before. One of the males gave the sharp double bark of alarm. Laurel hurried to finish the notation, not wanting to be interrupted. When she looked up, she found herself looking straight into Darren's gold-streaked eyes. She gasped and stumbled.

He laughed and caught her, his strong hand under her elbow. "Didn't think I could surprise you, not in the middle of a baboon troop."

"You actually came!" She sounded ridiculously

happy and eager, even to her own ears. "I mean, I saw your plane land, and I thought maybe you'd come to watch with me, but then when you didn't come out—"

"Ibrahim was involved in a big to-do with some people who'd brought in a dead baboon. I had to wait for him to finish before I could get a ride out."

She grabbed his arm. "What happened? Did Joan compensate them?"

"Joan dealt with them all right. She had no choice. They'd come with seven or eight men carrying machetes. She wanted that carcass and wasn't going to get it unless she paid them; not without open violence, and she's apparently not ready for that."

"Thank God for that anyway. Was she very angry?"

"Incandescent. I think Ibrahim volunteered to take me out here just to get away from her." His hand came over hers. "Laurel, it was the animal from this troop. I'm sorry."

Her throat closed, but she fought back the emotion. The last thing she wanted to do was cry about an animal in front of Darren. "I thought it was probably Chewbacca. We should tell Farah." Even in her own ears her voice sounded wooden.

Farah simply nodded when he heard. "It is the will of Allah."

Hot rage boiled up in Laurel, almost choking her. To blame this on God! Even on a faulty understanding of God.

Almost as if he read her thoughts Darren said, "I don't think so. We make a mess of the world with sin, and then say, 'It is the will of Allah?'"

Laurel felt like cheering. Farah gave Darren a puzzled

look, then lifted his chin and strode to the far side of the baboon troop.

"Muslim fatalism," Darren said and watched him go. "As if we don't have free will or some responsibility." He looked at Laurel. "Are you okay?"

The sympathy in his eyes tipped the balance. Tears stung her eyes, and she turned her head away. Darren put his arm around her, and for a second she relaxed into his strength. *No, I can't let myself respond to him blindly.* Then, taking a deep breath, she stepped away. "I'm okay now." Her voice was shaky and not very convincing.

"Would you like me to come back on a less difficult day?"

"No, don't go!" Her response was instant and from the heart and brought the heat of embarrassment to her face. She swallowed. "I'd like you to stay. You're here now after all, and…"

His hand tightened on her shoulder. "I'll stay. We'll make it through the day by God's grace. Both of us."

She looked up at him. "I didn't mean to force you into something. If you don't want to be here…"

"You're right. I'm not comfortable being here, but I did say I'd come." He gestured after the departing animals. "We'd better keep up."

Darren fit in easily. Keeping just the right distance from the animals, he was obviously more than competent in the bushland. His presence made Laurel feel calmer, safer.

"Cleo, she has found a tortoise!" Farah called.

Cleo twisted to approach backward, half sitting, looking over her shoulder at the little animal.

"What's she doing?" Darren was right at her shoulder.

"It's a submissive gesture. I guess she figures it's smarter to start humbly with something you don't know."

"A turtle?" Darren laughed.

Cleo turned and poked at the tortoise, then jumped back nervously, hands high. Gremlin watched cautiously from three feet away. The turtle had retreated into its shell. Carefully, Cleo put a finger into one of the leg holes. Then she bent and licked the shell. Now three other young baboons had joined them. They sat around the turtle like a committee meeting with a knotty problem.

Susan came over, sniffed at the turtle, and kept moving, obviously not interested. The older baboons were getting some distance ahead before the young ones left the turtle and ran to catch up.

Darren raised an eyebrow. "You called that little female Cleo, didn't you? I thought it was the thing for researchers not to give animals names, so one didn't try to foist human traits on to them."

She stopped in her tracks. "Did you learn that from Benson?"

"And others." He shifted as if the memory made him uncomfortable. "If they have names, why don't you introduce me?"

"Okay, that's Cleo, and there is Fupi, Argus, Drea." Even as she spoke, she felt an irritated helplessness. *If he'd already spent so much time with people who study animals, how is an afternoon with me going to make any difference?*

Cleo suddenly darted toward Argus, leaping high over him. The big male crouched and squawked. Darren laughed as Cleo ran from Argus's halfhearted threat and jumped in Laurel's direction. "That little Cleo is a bold brat."

"She is that." Laurel gave him a quick look, both surprised and pleased that he seemed so interested. *Maybe he's decided it won't do any harm to let himself enjoy the animals for a day.* She could hope anyway.

The day literally flew by. Darren had a good eye, picking up nuances in the interactions between animals. He and Farah talked easily, both in Swahili and English, but mostly he stayed close to her. When the animals settled in one area, picking wait-a-bit thorn pods, Darren sat on his heels the way the Somali did.

"How do you do that? I tried it and keep falling over backward. Most places out here have nowhere to sit, and I get tired of standing."

"I think you have to start when you're less than three years old and never stop. Most whites can't do it. They've sat in chairs all their lives."

"Didn't your parents have chairs in the house?"

"Nope, no chairs at all." His eyes were twinkling.

"Darren!"

He laughed. "Okay, we had chairs, but I spent as much time out of the house as in it. Like I told you, Mom didn't have much time for me. I was basically raised by my *aya.*"

"Aya?"

"Nanny, whatever. Sophia was a Kamba woman. I ran to her for security, played with her kids, spoke her language as soon as I spoke English. I'm not of mixed race, but I guess you could say I'm of mixed culture."

"So there's no hope for someone like me to really fit in?"

He raised one eyebrow. "Does Joan Doyle fit in with her Somalis? She came as an adult."

"And she's been here most of the time for over twenty years."

He nodded and stood up. "You're catching on now. That's why short-term missions are so futile. It takes a couple of years of very hard work to get fluent in another language, much less another culture."

Laurel frowned. "The church at home seemed to think it was a good idea to get people overseas short term."

Darren shrugged. "It is, for the people that go. They learn something about the rest of the world, become sensitized to the needs of others. As for really making a difference in the places they go…no, I don't think so, not unless they have a particular skill that's badly needed and not present in the country they visit, say orthopedic surgery or something like that. Even then, they're not really discipling. It's very rare that a month-long friendship really changes someone's life. If it were to happen, they'd still need to have committed support of a strong local church."

"Then it takes a lifetime of commitment to one place to really make a difference?"

"Are there any guarantees even then?" He was suddenly very sober. "A difference to whom?"

She held her hands out. "To the people. To the area. To the animals. A difference for God. I believe they all matter to Him."

He grinned. "I noticed."

He's not listening. She turned away from him. The troop was going a different way than they usually did. They were much closer to the ravine than usual. Movement caught Laurel's eye. Drea was off to one side, picking at something she'd found in the dirt.

Beyond her, something exploded, shooting forward. Laurel jumped then stared, her whole body rigid. A baboon scream sent shivers dancing down her spine and across her shoulders. Drea disappeared into a roiling tangle of fur, noise, and dust. *A cat? A leopard!*

The male baboons barked wildly, dashing toward the commotion. Laurel caught a glimpse of a big cat, crouched and running, dragging something. It flashed up a steep, rocky bank, a tide of baboons in hot pursuit.

One of the baboons grabbed at the leopard knocking it sideways. *They're going to kill it!* But then it rolled to its feet. Ears flattened, it shot into a narrow slot between tall boulders. The noise was deafening as every baboon in the troop seemed to be yelling at the top of its lungs. A feline growl rose above the cacophony, harsh and incredibly menacing. Laurel swallowed hard, forcing her tightly constricted throat to work. One of the males came flying backward over the heads of the rest.

"The leopard! She has taken Drea."

At Farah's alarm, Laurel turned her head to see him leaping up the hill in a wide loop around the confrontation. The boy stopped, poised on a boulder above the commotion.

It was only then that Laurel realized she had dropped her clipboard and was holding on to Darren's arm with both hands. She let go of him, scrambled for the clipboard, and tried to record the incident. This was important! Her writing was shaky, and her legs felt like they were made of Jell-O. A burst of noise made her look up. The leopard's snarl rose over a crescendo of baboon barking.

"If you shiver any harder, you're going to drop that clipboard again." Darren's hand on her shoulder brought her to herself.

"It's just that...I mean, I...I've never seen..."

His hand tightened reassuringly. "I've been in Kenya all my life, and I've never seen a leopard try to take a baboon either."

Laurel took a deep breath. "I've got to get where I can see better. I'm going up by Farah."

Darren came with her, and she was glad of his steady presence. As they reached Farah, another crescendo of barking and snarling erupted, but this time she could see what was happening. Leo and then Argus had dashed a little way into the cave after the leopard. Both jumped backward, twisting agilely millimeters from the leopard's claws.

"Farah, was that what the noise was before? Did the males challenge the leopard?" Laurel frantically sketched in the positions of the animals around the cave's mouth.

The pupils of Farah's eyes were huge with excitement. "Yes. Three times Leo has gone close, and twice Argus has done so. She is very angry, that leopard."

Laurel stopped writing midword. "She?"

"I know that one. The baboons have chased her before, but she never tried to take one. She has had cubs last year by fig tree ridge." He peered down the hill. The scene below had settled into a stalemate, the leopard snarling in the cave, the baboons pacing just outside.

"Look." Darren pointed at the bush below the cave. Laurel narrowed her eyes; there was something moving there. A second later a very shaky baboon walked slowly out.

"It's Drea," Laurel whispered. "They actually made the leopard drop her."

Several of the other baboons had seen Drea now. Susan made small sounds of greeting and was touching her gently. There was a deep gash on the young female's shoulder. Some of the baboons were moving off. Drea went with them, limping.

"So she didn't get any dinner after all."

"What?" It took Laurel a second to realize that Darren was thinking from the leopard's point of view.

"That cat is either young and foolish or desperate. Challenging a troop of baboons is foolhardy. She could have lost a lot more than her dinner."

Laurel shook her head, a vivid image of the graceful, fluid cat fleeing uphill from the baboons replayed in her mind. "She was beautiful. I wonder why she did it."

Darren shrugged, and Farah spoke up, "Perhaps it was that Drea came too close to the place she was lying. One cannot know these things."

"One can learn," Laurel said, half under her breath.

"But aren't there better things to do?" Darren asked.

Overwrought with excitement, she spun on him. "Look, you obey God the way He tells you to, and I'll do the same. Okay?"

He looked straight into her eyes. "It's a deal. Maybe He'll teach both of us something."

The baboons didn't stop harassing the leopard until

late in the afternoon. It was almost dusk by the time Ibrahim picked up her, Darren, and Farah. The acacia trunks looked golden in the rich evening light as they jounced into camp.

Darren touched her arm. "I've got to get in the air while it's still light. Will you walk down with me?"

He wants to be alone with me. She felt the old flutter of panic. *Think, don't just react, Laurel. I do want to talk to him.* She nodded and started walking. "Darren, why are you so uncomfortable doing this? Is it more than just a commitment to people?" *Is Jede right?*

He picked up a stick and shifted it from one hand to another before he answered. "I suppose you could say so. At one point in my life I was just looking for an excuse, an alternative to my parents' faith. Nature provided it…temporarily. Coming back into that world made me nervous. I wasted a lot of energy here once that would have been better spent elsewhere." He looked straight ahead, his face closed.

She bit her lip. "I can see now why you were reluctant to come."

"It was easier than I thought. Too easy. Nature is beautiful, seductive. I still don't feel immune—" He cut off his own words with a swift motion of his hand. Laurel waited in silence, and when he spoke again, his words came out weary. "I want to serve God, not get tangled up in distractions."

Distractions. Was he referring to nature…or to her? Swallowing the pain his words stirred in her, she nodded. "I understand, Darren. But this place—this world—God has created and the animals He's given us to care for, those aren't distractions to me. Caring for them is my service to God. He's the One who called me here, and following that call, being where He wants me...well, it brings me closer to Him."

He just shook his head sadly. "You're a special woman, Laurel Binet." He touched the tip of her nose. "See you later."

When he turned to go, her whole being reacted in protest. "No, wait!"

He took her hand. "What is it?"

"I..." What could she say? She shook her head. "Nothing. Never mind." But she found herself covering his hand with hers and holding on. *Use your head, Laurel. How can he help you?* But she couldn't make herself let go. "It's just that things are such a mess here. It's not your problem. I know that. I mean, you don't even think..."

"I wish I could make it better for you." He put his other arm around her and drew her close. He held her against him, cradled next to his heart, then, with a small sound deep in his throat, he let go.

She took a deep breath. "I'm okay now." *If only that were true...*

Darren gave a little grunt of laughter. "I don't know that I am." He ran a finger down her cheek, leaving a tingling trail of sensation. He hesitated, then gave a small nod. "Listen, Dad mentioned that a group from the Nairobi Baptist Church are heading to the coast for a week. Tropical beaches, and no baboons, leopards, drought, or burned children." He paused again, as though weighing his words, his eyes studying her face. "You obviously could use a break. How about it?"

"I don't know." It sounded so good, being with

Darren, away from the very things that kept coming between them...

Sure it sounds good. It would be a perfect setup—for doing a Lilith.

The thought jolted her, and she pulled back from him, but he only smiled at her.

"Just let me know. I really do have to go now. I've got about three minutes of light left."

A short time later she watched his plane disappear into the last glow of the sunset. She turned to walk away, her mind a whirl of emotions, so much so that she literally felt dizzy and unstable on her feet. *It felt so right to have him hold me!* She shook her head and tried to think clearly, but that seemed almost impossible when Darren Grant was the subject of her thoughts.

11

DARREN ADJUSTED THE THROTTLE AS HIS PLANE CLIMBED OUT OF Ndovu. His movements were sharp, jerky. He'd stayed out of the national parks and avoided really looking at the wild country since he rededicated his life to Christ. It just hurt too much. Then today, because of Laurel, he'd spent a whole day out there. He'd been a fool! *I gave that up. God is my Lord now!*

But what about Laurel? *She seems so sure that she can serve You, Lord, and still work there.* The muscles at the corners of his jaw bunched. *She can't be right.* He scanned the instruments and frowned. He was way off heading. The plane's heading was easy to fix, but was Laurel Binet going to do the same to his life? Holding her had felt so good…so right.

Not everything that feels good is good.

It had felt good to be in the wild, surrounded by nature, watching the animals again—but the power of that leopard wasn't anything compared to the power of Laurel's touch. He grimaced and glared at the instruments again. The way he was flying at the moment, he could use an autopilot to keep him on altitude and heading.

At least she's learned that things aren't as simple as she'd thought. He frowned, remembering her reaction to Chewbacca's death. Her grief had made his own chest hurt. *And it's going to get worse.* With the dry season progressing, the Meru boys would be sneaking farther onto Ndovu with their goats looking for less damaged land. The baboons would be ranging farther, looking for food, more likely to end up in gardens. *Can I do anything to help?*

His fists clenched on the yoke. He'd vowed to dedicate his life to God, to serve Him by helping Africa's suffering people. Just because he hadn't found the right way to fulfill that goal didn't mean he should compromise. Not even for a woman who touched his heart, his spirit, more deeply than he'd ever dreamed possible.

No. Everything he'd heard or read said you don't go into a relationship intending to change the other person, to make him or her suit you. Laurel was Laurel. He cared for her because of who she was. But who she was made her the wrong person for him....

His head ached. If he had any brains at all, he'd walk away from her, forget about her entirely. But then...he'd never claimed to be the smartest guy in the world. Just the most determined.

And in that vein, he figured the least he could do was check into the church trip. Laurel needed a break. *He* needed a break. What harm could there be in taking one together?

The next morning, Darren got a call. They wanted to know if he was interested in a contract with a tour company. Even as he set up the details, his stomach was tight with frustration. More taxi driving for tourists! Still, it was better than nothing, wasn't it?

"Hey, Darren." He looked up to see Stacy Hamilton at the door, his towhead looking almost white in the morning sun, and his perpetually sunburned face crinkled into a smile.

The two men clasped hands for a second, then Darren stepped back. "I was just thinking about calling you."

Stacy had been a high school classmate, lazy, a bit of a joker, but kind enough underneath. They'd played rugby together. Like most of his friends from the mission boarding school, Darren had lost track of Stacy during the rough years. Then three months ago, he had turned up in Kenya as a short-term missionary with the Southern Baptists. They'd spent several evenings talking about what had happened in their lives since high school. Darren had the distinct impression that Stacy had come to Kenya, not out of any real sense of mission, but because he didn't know what else to do and he didn't want to stay in the States.

"Okay then, I'm psychic. I sensed your thoughts on me. So what do you wish, O master?" Stacy bowed elaborately.

Darren chuckled and went along with him. "My mind was on you, O genie, because you attend Nairobi Baptist Church. I believe you have information about the upcoming trip to the coast."

"You're actually going to come with us? I thought you were too proud to hang out with expatriates." He deepened his voice and mimicked an old-fashioned preacher. "He is committed to spreading the Word of God, to shining the light in darkest Africa. All his actions, every resource at his command, bent to one great goal. He does not cohort with the frivolous, neither doth he dawdle with the foolish on sunny strands. He doth not—"

Darren crossed his arms over his chest and pinned

the other man with a stony look.

"Okay, okay—" he held his hands up in mock surrender and grinned—"enough with the looks that kill. What changed your mind about Nairobi Baptist? I thought you were committed to the AIC church you usually attend?"

"I am, but I met this woman who—"

Stacy burst out laughing and thumped Darren on the back. "A woman is your downfall!"

"Stace."

"Okay, okay, I'll be quiet."

"She's up at Ndovu Ranch working with Joan Doyle, and things are pretty rough there. I figured she needed a break, that's all."

Stacy just nodded, tongue in cheek. "So this woman, is she a Christian? Does she have a name? I don't mind women who're into wildlife, especially if wildlife includes me."

Darren rolled his eyes. "Forget it. Just get me the information on the trip, okay? Why did you come looking for me anyway?"

"The mission asked me to document the dry season. It's starting to get bad, and I thought some aerial photos would be great, especially since they'd pay for the flight. I mean, they did say they'd pay expenses. I wanted to know if you'd take me up a couple of times."

Yes! Darren jumped at a chance to do some flying that would not only help to pay the bills but might open people's eyes to the need here. "I'd love to. I don't have a flight booked until noon. How about now?"

Forty-five minutes later they were nearing Kenya Food's meat packing plant. Deep paths cut across the bone-dry ground. He could see clusters of cattle strung along the paths like oval beads. Trailing plumes of dust, they moved slowly. Here and there, a dead one lay—a small cow shape printed on the baked earth, framed by a dark stain. The herdsmen showed as tiny round beads. One or two were at the end of each string of cattle, walking in the blazing heat as they tried to get the cows to market before starvation killed them and made them worthless.

Darren's throat tightened as he looked. Many people waited until the last bitter moment, not willing to sell the animals that meant wealth, status, and sometimes even life itself, until it was clear those same animals would starve anyway. Now it was a vicious buyers' market. After they sold their cattle, the families would be left with almost nothing.

"The pattern of those paths and the cattle are going to look great." Stacy's voice was full of enthusiasm. "Let's fly over Nairobi Game Park now." Stacy kept his camera ready for a bit, then sat up. "It doesn't look half bad. No dramatic pictures of drought here. How am I supposed to use this?" He turned to Darren. "What's the deal? Did the park get more rain?"

Darren shook his head. "Wildlife isn't as hard on the land as goats and cattle are."

Stacy was squinting irritably. "Let's go somewhere that looks more dramatically dry." He stared down at the park. "I read something about wildlife and drought. They're designed to take the drought and not strip the land, aren't they? Yet I've seen pictures of dead wildlife from drought."

"It has to be worse than this. I hope it doesn't get

that bad this year." *Please, God.* Darren turned to climb over the Ngong hills. On the far side the Rift Valley gaped, and Lake Magadi gleamed white with soda. Hot air rising off the valley floor kicked the plane upward.

Stacy braced himself against the turbulence. "Why don't people farm wild animals then, if they're so much easier on the land?"

"You're not going to change thousands of years of thinking of cattle as wealth in a day." His thoughts turned to Ndovu. *But if we convinced the elders...* For a split second, hope lifted his heart—then he shook his head. That land was arid. Even carefully managed wild ungulates couldn't produce enough to support the big influx of people. *But with tourism to provide the rest of what was needed...* Could it be done? Not likely. Not without a huge influx of money.

He frowned and turned toward Limuru. Each tiny farm made its own pattern scratched in the red dirt. Even the few trees were so coated in dust that they matched the burnt ocher colors of drought. The bright green of the big tea plantations was dimmed to dun. The round tea bushes in even rows made the plantations look like corduroy.

Stacy was leaning out the door, taking pictures at a great rate. He motioned impatiently for Darren to circle again. "The earth tones are awesome!"

Darren watched the horizon as he pulled around. That bare earth did have a strong, spare beauty, but it meant children under three not getting the protein they needed for their developing brains. It meant women alone, trying to cope, while their husbands traveled searching for work of any kind. Work that usually didn't exist. It meant teenagers heading for the city and joining the bands of street kids. It meant families moving onto marginal land as had happened on the Wilson, land where wildlife had once lived.

If Laurel were here, maybe she'd understand. His chest felt tight and heavy. The new contract wouldn't leave him much time to see her in the next couple weeks.

At Ndovu, Laurel saw Darren's plane fly overhead and her heart had leaped. Almost immediately she'd seen the Cessna leaving. *Don't be silly, he has work to do.* Watching his plane disappear, she couldn't shake a bone deep feeling of disappointment. At the end of the day she was still blue.

It's just the dry season and the tension. But she knew that wasn't true. When she came into the compound, she looked for her mail. Her breath quickened, and her pulse rate increased when she saw Darren's writing. He'd left her a note! She slid her finger along the flap and flicked it open. It was an oddly formal invitation to the trip to the coast: *"I'm not likely to be seeing you often, as I've just signed a new contract that will keep my visits to Ndovu brief. God bless you. Darren."*

She stared at it for a long time, images filling her mind…a tropical beach, the ebb and flow of the surf, Darren sitting beside her, smiling at her.…

A warm flush ran from her center out to her extremities, and her hand tensed on the note. *Don't be an idiot. The last thing you need is to be in a place like that with Darren.*

She looked down at the note. Still…

A break would be nice, she couldn't deny that. A break from drought, hurting children, dying animals. It could be a time to pray and think, recuperate. She wouldn't have to be with Darren the whole time, there'd be other people, other Christians, and maybe a speaker.

She sighed and picked up her small stack of letters, noting one from Lilith and one from Julie. Eagerly she tore open Julie's letter, scanned the words, and smiled. Julie and David were doing great. Julie ended the letter by saying. "God gave me a man perfect for me. He'll have one for you too."

The smile left Laurel's face. There just wasn't a "perfect" man. Even a good marriage like Julie's took a lot of work and maintenance. A bad one, where there were differences, like between her father and Lilith…*and me and Darren.* She shut her eyes tightly.

Marriages like that didn't last. Or if they did, the people in them were miserable.

She opened the letter from Lilith more slowly. As she did so, Joan walked into the dining banda and sat down to look at her own mail. Laurel made a sharp, involuntary noise of surprise, and Joan looked up. "What is it?"

"Lilith is coming!"

"Your mother?" Joan's voice was sharp. "Are you sure?"

"That's what she says. She's coming to see the project she supports." She crushed the letter in her hands. "I suspected this, but I hoped I was wrong. You talked Lilith into giving you money, didn't you? You used me to get money from my mother."

Joan lifted one eyebrow. "Used you? Not any more than I use everything that comes to hand to further what I'm doing here at Ndovu. And I didn't do anything but ask. Your mother donated the money. Yes, I did use the address you put down for next of kin to look for financial help for the project. I do that with the parents of all the grad students, and I'd be a fool not to. I'll tell you one thing, I didn't expect the kind of response I got from Lilith Weaver. Most of the parents of my grad assistants send a couple of hundred dollars at the most. Lilith's response floored me. Your mother must be a very wealthy woman."

Laurel set her teeth. "Yes, she is." She had to get away to think this through. Head up, Laurel started for the door.

Joan laughed. "Ah, now we get some hubris, the pride of the rich offended."

Laurel turned. "I am not rich. Lilith is, but her money has nothing to do with me. My life and Lilith's run along different tracks."

"Are you so sure about that? She seemed happy enough to help you down this track. Wrote me a letter all about experiencing the central germ of life. Of the importance travel can have in bringing one home to the true center of self. Wanted me to loosen your locked, bourgeois mind and open it to the earth mother goddess." There was mockery clear in her tone, and she shook her head. "It takes all kinds, but money is money." She put both hands flat on the table. "Speaking of that, what will she want to see here?"

Laurel's fists were clenched so tightly her fingernails were biting into her palms. "I'm sorry, but I'm not going to help you separate Lilith from more money."

The look in Joan's eyes suddenly reminded Laurel of the way a sow bear's eyes looked when it watched a baby moose—or other prey. "So, are you going to try to put her off, get her not to come?"

Laurel sighed. "No, Joan, I'm not going to run away. I'll show Lilith what we're doing here. But she isn't easy—"

She cut Laurel off with a wave of her hand. "I don't really care what she's like. Just that she wants to keep funding the work at Ndovu. I want her happy and I want you to keep her that way."

It was clear that Joan would do almost anything to keep Lilith's money. Laurel pursed her lips, thinking. Was there any way to use this donation to encourage cooperation with the people on the Wilson? *A way to make things better for people* and *the animals.* That's what Jede had prayed for. Was this the answer? Would Lilith go along with it?

"What? What's on your mind?" Did Joan's voice actually sound a bit uncertain?

Laurel shook her head. She had to think about this. Pray about it. "Excuse me. I'd better turn in now."

"You've given up with your charity case then?"

Charity case? Laurel hesitated. Njeri and her daughter! They'd be waiting for her at Jede's place. "No, of course not."

Joan grunted and turned back to her mail.

Back in her banda Laurel picked up the first-aid kit, then paused and looked at Lilith's letter again. Slowly she sat on her bed and read it through more carefully. When Lilith came to Ndovu, Darren would almost certainly fly her in. *Darren with Lilith!* Laurel's stomach tightened into a hard knot.

As she left the compound, Farah stepped out of the darkness and walked beside her. "It is not good that you walk alone."

"I've been walking by myself all week and been just fine."

"Perhaps." Farah's robe flowed around his thin, straight form in the dim light. "It is good to help the needy. The Koran has said so."

"So you approve of what I'm doing?"

The palm of Farah's hand showed lighter as he turned it in a graceful gesture. "Even the children of infidels are to be pitied. But there are some who do not agree."

"You think one of your people would actually hurt me?"

"A woman should not walk alone!" As soon as they were in sight of Jede and Isaac's place, he faded silently into the darkness.

On this night not only Meli and her mother were waiting, but two other people—a woman carrying a baby with a raking, bubbly cough and a man with a high fever.

"They insisted on talking to you." Jede sounded tired and strained. "I told them that you couldn't help them. The baby sounds close to pneumonia, and I think the man has malaria. I tried to get them to go to the clinic, but they just sat down and stayed."

A flush of panic nearly made Laurel turn and run. "I don't know how to diagnose, Jede. How can I do anything for these people? I could end up causing their deaths! I know they don't like the clinic, but I can't help them. Really I can't!"

Jede spoke to them, but they only shook their heads and argued. Laurel offered to pay their fare to the clinic. Both finally took the money, but their demeanor remained angry and disgusted. Jede shut the door behind them near tears.

"Should I have tried to help them?" Laurel's voice was shaking.

"I told them you couldn't. I just wish…" Jede shook her head. "What's the use of wishing? At least we can help Meli."

During the confrontation, Njeri and Meli huddled in the corner as if they wished to disappear. Now they came forward tentatively. Laurel saw to her joy that Meli's arm was healing nicely. Njeri pressed three small, dirty, brown eggs into Laurel's hands and left quickly.

"Njeri came early to study the Bible with me." Jede rubbed her face. "She thinks her cousin might come with her tomorrow."

"Jede, that's great."

"But complicated. I wish the others hadn't started coming for medical help."

"Besides the fact that I can't help them, what's so bad about them coming?"

Isaac's step at the door stopped them. He heard the question though, because after he greeted Laurel, he answered her.

"Very likely those people believe that you refused to help for some reason of your own. They don't understand modern medicine very well, and you did help Meli. We're seen as your friends, so it puts us in an awkward position as well. The thing is, it's going to get worse. People are hurting for good food, and it will weaken their immune system. We don't have the resources to help everyone."

Laurel sank onto a wobbly wooden chair. "What can I do?"

Neither of them answered but just sat with her silently.

She looked from one to the other. Could Lilith's money be some kind of answer? Maybe if Lilith saw the need, she'd support building a clinic here. "Would you listen and give me your advice about something?"

"And our prayers." Isaac leaned forward.

Laurel told them about Lilith, her manipulative nature, and the fact that she'd donated money to Joan.

"She is coming?" Jede grasped her hand. "It will be good to meet your mother."

"Thanks, but it's even more complicated. I think Joan will do almost anything to keep Lilith's support. My mother wants some kind of a hold over me, and she isn't hard-hearted. Maybe there's a way to open doors here, do something substantial to help the people on the Wilson, and at the same time show them the value of keeping Ndovu wild."

Isaac stood up and paced the length of the room. "It would be very difficult to convince anyone here of the value of baboons or most of the other wild animals, for that matter. These people are in a fight to survive."

"That doesn't mean it shouldn't be done! When is following God's way easy?"

"I have been thinking about it." Isaac sounded very frustrated. "Nurturing a church here, really making disciples, already that is very hard. How can we make it harder by complicating it with animals?"

"Wait," Jede cut in. "I have an idea. What about the school? What if Laurel offered to take children to see the animals, and maybe help with the science classes? The children know the school isn't top-notch. They desperately want the kind of education that will open doors, get them away from this kind of poverty."

Laurel's eyes widened. "Would the teacher agree, and the parents?"

"Probably." Jede laughed. "Some of the braver ones anyway. There are all kinds of scary stories about how dangerous the Somali are, but the desire for opportunities is very strong. We could just ask for those who wanted to go."

Isaac was still shaking his head. "I can see some parents thinking that we're trying to send their children into danger. Perhaps Darren is right. The time for animals is past."

"No!" Laurel jumped to her feet. "God doesn't throw things away." *How could Darren have said such a thing?* "Look, I can't talk about this anymore. I've got to go."

"We'll pray about this," Jede called after her. "And I'm going to ask Simon, the teacher."

Laurel ran up the long hill in the dark. Tears blurred her eyes and she kept stumbling. She'd overreacted to Darren's words in a way that was much too revealing. Crazy! Why did God make him such a wonderful man and bring him into her life? She gulped for breath. It probably didn't matter anyway.

Lilith was coming. And Laurel knew the odds of her keeping her mother and Darren apart were next to nil. And she knew something more: Once Darren met Lilith, he was likely to drop her like a hot potato.

12

DARREN STARED AT THE SMALL, THIN WOMAN WHO CAME swirling toward him. Her black cape swished—thick, rich cloth swallowing the light. Clinking bracelets scattered glints of gold as her arms moved. Her hair was matte black, almost purple. *It's dyed, but what a color!* The woman looked like a crazed plum had attacked her.

Darren realized his mouth had fallen open, and he shut it as she came straight toward him.

"You must be Darren Grant. I'm Lilith Weaver."

Darren studied Laurel's mother, taking in the outfit, the overly dramatic way she spoke and moved. How could a mother and daughter be so different?

Maybe Laurel was adopted.

Lilith Weaver had reached out a thin, white, ring-encrusted hand to him and was waiting.

He blinked and jerked his hand out to shake hers; it was like shaking a handful of bird bones. "Welcome to Kenya."

"Peace be with you, my son." Her voice was rough as if she'd smoked too much.

Peace be with me? What next? As they traveled to the other airport, he watched her, trying to see through the facade. *At least Laurel will age well.* His jaw clenched. How Laurel aged was none of his business.

Lilith had leaned back and shut her eyes, breathing deeply. Was the woman actually meditating?

She said nothing until he helped her into the Cessna. Then she turned her big eyes on him, the same green shot brown as Laurel's. "Already I can feel the ambiance of Africa." She flung out her hands, pale butterflies in the sunshine. "All the dust and heat." She looked sharply at Darren. "Is Laurel sensing it? Are her eyes opened to the unique beauty?"

Darren blinked. "Ah, I think so. Now, if you'd just put on your seat belt."

"How is she? How is my Laurel?" A lot of the pretense had gone, and real concern showed in Lilith's voice.

Darren found himself liking her better. "I'm sure she's fine." *At least I sure hope so.*

The new contract had kept him very busy, and he hadn't had a chance to fly into Ndovu in the evening when he could see Laurel. *She'll be at the strip to meet her mother. I'll see her then.* He half smiled and touched the note in his pocket. Short and to the point, it still held some of the warmth that was Laurel. She'd thanked him for the invitation to come to the coast but hadn't said if she would come or not. The next part of the note looked as though it had been erased and rewritten several times.

"You'll be meeting Lilith and bringing her here. Under the facade is a lonely woman. She and I don't see eye to eye, but she is dear to me. Darren, please see her with God's love, and pray for me that I do the same." The last words were more slanted, the pencil had pressed harder.

Darren glanced at Lilith after he got the plane into cruise flight. She was facing the window, sitting rigidly upright, a pose of eager attention to the scenery. Her thin, white neck showed where her hair fell to each side. *Everything she does is an act.* He frowned. *Or seems like it.*

What on earth had Laurel's childhood been like with this woman as her mother?

I guess neither of us had easy childhoods.

As they circled to land, Darren could see the Jeep and several people. Very aware that Laurel was watching, he concentrated on doing a perfect landing. As he taxied toward the Jeep, he did a double take. Laurel was there, but so was Joan Doyle, and in the middle of a day of observing!

When the plane was on the ground, Lilith delayed just long enough to allow the Jeep to drive up. Then she emerged, settling her cloak and holding out her hand to him, as if she were a duchess being handed out of a coach.

"Laurel, my darling!" She fluted and enveloped Laurel in a swirl of black.

Stifling an urge to laugh at the theatrics, Darren moved quickly to the luggage compartment. As he took out the largest suitcase, he looked up to find Laurel's eyes on him. Joan and Lilith were between them and talking animatedly, but it was as if there was no one on the face of the earth but Laurel. And him.

Almost involuntarily, he took a long stride toward her, but Lilith took her daughter's arm, and the moment was broken.

Darren swallowed hard, his heart still hammering. Slowly he began loading Lilith's belongings into the Jeep. The women got in and Lilith turned. "Thank you for the flight. It was a joy to my heart! Such ambiance, such profound emanations from the wholeness of Africa, flying there above it all."

Lilith had held out her hand like a regal dowager

waiting to have it kissed. Darren shook it gingerly. "Uh, anytime, ma'am."

Past Lilith, Darren caught Laurel's embarrassed look and winked at her.

"Hmm," Lilith hummed. Darren looked at her to find her glancing from him to Laurel with a speculative look in her eyes. "Joan, could I be so bold as to invite Darren to come with us?" Lilith laid a hand on Joan's leathery forearm.

He expected an impatient rejoinder to the effect that he could come if he chose. Instead Joan said graciously, "Darren? You'd be welcome."

Something odd was going on, but so what if it gave him a chance to spend time with Laurel. He glanced at his watch. *Can I do that and make it back for my next flight?* He frowned. *Forget the next flight. They can wait a few minutes.*

"Thanks. That'd be great."

"Marvelous." Lilith rushed toward him, taking hold of his arm and leading him toward the Jeep. "Laurel, come and sit by this beautiful boy."

"Lilith, *please.*" Laurel was flushing wildly. She took a deep breath, which made the shadows play along the beautiful modeling of smooth, tan skin at her throat. "Darren is just a friend."

"Oh, for pity's sake!" Joan cut in. "Just get in the Jeep."

But Darren was still watching Laurel. *I'm making things worse for her.* "Look, I couldn't stay long anyway. I've got another charter in less than two hours. I'll come up another time."

"No, you must come!" Lilith climbed into the Jeep

and patted the seat beside her.

Darren ignored her. As Lilith was talking, Laurel had soundlessly mouthed, "Thanks."

"No problem." He mouthed back, then turned to Lilith. "I'd better not, not this time, but I'll be back, just as soon as I get a day free from the new charter contract. It was good to meet you."

Joan put the Jeep in gear. He took a couple of steps after them as they drove off, then rubbed his forehead with the heel of his hand. Seeing Laurel had confused him even more. He might as well admit it. He didn't want Laurel to change. Part of the attraction was her connection to the wild land he'd loved so much. *Doesn't that make her doubly dangerous?*

"Hello, brother!" Isaac was striding toward him. Their hands clasped warmly. "I heard your plane and came to greet you. We've missed seeing you. You've been busy with your new contract?"

"Laurel told you that?"

"She's a good woman." Isaac grinned. "Worth many cows. She speaks highly of you. Perhaps I could be your go-between to arrange things with her father. Jede would like that, and I'd enjoy traveling to Canada." He spoke tongue in cheek, teasing Darren with traditional African customs that even he and Jede hadn't followed completely.

Darren laughed. "I'll remember your offer."

"Did you know that she has been helping the school? She has already taken one group to Ndovu for a science outing. I can tell you, she has made me think new thoughts. The way she speaks of the Scripture concerning the place of mankind in creation. She confuses me."

"You're not the only one."

"Eeeeh! Is it like that? Indeed, women are a constant trial, even Jede. She listens to Laurel, and then preaches to me, quoting Francis of Assisi among many others. Perhaps we should all be monks like the good Francis. Until then, Jede has asked me to invite you over for chai."

"I can't, I've got a charter flight in an hour and a bit. How are things on the Wilson?"

Isaac shook his head. "Not good. Already the children are listless in school. Some of the very small ones have hair that is turning pale. They need more than the dry grain that is left. I have asked the church for help, but…" He shrugged.

"They have supplies for famine relief. Dad was telling me."

"The trucks are not available."

Darren's jaw clenched. He'd been in Africa too long not to know that answer was probably clouded by some kind of political or financial maneuvering in the power structure controlling those trucks. Forget ferrying tourists. He'd do the flight this afternoon and then see what he could do to get a truckload of high protein food to the Wilson. "Are you seeing an increase in illness yet?"

Isaac nodded. "Some, especially among the children. Laurel has been paying for the matatu fare to the clinic when we could not."

"She's doing that?"

Isaac patted his arm, the twinkle back in his eyes. "Truly I will pray for you, brother."

"You do that. I'd better get going, but I'll see what I can do about food."

As he flew back to Nairobi, Darren's head spun with what he'd just learned about Laurel. She was working with school kids, teaching them about nature. That fit her priorities, but paying matatu fare to the clinic? She was doing more than he was to make a difference. Isaac had said Laurel had made him think. She must have had a convincing biblical argument to get that admission from Isaac. *Could there actually be something to her convictions?*

"So tell me about Darren Grant. He really is delectable." Lilith had taken the other bed in Laurel's banda and was spreading her belongings liberally over the entire space.

And after that scene at the airstrip, he'll probably never come near me again. She frowned. When he said he was leaving, was he trying to be nice or trying to escape? He did sound sincere, but what if he was just being polite? Laurel didn't answer her mother's demand for information. *If I say nothing, maybe she'll drop the topic.*

"I saw how you two were looking at each other. Maybe he'll be the one to loosen your uptight attitude toward sex."

"You know where I stand on—"

Lilith waved a hand impatiently. "I know, I know, but you're in Africa now. None of your friends back home would ever know, and he is gorgeous. He practically exudes strength and virility. The tastiest tidbit I've seen in a long time."

"Stop it! Darren is not an appetizer."

"More like the main course, I'd say."

Laurel had been sitting cross-legged on her bed,

now she jumped up. "Lilith, knock it off! Darren's not a choice on a menu. He's...he's a good man. Someone with feelings and goals. Just like me." She paced across the room dodging suitcases. "As for whatever relationship Darren and I share, it's none of your business."

Lilith made a moue with her mouth. "Oh, dear, didn't even make it to first base with the dear boy, eh? Not even a little fling? How sad."

Laurel picked up a book—almost carried away by the strong urge to pitch it at her mother—but put it down again. "A *fling* is not on my menu. Any more than it's on Darren's. Believe it or not, Lilith, not everyone is as preoccupied with sex as you are. When we're together we have much more important things to talk about."

"Oh?" One of Lilith's carefully outlined black eyebrows lifted. "So you *have* spent time together. I thought there was something between you. I'll be watching with interest! Maybe I can encourage him a little...or a lot."

The old cringing embarrassment came over Laurel like a tide. She lifted her head and really looked at her mother. *Why does she do this to me?* She shut her eyes and turned that thought into a prayer. *Help me to see Lilith the way You do, and not as a blindly reacting child.*

When she opened her eyes, Lilith was staring at her curiously. "Do you feel faint, darling? I don't think Africa suits you." She leaned closer. "Do you wish you hadn't come?"

"It hasn't been easy, but no, I'm glad I came." Images flashed though her mind—giraffes against a sunset, Meli's shy smile, the taste of chai, Jede's kind eyes, Farah crouched on his heels, little Gremlin, and more often than anything else, images of Darren. *Would it have been better not to meet him?* Simpler certainly.

"So the money was a good idea." Lilith sounded positively smug.

"No, it wasn't a good idea!" She whirled to face her mother. "I just found out what you did a couple of days ago. You know I don't want you to spend money on me. I asked you not to years ago. Now I'm not sure if I got this job on my own merit or not."

"What does it matter? You got the job. The money did you good, whether you want to admit it or not. You just said you're glad you came. I spent this money on Joan Doyle's research project, not you. You would have sent it back." Lilith turned away.

Laurel stared at her thin back. *Is she really hurt, or is it just another manipulative ploy?* The thought took the wind out of her sails, and she sighed. "Lilith, we'll have lots of time to talk things through, but they'll be waiting on us for supper if we don't go over to the dining banda."

Joan made an obvious effort during the meal to be affable. Between her mother's pretentions and Joan's near bowing and scraping, Laurel felt like she was in a badly acted play. She listened as Joan raved about Laurel's contribution to the research; the first praise Laurel had heard from the woman.

As they left for bed, Joan detained Laurel for a minute. "Let your mother know she's welcome to sleep in tomorrow. I don't want another day of research disrupted. You can come back to spend time with her at noon."

It didn't work out that way. Lilith was up early the next morning all eager to get going. "Lilith, it's hot here, and the flies will be worse than they are on the compound. Are you sure you want to come out for the whole day?"

"Of course I'm sure." She straightened the covers on her bed with a jerk. "I didn't come all the way to Africa to see what I've been funding only to be defeated by a few flies!"

Joan was almost finished eating when Laurel and Lilith walked into breakfast. Joan looked up in obvious irritation at Laurel's lateness, saw Lilith, and forced a smile. "I'm surprised to see you up. Are you sure you wouldn't rather rest today? You must be tired from traveling."

By the tension in Lilith's body, Laurel knew she'd seen through that smile. Her mother lifted her chin and swung into one of her high-blown speeches. *She does that when she's feeling defensive!* The revelation literally rocked Laurel back on her heels. *But she does it to me, often. Do I make her defensive?* Laurel listened to Lilith with a weird feeling of looking at her mother as if she'd never seen her before.

"I'll enfold the experience of Africa, penetrate past it to fully experience a day in the bush. I want to let the spirit of Africa sweep over my spirit, the rhythms of Africa become my own rhythms, the sounds of Africa become part of my very heartbeat."

Joan's skepticism as she watched Lilith seemed to drive her on to further heights of rhetoric. To Laurel's relief, Joan's satellite phone rang.

"Excuse me." She moved to answer it.

Lilith let out her breath with a huffing noise. "Such an unsympathetic character. I would have thought that years in nature would have made her more spiritual."

Laurel looked at her mother, startled by her mother's insight—and how closely it echoed her own feelings. "Come and sit down and try some papaya." She drew her mother toward the table where Ambaro had quickly set another place.

"It's for you, Laurel." Joan handed her the phone. "It's Darren."

Feeling surrounded by ears and eyes, Laurel took the phone. Darren got straight to the point. "Laurel, look, I'm going to be driving a truck up. Should be there around ten-thirty tonight. Is there a chance we could spend a little time together?"

"Tonight? I'm not sure I can…" Disappointment swept her as she spoke; just hearing him on the phone made her feel good.

Lilith's knuckles bumped Laurel's cheek as she snatched the phone away.

"Mother!"

Lilith just smiled at her. "Darren, of course she'll spend time with you. She'd be a fool not to. She'll be waiting for you." With that, Lilith hung up the phone leaving Laurel staring at her, speechless.

Joan gave a bark of laughter. "I'm going out to the Jeep, come as soon as you're ready."

"Lilith! How could you *do* that?" Out of the corner of her eye she could see Ambaro watching with interest.

"I just didn't want you to miss anything because I'm here." Lilith put on her most serene smile and took a bite of papaya. "Mmm, really quite good and I'm sure full of healthful antioxidants. You must have some. If Darren is coming tonight, you want to be at your best."

Laurel wanted to scream, but her mother kept on eating, ignoring her entirely. Laurel squeezed her eyes shut and forced herself to take a deep breath.

Lord, give me strength. And patience... She opened her eyes and glared at Lilith. *And do it quick before I throttle my mother!*

13

"YOU'RE DOING *WHAT?*" THOR, HANDS ON HIS HIPS, GLARED AT Darren.

"Taking a load of famine relief food up to the Wilson. You have a problem with that?"

Thor paced across the hangar and whirled to face Darren. "You're insane! It's taken you months to build the connections for the contracts you've gotten this week, and you're giving them away. Besides your new tourist contracts, you've given three photo flights for an international magazine to Zebra Air. That magazine is going to go to them next time."

"Look, people are hungry up there. I had the contacts with World Food Aid to get the use of a truck."

Thor stared at him. "Get a grip, man. You're not one of those softheaded, bleeding idiots. Since when is a little hunger at the end of the dry season a new thing? It's happened for millennia. You've got to take care of yourself first or go under."

Darren crossed his arms. "It's not like that for me anymore."

"Give me a break! This trucking of food won't do much good. The kids get fed for a week and you starve. If God cared, why'd He let the kids go hungry in the first place? I don't think much of this God of yours."

Darren moved to argue then stopped himself. Thor wasn't going to listen to a discussion on the reason God allows suffering. *I know it comes from sin and can't be stopped until Judgment Day. I know in my head, God waits in order to allow more people to turn to Him, and I still don't get it.* If he didn't understand completely, trying to explain to an angry Thor wasn't going to work.

When Darren said nothing, Thor grunted and turned to walk away. By the open hangar door he paused. "Look, man, you throw away your business like this, don't go calling on me for help."

"I won't, Thor." Darren sank onto the old bench along the hangar wall and put his head in his hands. *Is this the right thing to do?* Thor was right; he could lose what business he had. He could have tried harder to get one of the agencies to take a load of food in themselves.

How much of this plan is a pure will to serve God, and how much is me wanting to see Laurel? He rubbed his hands over his face. *Or for that matter, to show her I'm helping the people on the Wilson, too.*

Lilith's black clothing seemed to attract flies. They were all around her as soon as the Jeep stopped. "They didn't show flies on the programs I've watched about Africa."

"No, they tend to skip some of the ugly parts." Laurel helped Lilith around a thorn bush.

Joan looked back at them. "Actually, the flies are much worse this year than they've ever been. It's the goats and cattle. Not only are they destructive and wasteful, but the flies come with them."

"So get rid of the goats and cattle!" Lilith flapped her cape at the pesky insects.

"I'd love to!"

The baboons scattered at the sight of Lilith's cloak.

Joan ushered her quickly away from the animals.

"You're going to have to stay back until they get used to you."

"But I don't want to be out here by myself." Lilith clutched Laurel's sleeve.

"You'll have a good view of how we observe the troop."

"Joan, I'll stay with her."

"But—" Joan crossed her arms, then sighed—"I suppose you're right. I'll get to work then." She strode off.

"So harsh and narrow." Lilith shook her head at Joan's back.

Harsh, yes. But narrow? Slowly Laurel nodded. *Lilith is right; all Joan cares about is the troop.*

The baboons moved constantly now, searching hard for anything. Because the baboons kept moving, the observers had to do so as well. Joan had instructed Farah to carry a little folding stool. Initially, Lilith had refused to sit on it but now was sinking onto it gratefully each time the troop as much as paused. Obviously thinking the job beneath him, Farah was at his most haughty. Speaking to no one, he stalked regally behind Lilith, standing as stiff as a post each time she sat.

"See that small baboon there." Lilith pointed at Gremlin. "It's thin. Even I can tell that, and I'm not an animal expert. Why don't you feed these animals properly?"

"We don't feed them at all."

"That's crazy! Look at this country. It's too dry to feed an anemic rabbit, much less thirty baboons or whatever. I thought you cared about animals."

Laurel held out her hands. "I do care for animals. I

care very much that Gremlin is in bad shape. He used to play so much and be really funny. But if we fed them, they would no longer be wild animals."

"So? They'd still act like baboons, wouldn't they?"

"Not like wild baboons. For me, not interfering is one of the hardest parts of being an animal behavior scientist. You don't treat wounded animals or feed hungry ones. Our job is to watch and learn."

"Scientist. Academic rubbish!"

"But Lilith, interference almost always does harm in the long run. Squirrels around campgrounds that eat too much human food aren't healthy. Bears that learn to scavenge campgrounds get shot. If we fed these baboons, they'd learn to look for food near humans and might start to raid gardens. The people around here are already hungry enough without that, and it would just get the animals killed."

Lilith grunted and stood up. "They're moving again." She nodded for Farah to pick up her stool and kept looking at him. "He's really quite beautiful." Farah gave her a direct, arrogant stare. Lilith's eyebrows went up. She leaned toward Laurel and whispered, "He doesn't understand English, does he?"

Trying not to laugh, Laurel answered, "Farah speaks English very well. Don't you, Farah?"

He inclined his head gracefully. "It is so."

For once Lilith seemed at a complete lack for words. She drew herself up to her full height, inclined her head to Farah, and walked off rapidly. Farah picked up the chair and paced after her. He looked smug.

By noon, the baking sun stood straight overhead, and a hot wind constantly rasped at them. Ant galls in the thorn trees whistled mournfully. Nothing seemed to be alive but the baboons and flies, thousands of stubborn flies. Joan seemed unaffected, as did Farah. Laurel could feel the gritty dust on her teeth. She pulled her hat down to shield her eyes. She wasn't comfortable, but she could cope. Lilith, on the other hand, looked very rough indeed. Dull and dusty, her black cloak flapped in the wind making her look like a raddled crow. Her normally pale skin was pasty. There was a big smear of dust stuck to the sunscreen on her left cheek. She'd refused to drink anything.

Laurel walked over to Joan. "I hate to bother you, but I think Lilith should go back before she gets sunstroke."

Joan grunted. "I've already called Ibrahim. See if she'll let you stay. You're wasting a good part of the day tomorrow anyway, and I don't want to lose this afternoon."

"Tomorrow?"

"The school kids. You told me you have another crew of them coming in."

"But that's not wasted time."

"Don't start again. Those people shouldn't be here in the first place!" She flapped her hand across in front of her face to chase off the flies. "If people would just leave well enough alone, the Meru would move when the first sustained drought killed off half their children."

"You don't want that, surely." Laurel's mind had gone instantly to little Meli.

"Don't I just?" Joan crossed her arms.

"It's not a war!"

"Oh yes, it is, and I know which side I'm on."

"It doesn't have to be war. People and creation have lived together for millennia. There must be a way."

"Stop your blathering and take Lilith out to meet the Jeep. Try to come back, if she'll let you."

Back at the compound, Lilith lay down on her bed with a sigh. "Are you sure you have to go back out there?"

"Joan asked me to." She put a pitcher of clean water where her mother could reach it.

Lilith caught her wrist. "But Darren is coming tonight. If you go back out there, you'll be as gaunt and haggard as that Joan creature. You need to be rested and at your best. Get some color back in those cheeks."

"Darren Grant is not my whole life, Lilith." *I'm not even sure he should be any part of it.*

Lilith smiled and touched her cheek. "Admit it. You want him in your life."

And that's the problem in a nutshell. Laurel turned to close the shutters. "I told you, he's just a friend."

"And I still don't believe you." Lilith lay back. "You go on out and watch your baboons. I am tired."

By the time Laurel finished work that evening, Lilith had slept and was feeling better. "That black woman brought me water to wash with. This place is positively medieval—a slim boy carrying my chair like a page, servants tending to every wish, and yet everything is so primitive. Couldn't Joan get running water here, and at least provide a shower?"

Hot and dusty herself, Laurel turned to the basin of water Ambaro had left for her as she did every evening. She plunged in her entire head, glad for her short hair. Coming up for air, she looked at Lilith. "But we're not at home; we're in Africa." She smiled. "Didn't you say I should assimilate the new and experience it to the fullest? Here it's dust, flies, and no running water."

Lilith made a face. "I'd rather assimilate Africa from a decent hotel. The one I stayed in the first night in Nairobi was quite adequate."

"So you don't feel that connection with the African bush?" Laurel couldn't resist teasing a little.

Lilith glared at her. "Actually I did. I'm not totally blind. Those animals are too much like us, the way they hug each other, even the look in their beady little eyes is too canny. One of the big ones gave me the most calculating once-over, like a skeptical banker. I think I'd rather take being stared at by primates in small doses, especially as they seem in danger of starving to death, or did I misunderstand?"

Laurel had stopped washing. "No, you didn't. They are in rough shape."

"Because of the drought?"

"Joan thinks if it weren't for the pressure from domestic goats and cattle on the land, they would be fine in spite of the dry weather." She finished washing her face. Was this the time to tell Lilith about what was happening on the Wilson?

"I don't like that side of the circle much."

Laurel had her face in a towel. "Pardon?"

"Death," Lilith said more loudly. "Just like loving and begetting. It's part of the circle. By the way, it's about time you got involved in the loving and begetting yourself."

Laurel stared at her. "A bit premature, don't you think? I'm not even married yet, remember?"

"What does that have to do with it? You don't need a husband; you've got me to help you. Being a mother would be good for you. Peel off some of the 'better than thou' layers."

"Better than thou?" *Is that how she sees me?*

Lilith pinned her with a look. "Well, better than mother, anyway. Believe me, you've made it all too clear. You're too good to spend time with me. Too good to enjoy sex. Too upright—and uptight—for any of the things I wanted you to try. Almost as self-righteous as your father, who rejected me for that slimy Sue woman—"

Laurel froze, defensive words just at the tip of her tongue, but Lilith hugged herself defensively. Suddenly she looked much smaller...almost pathetic. *Lord, I have You, and she's all alone. Help me.* She took a step toward her mother.

"No, Lilith. Not too good to spend time with you." Laurel reached out to her. *All these years I've been so blind, too wrapped up in my own pain to see she was hurting too.* Laurel felt like blinders had just dropped off her eyes. *All the pressure, the attempts to remake me—she was just trying to prove she was okay herself. Why didn't I see that sooner?*

Lilith twisted away. "I don't need your pity."

"Will you accept my apology then?"

"Apology?" Lilith turned, and the astonishment on her face stirred shame in Laurel's heart.

She nodded. "Not for being who I am, but for staying so far away from you. For making you feel as though I didn't want to be near you."

Lilith stared at her for a second, then grunted in a noncommittal fashion. "We'd better go and eat."

After supper, Joan began to tell Lilith about the importance of the work at Ndovu.

Lilith shifted in her chair, then picked at her thumbnail. Laurel watched her. *She really couldn't care less about what Joan is doing here. She only sent that money because of me.* Her mother's pushing didn't sting so much now, not after she'd seen the uncertainty and pain behind it.

Lilith crossed and uncrossed her legs, looked at Laurel, and rolled her eyes. Joan was too engrossed in her lecture even to notice. When she started in on the damage done by the goats and the squatters, Lilith reacted. "So why are baboons any better than goats? Even if they bring flies, the goats do someone some good."

"Good?" Joan bleated the word, sounding almost like a goat herself. Then she shut her eyes as if she were in pain.

Lilith looked at Laurel, eyebrows high, belligerence sparking in her gaze. "They belong to someone, don't they? I know you think studying wild animals is worth doing, but primitive people are interesting too. I want to get to know the local natives."

Laurel cleared her throat. "Um, Lilith, it's not like—"

Joan interrupted. "If that's what you'd like. We could walk over to visit with Ibrahim and his people after supper."

"I don't mean the people who work with you. For pity's sake, they speak English. I mean the natives, the ones you called squatters."

Joan looked as if she'd bitten into a rotten egg, but she remained determined to keep Lilith happy. "Laurel will be taking a group of their children to see the baboon troop tomorrow. I doubt if they'll be what you seem to expect." She leaned forward abruptly. "Lilith, I appreciate your support very much. It's essential that you get a clear picture of the conflicts here. The wild land on Ndovu must be preserved, and the squatters are a threat."

"Do they have to be?" Laurel found her voice was shaking slightly. Both Joan and Lilith turned to look at her. Praying for help, she plunged on. "I've been thinking. There has to be a way. Maybe somehow set up an organization that was affiliated with the research here. It would benefit all the people who live nearby, give them a stake in keeping Ndovu wild." Joan was glaring at her, but did Lilith look interested?

Laurel twisted her fingers together, fighting to find the right words. "Joan, you know that there can't be wilderness when the people around see no good in it. You know that. It's accepted dogma that a wilderness area needs local support. We could build that here. We could make a school for kids, do seminars to teach alternative dryland farming practice, maybe do some ecotourism that would put money into local pockets."

"It wouldn't work here!" Joan swept a hand downward.

"It would if God opened doors." *I can't believe I said that to Joan Doyle and Lilith.* "The people on the Wilson are hungry. If we helped feed them, it would reduce the pressure on Ndovu."

There was a brief silence, then Joan laughed uneasily. "As you can see, your daughter and I disagree about some things. I need to be up early. I'll just bid you good night."

Lilith stood up as well. "I'll hit the sack, too. Laurel will want to wait up for Darren." She winked and left Laurel alone.

Laurel sat very still. Neither Joan nor Lilith had responded to her ideas. *Did I blow it by talking too much or too soon?* If they hadn't listened, would Darren? Was it all an empty dream? *Please let him listen, and let this work.* She bit her lip. He was going to be here in an hour or so. *I'm going to have to apologize for what Lilith said on the phone.*

Laurel tried to read a book but gave it up after a frustrating hour. It was after eleven. *Did he get into some kind of trouble? Maybe he's just practicing "African" time.* Laurel jerked to her feet. *He can wait until tomorrow.* She paced around the room, sat down again, and stared at the wall. *Where is he? He drives me nuts!*

Laurel picked up the book and stared at it for another forty-five minutes without remembering a word she'd read. "This is crazy. I'm going to bed."

14

LAUREL SLEPT UNTIL THE DAWN BIRD CHORUS WOKE HER. IT wasn't a morning she had to be out observing the troop by the time the sun came up. She let her breath out with a sigh. Lilith was only a thin heap seen through the haze of the mosquito net over her bed.

The growl of a big diesel engine in the distance made her frown and lift her head. Darren had said he was bringing in a truck. *Is that him?* Quickly she slid out from under her mosquito net, dressed, pulled a brush though her short hair, and went out. Ambaro was over by the dining banda. Laurel waved and Ambaro waved back with a smile. *"Chakula iko."*

Laurel knew enough Swahili now to recognize the word for food. "Thanks."

The truck sound that had gotten her out of bed had stopped. Laurel longed to ask Ambaro if she'd heard it or knew what it meant, but she didn't have the words. Slowly she walked toward the dining banda.

"Hey, Laurel!"

Darren. She spun around to see him waving from the lower end of the camp. *He came!* Without thinking she ran toward him only to come to a stop staring. "What happened to you?"

He grinned, white teeth flashing a contrast to his incredibly dusty face. Even the smile wrinkles in the corner of his eyes were coated. "Sorry I didn't make it last night. Had to winch the truck out of three dry riverbeds. Flying has made me soft."

Laurel almost laughed. Darren Grant looked anything but soft. Everything about him spoke of lean
strength, confidence, and power. He grinned at her
through the dirt smudges, the dark stubble on his
cheeks creased with those incredible dimples.

"Yeah, soft. I should have known how bad that road
is, but flying is the easy way around."

"I'm sorry for the way Lilith spoke to you. I never
know what she's going to say."

"Not easy having her for a mother?" His eyes were
sympathetic. "I'd say you were the one who was hurt. I
tried to say that I didn't want to push you, but she'd
hung up. If you'd rather not talk..."

"But I do. I've got this idea of how things might be
made better on the Wilson and here at Ndovu. I've been
so worried."

"Worried for your animals?"

"Yes, and for the children. The little ones..." She
ducked her head. *He'll just say I can't care about them and
the animals.*

He touched her arm gently. "I know what you mean.
Come with me. I've got something to show you."

"I can't. Jede is going to bring a bunch of school kids
up this morning."

"It's not even seven. They can't be expected yet." His
hand was still open. "Come and see. Please?"

She reached and took his hand, feeling the warm,
strong fingers close over hers. The action had been auto-
matic, but she didn't regret it. His hand over hers felt so
good.

As they walked down toward the airstrip, Darren
looked at her several times as if he wanted to say some-

thing. As they came around the last bend in the dusty track, a huge Mercedes truck came into view. Obviously designed for punishing roads, the thing was so covered in dust she could barely see the blue paint.

"You drove *that* here? Why?" The logo on the door suddenly registered in her mind. It was the name of a well-known Christian relief agency. "It's food. You brought food in! Oh, Darren." She threw her arms around him.

"Hey, careful. I'm filthy."

"Do you think I care?" The tears stinging her eyes startled her, and she ducked her head, swallowing hard.

Darren put both hands on her shoulders and stepped back, looking into her face. "You *are* crying." He shook his head, his eyes tender. "Ah, Laurel...do you care so much?"

"It's been awful. I took out a bunch of school kids to see the baboons. Some of the smaller ones were just out of it. They had potbellies from malnutrition, like those horrible famine pictures you see on TV. I saw one kid try the acacia pods the baboons were eating, then the whole bunch was doing it. Joan was furious! Today I'm going to feed them first no matter what she says."

"That might prove a bit complicated, but it's a kind idea. Come on, let's get this food down to the church." He looked at her again and grinned. "I think maybe you should wash your face first, though. I've got some water in the truck."

She climbed up on the running board to look in rearview mirror. "Oh, wow!" Her face was filthy from the dust on Darren's shirt and streaked with muddy tear tracks. Her clothes weren't much better. She swatted at them and most of the dust came off. Darren handed her a rag and a water bottle.

"That's what you get for hugging me."

They both laughed. As she wiped her face, Laurel felt happier than she had in weeks. She looked in the mirror to see if she'd gotten rid of most of the dirt when she suddenly remembered her mother.

"Wait. I've got to tell Lilith where I am." She jumped down. "Why don't you go on down? I'll meet you at the church in a few minutes. That's where the school meets, so I won't miss Jede and the kids."

"See you there." He swung into the cab, then called through the open door. "Bring Lilith with you."

As the truck ground into gear, Laurel gave a little skip, and then ran back toward the compound. Lilith was up and dressed, eating breakfast. Seeing the food, Laurel was suddenly very hungry.

"Darren's here!" She grabbed a piece of bread and took a big bite.

"Where?" Lilith looked toward the door.

Laurel waved her hand at her full mouth and swallowed hard. "Down at the church. Oh, Lilith, he trucked food in! I'm so happy. Now the kids will be okay. I'm going to go down and meet him there. Will you come?"

"To a church? You know I don't do that."

"Please? It would mean a lot to me. Besides, the building is a school too, and this isn't a church service." She laughed. "I suppose it is in a way, actually, a service of the church. But nobody is going to sing hymns or anything; at least I don't think so. They're going to be distributing the truckload of food Darren brought."

"Only to the faithful, right? Everyone else is out of luck." Lilith crossed her arms and glared at Laurel.

"I'm sure the supplies go to everyone. Jede and Isaac

wouldn't leave people out just because they don't go to church. Please come. You'll see."

"You promise no one will preach at me?"

"I promise." Laurel was making peanut butter sandwiches as fast as she could. If she was hungry, Darren must be starving. She stopped. Darren might be hungry, but he wasn't actually starving, not like some of the people who'd be coming to get the food he'd trucked in. She looked at the sandwich in her hand and put it down.

"What's wrong? You look as if that sandwich just bit you."

"I just realized Darren wouldn't be able to eat it anyway, not in front of people who are really hungry." She stared at the food on the table. This last month, food had meant something totally different to her than ever before. For the first time, when she thanked God for her food before a meal, she meant it fervently.

"If you're finished meditating on those sandwiches, shall we go?" Lilith stood up.

"I'll just wrap them up for later."

As they headed down the hill, Lilith repeatedly rubbed her arms as if she were cold, even though the African sun beat down like hot honey as it swung higher into the sky. "I'm not comfortable going to a church. There's a power in churches that just doesn't like me."

Laurel checked midstride. "Doesn't like you? Lilith, God loves you."

"Don't give me that bull! I'm not an idiot. You've heard some of the things your father has said to me. He, for one, has no illusions that God likes me. Not one person from a church has done anything but judge me; tell me I'm wrong."

She means me as well. The realization saddened Laurel. "What about Edwina? She went to church." An older woman who lived down the road when Laurel was little, Edwina used to bring over baked goods and visit. She was the one who'd given Lilith seeds for the morning glories that bloomed all over the front of the house. Edwina's love for Christ was one of the things that had made Laurel ready to respond when she was sent to a Christian camp by her father.

"I think she was truly a wise woman, a wicca type. She only went to church because it was expected of her. I'm sure of that."

Laurel opened her mouth to argue and shut it again. If Lilith wasn't ready to admit a truth, she simply remade reality. Laurel sighed. "Look, I'm not trying to make you come. You can go back if you want. I'd really like it if you came. I promise no one will preach at you. I won't let them."

"You'd do that?" Lilith's face was wary.

"I will."

Lilith smiled and took Laurel's arm in a way that was definitely proprietary. "You're going to be on my side for once. In that case, let's go."

They could hear the buzz of many voices well before they arrived at the churchyard. "That's a church?" Lilith stared at the tin-roofed, open-sided building. "Nobody from there could be too high and mighty." But the tightening of her grip on Laurel's arm let her know Lilith was still nervous. Suddenly she pointed. "There's Darren organizing the natives. See, he's over there."

Even as she cringed at Lilith's choice of words, Laurel's heart gave a quick skip at the sight of Darren. He was a full head taller than the people crowded around him. The group seemed to be mostly men. Some were shouting. Darren and Isaac seemed to be trying to make some point. It didn't look like the sort of conversation one should interrupt.

"Darren! Over here!" Lilith's high-pitched yell pierced Laurel's eardrums and made her want to disappear as everyone turned to look at them. Darren raised his hand in a quick wave and turned back to the people around him. The sound of talking, which had stopped dead, began again with a burst of noise.

Lilith snorted. "Ignore us, will he? Well, I'll see about—"

Laurel grabbed her mother, preventing her from marching into the group. "Lilith, they're talking. Please!"

She gave a little grunt. "People have ignored me and put me down all my life, but they shouldn't do it to you."

"He isn't. He's just busy." Watching her mother, listening to her, Laurel realized that like Lilith's speeches, her rudeness stemmed from insecurity. She was sure people undervalued her, so she demanded what she thought was her fair share of attention. "He'll come talk to us when he can. I'm sure he's not putting us down."

Lilith didn't look placated in the least. To Laurel's relief, Jede came over. "I didn't see you. This is your mother?" She took Lilith's hand with both of hers. "You have a wonderful daughter. She's kept me sane. I'm so glad to meet you!"

Lilith blinked uncertainly. "Thank you."

Jede spun back to Laurel and threw up her arms. "Isn't this wonderful? Now the children will be okay."

"What's going on?" Laurel pointed at the group

around Darren. "Is there trouble?"

"Not really. Some of the people want to start distributing food now, but others, Isaac and Darren included,
think we should wait until all the church elders are
here."

"So it's going to take a while?"

Jede laughed. "Doesn't everything? After the elders
come, they'll talk and figure out a system of distribution
that seems best to them. We'll have to pray hard that
they decide to start with the neediest, not the most polit-
ically expedient."

Lilith's chin went up. "I should have known, even in
a church with no walls, Christians are the same sanctimonious hypocrites everywhere. They'll only give food
to the church people."

Jede gave Lilith a startled look. "No, to the whole
community! We're not perfect, but hopefully, God can
work through some of us showing His love. Laurel certainly has done that for me."

"But then you're another Christian. It seems to me,
you people talk a lot about helping the world, and then
mostly pat each other on the back and cut other people
down."

That did it. "Lilith! You can say what you want
about me. Yes, Dad gave you a rough time, too, but don't
tar others with the same brush. Edwina stuck by you as
a loyal friend for years. Darren managed to find a truckload of food somewhere and struggled all night to drive
it here because these people are hungry. Jede and Isaac
are here helping. Being a Christian doesn't mean we're
perfect, but we do care. God's love is not a fairy tale!
What are *you* doing to help these people?"

When silence met her outburst, Laurel could feel her cheeks flush. She'd probably only increased Lilith's antagonism toward Christianity…but somewhat surprisingly, Lilith didn't snap back. She stared at Laurel in surprise, opened her mouth, shut it again, and looked around.

A burst of noise from the school kids drew their attention. They were shouting out some kind of chant. It took her a couple of seconds to recognize the times table in English. She'd met the teacher, Simon, a young man much puffed up by his own importance. Now he had an audience, and he redoubled his efforts, strutting back and forth, banging the rickety table that served as a teacher's desk, and leading the chant loudly. He held up his hand, bringing the chant to a halt, and pointed to one of the taller boys.

"Is that some kind of mystical chant?" Lilith was staring intently at the school children. "They've even got uniforms or remnants of them. How charming."

The condescension in her voice made Laurel cringe. She caught Jede's raised eyebrow and shrugged apologetically. Movement in the group around Darren caught her attention. They turned almost in a body and walked toward the truck.

Darren left the group and came toward her. Dimples creased his cheeks. "You came! That's great." He shook Lilith's hand. "Welcome." A yell in Swahili from the top of the truck turned his head. Laurel looked up to see a black man in a torn shirt gesturing impatiently. "Excuse me. I've got to help unload the truck." Darren took a long stride, grabbed the top of the truck box, and swung up in one lithe motion.

"Wow," Lilith said the word almost into Laurel's ear. "He is amazing."

"Lilith, don't." Laurel kept her voice down.

There were shouts, and then the scene resolved itself into an organized work crew. Isaac was on the ground directing the building of a stack of gunnysacks. Darren carried two of the heavy sacks at a time. Laurel found herself watching him move, powerful and lithe as a leopard.

"There aren't very many men here compared to women and children."

"No, they're mostly off looking for work in the towns and cities," Jede answered Lilith.

"Dump the women with the kids and have a good time?"

Jede shrugged. "You're right about some of them, but many do send money and come back as often as they can."

Someone coughed right beside her. Laurel turned to see one of the schoolboys standing there, poker straight. A slim, black shoulder showed through a tear in his blue uniform shirt. He threw back his head and announced in a loud, singsong voice. "If it will please you, the children for watching those baboons are prepared." A burst of giggles came from the smaller school children. The boy turned stiffly, all precarious dignity.

Laurel tried to bolster his confidence. "Thank you. You speak English very well."

He gave her a stiff nod, with just the beginnings of a delighted grin showing. "Is it that we will go this day?"

"Yes, of course. Jede, can you still come to help?"

"I'd love to. I don't think I'm needed here. Isaac and

Darren will work things out with the elders."

"Isaac will do fine on his own." Darren came over. "If you're still going out with the school kids, I'm coming too."

"See, I told you." Lilith poked Laurel in the ribs.

Darren looked at her and grinned—and his smile was so clearly protective of Laurel that Lilith stepped back.

Laurel looked away from him before she melted completely.

Jede cleared her throat. "The children will be glad to have you, and we will too."

Lilith and Jede are trying to push Darren and me together. Should she try to stop it? Tell him not to come? But she wanted him to change his mind about the worth of helping animals, about her priorities, and watching the kids see things for the first time might help.

"And you, Laurel?"

"Of course you're welcome." Despite her roiling thoughts, she managed to get the words out steadily enough. *I'll just have to keep a tight lid on my feelings. If I can.*

15

"You will come also?"

A gaggle of nine excited school children had come over. The taller boy was looking up at Darren with a huge smile on his face.

Darren answered in their own language and the whole group burst into giggles.

"He's good with kids too," Lilith said in Laurel's ear.

She makes Darren sound like a dog I'm thinking of buying. To Laurel's relief, Jede started to introduce the children to Lilith, asking them to say their names. The girls especially tended to giggle and look down, covering their mouths with their hands and answering almost inaudibly. One by one the children shook Lilith's hand. Initially Lilith seemed startled, but as each child came to her, slowly she began to smile.

Three of the boys crowded around Darren, talking nonstop as they started up the hill to Joan's camp on Ndovu. The girls surrounded Jede.

Lilith stuck close to Laurel. "They're nice kids. Dirty, but nice. And they actually seem quite intelligent." It was the same comment Lilith had made about the baboons.

Laurel lowered her voice. "It's pretty hard to take a morning shower when you haul your water by hand from a source several miles from home. Listen, these are people like you and me, and some of them speak English."

"Excuse me for existing! I was trying to be nice, if you didn't notice." She stuck her chin in the air and moved to the far side of the group.

How am I supposed to respond to that? A gentle touch on Laurel's sleeve drew her attention. It was Sophia, a girl whose dark skin had rich red highlights. "My mother, she greets you."

"Do I know your mother?" Laurel tried to speak clearly and space her words well apart so Sophia would understand.

"Of course you do." Jede looked back at her. "Sophia is Meli's big sister."

"Oh. How is Meli?"

"She is well, and now that the food has come, my small brother will be well also."

Lilith came over and demanded an explanation. Her face grew thoughtful as she listened. Sophia had taken Lilith's hand and skipped alongside. Lilith managed to look profoundly uncomfortable, surprised, and pleased all at the same time.

Laurel found herself watching Darren with the boys. One of them mimed a plane landing badly, bouncing on the strip. Darren shook his head, and with his hands mimed a very smooth landing, then pointed to himself. The whole group burst into laughter.

At the compound, Ambaro stood at the door to the dining banda, wooden faced with disapproval. Several Somali men, including one that Laurel had never seen before, lounged nearby. Darren went toward them instantly, calling out a greeting. Laurel tried to usher the school children into the dining banda where she had the food for them. They wouldn't go. Instead, they stood in a tight group, glancing at the hostile faces.

Darren greeted each of the Somali men formally,

shaking hands elaborately. What sounded like an argument developed immediately.

"Jede, this is impossible." Laurel could feel two of the smaller children pressed against her. "What are they saying?"

"They don't want the kids here. Darren is saying that they're only children. That they've come to watch the troop." Her mouth tightened as one of the men said something loudly, and the whole group laughed. Darren looked as though he'd bitten into a rotten apple, but the tension seemed to have relaxed.

An older boy in the group of school children yelled and started to run forward. All the other kids held on to him.

The men laughed louder, and one made a comment. The schoolboy subsided.

Laurel looked at Jede.

"That first man, he said, 'To please you, Mr. Grant, we will allow these to watch their cousins.' James—" she pointed with her chin at the taller schoolboy—"wanted to fight him. The man said that at least he had some backbone. I think they are less angry now because of James."

"Because he wanted to fight them?" Laurel asked incredulously.

"They value courage."

Lord, You take care of things in ways I don't understand, but thank You. And thanks that Darren is here. She had an uncomfortable feeling that without Darren, those men would have simply driven the children away.

Lilith was staring wide-eyed at the Somali men. "I don't know what's going on, but let's get out of here."

"I'll just grab the food." Laurel darted into the dining banda. Ambaro had put the food away! *It's getting worse with the Somali and the Meru.* Laurel grabbed several loaves of bread, fruit, and peanut butter. *Is Ibrahim even going to take us out to the troop in the Jeep like he did last time? If he doesn't, I'm not sure I can remember the way…and if I can, what will I do if I get stuck in the sand?*

She ran back out. Ibrahim had driven the Jeep over. He and Darren were talking.

"Darren is offering to drive. Ibrahim refused." Jede rubbed a hand over her face. "I don't think he wants us loose on Ndovu without supervision."

One of the smaller children began to cry. James poked him hard in the ribs, saying something, and the little boy snapped to attention, mouth still wobbling but fighting hard. Darren put a hand on the child's shoulder.

Ibrahim beckoned impatiently for the children to get in. Everyone piled on—adults on the botton, children on top. Laurel ended up sandwiched between Lilith and Darren, with Sophia and another girl on her lap. Darren's arm was behind her.

He leaned over and spoke softly in her ear. "I can't say you lack courage, but are all your schemes this harebrained?" His eyes were laughing.

"It wasn't this bad last time."

"What is *harebrained?*" Sophia asked.

"Head like a rabbit," Darren said straight-faced.

"Memsahib Binet has a thing with a head like a rabbit?" James, who was wedged between Darren and the door, asked incredulously.

"Considering something she told me this morning, she probably has several." Darren nodded.

"Always has," Lilith said dryly, playing along. "Lots of harebrained schemes."

"Hey! Not all of them." She couldn't help laughing with them.

Jede turned, looking through the elbows of the kids on top. "I agree with you, Laurel. Difficult and harebrained are not the same thing."

Darren raised an eyebrow. "That's true."

"I do not understand." James had leaned forward as far as he could and turned to see their faces.

"It is nothing. Only silly talk." Darren's calm words reassured her.

"One day I will learn the English so that I can hear silly talk." James folded his arms and set his chin.

Laurel could hear Ibrahim talking to Joan on the radio.

"Farah will guide you," Ibrahim announced as he stopped the Jeep. "He is just coming."

"Good, that will give the children time to eat." Laurel reached for the food as they climbed out. The children were glancing nervously at Ibrahim, so she led them a little ways away.

"I do not wish to eat this food." James turned his back.

"Why is that?" Darren asked, squatting on his heels.

"It is the food of the Somali."

"It's from the store," Laurel protested. *If he won't eat, none of them will.*

"Are you afraid?"

"No!" James stepped forward, took several pieces of bread, and began eating rapidly.

Thank God for Darren. Once again, he'd defused the situation.

Jede asked the blessing, and the food disappeared with incredible rapidity. Two children still refused to eat. Sophia left Laurel, sat by one of the stubborn ones, and started to talk earnestly. Jede was sitting very close to them, and Laurel saw her smile at Sophia's words. She leaned forward and added something.

"Well, what was that all about?" Lilith demanded. She was perched like a black crow on a big rock.

"Sophia told them that they shouldn't be afraid. The Christian God is stronger than anything. No curse could bother them anymore because I thanked God for the food," Jede explained.

"Huh. So why didn't James want to eat it?"

James had been looking from one to the other, concentrating hard at understanding the English. Now he cut in. "I do not eat the food of those who hate me, but this is from the little store."

"Why did you come to see the animals?" Darren glanced at Laurel as if to say, *Listen to this.*

"I have come here because I am not afraid. Also I wish to hear English. Not for animals. I am not foolish!"

"I came because Laurel has helped my sister." Sophia ducked her head, and her eyes darted toward Ibrahim. "I am afraid."

Another girl spoke. "I came because of Jede. She is my friend, and Laurel is her friend, so I came. She said the animals are not what she thought before, so I came to see."

Laurel frowned. *Doesn't Darren know that I don't really care why they came, so long as there's any chance they might see something of God here, something to open their eyes and their world to include the value of creation.* She sighed. How could he? He was just as blind as the kids.

Farah appeared, stalking through the grass. "Joan has said they must stay well back. No one is to take the food of baboons." His eyes slid over the school children. James glared at him like a terrier ready to fight.

Silently, Laurel prayed for help. *May the beauty of Your wild land touch one child. And help me to show them Your love.* If this could work, maybe Darren would open his heart and really listen to her.

The first hour that morning was very tough. The children huddled together looking at Farah and the baboons warily. Joan stayed resolutely remote, only speaking to them once to tell them fiercely to stay well back. Darren walked along, talking softly to the boys. He glanced up at her and lifted a sardonic eyebrow.

Laurel's stomach hurt. *Is he right? Is this totally hare-brained like he said?*

At least Lilith seemed contented. Sophia and two smaller children stayed close to her. She looked both purposeful and serene, as if determined to comfort them. The baboons paused near a hundred foot sheet of horizontal rock, buff granite with orange water stains. Laurel collected the children around her on the rock.

Jede had settled down on the rock with her legs stretched out in front of her and her hands in her lap. Seeing her posture, Laurel, who'd started to sit cross-legged, quickly corrected herself and copied Jede, as did the girls. *She told me it's the only modest way for a woman to sit on the ground.* The boys were sitting, crouched on their heels like Darren. *I have so much to learn!*

"Why don't you tell them about the family groups, Laurel?" Jede prompted.

"They have families?" Sophia blurted, and then covered her mouth. The other kids giggled.

"Even a goat has a mother and father. How not?" an older girl answered her. The giggling grew, and Sophia looked like she wished she could disappear.

"But does a goat have a group of relatives who stand up for one another?" Jede's question stopped the giggling.

"The mother goat will protect her baby," Sophia answered doubtfully.

"A mother and child are not a family." James slapped the rock in emphasis. "An animal does not care who is its father."

Farah had moved quite close, still observing the baboons, but obviously listening. Now he looked at James. "There are some who call themselves human who do not know their father."

James bristled. "I know my father!"

Laurel cut in quickly before things got completely out of hand. "You're right, James, the baboons don't seem to know or care who their fathers are. But they do have families."

Out of the corner of her eye she could see Darren, on the outer edge of the group, watching her with disturbing eyes.

I won't let him rattle me! Laurel lifted her chin. "Farah, would you describe Gremlin's family for us?"

Farah gave her a startled look, then stretched himself to his full height, and with a slightly didactic manner began to explain. "Gremlin, he is that small one there. His grandmother is Susan, the mother of many, but his mother has died. His sister, she is helping him.

See, she is there." He pointed to Cleo with his chin and waited until the schoolchildren had all seen who she was.

"But she is small!" Sophia protested.

Jede asked the group if they knew any adults who were helping to raise a child that was not their own. Almost all the hands went up. As the stories poured out, Laurel realized that the extended family was much stronger here than in North America. Her mind went back to James's words. *"A mother and child are not a family."* She would rather stay single than risk getting into that situation as Lilith had.

She looked around for her mother. Lilith was standing almost behind her. *I should have brought that camp stool for her.*

A hand on her arm brought her back to the present. Sophia was trying to get her attention. "You said they do not know father. Look there." She pointed. Susan groomed Argus, one of the big males. In Argus's lap was Twende, Susan's youngest. Before Laurel had time to answer, Twende suddenly darted away from Argus and tried to snatch a seed pod that Gremlin was opening. Gremlin screamed and darted into a thornbush. Balancing precariously on the very tips of the branches, he dodged Twende's grabs.

The children laughed delightedly. Cleo waded in, giving Twende a whack. This was too much for Twende, and he ran. Cleo sat down looking satisfied. Everyone laughed again. "That one, she is a good sister," Sophia said as they watched Gremlin come to Cleo for a reassuring cuddle.

The tension was broken, and for the rest of the day

the children talked happily. Even Farah seemed less antagonistic. Only Darren remained remote. He'd pulled back and walked at a small distance, watching her and the school children. *Like I watch the baboons.* What was he thinking?

Lilith had a small huddle of children around her. There was a burst of excited talking from the group, and Laurel dropped back to walk alongside.

"What's so interesting?"

Lilith was smiling. "I just told them that I like baboons better than cows. They acted like I said something revolutionary."

"Cows are the animals for wealth," James explained. "Of what good is a baboon?"

"To give pleasure to God." Jede gestured at the troop. "The wild things, they are God's cattle, and He gave them to us to tend."

Wow! She said that well, in a way that will make sense to these kids. Jede really did understand. Why couldn't Darren?

There was a short silence, and then Lilith laughed. "God's cattle? If I believed in one big paternal God, I'd say He should have fired us a long time ago. If our job is to tend nature, we've failed."

Sophia ignored Lilith and looked at Laurel. "Is this so? Are the wild animals truly God's cattle?"

"Who made them?" Laurel looked from one to another waiting for an answer. *Can Darren hear this?*

"Allah is creator!" Farah cut in.

The others nodded. James put his hand up waving for attention. "A boy who is careless with the goats and cows is beaten."

The whole group stiffened uneasily. "But what are we to do? They eat our gardens. My uncle killed a baboon." Sophia crossed her arms defensively.

"Do cows and goats get into the gardens?" Jede asked.

There was a chorus of assent.

"Why?" Jede seemed purposeful in her questioning.

James answered her. "Because the boys have not taken them to good grass. They are hungry."

"Are we to herd baboons?" Another child asked incredulously.

"Perhaps it is that they have need of a space to live." Sophia's voice was soft and nervous.

Yes! Laurel felt like cheering aloud. But to her surprise, Lilith beat her to the punch.

"That's right!" Lilith stood, sweeping out one arm so that her cape swirled. "That's exactly what Joan was telling me. She's very worried that the more people come near, the less room there will be for baboons and for all the animals. You've grasped the essence. All of the earth mother's children should have a place to paint their pattern, dance their part in the dance of life. Even the insects have their song to sing in the great symphony of life." The children were staring at Lilith with startled eyes. They couldn't have caught more than one word in three.

No, Lilith. Not the earth mother! Darren shouldn't hear that. She looked in his direction. He'd crossed his arms. *Closed body language.*

Laurel jumped when Lilith suddenly bellowed, "Joan! Joan Doyle! Come here!"

Laurel cringed at the command in Lilith's voice. "Lilith, Joan is busy."

Lilith made a shushing motion with one hand and bellowed again. This time Joan came over. Several of the children chorused a greeting, but she ignored them like just so many of the pesky flies. "Can I help you, Lilith?"

"This child understood. She understands that the troop on Ndovu needs land. Education really is the answer."

"One child agreeing the wild animals might have a right to live does very little to make things better. Now if she were president—"

All the kids laughed, and Joan raised an eyebrow. "Excuse me, but I want to finish what I was doing." She strode away, leaving silence in her wake. Farah followed her. It took a few minutes for the children to begin talking again, but they were too full of questions to stay silent for long. All their lives they'd lived next to the animals, but they knew almost nothing.

Darren just kept watching. If they asked him a direct question, he would answer, but otherwise he was silent.

Seeing a chameleon on a branch, Laurel picked up the tiny, slow-moving reptile. Several of the girls screamed, and all of the children backed away from her rapidly. The little thing looked like a tiny triceratops with a serrated back and long prehensile tail. "What's wrong? It's just a chameleon. Look how its eyes move individually."

Jede backed away. "They're poisonous. At least I always thought so."

Nothing Laurel could do would convince any of the children to touch it. When Jede reached out a tentative hand, the whole group exclaimed in a mixture of horror and admiration. Lilith wanted to take it back to the compound. "It looks as if it holds secret power."

"It's just another of God's creatures, and better off here." When Laurel released it, three of the kids stayed close staring at it for a little while. Somehow they got started trying to see how many different kinds of creatures they could count.

"Truly God has many cattle!" James said at the end of the day.

Back at Joan's camp, Jede offered to walk back with the children. "There's no reason you should have to come." The group left, calling good-bye and thank you.

"It was an amazing day, but I'm going to go to our banda and rest until supper." Lilith turned to leave.

They've deliberately left me alone with Darren. He was standing to one side and slightly behind her. She didn't turn. "You still think that was a harebrained scheme, don't you?"

He put a hand on her shoulder. "I admire you for it."

She spoke without moving. "Why?"

"I'm beginning to understand your values, why you're not lying when you say you care for people and creation."

She turned to face him, taking his hand in both of hers. "Really?"

Darren gently squeezed her fingers then withdrew his hand. "Maybe a little, but that doesn't mean I agree."

"But how can you not?" She shook her head.

"Hey, don't look so discouraged. You did give me food for thought, and hopefully, you're still learning too." He smiled. "I saw that you've learned to sit properly."

"It still makes my tendons ache."

"Learning is like that." He touched the curve of her cheek gently, and she shut her eyes. *He's right, learning hurts. Just being near him affects me.* But it felt so right. *Be careful, feelings can trick you!*

He lifted her chin gently with one finger. "I've got to take the truck back, and then fly some charter contracts. You will come to the coast, won't you?"

She wanted to. Oh, she wanted to. But she'd already decided it wasn't the wise thing to do....

Help me, Lord.

"Tell you what, why don't you explain what you've decided and why. Then I'll do the same. Okay?" His eyes were calm and steady.

That made sense. At least they could talk it through. "Okay."

"Good." He touched her gently on the end of her nose and turned to go. But as Laurel started walking, she couldn't help wondering if she'd just made a mistake.

16

"SO?" LILITH DEMANDED AS SOON AS LAUREL WALKED INTO the banda.

"I said I'd go to the coast with him."

Lilith crowed. "I knew he'd break you down."

"Hey, it's with a church group. We won't be alone."

Lilith shrugged. "Oh, well. Still, better than nothing. But don't take him too seriously. Love should never be earnest. Can't you just have fun?"

Like you did with the men that were in the house for a night or two? Laurel turned her head away.

Lilith sat on her bed. "You know, those children today, I think they quite liked me."

"I'm sure they did." Laurel's shoulders had relaxed at the change of subject.

"I think I have a natural affinity for primitive children." Lilith settled herself complacently on the bed. "Maybe I'm primitive too; that's why we got along so well. That field trip was a great idea."

"I'm glad you approve. I'm just about positive that Joan let that trip happen because of you. I think she said yes when I asked her because of the money you'd donated. She wants more from you and thinks I can influence you."

Lilith gave a bark of a laugh. "Little Laurel is using money for leverage now. You're learning. It's amazing what people will do for money." She frowned. "Well, most people. You never would do what I wanted when I offered money."

"Maybe I shouldn't have asked her, but the idea seemed so right."

"Don't worry about it. I approve, and I'm the one who's paying. The one who has the money calls the shots. It's as simple as that. I'm sure whoever was funding this baboon thing before had conditions on the funding."

"That's true enough. But…"

"If this bothers you so much, I'll just ask her if she'd rather have the funding *and* the field trips, or no funding. I'm sure she'll say she wants the funding. Unlike you, Joan wants money badly enough to do things my way."

"Making criteria for funding a project is different from trying to control a person's life." Laurel held out her hands. "Maybe you just didn't realize that. You didn't know how abandoned I felt when you wouldn't help with sports or any of the things I wanted to do or to wear. If I didn't do exactly what you wanted, you cut me off."

Lilith's pale face flushed, and her eyes glittered. "You think *you* were rejected. When did you ever approve of a single thing I did or a single thing I was?"

Her mother's words hit Laurel like a punch in the gut. *But you were the mother. The one who was supposed to be an adult.* Laurel dropped her hands and sank onto her bed. "I didn't see you as someone who might be hurting and lonely. I was afraid of your power over me and pushed you away. It looks like we've both been longing for the other's approval. Lilith, I care for you very much."

Lilith ducked her head. "But not for what I believe or how I act?" She asked in a very small voice.

"Couldn't we just agree to be different?" Slow tears were trickling down Laurel's cheeks. "Any strength and hope I have comes from God. I want that kind of security and love for you, too."

Lilith's head came up. "I told you, God doesn't like me!"

"Ask Him. Ask Him if He likes you."

"As if He'd answer. What will it be, a booming voice from the clouds?" She snorted.

Laurel fought to stay calm in the face of Lilith's mockery. "I don't know how He'll answer you. But I know He will."

Lilith shook her head. "What will He do? Send a man like Darren Grant into my life? Is that one of the ways you can tell He loves you?"

Laurel flinched, then let out her breath slowly. "I don't know what God is doing with Darren and me, but I can't see how it could be more than maybe learning a bit from each other. But that's us. God will speak to you in whatever way is best for you. Because He loves you."

"You mean that, don't you? You're not just baiting me or trying to side with your father against me?"

"Side with my father?" Laurel's voice came out in a startled squeak.

"That's what I thought this whole Christianity thing was about." Lilith's eyes narrowed. "You've been preaching ever since that first summer you spent with him."

"But I didn't spend it with *him*. He dumped me at different summer camps, remember?" Laurel hugged herself tightly, choking back the hurt that memory still caused her. "God's love was the only thing that kept me sane."

Lilith stood and swept her cloak off the bed. "You know, this Darren reminds me of your father in some ways." She shook her head half smiling. "They're both rather—" her smile broadened—"*irresistible*. They have something special about them. Something you can't get out of your head."

Or your heart. Laurel agreed silently.

"Your father was...remarkable. He simply swept me off my feet." She settled the cloak around her and sighed. "Pity I didn't realize how little we had in common until months after we were married."

Her mother's wistful tone tugged at Laurel's heart. *She sounds as though she actually loved Dad!* But before Laurel could comment, Lilith waved her hand, as though sweeping the air in front of her. "Listen, Laurel, men are better playthings than partners. You can never see who they really are until it's too late. Be careful with Darren, loosen up, enjoy, but don't take him too seriously. I couldn't see the pompous idiot under the beguiling facade your father presented to me. I thought he was courteous, old-fashioned." She gave a short, bitter laugh. "More the fool, me. He certainly showed his true colors in time. Have I ever told you how he humiliated me in front of all our friends?"

And so began another tirade against Laurel's father. By the end, she was almost shouting. Laurel felt raw, Lilith's barbed words assaulting her as effectively as glass shards embedded in the straps of a cat-o'-nine-tails. She struggled to tune out the outpouring of hate and anger, went to the basin, and started to wash her face. The cool washcloth felt incredibly good on her tear-swollen, dirty face.

Lilith's tirade slowed and came to a halt. There was silence, except for the sound of the water in the wash-basin. Laurel felt Lilith's hand on her arm. "I just don't want you hurt the way your father hurt me."

Laurel stood stiffly without turning. "And you think keeping men at a distance, using them only as...*play-mates* will keep me safe?"

Lilith patted her shoulder. "That's right."

"But they did hurt you, all those men. I saw you crying when they left."

She shrugged. "So, I'm not perfect, but none of them hurt me the way your father did. I just want you to be happy."

Laurel shook her head, the slow tears still coming. "Oh, Lilith."

She could hear Lilith sigh, then her mother put an arm around Laurel and squeezed her shoulders. "Okay, if it's what you want, I'll ask this God of yours. He won't answer, but I'll ask Him just the same. Does that make you happy?"

Laurel dropped the washcloth with a splash and hugged Lilith hard. "Yes," she whispered into her mother's hair, "it makes me very happy."

A knock on the door made them both swing around. Laurel grabbed a towel and rubbed at her face, hoping to hide the marks of her tears. The knock came again.

"Come in."

Joan just put her head in. "Breakfast will be half an hour late. Ambaro has asked for several days off to visit her sister at Saba." She raised one eyebrow. "It might be good to remember sound carries on a still night." She retreated, closing the door behind her.

Lilith rolled her eyes and echoed Joan's last words, imitating her tone of voice. "She is so uptight. Well, she'd better not be so high and mighty with me, or she'll lose her precious funding!"

"I don't think she was trying to be rude."

"Huh. Just putting me down for being noisy. Well, I'll be noisy if I want to. She doesn't think much of me, but she'd better be careful."

"Is that why you always fought with my teachers?"

"What?"

"Because you felt bad when they didn't like you?"

"Not bad, just plain mad." Lilith frowned. "It was you not liking me that made me sad." She crossed her thin arms. "Maybe I can change that. You asked me this morning what I was doing to help these people."

"I was just reacting to what you'd said about Jede. I didn't mean—"

"Oh yes, you did, and I'm telling you. That project you were talking about to Joan, the one with schools and so on? I'm going to make that happen. Everyone will have to admit I'm worth something, even that God of yours."

Laurel's mouth fell open. Part of her wanted to grab at the chance. "You don't have to do anything to be worthwhile. God loves you right now."

Lilith tipped her head back. "Don't give me that. I know what people say. I'm touchy, aggressive, eccentric, and a witch to boot."

"So? Most days I'd like to wear a big sign that says, Be patient with me, God isn't finished with me yet." Laurel held her mother's thin hands in hers. "I desperately want the project to happen, but you don't have to do a thing to be loved by God. Lilith, you are a worthwhile person."

She stared warily at her daughter. "It's nice to know you think that, assuming, of course, that what you're saying isn't just so much religious rhetoric. Meanwhile, tell me about this idea of yours."

"Okay, but it all starts with God's love. See, caring for God's creation lets me feel closer to and loved by Him."

"Is that why you're so much into science?"

Laurel nodded. "Anyway, I want to find a way to let other people see that, not just sit alone studying creation. But everywhere it seems like people are taking sides, either for nature and against humans or the other way around. Joan calls people cancer on the earth, and Darren—"

"Darren again, is it?"

"Lilith!"

"Go on."

Biting back her frustration, Laurel continued. "He thinks that there's so much need here among the people that focusing resources anywhere else is wrong. If I could only show him that people and creation belong together, then maybe..."

Her voice trailed off and Lilith laughed. "Men always think they're right. By all means, let's show the fool."

"That's not what I meant!"

"Just what do you want? A man who shares your dream? Good luck." Lilith laughed bitterly and turned to get ready for bed.

Laurel watched her. *A man who shares my dream? Not just my dream, our dream. I could learn from him too.* Was that so impossible? Her head said Lilith was wrong. *The Bible says she's wrong, and look at Julie and David. They're so happy working together with their Christian guiding outfit. They definitely share a dream.* Still, the knot in Laurel's stomach only tightened.

17

LILITH, DIRECT AS EVER, TACKLED JOAN AT BREAKFAST THE NEXT morning. "I want to ask you a question."

Joan stopped with a bite of porridge halfway to her mouth. She slowly put down the spoon. "Yes, what is it?"

Laurel put her spoon down abruptly and started to speak, but Lilith cut her off. "Just this. Would you rather have school trips and so on or have me cut funding?"

"I'd rather have the squatters gone!" Joan's eyes narrowed. "Are you going to heap more demands of some kind on me?"

"Wait." Laurel tried to keep her voice calm. "Maybe I shouldn't have pushed the school trips this way. I just felt it was so important to reduce the hostility—"

"You are a dreamer if you think the foolish little school trips will help reduce any hostility between the Meru and my work at Ndovu. A pretty young woman with romantic dreams." Joan snorted. "Dreams tend to get tarnished by the harsh reality of Africa. Oh, speaking of romantic dreams, Darren Grant called. He's going to be coming in on Friday. He wants you to go out with him, some trip to the coast he said you'd agreed to. Next time you might ask permission first. You are supposed to be working for me."

Lilith cleared her throat sharply.

"Oh, I know. I've got to keep you happy or lose funding." Joan's voice was bitter.

"Joan, I'm sorry I didn't ask about going to the coast before. If it's impossible, I can stay here." *Is this a way out without running? But I want...*

"Don't be ridiculous! You can go to the coast." Lilith stood and faced her. "Go, enjoy Darren and get him out of your system." With a swirl of her cape, she turned to face Joan. "Now that that's out of the way, do you want to talk to me about the conditions for a long-term funding agreement?"

The look on Joan's lean face could only be described as a snarl, but she led the way to her office. With a splitting headache, Laurel headed out to spend the day with the baboons.

Through the long, dusty day, Laurel did her job and ached inside. What if by letting herself spend time with Darren, she was just setting herself up to make a huge mess of her life the way her mother had. *She told me how hot Dad was.* Lilith had said she didn't realize how different Laurel's father was from her. *I don't even have that excuse. I know we don't see eye to eye.*

But what if that changed? *He said I'd given him food for thought....* Laurel shook her head and focused on the troop. Her lips tightened. *But was it enough? Will it make any real difference to him...to us?* Laurel's throat tightened on her fear that the answer was a clear, resounding no. The sun beat down, shriveling hope. In the dryness, her fears flared unchecked, like a spark in the brittle, dry grass of Ndovu tinder. If only it would rain! At least Gremlin might survive, and the Meru would get a crop in.

The baboons were listless. Cleo was limping for some reason and paying almost no attention to Gremlin. Laurel watched the two of them. Nothing was working out. *My dream has turned into a fight between two self-inter-*

ested women. How can this be what Jede and I prayed about?

She bowed her head. "Lord, if You would turn this mess into something good and not evil, something that helps, please do it." *Maybe Darren is right, this scheme has a rabbit's head.* She half smiled remembering the puzzled looks on the children's faces when he'd said that. *He's so much fun.*

What is he going to say when he hears about the project? How can I do it even if Joan agrees? I couldn't even have taken the school children out last time without Darren's help. Laurel could hear little crackling noises in the brush, as if the land was audibly shriveling up. The heat was sucking all the life, all the hope out of everything.

Laurel had let Farah carry the radio, as it made him happy to be in charge of it. She glanced up at the sound of static, but his conversation with whoever had called was in Swahili. He put it carefully back into the case on his belt and came over.

"Ibrahim is coming. You are to go back. Joan has said so."

"Did she say why?"

Farah shook his head. "Perhaps Darren Grant has come."

"No, Darren said—" Laurel caught herself, and then saw the twinkle in Farah's eyes. *He's teasing. Am I that obvious with how I feel about Darren?* Apparently, she was.

When Ibrahim arrived, he was unusually silent, almost hostile. He dropped Laurel off at the door of her banda and didn't look at her when she thanked him for the ride. As she got out beside Lilith, he drove off rapidly.

"What's wrong with Ibrahim?"

"We won!" Lilith flung her arms out. "Ibrahim tried

to argue Joan out of working with us, but she shut him up pretty smartly. She told him she is an animal behavior scientist not a political ally in some tribal argument over land rights. She would do what she needed to do to keep Ndovu wild. He didn't like that much."

Laurel's mind spun, trying to come to grips with this new information. "What exactly did Joan agree to?"

"She said you and she could hammer out details after the trip; whatever system you want as long as Ndovu is kept wild. She'll do anything to keep on studying her precious baboons."

"I'm not comfortable with forcing Joan to do something that she obviously hates."

"Just what do you want? Lightning from heaven? This is what you wanted, isn't it?" Lilith was looking at her from desperate eyes.

Laurel reached out to touch her mother's arm. "Thank you for caring and trying to help."

Lilith only grunted, but she looked slightly mollified. "Well?"

Can this work? Is this what You want, God? "I'm not sure what to think, but maybe I could start finding out whether it's even possible. For one thing, we'd have to make sure that the school was for the Somali people, too."

Lilith's expression lightened. "I think you'll find most ideas are possible with enough money behind them. Oh, one other thing—I'm not sticking around. We called another charter company, and I've got a flight out to Nairobi right away. That's why I made Joan call you back. I've finished packing, and the plane should be here any minute. Darren wasn't available, too busy hauling food to the hungry to mind his own business properly. Both of you are dreamers."

"You're leaving? But—"

"I'll see you again before I leave Kenya." Lilith headed into the banda. "Come help me carry my stuff out." She turned with her hand on a suitcase and gave a wry smile. "Joan Doyle has mixed feelings toward me right now. She was eager to recommend some excellent tour companies. She assured me that I wouldn't have to walk in thornbushes or put up with so many flies."

Laurel reached for her mother's hands. "Joan might want you gone, but I don't."

Lilith gave her a sharp glance. "I believe you mean that." Her voice suddenly shook, and she turned away quickly.

Is she crying? Laurel took a quick step and put an arm around her mother. Lilith turned and hugged her hard. "You know, you didn't turn out so bad, after all." She laughed shakily and stepped back, tears in her eyes. "Despite your preoccupation with God."

"I do care about you, Mother." She squeezed Lilith's hands.

Lilith coughed and turned away. "Enough of this. Come along, help me carry my things. Ibrahim is going to be here any minute, and we don't want to keep his excellency waiting."

"He does have a certain presence, doesn't he?"

Her mother laughed. "Oh, and then some. I think he was an emperor in another life—Nero or someone like that. He certainly has the aura."

After one last quick hug down on the airstrip, Laurel watched her mother's plane fly away. *Lord, please be with her. Answer her prayer and show Yourself to her.* She stood for a long time watching the sky even after the plane was out of sight. *Help me to be wise, and not repeat her mistakes.* She sighed. The hot wind lifted her hair. She could hear the sound of goats in the distance. Laurel took a deep breath and turned to go back to camp. *I'm in way over my head. Just help me make a difference for You in this place, Lord.*

When she got back to the compound she looked for Joan, but the woman was nowhere to be found. Obviously, she wasn't ready to talk to Laurel. With an uneasy heart, she sat down and tried to work out the details of her dream. *I don't know enough!* Laurel threw down the pencil. *The school curriculum here, what the government will think, if the church will help—I don't know any of it.* She crossed her arms and glared at the table. She had to figure out how to get the Somali and the Meru involved.

If only there was someone to plan with her, someone who knew Kenya and loved God. *Someone like Darren.* She stood and started to pace. *Would he?* He was looking for a way to work with one group of people. A way to make a difference. He'd said so. *This would make a huge difference if it works. He'd have to see that.*

She sat down again, picked up the pencil, and made a rapid random pattern of dots on the paper. *He even said I gave him food for thought.* She clenched the pencil and wrote: Ask Darren for advice. She scratched out the word *advice* and wrote *help,* circled it twice, and frowned furiously. *I've learned so much. Why won't he?* She stabbed the paper so hard her pencil tip broke.

She shut her eyes, and her mind was suddenly full

of memories of Darren. The way his grin flashed in his tan face, the lithe strength as he vaulted onto the back of the truck, the feel of his mouth on hers. An aching longing filled her.

A shiver whispered through her, and Laurel pushed it—and her errant thoughts—away. She couldn't let herself give in to either.

The next several days were baking hot, but there was a difference—clouds were rolling across the sky now, like hope just out of reach. On Thursday afternoon she even heard thunder. There was a hushed, airless heat. Even the baboons seemed to be watching the sky, looking up at the clouds periodically. None came close, no shadow cut the heavy sun. Laurel felt as if she would explode if it didn't rain soon.

Cleo's limp was worse, and Gremlin was withdrawn, thin, and dejected. Even the big male baboons had quit threatening each other. Her only consolation was knowing that human children were no longer hungry. In Canada, Laurel had longed for spring, but that longing paled into insignificance compared to the longing for the rains. It was a constant topic of conversation.

"If the rains do not come, perhaps the Meru will leave." Ibrahim glanced sideways at Laurel as he drove them out to the troop one morning. "If there is nothing here for them, they will go. This is not their place. There must be nothing for them here! You must not make this school."

Laurel shifted uneasily in her seat. "Ibrahim, if there is a school, it will be for everyone—Somali people as well as Meru."

Ibrahim frowned and Joan cut in. "Until there are

some concrete plans, you have no right to make empty promises. These people have lived at odds for *hundreds* of years, and you think your little foundation is going to change that? You're ridiculous!"

Laurel flushed. "I may be, but God isn't. And if He is in this thing, anything can happen. Especially peace."

"Who can know the will of Allah?"

At Farah's sudden comment, Laurel turned to look at him, but his expression was blank. *Was he trying to defend me?* Joan and Ibrahim seemed equally suspicious. Ibrahim especially glared at Farah, but he looked back proudly. "That is the teaching. Allah does as he wills."

Ibrahim grunted, and Joan made an irritated gesture. "I'm surrounded by religious fanatics. I prefer the baboons."

Ibrahim brought the Jeep to a stop, and they all climbed out.

"Look." Farah pointed to a small, twisted acacia thorn tree. Laurel could see nothing, but he beckoned impatiently. "The flowers, they come. Always before the rains, they come."

On the tips of the dry, leafless, branches, tiny buds were swelling. One was partly open showing dull yellow fluff. "Does that mean the rains will come in the next couple of days?"

"Perhaps." He shrugged expressively.

Joan had bent eagerly over the tree. "At least the buds will give the baboons a nutritious food source." She looked up at Laurel. "Yes, the rains will come, but whether they are light and patchy or rich with water, who knows. The buds can open, then dry out and die from lack of water."

Dry out and die. Was that what would happen to her hopes?

18

THE STEERING WHEEL OF THE HEAVY DIESEL TRUCK VIBRATED under Darren's hands. Tinny, syncopated music blasted from the radio in the lap of the Kenyan sitting against the door of the cab. Darren could hear the people perched on top of the load singing.

Thor was right; he was losing business because of this, but what was the use of doing something halfway? He'd truck food until there was enough to last until the crop after the rains provided for them. It would take another couple of loads. More if the rains held off. In spite of the risk to his business, he was content with this trip. *And how much of that comes from the fact that you know you'll see Laurel?*

Dust billowed in the windows and swirled into the cab as he brought the truck to a halt in Saba. The singing switched to the general commotion of arrival. People began to climb down, clothes fluttering in the wind as he watched them in the rearview mirror.

"Eh, thank you, brother!" The men crowded into the cab shook his hand enthusiastically, yelling over the noise of the radio. "Go with God!"

He had given rides to those who wanted to travel. To him it was natural that in a country with few private vehicles, every vehicle on the road would be a target for hopeful travelers. Now he answered farewells and shook hands, but his mind was already with Laurel.

He shoved the truck into gear. Images of her played in his mind: her big, dark eyes looking up at him; the graceful shape of her forearms as she pointed out the different animals she loved; the flashing joy of her smile when she knew there was food for the kids at the Wilson; her warm, soft mouth on his. He swerved, barely missing a goat. *Get a grip, man!* He forced himself to concentrate on muscling the heavy truck safely down the rough track.

He turned the truck and headed for Isaac's church on the Wilson to unload. The school kids poured out of the church, dark legs and arms flashing in the sun. James jumped up and grabbed the rearview mirror, hanging on and riding until the truck stopped.

"Eeeeh, James, you will surely die an early death." Darren shook his head, half laughing at the boy.

James flashed him an impudent grin and dropped down. Darren opened the door to a storm of high-pitched greetings and laughter. He answered them as he vaulted onto the back of the truck. The sooner the truck was unloaded, the sooner he could look for Laurel. The schoolteacher walked over. He flipped a sack off his back and reached to shake Darren's hand. "So, Simon, how have the field trips gone?"

"They have gone well. Perhaps even I will go the next time and become a student of baboons." He grinned. "The children have told me many interesting things they are learning from Memsahib Laurel. Perhaps she is a wise woman."

Darren tipped his head. *If she's impressing Simon...* But what if it was all wrong? What if Laurel was leading all these people into the same mistake he'd made when he turned away from God?

He turned abruptly to go back for another sack.

Simon tried to stop him. "Come and rest. James has run to find Isaac and the other men."

Darren shook his head and kept going. *Laurel isn't running from God. I would recognize that.* He had to talk to her, figure this out. Both of his fists closed on a sack, then seconds later on another. He worked at shifting the load as if that would shift his confusion.

Some of the older kids began to help, working together to carry a sack from the truck. James came back at a run. "Isaac asks, can you take part of this food to the people across the ravine? It is far for them to walk to this place."

"How much?" Darren asked still moving.

James shrugged. "I do not know. Isaac is just coming."

Sweat was running into his eyes. Darren wiped at it and hoisted another two sacks. When he deposited those two on the growing pile, Isaac was there. "You're working like a donkey," Isaac said as they shook hands. "What dog has bitten you?"

Darren glanced involuntarily toward Ndovu, and Isaac chuckled. "Perhaps the dog is called woman?"

Darren worked faster and harder.

"She is a good woman that one." Isaac's eyes were twinkling. "She should bear you many healthy sons."

Darren froze. *Laurel, the mother of my children?* The heavy sack, half lifted, thumped him in the shins, nearly knocking him off his feet. A jolt of reaction shot up his spine—an odd, exhilarating combination of joy and terror.

"Be careful, my brother!"

Darren recovered his balance. "Then be careful what

you say. How much do you want me to leave on the truck?"

"There are thirty families, so do as you think best."

As he pulled away from the church a few moments later, he glanced at his watch again. Laurel might have come back into the compound for lunch. Should he take the sacks across the ravine first, or go see if she was there? He turned the truck toward Ndovu. The Jeep was at the compound, but neither Joan nor Laurel were around. Darren set out to find Ibrahim. A few minutes later he and Ibrahim were bouncing across the desiccated grassland.

"So what is the news?" Darren asked settling into the seat. "How is Laurel?"

"Her mother has left. That one is not a woman of peace."

"What do you mean?"

"It is not my affair to speak of it." He spat emphatically into the dust. Darren tried twice to get more information about Laurel, but Ibrahim would not answer his questions. Obviously, Lilith had offended him in some way. Laurel's mother wasn't someone who was careful about what she said. *Probably just some careless statement.*

"They are just there." Ibrahim jerked his chin toward the south. "I will wait for you. It is good that you take Laurel away from here."

Darren looked at Ibrahim for an explanation, but he wouldn't meet Darren's eyes. He shrugged and headed through the thorn brush with long, ground-eating strides. As the troop came into view, Laurel glanced up as if she could sense his presence. Their eyes met. Her cap of dark hair shone in the sun. Hot noon light outlined the contours of her body and lit her tentative smile. He stood looking into her eyes, both of them completely oblivious to anyone else.

Joan cleared her throat loudly.

Laurel started, blinking as though coming out of a trance. He knew how she felt. He moved toward her and took her hand. "You said you'd come out with me to the coast. Can you come now?" Suddenly he felt foolish, vulnerable.

Joan cut in before Laurel had a chance to answer. "Go on. I could do with you out of my space for a few days."

The look Laurel gave him was uncertain.

"Laurel?"

She nodded and went with him, but on the walk back to the Jeep, she wouldn't meet his eyes.

"Laurel, are you afraid of something?"

Her shoulders jerked. "Do you want a list?"

"That's not what I meant. I mean right now."

"So did I." She was walking quickly, moving gracefully through the bush.

"Okay, give me the list then. Maybe I can help." The look she gave him was almost that of a hunted animal. He stopped in his tracks. "Are you afraid of me? I wouldn't hurt you."

"That's probably what Lilith thought about my father too." She shook her head. "You and I are so different."

Thornbushes kept getting in the way, so he couldn't walk alongside her. "Laurel, you're a special person. I don't want to hurt you. Ouch!" The branch of a wait-a-bit thorn had caught him across the back.

She stopped to help him get loose. The contact ran over him like warm rain. Her eyes were wide and her breath quick. They stood very close for a second, then she turned her head aside and stepped back. "You confuse me, Darren Grant."

He laughed. "I confuse you? Isaac made some crack about you and me, and I just about fell off the top of the truck." He held out his hands. "Look, Laurel, I didn't expect this either. You're right, we have differences. But for now, can't we just let ourselves enjoy being together?"

He saw the smooth skin of her throat move as she swallowed hard. She shut her eyes for a moment. "Just have fun? Lilith would like that."

A frustrated huff escaped him. "That's *not* what I meant. If there's to be anything between us, it will be a lot more than a casual encounter." He could feel his palms sweating.

"I don't know, Darren. I really don't know." He wanted to touch the smooth line of her cheek. Her eyes were huge. "I do want to talk, to ask you about some things."

She was so close. *Take it easy, Darren.* He took a long, slow breath. "How about we start there then. I'm not sure how much we'll get to talk in the truck."

"Truck? You brought another load of food in?"

The joy in her eyes made him smile. "I did. You may be pretty sick of that truck by the time we get to Nairobi."

"Hey, no problem."

Half an hour later she was a bit wide-eyed when he took the heavy truck over the lip of the ravine, but she braced herself. Coming across the packed sand of the dry riverbed in the ravine, he accelerated gradually, careful not to let the tires start to spin in the sand.

"Hang on!" The heavy truck bucked and lurched as it plowed up the bank on the far side, but they made it.

"Wow. I can see why you usually fly." She was laughing. "Four-wheeling in a three-ton truck. Wild!"

"Too wild?" The question had been light and teasing, but he found himself waiting for her answer with considerable anxiety.

She shrugged. "Not if I get to learn how to drive this thing myself."

He laughed. Her quick humor and grin warmed him, melting away his anxiety.

"Watch out!" As Laurel called out, he spotted the children dashing across the track. Two little boys playing chicken with the truck! His foot came down hard on the brake. The big truck skidded in the sand, barely missing the kids.

"They're grinning and waving at us." Laurel had twisted around to look back. "They did that on purpose!"

"Yes." His voice was grim. As the diesel shuddered to a halt, one boy was already running. An older girl was holding onto the other one as he struggled to get away. Darren jumped down from the cab.

Laurel was just a second behind him. "That's Sophia! I know her from the school."

The boy kicked Sophia hard in the shins, broke loose, and ran. Sophia looked like she wanted to join him but stood her ground. As she recognized Laurel, she ducked her head. "My brother, that one, he is bad."

"Your brother is crazy!"

Sophia twisted her hands together. "If he hears, my father will beat him."

"Beat him? Oh, Sophia, surely not." Sophia's distress was echoed in Laurel's eyes, and Darren's anger waned.

"I won't talk to your father this time, but listen." He bent to her level. "Tell your brother if he does that again, I will personally come to your house and speak to your father. If I hear that he ran in front of *any* vehicle, I will come. Understand?"

Sophia nodded emphatically. "I will tell him. Is it that you are bringing food?"

"That's right."

The girl's face lit with a huge smile. "I'll go to tell the people!" She turned to run, then faced them skipping backward. "Laurel, you have brought good things! The days in God's wild land and now food!"

The next half hour was hectic as they unloaded the sacks. Sophia's father appeared and started an argument about distribution, which was only solved after careful diplomacy. Darren found that even as he tried to smooth things over with the men, his eyes were drawn to Laurel. She was talking animatedly with Sophia, her mother, and little sister. Her dark hair swung as she gestured. *Thor was right; she has the grace of a gazelle. She's both graceful and kind.*

To his great irritation two men asked for a ride to Nairobi. He couldn't in good conscience refuse them. *Besides, what would I say? No, you can't come. I want to be alone with this woman?* That would certainly be interpreted in a way that wouldn't be good for either his reputation or Laurel's.

"Laurel, a couple men have asked for a ride. We

won't be able to talk much; I hope that's okay with you."

"Of course." She grinned at him. "I'm not sure I could stand being alone with you in a truck for hours and hours anyway. This will be easier."

Shifting away from the strangers, Laurel ended up against him, the contours of her leg warm against his. She looked up at him, her eyes wide, her churning emotions evident in their depths.

He grinned. "Easier?"

She laughed at that. "Maybe I should go sit over by the other door."

"No, I like you right here." He wanted to put his arm around her, keep her there next to him.

How long do you think that would last?

The question surprised him, but not nearly so much as the response that rang through him.

What he wanted from Laurel wasn't today, or tomorrow—nothing so rational or reasonable as that. What he wanted was crazy, insane, totally impossible... and totally undeniable.

He wanted forever.

19

RIDING PINNED AGAINST DARREN THIS WAY, THIGH TO THIGH, was the most uncomfortable position Laurel could remember being in.

Not just because her movements were restricted, though that was irritating. No, the worst part was that she had to constantly resist the urge to snuggle against him. Honestly!

His arm brushed hers when he turned the wheel. *The hair on his arm would be dark in the winter, but here it's just a deep gold.* She wanted to touch that tan skin, smooth corded muscle...

Oh, help! She swallowed hard and looked out the window.

One of the other men in the cab asked Darren something in Swahili. He answered, and a long conversation developed. She could only catch one word in ten. The truck pitched and bucked, throwing her repeatedly against the African man next to her or Darren. The African man let his eyes slide over her in a way that made her skin crawl. She braced her feet and pushed her back into the seat, trying to stay still. It was no use. Finally she simply relaxed against Darren. She glanced up, but he didn't react. Or did he? The corners of his eyes were smiling, as if something had made him happy.

It felt so good to be with him, touching him. *And it's not like I planned this or can even help it.* She leaned her head back and shut her eyes. *Lord, help me. Was I foolish*

to come with Darren, to let myself be around him like this?
She sighed. Probably. But foolish or not, she'd wanted to
come. More than she'd wanted anything in a long time.

If nothing else, Darren was giving her a far better
understanding of Lilith, of the powerful attraction with
men that she was always talking about. Laurel had felt it
before, of course...but never like this.

Silently she prayed for Lilith, for the people on the
Wilson, for the wild land on Ndovu. Her thoughts, her
prayers were only the top level of what was happening
inside her. The deeply disturbing and comforting feel of
the warmth of Darren's body next to hers was the theme
of her inner symphony.

Through half-closed eyes, she watched the play of
muscles in his forearms as he fought the heavy vehicle
through a road that looked impossibly narrow and broken. He was very good at it. Once he looked over at her
with such a knowing smile that her mouth went dry.

The thin man near the door looked outside and said
something sharply. The conversation got quite urgent
with all of the men glancing to the northeast. Laurel followed their gaze and did a double take. It was the odd-
est cloud she had ever seen. Still quite far away, the nor-
mal thunderhead was perched on what seemed to be a
roiling brown-gray wall.

"It is rain," the man said in heavily accented English.

"Is it raining on the Wilson and Ndovu?" She
ducked down to stare out at the cloud with the rest of
them. "That really is rain, not just a dust storm?"

"Don't know. Maybe." Darren muscled the truck
around a bend.

"We need the rain so badly—the people on the

Wilson, Jede, the animals, everyone. It has to rain. It just has to."

"Now you sound like a true African." A grin creased Darren's lean, tanned cheeks.

The man next to her said something emphatic in Swahili, gesturing excitedly at the road. Laurel shrunk back to get away from his elbows. Darren laughed. "Hold on, Laurel. We've got some real driving to do." He accelerated to what seemed an insane speed.

"You're crazy! We'll break an axle."

"Maybe, but this truck is pretty tough, and we don't have a load on."

She was bouncing around like a piece of popcorn in a hot pan. Darren was focused on the road with a manic grin on his face. *He loves this!* She wedged a foot against the dash and pushed her back hard into the seat trying to stay put. "Why are you doing this?"

"If the water comes down, we shall be stopped," the man in the middle answered.

"Stopped?"

"There is a river which is now dry, but the rains will fill her." He gestured with a thin, black arm at the cloud.

She gasped, vacillating between exhilaration at the wild ride and terror, as the truck tipped violently to one side. The riverbed came into sight, still dry and sandy. Darren whooped aloud. "We beat it!"

The other men cheered. Laurel only managed a croak, and then clutched at the seat as the truck dove down the side. It plowed, growling, through the sand. As they crested the far side, there was a loud bang, and it listed to one side.

"What happened?" Her voice shook.

"We just lost a tire." He grinned. "At least we got across."

Laurel wanted to kick him. He'd terrified her and driven so wildly he'd blown a tire, and now he was grinning? The African men were already climbing out, unperturbed.

With the noise of the engine silenced, Laurel was aware of the baking emptiness around them. Darren opened his door and jumped down, his movements quick and purposeful. By the time she stepped down into the thorny sand, he was already pulling a huge jack out of the truck bed.

"That jack isn't going to do much but sink into the sand. I'll find you a flat rock."

"Just a sec, there might be something here." He started to get out the spare tire.

"And maybe not?"

He grunted, still working at the tire.

"I'll go look. It will give me something to do." She headed for the riverbed.

"Be careful." His head was up, looking at her, eyes worried.

I've been walking in the bush every day for months. What's he worried about? She shook her head. He hadn't seemed like the overprotective type. The cloud was closer now, the air still and oppressive. Laurel crossed to the far side of the riverbed to a rocky outcrop in the sand. A rushing noise like distant wind made her look up, but she saw nothing to alarm her. She bent to pick up a rock.

"Hatari!" One of the African men was screaming and beckoning at her from the far bank.

She picked up the rock and started back. The rushing noise got louder. Glittering tendrils of water, like the little trickles that start down a ditch after the rain, darkened the sand, shallow and pretty. *It did rain!* The water would feel so good on her hot feet.

"Run! Laurel, get out of there!" Darren was bellowing.

Laurel looked up in time to see him leaping down the far bank. What was his problem? The first trickles of cool water touched her feet, swirling through her canvas runners. Darren charged toward her sending up sheets of water as he dashed across the fingers of wonderful wetness.

Suddenly the water wasn't so gentle. Calf deep, it swirled and tugged at her ankles. Now she did run, lifting her feet high as she dashed, splashing toward Darren. In seconds the water was knee deep. A chunk of driftwood hit her, and she stumbled, tangling her legs in the branches. She ended up sitting in the water and kicking frantically to get her legs free. *Thud!* Something hit her shoulder, becoming visible as it dragged past her, a hunk of tree. She kicked hard, but her feet were stuck. The whippy ends of thorn branches stung her cheek. Her head went under.

Gritting her teeth, Laurel kicked with all her might. Her right foot was free; she shoved at the mass on her left, and it came free, too. For a split second she thrashed blindly. *No! Don't fight it. You've played in white water. Feet out in front. Paddle with your hands.* She managed to do that, and her head came up. *Thank you, Lord!*

She gulped for air and tried to get her bearings. Now she'd have to work her way gradually to the edge. Only this water was filthy. A vine wrapped around one arm. Her head went down again while she shook it off. Up again, taking gulps of air, something clipped her over the ear.

Darren was suddenly beside her, taking great leaps through thigh-deep water. She grabbed his outstretched hand. He dug in his feet and leaned back. The river tugged wildly at her, and their hands began to slip.

"Move with the water!" She shouted the words just before she got a face full of muddy water.

He listened and took huge strides alongside. His arm came powerfully around her waist, lifting her. With him there, she managed to get her feet on the bottom. His strength was astounding as he pulled her across the current to the shore. Once there, he simply picked her up and climbed the bank. Cradled as she was in his arms, held tight against his chest, she felt a sense of safety, of security unlike she'd ever known before.

At the top of the bank, Darren stopped. His face was very close to hers. "Are you all right?" Through their wet clothing she could feel the warmth of him.

"Yes." Her voice was less steady than she would have liked.

Laurel moved to try to get back onto her own feet, but Darren's arms tightened, and his mouth came down on hers. It was not a gentle kiss, but full of anger and passion.

Abruptly he broke off and set her on her feet, keeping an iron-hard arm behind her. "Don't you ever do that again!" His arm tightened. "Just what did you think you were doing, standing in the middle of the riverbed smiling at the water? Next time I tell you to move, you move!"

Laurel twisted away from him. "Excuse me. I would have been just fine!" Her voice was shaking with emotion. Weaving slightly on rubbery legs but with her chin lifted, she faced him.

He crossed his arms and glared at her. His chest was heaving, and his hair was slicked across his forehead, dripping in his eyes. "Just fine? I saw you go under twice."

"I had my head up. I was moving with the current. *You* didn't know to do that." She glared at him.

"There was half a tree aimed straight at your head when I dragged you out of there. You would have—" He turned his head away.

Would I? Did he just save my life? Her knees felt as if the bones had suddenly turned to river water. She reached to touch his arm and froze. Out of the wet, curling hair on the back of his head and down his tanned neck, a wide slick of blood soaked his shirt.

"Darren, you're hurt!"

He reached up and touched the back of his head, looked at the blood on his hand, and shrugged. "Something hit me when I grabbed your hand out there. You were right to tell me to move with the current." He looked at her. "Hey! Don't go sheet white on me like that. I'm okay."

She staggered, and his arm came around her waist. A yell in the distance brought Darren's head up. She could feel him tense, then he answered with a bellow that coursed through her. When she flinched, he smiled down at her. "Sorry. Didn't mean to blast your ears. That was the guys from the truck. They should be here in a minute."

"Darren, let me look at your head."

"Don't worry. I'm fine." He yelled again, letting the two men know where they were.

She pulled away from his arm. "Stop with the macho 'I'm fine' thing. There's blood all down your neck. Let me see."

He gave her a grin. "Yes, nurse, by all means, ma'am." Then he got on one knee and bowed his head. "At your service."

Laurel hissed between her teeth, partly out of irritation and partly at the gut-twisting sight of Darren's blood. She touched his head, lifting his hair. He was cut because of her.

"Ouch! Am I going to die?"

She let out her breath in a half laugh. "I doubt it, but you've got a half-inch gash in the middle of a big lump. You need stitches."

"Nope, I'd rather have a scar to remember you by."

Before she had a chance to respond, he had already turned to meet the first African man.

"God has kept you safe!"

"He has." The confidence in Darren's voice stirred Laurel deeply. She might doubt his reasoning at times, but she could never doubt the sincerity of this man's faith in God.

The other man arrived seconds later. "Eeeeh, sorry! Sorry!" He took in their bedraggled state, then said something and pointed at the sky again.

Darren's arm came around her, and he started for the truck, almost running. A blast of hot wind full of grit hit them. The sun was suddenly blotted out, and the air turned almost black. Laurel squeezed her eyes shut as stinging dirt hit her face.

"It's the gust front of the storm!"

It was hard to hear Darren over the roar of the wind, so she just nodded and leaned into his strength. It was either that or fall flat on her face. In the cab of the truck, the pressure of the wind and stinging dirt suddenly stopped. Out the windshield she could see great swirls of dirt tearing by the thrashing thorn trees.

"I'm going to finish changing that tire. We've got to get out of here before the road gets too soft to travel."

"Can I help?"

Darren shook his head. "You've had quite a shaking. Relax for a couple of minutes."

And you haven't? She watched him go and sank back against the seat. Through the gusts of dirt she could see the filthy, swirling water of the river boiling past. The flying dirt made a noise like hail on the upwind side of the cab, and thin eddies of dust smoked in around the door frame. *God, I don't know what You're doing with my life, but thanks for keeping me alive, and thanks for Darren.*

The truck was rocking under the impact of the wind. How could the men get anything done in this? Laurel looked at the rearview mirror but could only see a huddle of backs. A few huge raindrops smacked against the windshield, leaving long streaks of mud that dried in seconds. The door burst open with a gust of wind and grit, and the men piled into the cab. Darren put a hand on her shoulder. "You okay?"

She nodded, wanting to lean against his solidly comforting presence.

"We're going to have to really move to get out while the roads are still passable."

They almost made it. Rain hit them just before they

reached pavement. The last ten miles of dirt road took more than an hour as Darren slowed to a crawl, wrestling the big diesel through slick, red clay mud. Over and over it seemed they were about to be irretrievably stuck, but every time he managed to fight through.

Shaken and filthy, Laurel watched the volume of traffic increase as they neared Nairobi. Then they were in the cluttered side roads. The African men left them with enthusiastic handshakes and good wishes.

Darren turned to her. "We have a choice to make. We've got a couple of hours of daylight, long enough to fly to the coast. But if you're too tired, I could find a place for you to stay in Nairobi, maybe at a mission guest house." In spite of the dirt and blood on his skin, he looked wide awake and ready for anything.

She'd done enough of the fainting violet stuff already. "If you're ready to fly to the coast today, I'm up for it."

"Are you sure?"

She lifted her chin. "Look, we have rooms booked there. Here we'd have to pay more money or else intrude on someone, right? So it would be stupid not to go. What's another two hours?"

He laughed. "You're an amazing woman, Laurel. Okay then, we fly."

At Saba, a small town near Ndovu, the torrential downpour had cut vision to almost zero. There was no time for the deluge to soak into the parched ground. Water sluiced across the hard surface, sweeping debris with it. Sticks, dirt, sand, animal and human waste tumbled in the rivulets over the bank and into the river.

That evening in the quiet after the storm, Ambaro stepped gracefully through the mud. With the other women, she was going to draw water for cooking, washing, and drinking. All were happy. Her sister had born a boy child, and the rains had come. What could go wrong now?

The answer came with a vengeance.

The next day on the trip back to Ndovu, Ambaro's daughter began to complain of not feeling well. By the time they arrived, it was clear she was seriously ill.

As she watched her child suffering, Ambaro could only mutter fervent prayers for mercy…but Allah didn't seem to be listening.

20

LAUREL OPENED HER EYES, AND FOR A SECOND SHE WASN'T SURE where she was. She stared at the unfamiliar ceiling. A few resting moths punctuated its smooth surface, their patterned backs like tiny triangular stickers on a large, white page.

I'm at the coast with Darren. A flash of fear and excitement made her stomach quiver. Stripes of bright sunlight came through the shuttered windows. She had the delicious feeling that comes after a long, deep sleep. She stretched between the smooth sheets. *Ow!* More than one spot ached from that episode in the river. Other than that, she felt fantastic. It took her only minutes to pull on a swimsuit and skirt. Forget breakfast, she wanted to see the beach. *And find Darren.*

They still hadn't really talked. It had been too noisy in the plane, and she'd been exhausted. Still, the bond between them had strengthened, as though there were a deep, basic understanding developing between them. A kind of oneness.

She took a deep breath and opened the door. In the night, she'd gotten a vague impression of white sand gleaming palely next to a moon-silvered sea. Now the colors were vivid primaries.

Laurel walked down a sandy path through rustling palms. She squinted as the sunlight off the blazing white beach hit her face. The sea spread out in front of her, a glowing blue-green under a royal blue sky. The air smelled of brine, seaweed, and a wild vastness. It was like a travel poster, only a thousand times more vivid and alive.

"Hi, sleepyhead; catch." She just managed to snag a Frisbee Darren sailed toward her. Automatically she sailed it back to him. With a fast backhand he passed it to one of the others and ran to her. Darkly bronzed, Darren was the perfect finishing touch to the poster. Well, almost. Frayed khaki shorts might not match the travel poster image, but they looked incredibly good on him. "So what do you think of it?" He gestured at the ocean.

"It looks like a travel poster, too good to be true."

He stepped back, made a frame of his hands, and let his eyes dwell on her for a second. "I'd say so."

She felt the heat of a blush in her cheeks.

"Hey, Darren!" One of the guys, blond and gawky, flipped the Frisbee in their direction. Darren took two strides and leapt for it. He looked back at her. "Come on and meet the others."

The day passed in a blur of sun, sand, and laughter. There were about fifteen in the group. In the afternoon they crammed into someone's Volvo and drove to Dianni Beach to rent windsurfing boards. Ndovu and the problems there seemed as far away as the moon. Yet every now and then, Laurel would remember and wonder if it rained on Ndovu, but then something else would snare her attention.

It was like an afternoon out of a dream. Images stood out—Darren's strong arm around her as he showed her how to pick the sail out of the water; the joy in his eyes when she finally got the knack; and the exhilaration of moving fast over the warm, blue waves. She stayed out of the area where the waves were breaking, but Darren didn't. He played, making his board leap and twist above the surf, but he watched for her and came back to her laughing.

Bright sunlight outlined his muscles with hard curving lines as he came toward her. "You're doing great!" He pivoted his board and brought it next to hers. Saltwater glittered on his lashes.

"Tomorrow I'll be out leaping the waves, catching the wind off their crests, and flying with you, right?" She wobbled as a gust of wind caught her sail.

"Right." He slid his board past her and whipped back on the other side, tacking sharply. Looking at her, he didn't see one of those basketball-like buoys. His board hit it sharply and swung into hers. The impact sent her completely off balance, so she took a running step onto his board, then they were both in the water.

He came up, his arm under her elbow, but Laurel twisted away and dunked him.

"Hey!" He dove and grabbed her ankle, pulling her under with him. In a wild tangle of limbs, he kissed her. She had a tingling impression of warm lips, strong muscles, and sea salt. Both came up, gasping for air. His intense eyes, gold streaked in the sun, made her insides shiver. She'd responded to him so simply, gladly in the sun warmed water. She ducked under the water and came up on the far side of the board. "Why did you kiss me?"

"I wanted to." He grinned at her and vaulted onto his board in one smooth motion. "We can talk more later when we've had time to think."

That evening they walked together on the beach.

Ghost crabs slid out of their way, pale shadows on the silver sand. Wind lifted Laurel's hair, and Darren took her hand. His warm, strong fingers intertwined with hers. She felt distant from herself, suspended in time, almost as if she stood at the edge of a cliff....

The thought brought to mind the time she'd gone cliff diving. It had felt like this...an intense mixture of fear and anticipation. *Is this Lilith's trap?* Her throat tightened and she stopped walking.

Darren turned toward her. "What is it, Laurel?"

"Who are you?"

He let out his breath in a half laugh. "I'll never figure you out. What do you mean?"

Her question sounded silly now. *Do we really belong together? Can I trust you?* That wasn't any better. She opened her mouth, but nothing came out.

The moonlight showed the planes of his face, but she couldn't see his eyes clearly. He stood still, looking at her. "No, I'll try to answer. What do you want, a kind of thumbnail biography, or...?"

"No." She hesitated. "It sounds kind of silly, but I meant who are you deep inside, right now. Maybe no one can answer that. I'm not sure I could."

He looked away from her, then the words came slowly. "I doubt if anyone really knows himself that well, but I do know what I want. The apostle Paul called himself a servant of God. That's what I want to be. Not that I'd have the gall to introduce myself that way—Darren Grant, servant of God. Believe me, I know I don't live up to it." He clenched his fists. "But I want to bring hope and light to people who have none. I've been in that dark place. The thing is, I'm still working out how to do what I think I've been called to do."

Laurel touched his arm. "That's what you were doing trucking the food in."

"I suppose, but I want some kind of plan. I know I'm just one guy, and Africa is a huge place, but I want to make a difference, long term." He gave that half laugh again. "The Bible says God has something for each of us to do. I think it's in Ephesians. He chose us from before the creation of the world and designed good work for each of us. I'm still trying to find what that good work is for me. But one thing I do know, flying small charter just isn't cutting it."

Laurel's heart quickened. "You really are looking for something else?"

"There's got to be a way! I've thought about traditional missions, but I'd have to go back to the States and try to raise support, jump through all the hoops they set for people who've never lived here, orientation and so on." He turned and looked out to sea. "Maybe that's what it will come to."

Maybe God is getting him ready to work at this foundation He's making happen. "Darren, listen." Her throat was tight. "Some stuff has happened at Ndovu. It looks like there's a chance to set up a foundation, and Lilith wants to donate the money for it."

"She's that wealthy?"

"Yes. She's doing it to please me, but I think maybe it's God's idea. See, Jede and I prayed..." She shook her head.

"You and Lilith are working some things out in your relationship then?" His eyes crinkled on the corners, and he took her hands. "I'm glad for you."

"Lilith said she'd pray and ask God to show her He's real. I think she will."

"That's great." His hands gave hers a little squeeze. "And…?"

"I wouldn't take money from her for years, not since high school. But this… Maybe it's the chance to accomplish what Jede and I've prayed about. Lilith wants me to set it up, but I don't know enough. I can't do it alone."

"What about Joan Doyle? She isn't exactly the spectator type. She knows Kenya well enough. Why would you need someone else?"

"Joan is kind of an unwilling participant. She wants Lilith's money to preserve Kopje Troop's habitat, and so on, but this is for people, too, both the Meru and the Somali. It could include schools, a clinic, whatever the people need, but especially a way to teach how God meant for people to care for His created world. I was hoping that you…"

Darren was suddenly very still. His head was turned so that his eyes were in deep shadow. "So the goal of this thing is caring for nature, for animals, right?"

Laurel stepped back. "The goal is to see what the Bible says about that. It would be a foundation to take care of the wild land at Ndovu, but not just the wild land. Like I said, it's for the people, too. I want it to be good for both and work with the local church."

He stood rock solid. "But which comes first?"

"Neither one without the other. God put us in charge of His creation. It has to come together. God's people and His land, healthy together, in tune with Him." She kicked a lump of sand. "Don't be so stubborn. It's not either-or."

"When so many people are suffering, isn't it?" Darren crossed his arms, hands fisted. He started to say something else, stopped himself, then shook his head. "Thank you for thinking of me. That was a compliment, but I think I'd better go in."

"Don't walk away from me! You said you wanted to hear what I had to say. Are you going to listen or not?"

Darren grunted as if she'd punched him. He turned back, his hands still fisted. "I don't want to argue with you, Laurel."

"Argue already! I'm ready if that's what it takes to get you to listen to me. Say what you're thinking! Anything is better than this crazy dance we're doing."

She could see his chest heave as he took a deep breath. "Blast it, woman! You are dangerous. Don't you see? The things you're talking about, the things you care about...I can't see my way clear to spend my time on that." His gaze bore into her, and he took a step toward her. "But I can't just walk away either."

She swallowed the lump that had suddenly lodged in her throat. "You can't?" The words were hushed, choked.

His brows arched, and humor twinkled in his gaze...until it was replaced by something else. Something far more intense. "No, Laurel, I can't. I want you. More than I've ever wanted any woman in my life."

Laurel gasped and shook her head blindly. "Darren—"

He caught her, pulled her close, and kissed her. A rough, urgent kiss. Her knees nearly gave way, and, almost in spite of herself, she responded.

A low growl sounded in his throat, and he pushed

her away. They stood, facing each other, laboring for each breath.

His voice was low and harsh. "I tried to stay away from you, but then I started to hope that it could work. Maybe I've been grasping at straws...." He gave a shake of his head. "Read Romans, chapter 1. Look what happened to the people who put creation first, before the Creator."

Laurel was shaking from head to foot. "I have read it, Darren. I know what it says. And what it doesn't say. And I know what Genesis 1 and 2 tell us—that caring for creation was the first job God gave humanity. People *and* the land, the animals...*all* of God's creation belongs together."

There was no way she wanted Darren to see her cry. Not now. She turned to run, but he caught her arm. With all her might, she twisted away. "Let me go, Darren. This was a mistake. I never should have come. I'm going back to Ndovu where I have something useful to do."

"And just how are you going to do that?" He blocked her path.

"Bus, train, matatu, plane. I don't care." She dodged past him and ran for the lodge, the sand sliding under her feet as tears blurred the lights ahead of her. In her room she started pitching things into her backpack, but she couldn't see through the tears. She dropped what was in her hand, fell onto the bed, and sobbed.

His growl echoed in her head. *"I want you more than I've wanted any woman in my life...want you more...want you more..."*

She slugged the pillow and clenched her teeth against the ugly sound in her throat. There was no denying it, she wanted him, too. *So what! Wanting doesn't mean giving in. No matter what Lilith says. Darren will live his life; I'll live mine. I'm getting out of here!*

Lilith was right. Caring for a man just set you up for pain. Laurel was a fool to think that she and Darren could share a dream.

Taking a long, ragged breath, Laurel stood up and finished packing. She splashed cold water on her face and marched out carrying her pack. At the door to the main lodge she hesitated. Getting back to Ndovu wasn't going to be a picnic. Kenya wasn't exactly safe for a white woman traveling alone, and she was still not fluent in Swahili. Laurel swallowed hard and lifted her chin. There were taxis and also buses. She'd seen them. Surely the woman at the desk could tell her how to catch the bus to Nairobi. She shook her head. That wouldn't help. She had to get all the way to Ndovu. Joan had found another pilot to bring Lilith out. She'd find one, too.

No one was at the front desk. A Kenyan man walked by, one of the hotel employees. "Excuse me."

He turned to look at her.

"I need to find a charter plane. Could you tell me how I can do that?"

He shrugged. "Perhaps at Dianni there would be such a thing. It is not good that you go at night. In the morning it will be better."

In the morning it will be better. Not likely! Laurel set her teeth. She'd seen the Dianni Beach Hotel while they were walking the beach. It was only a couple of miles away. *I'll walk. My pack isn't that heavy.* As she trudged through the sand, it seemed to get progressively heavier. Her mood swung between anger and tears. The sand dragged at her feet. Maybe she should go back. Bolting like this was probably foolish. *At least I could wait until tomorrow. Tomorrow there would be time for arrangements and explanations.* She slowed. Darren's words echoed in her head. *"You're a dangerous woman."*

"As if I'm some sort of toxic chemical," she muttered and marched on. She was *not* going back! The man at the desk in Dianni insisted that there was no way to find a plane in the middle of the night. Laurel booked a room.

"If you can find a way to charter me a small plane tomorrow morning, I'll pay you well for the service."

The man looked at her sharply, then nodded. "Tomorrow, if it is possible, it will be done."

Laurel finally fell into a heavy sleep near dawn. The phone by her bed rang, jerking her into wakefulness. "Yes?"

"Mademoiselle, as you requested, the pilot awaits you. He is here."

"Good, I'll be right down."

Laurel rubbed her face and then hurried to take a quick shower. As the water sluiced over her body, she shut her eyes. At the thought of Darren her whole chest ached. Her diaphragm heaved in something close to a sob, but she clenched her teeth. "No!" The word was muffled by water in her face. "I'm finished with him." Her chest heaved again and she gulped. "I won't cry. I won't!" Roughly, she toweled herself dry, pulled on clothes, shoved a hand through her wet hair, slung her pack over her shoulder, and hurried to the front desk.

The man at the desk looked up and smiled. "Good morning. The pilot is just there."

Relieved, Laurel turned and then froze.

Darren Grant met her angry gaze with a slow, lazy smile. "Well, well. Fancy meeting you here."

21

THROUGHOUT THE NIGHT, DARREN HAD PACED THE BEACH, THE ache in his chest growing. *I wanted to listen to her.* But Laurel had asked him to help her at Ndovu, working with Joan Doyle! Deciding to listen to her defend something that he felt was wrong was hard enough. But to be suddenly asked to be part of her wild scheme—it had been like being punched in the jaw.

If only she were right. *Can I let myself drown in the beauty of nature and still follow God with my whole heart?* He turned to face the ocean and let the breeze stroke his hot forehead. Was it actually possible? *I am going to read those passages again. I couldn't have gotten this all wrong, surely.* He frowned. Maybe for Laurel it was all right, but nature had been an idol for him. Could it ever be anything else?

Darren didn't go back to the lodge until almost dawn. The manager of the Dianni Hotel approached him. "We have a guest who has an urgent need to charter a plane. Can you do it?"

I don't want to be here without Laurel. "Why not? I'll come and see what he wants."

At the Dianni, he rocked backward, catching himself with a hand on the wall. *It's Laurel!* He realized his mouth was open and shut it abruptly. She had frozen midstride and stared at him with wide, hurt eyes. Her hands fisted.

He'd said the first thing that came to his suddenly dulled mind: "Well, well, fancy meeting you here."

Her response had been as heated as his had been mocking. "How *dare* you follow me?"

"Follow you? Please." The muscles in his jaw bunched. Seeing her again made the ache in his chest worse. *God, why did You bring her into my life at all? Now we're going to be in a plane together again.* His voice came out very flat. "I had no idea you were at Dianni."

Laurel spun on the East Indian manager. "How did you find this man? Did he come to you?"

The manager shook his head. "No, ma'am, no! It is I who found him. You wanted a charter pilot. I looked at the airport and saw his plane. I then traveled in the night to find this man who can fly you. Shall I send him away? I do not think there is another. Not to be found on this day."

Laurel turned back to face him, eyes narrowed. "You didn't plan this?"

In spite of himself, Darren wanted to laugh. It was so ironic. "Not by a long shot. I didn't even know you'd left the lodge." *I won't tell her I worried about how she'd get safely to Ndovu on her own or that I was planning on offering her a ride with me on this charter.* Not that he had thought the offer would be well received. Judging from her present reaction, he'd been right.

The manager cleared his throat loudly. "Do you wish me to send this man away? If so, please to remember my most heroic effort in finding him."

Laurel turned her head and looked at the man, then back at Darren. She was very pale, and there were huge circles under her eyes. Darren had a sudden impulse to comfort her. Over and over in the night he'd agonized over his words. *She held out her dream to me, and I swat-*

ted it like a fly. Even if she was wrong, he shouldn't have done that. He made a tentative movement toward her with one hand, as if to reach out.

Laurel stepped back quickly. "You *said* you wanted to keep away from me. Flying me to Ndovu doesn't exactly fit the bill."

"Look, I was upset at the time." He ran a hand over his face. "I'd be glad to fly you back to Ndovu."

"So I can get on with my misguided life?" Her voice rose like she might cry. "I have to get back there."

He held out a hand. "Listen, I want to—"

"No! Don't talk to me. Just fly the plane and leave me alone!"

The manager had been listening closely, now he nodded emphatically. "Good, good." He ushered Laurel toward the desk. Her movements were short and jerky as she paid the bill. When Laurel left to get her pack, the manager grinned at him. "She has much spirit, that one."

"Yes, she does." *God help me with this. Even if we can't see eye to eye, I don't want her hurt.*

"It is better to get a quieter one for a wife, but the others, they are interesting diversions, no?"

Darren turned on him, fists clenched.

The man went pale and backed away rapidly.

I'll be up for assault if I don't relax. He took a deep breath, then Laurel walked in, her whole posture tense and unhappy. *I bet she didn't sleep any more than I did.* He reached to take her pack. She turned away from him, insisting on carrying it herself.

True to her word, Laurel said nothing at all, didn't even look at him as the hotel van took them to the little airport. In the air, it didn't change, she wouldn't respond nor would she fly the plane when he offered. Pale and still, she stared out the window. He wanted to argue, to explain. *But I agreed to leave her alone.*

The ache in his chest threatened to choke him, and he began to be angry again. *How can she be so stiff-necked? Freezing me out like this?* By the time they were circling Ndovu, he wanted to shake her. Apologizing was the last thing he felt like doing. *But this might be my last chance to talk to her. I've got to try.* He tightened his hands on the yoke and kept the little plane circling.

"Look, I've been quiet for hours, but I have one thing I have to say. I'm sorry I was so harsh last night." He found he was sweating. He blundered on, trying to keep his voice less angry. "I will read those Bible passages, and then maybe we can talk."

"I don't think so. Lilith made a big mistake, and I'm not going to repeat it. She said the chemistry between my father and her was mind-boggling. It blinded her to their huge differences. Being around you is too hard." Her voice was shaking. She'd turned her head away, so he could only see the curve of her cheek.

"What do I have to do? Beg on my knees? It's a little cramped up here for that."

Laurel kept her face turned away. "Please land the plane and let me go. Find another job where we won't see each other." He could see her trembling. "God does have something good for you. I know it. But please, leave me alone."

Darren gritted his teeth and pulled the plane around into a tight approach. Usually he flew over an unpaved runway slowly, looking for evidence that the surface was good, especially after there had been rain in the area.

This time he didn't bother. As soon as the wheels touched, he knew it was a mistake. The drag and skid of heavy mud under the wheels twisted the plane to one side. By habit, he'd kept the nose wheel off the ground as he did in every soft field landing. Now he muttered under his breath, cut the engine, and fought with all his strength to keep the plane straight and the nose up as they jerked and skidded down the runway.

He almost managed it. The nose wheel had touched; the propeller had almost stopped rotating. Then the nose wheel stuck on something and buckled. The jerk threw them forward in their seats. The plane made a violent half circle and was still. The only sound was the ticking of cooling metal.

He looked at Laurel. "Are you okay?"

She was staring at him with huge eyes. "I'm fine, but your plane! What will you do?"

Most women would freak out, and she's worried about me. He shut his eyes. *If only…*

"Darren, are you okay?"

He gave a half laugh. "Yeah, I'm just fine. You're furious with me; I've got a busted airplane; and I have no idea what to do with my life, but physically, I'm great." He undid his seat belt. "Look, this isn't your problem. I'll take you up to Ndovu, and then find some people to help me push this off the runway."

"I can walk up by myself. In fact, I'd rather do that." Laurel got out of the plane. He followed and pulled her pack out of the cargo area. For an awkward moment they stood facing each other. He started to speak, but she motioned him to silence. "No, don't say anything. I'm sorry it had to turn out this way." *She's trying not to cry.*

Abruptly she turned away and walked off, slipping a bit in the heavy mud.

He went after her. "At least let me carry your pack."

She waved him off without looking at him. She *was* crying.

"Laurel."

"Please, leave me alone. I can't stand this!" Turning, she set off up the road, almost running in spite of the heavy mud and her pack.

His hands clenching and unclenching, Darren watched Laurel stumble and run away from him. *Do I have any chance with her at all now? Why couldn't I have listened and kept my mouth shut?* But should he, if she was so offtrack in her priorities?

He sighed and looked at his plane. At least this he could do something about. The front wheel strut had buckled, and the fuselage was dented. He ran a finger down the edge of the prop. Undamaged. At least it hadn't hit the ground, so he shouldn't need a new driveshaft.

He climbed into the cockpit and tried radioing Nairobi. Usually he had to be a couple of thousand feet up to make contact. Nothing. He stepped back out, crossed his arms, and stared at the damaged craft. *I should walk up to Joan's camp and ask to use her satellite phone.*

Darren's jaw clenched. Laurel would be there. *She'll turn away from me again.* Tomorrow was soon enough. She'd be out with her animals for sure then. *Animals...* His stomach hurt. Unbidden, images of the awakening after the rains came into his head: baby impalas, like golden Bambies, in emerald grass; weaverbirds taking baths in a puddle; long skeins of pelicans, geese, and ducks in the sky as the European birds came south; fox kits blinking in the sun with soft, startled baby eyes. *It's so seductive. Could God ever really give it back to me?*

Laurel seemed so sure she was right. He ran his hand through his hair. Nature had been an idol for him and a major waste of time. It was obviously Joan Doyle's god, but what about Laurel? *I've assumed that she's making the same mistake, but what if she isn't? Could I be wrong?*

He muttered the old cliché about assumptions. Blindly he sat on his heels and tried to think. Instead, wild emotions clouded his brain. No matter what was true about nature, Laurel had made it very clear she didn't want him in her life. He'd made a mess of everything. His throat closed. It felt as if someone was tightening a steel band around his chest. He stood up and strode down the path.

He would read those passages of Scripture she'd mentioned. *I owe her that much. Then I'll just get on with my life.* His mouth twisted bitterly. Get on with his life? Without Laurel? What life? Flying small charter with a broken plane? His scruples about keeping God first had lost him Laurel, and maybe he'd been wrong the whole time. Now he had nothing, not even a way to make a living.

Laurel was very glad for the walk up the hill. It gave her a little time to compose herself. Taking deep breaths, she forced herself to stop crying. *God, I need Your help. Please!* Over and over she repeated the word *please* as she walked up the hill. As the buildings came into sight, she hesitated. *Okay, I'm back in this world.* Deliberately she turned her mind to the animals in the troop. How was Gremlin doing? Had the rains helped yet? Holding that thought, she focused on it with all her might. Anything was better than thinking about Darren right now.

At the compound she went straight to her banda. To her relief, the water jug was full. She dumped her pack on the bed, poured some water into the basin, and splashed cool water onto her burning eyes.

The banda door opened behind her. Hearing the sound, Laurel turned.

"Joan, what are you doing here in the middle of the day?"

"Checking our water supply. You're back early."

"Yes." Laurel had no intention of explaining anything to her.

Joan didn't seem to notice. She looked very keyed up. "When you came, you had your full spectrum of inoculations including cholera?"

What an odd thing to ask. "Yes, of course."

"Good. Meet me in the dining banda in half an hour. There are some things we need to go over." She turned on her heel.

"Wait! How are the baboons? Is Gremlin still okay?"

Joan stopped, and her voice warmed slightly. "They're doing better. It rained two days ago, and already there are some green shoots. At least some good has come from losing the support of UCLA. It's lovely not to have to go back and teach. Using the Somali ponies to get through the mud is going to work. Hurry up and get changed. We have work to do."

Suddenly, Laurel felt very tired. *How can I do any*

good here without help? Without Darren. *I can't do this.* Saying a silent prayer for help, she changed and walked slowly toward the dining banda.

Joan looked up as she entered. "What's with you? You look like your best friend just died." Her eyebrows went up. "Aaaah, you're back early. You and the flyboy had a fight? Young love gone sour, is it?"

Laurel clenched her teeth. "You said you wanted to go over some things with me?"

"And your love life isn't one of them?" Joan laughed, then sobered quickly. "If your idea is going to work for our mutual benefit, we do need to get along. Lilith made it very clear that, other than the actual observation of the Kopje troop, the direction of this foundation she intends to set up is to be in your hands."

Joan paused, watching her warily. She was waiting for some response. Laurel felt like a player in a game with very high stakes, a game whose rules she didn't know. For a second she debated telling Joan she'd changed her mind, that she'd be leaving Kenya. *I don't even want to try, or be here. It's too hard!* But what would she tell Jede? She swallowed, silently prayed for courage, and took the plunge.

"Lilith told me the same thing. That I'd be in charge of the other functions of the foundation." She held Joan's eyes.

"And just what did you plan for those? Or haven't you gotten that far?" *Why couldn't Darren just have agreed to help me?* Laurel knew she was well out of her depth. Still, she felt obliged to try. "I have no solid plans, but I do have some parameters. First of all, everything would be based on biblical principles."

"Everything? What is *everything* exactly?"

"Ah, there would definitely be a school, good teachers, excellent curriculum that would fit in with the Kenya school system, but strongly emphasize care of the land." Laurel was thinking on her feet. "Not just wild land, but cropland too. We'd fund research on how to maintain and utilize arid land, maybe investigate game ranching, work with people who've already done research. We'd have to find a way for local people to make a living without destroying the area. I was thinking eco-tourism might take up the slack and provide resources to support the population without stripping the land."

"This school, would it be simply a research center, perhaps a branch of the university of Nairobi?"

"Not just a research center. It needs to be a good school for local kids as well." *If this is going to be worth doing at all, God has to be first.* If only she had the right words. She tried again. "Mostly, we'd need to work with the local church. It would be great to tie in with Bible colleges, offer courses that would be accredited with them as well."

Joan coughed, as if choking on that idea. "And just how would you deal with the Somali if you drag local churches in? You've been here long enough to know their reaction to Christianity."

"I don't know. Not yet. But God does, and He'll help us figure it out. Maybe we could get them to teach the old nomadic patterns, how they kept the land healthy and how they didn't. I understand that Muslims see Christians, as well as Jews and themselves, as 'people of the Book.' That could be a basis for cooperation."

"You have no idea the depth of animosity you're dealing with here!" Joan took a deep breath. "Why don't you focus on just the Somali people first? Forget the biblical stuff and focus on land management and an excellent school for the Somali children. That I could live with."

Laurel shook her head and started to speak, but Joan cut her off. "We're not going to settle this in a day or even a month. Meanwhile, we've got work to do. Let's think about it and talk later. Ibrahim will take you out to the troop. I've told him to bring you a horse. You can join Farah. I have to take care of something here first." She marched out of the room, her steps jerky.

Laurel sagged into her chair and bowed her head. "God, please help me. She's going to fight every inch of the way." Her voice was only a tiny whisper. Slowly, she stood and followed Joan through the door. Ibrahim was walking toward her leading two small, scrawny horses. Not surprisingly, his manner was cold and formal. Still, his hostility made Laurel feel even more discouraged.

"Jambo, Ibrahim." Jede had told her how important greetings were in Swahili. Laurel searched for the words. *"Habari yako?"*

Ibrahim answered formally and in English. "We are well, except that the daughter of Ambaro is very ill."

"Oh no! Khadiija is sick?"

Ibrahim shrugged. "It is the will of Allah. Children die."

"No!" The protest was almost involuntary. "Maybe I can help." She started toward Ambaro's house.

"No, memsabu. Joan is already there. She has asked for you to go to the baboons." He led a horse forward and held it, waiting for her to mount.

Joan is with them. She probably knows more than I do.
Laurel swallowed and focused on the horse. It was a
dusty dun color. "But it's so skinny."

"She is a good mare. Now that the rains have come,
she will become fat and shining. She is strong. See, I will
show you." Still holding the reins of the other horse,
Ibrahim vaulted onto the mare's back and sped away,
both animals going at a dead run, flinging gobs of mud
into the air. He swung wide and tore back, stopping only
feet from her. The mare threw her head up, gaping
against the pull of the harsh bit in her mouth. Ibrahim
jumped down. "See, I have found a *wazungu* saddle for
you."

Wazungu? Oh yeah, "white people." The mare was
wearing an extremely dilapidated English saddle. Laurel
had only ridden in western saddles. She swallowed hard
and took the reins. *Here goes nothing.* The little mare
stood quietly enough while she mounted. The horses'
feet made plopping sounds in the mud. In spite of their
small size and prominent ribs, both animals seemed
bright and determined.

"Was it that you had a good journey with Bwana
Darren?"

"It was good to see the ocean. It is beautiful." Her
throat was suddenly tight. What if he came back and
tried to talk to her again. She shut her eyes. *I couldn't
stand it!* "If Darren comes looking for me, I do not wish
to speak to him."

Ibrahim frowned and said nothing more until he
pulled his horse up. "The baboons are just there." He
pointed. "They still fear horses, so you must walk now."

She gave the mare one last pat and set out. Now that she was almost there, she was eager to see Gremlin and the others. One of the baboons barked in alarm as she came into sight. The others looked up and then relaxed.

"See, they know you are their friend." Farah came forward to greet her. "Look, Gremlin is happy."

At least Farah sounded glad to see her. She was so relieved to find one friendly face that tears sprang to her eyes. Gremlin had stood on his hind legs to get a good look at her. He bounced like he was a kangaroo for a few steps and turned a clownish somersault. Cleo clouted him and scolded. "They're better already!"

"Yes. It is good."

Laurel slid easily into the familiar pattern of watching and recording. The land was singing. There was no other way to describe it. Green shoots were everywhere. The bushes were loud with birdcalls as the male songbirds marked out their nesting territory. Frogs called from the puddles, and insects were buzzing everywhere.

"The rains have brought gladness," Farah said when a wild game of tag erupted in the troop.

"It changed so fast." Even the sky was full of banners—huge, white cumulus clouds gleamed against the fresh washed blue. Laurel could not join the song. Her brain and body seemed set on playing back images of Darren, the sound of his voice, the smile in his eyes, the feel of his mouth on hers. The memories caught her unprotected, jabbing like sharp sticks up under her ribs. She tried to force herself to snap out of it. When that didn't work, she focused on talking to Farah, using the little Swahili she knew.

Farah laughed and participated gladly. Laurel tried

to remember all the ways Jede had told her to ask for news. "How are your brothers? How is your farm? How are all your affairs?" Farah answered that all was well. That was the traditional answer, but when they were finished he asked in English, "Have you heard that Khadiija is very sick? When she was in Saba, she became ill."

Laurel nodded. "Ibrahim told me."

"Perhaps she will not die. Joan has given her good medicine. Ambaro must give her water many, many times. Ambaro does so because Joan has threatened to send us all away unless it is done, but it is foolish. How can one change the will of Allah? If he wills, she will recover. If not…" He shrugged.

Laurel's mouth tightened. *Fatalism again.* "Does Joan know what's wrong?"

Farah frowned. "She said Karara. Joan is very angry and has made us put much *dawa* in the drinking water. She has driven everyone away from Khadiija except Ambaro."

"Karara? Oh no! You don't mean cholera?" Farah nodded and Laurel's stomach suddenly hurt. She'd read about how cholera killed hundreds on a wagon train going West in 1890. There were horrible descriptions of children with violent diarrhea and vomiting. They got dehydrated, just shriveled and died, and it was all from water contaminated by human excrement.

That's why Joan was worried about the water. "Farah, have you been inoculated against cholera? Have the others?"

"I do not know this word *inoculated.*"

"Given a needle to prevent cholera." She mimed giving herself an injection.

"Perhaps this is to be done. She has called some other pilot, one with—" he slowed and enunciated carefully—"a helicopter to bring dawa for this thing."

"A helicopter? Here?"

"It is said that perhaps soon it will come, but Joan did not know the time. She was also angry concerning this and has said all of our people must come when we hear this thing arrive. I have never seen such a thing. Is it very wonderful?"

Laurel smiled. "I suppose you could say so."

"Only Allah knows what will happen. It is foolish for a woman to think she can stop death."

"But didn't God give you a mind to decide things?"

Farah gave her a puzzled look, and suddenly Laurel wanted very much to do something right. Even if nothing else in Kenya turned out for her, maybe she could make a difference to one person, to Farah. She searched her mind for words that would explain. Darren said people here thought in allegories.

"If you see a river with a bridge. Do you cross the bridge or just walk into the river."

Farah gave her an intent look. "I go on that bridge."

"If someone saw the bridge but ignored it and fell into the river, should he blame that on God's will?"

"So this needle, it is a bridge across the sickness?"

"I think so." Suddenly the picture she'd seen as a child of the cross of Christ as a bridge to God came into her mind. *God is helping me. Please don't let me blow this.* "Farah, can I tell you about an even more important bridge?"

He nodded, looking puzzled.

She bent and, writing in the sand, drew two circles.

"Okay, this circle is God. This one is people. How can we come to God?"

"We do his law."

"Can you do it perfectly?"

Slowly, Farah shook his head. "Perhaps it is that the holy men, the saints, can come to Allah."

"No one can. Justice must be done; sin must be paid for. But God didn't just abandon us to pay for our own sins. He sent His own Son to earth as a man. Jesus Christ took the consequences of all the wrongs we've done. You've heard that He was killed, crucified, but it was worse than physical death. He actually took our punishment. We need to accept His gift of salvation."

Farah listened intently when she quoted John 3:16, but he seemed uneasy, shifting his feet and glancing nervously around. "I will think about this thing. Joan Doyle, has she walked on this bridge?"

"I don't think so."

He nodded sharply. "And Darren Grant?"

"Yes. He has crossed it." Laurel's throat tightened suddenly. *He would have probably done a better job explaining, too.* But Darren wasn't here, so she would just have to do her best. The land was green and sang with joy, but Laurel felt dry as dust, and very far from song. She'd had a chance to speak of God's love, but she felt so alone.

22

DARREN STRODE PAST THE PATH THAT TURNED TO JEDE AND Isaac's place. He wasn't ready to talk to anybody. Jaw clenched, he kept walking on and on. It would be so easy to say yes to flying for Spiro. At least he'd make a living that way. A verse echoed in his head, *"What does it benefit a man to gain the whole world and lose his soul?"*

So what was he supposed to do? Just quit trying? *You want me to lose Africa too?* Darren grunted as though he'd been punched and started to run. He barely noticed the people who stared at him as he loped past them. He needed to be alone. Speeding up, he turned back onto the deserted land of Ndovu Ranch. He fought the slick, clinging mud as if it were a personal enemy. Boys herding goats called to him in high voices. A small band of Thomson's gazelles darted away. Vervet monkeys chittered in warning.

Finally, chest heaving, he squatted on his heels on the edge of a lava cliff. An ibis flew over with its ringing cry, *"Manga! Manga!"* Still as the stone he perched on, Darren looked out across the land. Just being alone here calmed him. Slowly he took a deep breath. *God, I don't want to turn away from You.* The calming feeling of being surrounded by beauty and love intensified. Darren frowned. He'd known something of this comfort in nature when he'd had his back turned to God. *Can I trust this?*

He pulled a tiny, battered Bible out of his back pocket. Since he returned to God, he always had it with him. He stared at the little book on his callused palm. Laurel's words from the fight on the beach came back to him. *"You read Romans 1 then, and look at what it really says about creation."*

He opened to the passage. Words that he'd barely acknowledged before seemed to jump off the page at him. "What may be known about God is plain to them, because God has made it plain to them. For since the creation of the world God's invisible qualities—his eternal power and divine nature—have been clearly seen, being understood from what has been made."

Darren stared across the land. Beauty met his eyes. Big clouds muscled their way upward into the afternoon sky. As a pilot, he knew the power in those shining white towers. The silver gray curtain of a rain shaft hung below the flat, bruised bottom of one monster. Again Darren looked back at his Bible, then up at the power around him.

God's qualities? What had Laurel said? *She feels God's love through nature.* God's love? Had he gotten it that wrong? Darren stared blankly at the page. *But it was a false god for me. I did turn from You.* Could God really give this back, all the joy? Was it really worth spending time on when people were hurting?

His hands were shaking, making the words on the page difficult to read. "Lord, I don't want to be distracted from serving You, from helping people You love. You mean more to me than all this." His voice was a hoarse whisper. "Help me now. I don't want to get pulled off base because of my feelings for Laurel."

His chest heaved in a deep sob. Another verse came back to him, a verse he'd heard since childhood. *"The heavens declare the glory of God, the skies proclaim the work of His hands."*

"Your hands, Lord?" He looked up at the gleaming edge of a thunderhead. *Can I trust this?* Laurel had said something about Genesis. His fumbling fingers found the place. "The Lord God took the man and put him in the Garden of Eden to work it and take care of it."

"Man's first job." That's what she called it, tending creation. *If it was the first job You gave us, it can't be wrong, not if I focus on You.* Darren gave a choked laugh. "The whole time I thought I was running away from You, it was Your glory. You were there all the time!" He stood, facing the wind, tears running into the stubble on his cheeks. After a time he calmed, the wind felt cool as it dried his tears, as if it were God's hand, gentle on his face.

"Why didn't You show me before?" He asked the question to the air. "Why did You have to wait until I'd driven Laurel away?"

There was only a deep sense of God's presence. *He was always here. Nothing has changed with Him. I just had my eyes held shut. I didn't even really look at Scripture on creation because I missed it so much.*

Darren swallowed hard. Without Laurel, he might have never opened them, never let himself see God's beauty in creation. He had to find a way to talk to Laurel again, to let her know that he now understood a little of what she was trying to do.

Darren turned and headed purposefully toward the main compound on Ndovu. As he walked, the beauty around him seemed to sing to him, only this time he was not afraid of the song. No longer was it a siren song drawing him away from God, but the living poetry of God Himself.

Laurel was right. There must be some way to keep this song alive. What had she said? Work toward the pattern that God had intended for mankind and creation? Something like that. Even as he thought, his stomach tensed. It wouldn't be easy. Laurel had no idea of the complications, the politics, and rivalries that would be involved.

That's why she asked for my help. He'd turned her down without even giving her a decent hearing. *I'll apologize. Make her listen somehow.* Darren began to run again, only this time his pace was much more controlled. He steadily ate up the ground between him and Joan Doyle's compound.

Slowing to a walk, he entered the area and turned toward Laurel's banda. No one was there. Darren walked toward the Somalis' living quarters. *They'll know where she is.* Ibrahim came to meet him.

"I am to tell you she does not wish to speak with you." Ibrahim's face was deadpan.

Darren's stomach contracted into a cold knot of lead. "Where is she? I must find her!" In his desperation he stepped toward Ibrahim with clenched fists.

"Wah!" Ibrahim jumped back laughing. "Surely I will tell you, brother. Such a man as you will not be stopped by a woman's stubbornness. She is with the troop. We shall go out together on horseback."

Darren had to force himself not to urge Ibrahim to hurry. Anything he did to ruffle the man's dignity would only slow the process. He bit back the questions on his tongue. Three horses milled in a fenced area. Ibrahim caught one easily, but the others spun away, dodging and running.

"Just go! Leave these horses. Find Laurel and bring her here."

"No, I will catch one for you." Ibrahim moved again to corner one of the fiery little animals. "You can then catch your woman yourself. Perhaps she has the same spirit as these horses, and it will not be so easy."

Darren was grinding his teeth. "Brother, tell me where the path is. I will go on foot."

Ibrahim didn't even look up. One of the mares had stopped and was facing him. Cautiously he moved toward her, his robe blowing in the wind, one slim, brown arm outstretched. Darren watched, holding his breath. At the last moment the mare spun away, kicking up mud as she accelerated. Ibrahim walked after her.

"Brother! Tell me the path."

"Haraka haraka haina baraka." Ibrahim called the old proverb over his shoulder and kept going. *Hurry, hurry has no blessing!* Darren grimaced. It wasn't a proverb he wanted to hear at the moment.

Ibrahim approached the mare, and this time she stood still. *Finally, praise the Lord!* Ibrahim saddled his horse, but Darren simply vaulted on bareback. "I'm fine this way. Let's go!"

"As you wish." Ibrahim was definitely laughing at him. "Perhaps you will not be so comfortable."

Within minutes, Darren knew the man was right. This mare had a backbone that felt like an ax blade. He kicked her into a canter, and both men sped out onto the grasslands, the galloping horses throwing up great gobs of mud.

Argus's sharp bark of alarm brought Laurel's head up. The whole troop froze, then scattered, babies leaping onto their loping mothers. Gremlin scrambled behind, screaming in panic. Two horses shot out of the bush, thudding to a stop.

Laurel flinched and moved back, staring. Darren! He'd bolted straight into the troop on a horse, and Ibrahim had brought him. "What in the world are you doing?" She turned to Ibrahim. "And you? Have you both gone mad?"

Ibrahim was grinning like she was an amusing child. "I brought this man because he wishes to speak to you. It is better that a woman bear children than chase foolish plans."

He wants me gone, and he thinks Darren will take me away from here. Laurel gritted her teeth, choked with warring emotions.

Darren had slid off the mare and was standing beside her. "Sorry about spooking the baboons."

"I asked you to stay away."

"Not before I tell you that you've opened a locked door for me. A door that will give great joy no matter what happens between us." He stood unintimidated, feet firmly planted, eyes steady.

"A door?"

He nodded. "A door opened so that I can now praise God for His creation and enjoy it without guilt or confusion. I'm not afraid it will suck me away from Him anymore."

Ibrahim gave Farah some kind of order. Darren

looked up sharply. For a second she thought he was going to argue with the two Somalis. Ibrahim and Farah vaulted onto the horses.

She called out almost involuntarily, "Wait! Don't leave me!"

Ibrahim grinned, gave Darren a salute, and the horses cantered into the bush. The sounds of the retreating horses faded, and silence enfolded the two of them. Even the baboons were gone. She was alone with Darren Grant.

"Please don't be afraid, Laurel. I didn't ask them to leave." His voice was uncertain. "Would you give me a chance and listen?"

She backed away from him. "I can't."

"Okay, how about we keep it impersonal? Would that make you feel better?"

She shook her head blindly. "I don't know. But if I understood what you said a moment ago, I'm really glad for you." She wanted to touch him, hug him. *No, I'll just hurt both of us. How can I tell how much he's changed? I want to trust him too much!*

He started to reach out to her. She retreated quickly. "Please, don't crowd me."

He put his hands down. "You asked for my help with this scheme of yours. I'm ready to do that if you still want me."

"But I don't even know if it will work. I'd just go back to Canada, but there's Jede and little Meli and—" The words caught in her throat as the realization hit her. "Darren, they could be in danger! There's cholera!"

"Where?" His whole body was rigid. "How do you know?"

"Farah just told me Joan thinks Khadiija has cholera. He said she's asked for someone to fly in with a helicopter and cholera vaccine, but they don't know if or when it's coming."

"The water at Ndovu is contaminated with cholera?"

Laurel shook her head. "Farah said she got sick on the way back from Saba."

"And Joan has obviously reported it. Good. She knows the precautions and will enforce them. It's not unusual at the beginning of the rains." He hesitated. "You're sure Farah said vaccine was on the way?"

She nodded. It was hard to look at him, have him so close. She wanted to reach out for reassurance and bit her lip hard. In spite of the heat, she shivered. A tentative baboon contact call made her glance down. Gremlin had come close and sat near her feet.

"Looks like you have a friend." Darren's voice was so kind that tears stung her eyes. She couldn't stand this much longer.

"Laurel, I have to go. I have to warn Jede and Isaac that there's cholera in the area again."

"I know." Her mouth felt stiff, and the words came through with difficulty.

"And should I talk to them about this foundation, what they think would work? Maybe the Somali elders, too?"

Laurel bit her lip. *I did ask him to help, and I need it.* "Thanks." She wouldn't meet his eyes.

He turned to go, and then hesitated. "Please don't be afraid of me. I wish you no harm. In fact, I care for you very much."

"Darren, don't." Tears sprang to her eyes, and she turned away.

"I am not your father, and you aren't Lilith. Think about it. I'll go now, but open up and give me a chance." He stood waiting for a moment, but she couldn't trust herself to look at him. Finally he sighed. "I'll go now."

He ran off into the bush, leaving her staring at his back and crying. Gremlin plucked at her pant leg. She looked down at him, and he made a distressed sound. She sat on the ground and hugged her knees. "We're both lost, you and me." Gremlin could be brought back to the troop, but what about her? She looked again in the direction Darren had gone. *He said he's changed, that You've changed his heart about nature, Lord. I want to believe him so much...too much.*

She shivered and hugged her knees more tightly. *Lord, help us.* She took a deep breath, got to her feet, and began to search for the rest of the troop. She focused on praying for the animals, for the sick child, for the coming struggles, and the foundation....

Anything to take her mind off of Darren Grant.

23

"SO, IBRAHIM SAID YOUR FLYBOY RODE OUT TO SEE YOU THIS afternoon." Joan was watching Laurel as she walked into the dining banda.

"Yes, Darren came out." With an effort, Laurel kept her voice level.

"Lovers reunited?" Joan laughed, and Laurel's stomach contracted. "Look, why don't you and your lover boy take off and enjoy yourselves?"

Laurel shook her head. "Joan, it's not—"

"Of course it is. You relax. I'll talk to the government and to Kimathi about getting the school started and maybe linked with the University of Nairobi."

She wants to keep control. Laurel turned her head away. *Forget the wrangling over power. I don't want to think about Darren either. A child is sick.* "Does Khadiija have cholera?"

Joan crossed her arms. "I think so."

"Is she getting better?"

"She's through the worst of it." Joan's mouth tightened. "I'll not have my staff decimated by this! I need them to keep the study going."

Keep the study going. Is that all that matters to her? "Farah said a helicopter is coming with vaccine."

"It's supposed to. My name isn't exactly roses with anyone in power, and they couldn't give a fig about the Somalis. I was reduced to calling a mission for help, and I'm not sure they believe me. They'll go to Saba first, so we'll have to manage as best we can." She stood abruptly and paced the room. "If you care about the Somalis so much, why make trouble? Surely you can see it's not fair to throw them out and bring in their ancient enemies instead."

"I don't want to throw them out." Laurel fought to keep her voice level.

"And just how do you intend to run a school that's accredited with, of all things, Bible colleges without doing that?"

"Maybe two tracks, both offering an excellent version of the standard Kenyan curriculum with extra environmental studies, but only one track would offer the Bible as part of the program. I don't know. We've barely even begun to think—"

"We? And just who is we?"

She stared at Joan, torn between despair and the crazy urge to laugh. She was already thinking of Darren and herself as a team. She shook her head.

"What, cat got your tongue?" Joan looked around the room. "Where is our food?" She shoved back her chair and bellowed, "Amina!"

"Who is Amina?"

"Another of Ibrahim's daughters-in-law. She was supposed to do Ambaro's job." She paused and bellowed the woman's name again.

Farah stuck his head in the door. "Ambaro is ill since a small time ago, memsabu. Amina is caring for her, to give her much water the way you taught with Khadiija."

"Ambaro is ill!" Joan leapt to her feet and ran toward the door.

Laurel followed. Joan was yelling for Ibrahim and

the others. Before long, a wide circle of graceful Somali forms gathered in the dim light. Laurel couldn't follow what was said, but the tone was emphatic in the extreme. One of the other men protested, but Ibrahim stood by Joan. The group started to disperse, and Joan marched toward Ambaro's house.

Laurel followed. "I can help nurse her. I've been vaccinated."

Joan stopped abruptly. "You stay away from my people with your do-good attitude. Amina is probably already exposed. She can do the filthy nursing! I've told the others that I'll banish anyone who comes near. That includes you. Why can't the cholera go where it would be of some use!" She turned and marched into Ambaro's banda.

Laurel frowned and watched Joan go, a woman totally dedicated to one goal. Walking toward her banda, Laurel silently prayed for Ambaro.

Farah stepped close to her out of the darkness. "There is much talk concerning this school which may be planned. Darren Grant was speaking to the elders." He gave her a quick glance, eyes flashing white. "Perhaps it is that I would come if my father permits."

"You would?" Impulsively she reached to grasp his hands.

He dodged. "Darren Grant has said I must tell you to go to the house of Jede and Isaac this evening." He slid away, melting into the shadows.

Darren is helping, and already doors are opening. Could what seemed so impossible actually become possible with Darren's help? Before Laurel went to Jede's house, she washed from head to foot and changed her clothing. She wanted no risk of spreading cholera to the people on the Wilson. As she dressed, she tried to keep her mind on that...and not on Darren. On her way to Jede's, she thought of the cholera threat and instantly saw Darren's worried face as she told him about it. How would he react to the news about Ambaro?

She walked faster. *How can I trust myself to work with him as a business partner?* The moon printed shadows of thorn trees across the path. She stumbled on a bump hidden in a shadow. *I'm not ready for anything else.* She couldn't leave or even refuse to work with him. That would endanger any chance of Lilith's money helping people at Ndovu and on the Wilson. There had to be some way to keep him at a distance without abandoning either place.

Jede called her name softly and stepped out of the darkness. "The men are talking, so I came out to meet you." She took Laurel's hands in both of hers. "I've been worried about you. Darren told us."

"That Joan thinks Khadiija has cholera?" Her voice sounded tight even in her own ears.

"Yes, but that's not what I meant." The light from the house windows outlined Jede's sensitive features. "He's a good man."

"Jede, please! I know that." She coughed to cover the break in her voice. "You don't understand. Darren and I are so different. My mother ended up married to a man she had nothing in common with just because she thought she loved him. Sure I like Darren, but that isn't enough."

Jede shrugged. "Mabye not. Still, I was praying for you while the men talked. I felt strongly I was to remind you of Joshua 1:9: 'Be strong and of good courage; be not afraid, neither be thou dismayed; for the LORD thy God is with thee withersoever thou goest.' I don't know why. Do you?"

Because I'm so afraid of repeating Lilith's mistake? She wasn't willing to go there. "Maybe just to encourage me. Thanks, Jede. About the cholera, is anyone sick on the Wilson?"

"No, we've convinced them to be more careful with water, or at least many of them. Darren and Isaac don't expect any problems with that. They'll be waiting for us. Come, let's go join them. It would probably be better if we only speak to answer questions. Three of the most powerful elders are there, and they're more comfortable talking to other men."

"That doesn't bother you?"

Jede laughed. "Sometimes, but I'm more interested in getting something useful done for God than demanding my rights, whatever those may be."

The men were sitting around the table. They stood and shook her hand as Darren formally introduced her. He paused and translated what he'd said, his eyes gentle on her. "I told them that you've brought blessing to this place, and opportunity, and that you're a very special person."

Heat rose in her cheeks. Just seeing him made her heart hammer uncomfortably. He switched back into Meru and kept talking. Two of the elders hummed the soft *eeeeh* of agreement, but the other watched with wary eyes. Isaac motioned for her to sit next to Darren. Uncomfortable, she did so, pulling her chair back as far as she could. Jede brought her a cup of chai and sat beside her. "I'll translate for Laurel."

The thin, old man with the wary eyes immediately stood and burst into a long speech. Jede pulled her chair close to Laurel and spoke softly. "He says once there was a mongoose and a cobra that were enemies. Each time the mongoose met one of cobra's children, he would dodge the strikes of the deadly snake and kill it. He and his children would feast that night. Each time the cobra met one of mongoose's children, he would approach softly and strike. He could rest with a full belly for days. Months and months went by. The two tried over and over to kill each other, but to no avail. They grew tired of the endless vigilance. Then a rabbit came from another country and said, 'I will begin a school. In that place your children will be friends and learn together.' Warily the two agreed. From now on the mongoose and his children would eat only rats, and so would the cobra. All went well until one of cobra's children came to school tired. He slept, and when one of mongoose's children touched his shoulder, he struck out of reflex, killing the mongoose's child. The brothers of the mongoose killed that cobra. Still, to this day, mongoose and cobra are enemies."

The old man looked pointedly at Laurel. Under that gaze she felt very much like a rabbit from another country. He slowly sat down, his point made. Laurel's stomach felt like a hot cannon ball. Was Joan right? Was she just a naive fool who was bent on making a mess?

Darren answered, his deep voice calm and thoughtful. Jede translated his words softly into Laurel ear. "But are we animals to be driven by instinct?" Darren let the question hang there, then gestured in her direction.

"This woman offers your children schooling you could never afford. Will you throw away this opportunity?"

He was so competent, so good to have beside her. *And it seems like he really has changed his mind.* She sucked in her breath. *What if he's only working for the school and for peace?* Would he defend the wildland when it came right down to it?

She set her jaw. *Whatever he does, I'm not going to leave the wildland out.*

One of the men asked a question, and Darren passed it on to her. "He wants to know if this foundation will buy them better seeds that will grow in dry ground."

"Tell him I hope to include information and funds for dryland farming that will do less damage. Tell him that the health of the ecosystem and the animals and plants that belong here is part of this. I'm sure God wants them cared for, too, not as a tag on, but as an integral part of how we live on the land He's given."

Darren raised his eyebrows slightly. "You might want to take it slowly with that. If you want them to participate, sell them on it gradually, maybe from the ecotourism angle."

Good advice, or is he hedging? She looked at Jede, who nodded.

"Okay, put it the way you think he'll understand, but I'm not going to leave the wildland out. If you can't live with that, you shouldn't be part of this."

Jede put a hand on her arm, and one of the men cut in, obviously questioning what had been said. Darren looked at her for a second longer, then turned to answer.

Laurel shifted in her chair. Was she just looking for an excuse not to have to deal with Darren as an ally?

There were more questions about the school and about involvement with the denomination to which Isaac's church belonged. The talk went on and on. The elders made their points in careful speeches, often using allegories as the first one had. Darren replied in kind. The contours of his face, sculpted by lamplight, moved expressively as he spoke.

Jede caught her watching, smiled, and whispered, "He speaks well, does he not?"

Laurel looked away from her friend. To her relief, the meeting seemed to be winding down. The men stood and shook hands, their hard, dry hands on hers. Darren came with her outside, and Laurel had the strong impression that Jede was deliberately detaining the others.

"Don't look so tense. I think we're well on the way to having them convinced." He smiled. "That only leaves the government, the church denomination, the landlords, and the Somali people to get on our side."

"Is it crazy? Should we just forget it?"

"Not on your life. If God chooses to open doors, we have a chance to do something remarkable here. He's already used you to do that for me." The tenderness in his tone made her want to weep. "You have no idea how much I owe you for that."

I've learned so much. Why shouldn't I believe him.

Because you're afraid....

It was true. Every thought that the barriers might be gone from between them—every word and action that brought them closer together just magnified the sense of standing on the edge of a cliff. She actually swayed on her feet. He was so close. She reached out, almost touch-

ing the strong line of his jaw. *No!* She tore her eyes away
and looked at the ground.

"I'd better get back. I won't come down here again.
There might be a chance of bringing cholera."

"I doubt it. Laurel, please…"

"No, I can't risk it." Even as she said the words, she
knew that he sensed the double meaning.

Walking back, she prayed for Ambaro and Khadiija.
She prayed that the vaccine would come soon. Her
prayers were edgy, preoccupied, and she could not let
herself relax and trust God. Anytime she loosened her
guard, Darren's image filled her mind. The dizzy void,
the feeling of losing control, loomed in front of her.

Trusting God was one thing, but trusting a man?
Human beings, no matter how wonderful, were flawed.
And I'm not looking at him objectively. I know I'm not.

She lay for a long time in the darkness before she
slept. It started to rain hard, and the sound of the rain on
the roof finally lulled her to sleep. When she woke, she
rose to splash cold water on her face.

She could see a light in Ambaro's banda. *Maybe I can
help.* Quickly she dressed and went out. The dim golden
light of a lantern touched the still figures she could see
through Ambaro's open door. She came closer, and the
smell of the room hit her. She stepped back, gagging.

Ambaro lay on one pallet. Amina was crouched on
her heels beside Ambaro but seemed to be asleep. As she
watched, Khadiija climbed out of the other bed and tried
to cover a mess on the floor with some filthy towels.

"Stop!"

Laurel nearly jumped out of her skin. A Somali man
she'd only seen a few times was just behind her, spear

poised. "It is forbidden to enter!"

She looked back. Amina was on her feet. She bent and began to help Khadiija to clean up, pitching the filthy cloth onto a heap of rags by the door.

"Get away!" The Somali man loomed close. At least that was what she thought he said. She didn't have enough Swahili to argue. She nodded and started to back away. A flashlight suddenly shone in her face. Joan was in the door of her banda. "What is it?"

The guard replied quickly.

"Laurel, if you're up, do something useful. The notes from yesterday are in the dining banda. Go update the computer files." Joan had on a caving flashlight, one that sat on her head. The effect was eerie, as if the woman's head was glowing. *She sounds tense, wired.*

"Leave them." Joan's voice was brittle. She came out of her banda threateningly. The man leveled his spear at Laurel's stomach. Left with no choice, she turned and walked stiffly toward the dining banda.

She'd just booted up the computer when Joan appeared. "Bring up the ID files."

Laurel did so. Joan looked over her shoulder, demanding to see one animal's file after the other. She insisted that the photos of each baboon stay on the screen while she studied it: Scruffy Susan, the imposing Argus, Cleo who managed to look impish even in a photo. Gremlin's latest picture must have been taken at the heart of the drought. He was one very bedraggled urchin.

Joan insisted that they look through the files of the baboons that had died. Chewbacca's image made Laurel catch her breath, then there was a big section of animals

Laurel had never seen. She glanced up to see Joan with tears in her eyes. Impulsively, she reached for Joan's arm to comfort her.

Joan's hand clamped onto hers like an iron-hard pincer. "You're a thief! You're taking over my project, my people, my animals. You have no right."

Laurel's mouth fell open. Wincing, she tried to pull away. "No, I love them too."

"These are mine!" The woman dropped Laurel's hand and stalked out of the room. Through the open door, Laurel saw her walk to Ambaro's banda. There, she stood just inside, staring at the heap of filthy cloths.

Laurel frowned and got back to work. At least filing data gave her a way to focus her mind. Joan reappeared at breakfast looking much more composed. After the meal, she stopped Laurel at the door. "You'll be observing alone today. There are some things I need to do. But first, I need some information from you about your goals. You're set on helping the people on the Wilson, right?"

Laurel nodded warily.

"Let's start with their water supply. Most get their drinking water from the borehole dug two years ago, is that right?"

"Yes." *What is going on?*

"Will they be using surface water now that the rains have come?"

"Jede told me she and Isaac were trying to encourage people to use the big well. It's less likely to be contaminated, but how can I tell what they'll do? What are you thinking?"

"Just want to know where we're starting. Water supply

is extremely important in a semiarid situation." She went on to give a very competent lecture on the importance of setting up and maintaining a good water source. Joan halted her lecture and looked out the door. "Ibrahim is ready for you. Go now."

As they left, Laurel was relieved to be doing something routine. She'd been through too much, had her heart torn in too many directions, too many ways, to deal with much more. Routine was a salve for her raw, screaming nerves. Gremlin was even brighter than he had been. In fact, all the young baboons were often playing again. She smiled at the sight of a long line of baboons, tails in the air as they bent to drink in a puddle.

"Is it that baboons can get cholera from dirty water also?" Farah asked.

Laurel looked at him and frowned. "I never heard of such a thing." And yet, there was something in his words that left her feeling on edge...nervous.

"Joan would not like that. Perhaps she values this animals more than men. If those on the Wilson die, she will be pleased."

Laurel froze. Joan had asked about the water supply on the Wilson! Then she'd walked that direction after stopping in Ambaro's banda.

"No! It can't be. Not the well on the Wilson!" *Father...O God, surely we're wrong! Even Joan wouldn't deliberately contaminate the water with cholera, would she?*

She knew the answer even as she asked the question: Yes. That was exactly the kind of thing Joan would do. Hadn't she said, over and over again, that this was a war?

"What is it?" Farah was staring at her with concerned eyes.

"I've got to go back. I've got to find out!" She turned and ran in the direction of the compound.

"Wait!" Farah came after her, loping with ease alongside as she struggled and slipped in the mud. "What is it that you do?"

I can't tell him. What if I'm wrong? She stopped and faced him. "I know this seems crazy, but I have to go back. Right now."

"I will call Ibrahim to bring the horses." He took the radio off his belt. No one answered.

Laurel shifted from one foot to the other. If Joan was taking filth from Ambaro's sickness to contaminate the well on the Wilson, Laurel had to hurry. She'd have to tell Jede before anyone drank that water.

"Farah, I can't wait. I'll follow the tracks we made coming in. If you do contact Ibrahim, tell him that. He can meet me partway. Ask him to find Darren. I need Darren."

He nodded and she turned to go. "Laurel!" Her name sounded like *Lalo* in his mouth. "Be careful! Many dangerous creatures also are glad in the rains."

Dangerous creatures! Just what I need. Still, she didn't pause, but saying a quick prayer for help, she ran on.

24

DARREN WALKED BACK UP TO NDOVU. *I'VE GOT A REASON TO BE here she'll accept. I'll talk to the Somali elders again. I've got to see Laurel, talk to her.* But she had already gone out to observe when he arrived. He'd just have to make the discussion with the elders last until evening. That shouldn't be too hard. The Somali loved to talk.

He bowed his head as he walked. "Lord, Laurel is so determined to serve You in the way she thinks You want. I love her." *I mean that.* He stopped in his tracks as the realization hit him. *I do love her.* He took a deep breath. "I want to be with her the rest of my life." He swallowed hard as Isaac's words came back to him. *She'll bear you many fine sons.* "That too."

He crouched down on his heels and clenched his hands. "God, if there is any way, soften her heart toward me. I know she cares. I know it!" Darren bowed his head, covering his face with both hands. The next words wouldn't even come out aloud. *Please don't let it be that I've ruined every chance we might have had by my reaction to her at the coast. She's so scared. Open her heart to me.*

He eased himself to his feet. *And help me know how to share her vision for the foundation. It means so much to her....* As he walked, he rehearsed what he would say to the Somali elders.

Many hours later, he was crouched on his heels in the shade of an acacia tree with Ibrahim and several other Somali men. The radio on Ibrahim's belt crackled, but the man ignored it, being in the middle of a complicated allegory. A few minutes later it crackled again. Darren straightened. Had he heard Laurel's name through the static? Still, Ibrahim ignored it. A third time it came to life, and this time he stood and answered with a flourish.

It was Laurel's name! Darren stepped closer, watching intently.

"I will tell him," Ibrahim said and turned to Darren. "Your woman, she is running on foot to the compound. We are to meet her."

"What's happened?" It was all Darren could do not to grab Ibrahim by the shirtfront.

"Farah said she spoke of cholera and the Wilson, and then she ran." Ibrahim shrugged. "Perhaps she is mad. But she asked for you. Farah was to find you, get your help."

"Not likely!" *What could have upset Laurel that much?* "I've got to find her." He spun and ran toward the corrals. The morning was very muddy. It wouldn't be hard to follow the horses' tracks. Ibrahim called him, but he didn't look back.

Darren ran hard, his eyes searching the gray-green thornbush for a sign of Laurel's figure. *She asked for me.* His heart surged with joy, and he pushed himself harder. He wouldn't fail her this time. The thud of horses' hoofs behind him brought his head around. Two of the fiery little Somali horses were coming at a gallop. Ibrahim's robes flew out behind him as he jerked both to a halt and gestured at the riderless one. "Horses are faster."

Darren nodded and leapt on. Both lined out at a gallop, Ibrahim in the lead. *This isn't the way we went out with the Jeep!* Darren stuck his heels in and came even with Ibrahim. "Where are you going?"

"There is a shorter way to come more quickly to where she is walking."

"What if we miss her?"

"Then we will return and catch her from behind." Ibrahim dug his heels into his animal. Great chunks of mud flew up behind them. No horse could keep up that pace for long, and they soon dropped into a ground-eating trot. "Just there." Ibrahim pointed with his chin. "By that rock. That is the place we join the longer way."

Ten minutes later they rounded a huge boulder. Darren looked at the ground and hissed through his teeth. Laurel's tracks were printed clearly on the muddy earth—tracks returning toward the compound. He spun the horse around and spurred it into a canter. Something drastic must have happened to make her come back alone like this.

Ibrahim followed, cantering alongside. Darren turned to him. "You go on back the short way and see if she's in the compound. Come back this path toward me if she isn't."

Ibrahim grinned at him. "You will catch her alone. Perhaps I should not come back to you?"

He had a point. *I do want to be with her alone.*

Ibrahim laughed at the look on Darren's face, spun his horse, and dug his heels in, robes flying over the little stallion's skinny rump. Darren checked the mare to a trot and focused on following Laurel's tracks.

Gasping for breath, Laurel had crossed the compound of Joan's camp at a stumbling jog. Her hands and knees were muddy. The pad at the base of her left thumb throbbed steadily. She dropped to a fast walk and dug futilely at the big thorn embedded there. No luck. Laurel made a face and started to jog again. What was mud or falling on a thorn compared to the danger of a cholera epidemic?

Please, Lord. Let me be wrong about Joan. But something deep inside told her she wasn't. Laurel shook her head and tried to speed up. All the way in, she'd been alternating between disbelief and horror. She had to find Joan. That was the only way to learn the truth. *If I'm wrong, everyone will think I'm insane, tearing back here covered in mud and panic.*

She dropped to a walk again. *So what if they think I'm crazy? I can't be silent and risk the lives of hundreds of people.* Grimly she plugged along past the airstrip. She seemed to be stuck in slow motion. Ahead on the path, she saw a little group of children. As she got closer, they stopped walking and stared at her open mouthed.

"Have...you seen...Joan...Joan Doyle?" The words came out between gasps.

The children backed away from her, then turned and ran.

"Wait! Please wait!" They didn't even pause. Frustrated, Laurel blew out a breath that was close to a sob. She must look frantic. No wonder the kids were scared.

The oldest turned and stood still, and she recognized him—James, from the school field trip. She hurried toward him. Laurel saw his chest rise and fall as the boy took a deep, steadying breath.

"What has happened that you run like this? Is someone dead?"

Laurel shook her head. *I can't say anything. It could make so much trouble if I'm wrong.* "James, please, have you seen Joan? I need to find her immediately."

He jerked his chin in the direction of the other boys who were watching warily at a distance. "One of those has said his sister told him that Joan Doyle was at the well when she went to get water. Joan stood watching as if she waited for something."

A wave of shivers passed over Laurel making her knees feel weak. Joan had gone to the well! *God, what can I do? Help me!* No one should drink that water, not until it could be tested safe, but how? And what if she was wrong? What if Joan really was concerned for water safety?

"Perhaps I could run to bring Joan Doyle to you?"

Laurel hunched her shoulders together in indecision. The straps of her backpack pulled against the movement. *My backpack! I've got pen and paper.* In a second she had it off. Careless of the mud, she dumped the pack on the ground and knelt, scrambling for writing material. "Could you take a note to Jede for me?"

The boy nodded warily. Laurel started to scribble her suspicions, and then stopped. If she was wrong, it would make things so much worse between Ndovu and the people on the Wilson. She wadded up the paper. Leaving smears of mud, she started another note. "Jede, please find a way to stop the people from using the well until we know the water is safe. I can't explain, but I ask you this in Christ's name. Laurel."

She folded the note tightly and pushed it into James's hand. "Hurry!"

The boy gave her a white-eyed look and ran off, covering ground faster than Laurel could ever hope to. Shoving the now muddy pack onto her back, Laurel hurried down the path to the well. Maybe Joan hadn't done anything yet. *Maybe I can stop her. Maybe she's still waiting until she's alone...until there are no witnesses.* Laurel swallowed hard. *Maybe James is right and I am crazy.*

Laurel passed other people on the path. All stared at her open mouthed as she slogged past at a dogged run, covered in mud and gasping for breath. There was muted breathing, the padding of feet, and giggles behind her. She glanced back to see that she had a fair contingent of children following her. *Great. How am I supposed to confront Joan if I have an audience?* Listening children would pass on what they heard. If she was wrong, her words would spread; the damage she'd tried so hard to avoid by keeping silent would happen.

Silently praying for help, she plowed ahead. A white woman on the path. Joan Doyle was coming toward her! Laurel stopped, frozen in her tracks.

Joan's eyes were narrowed. "What is it? Is there trouble with the troop?"

"No, the troop is fine. I need to talk to you."

Joan frowned. "I don't have time for that! You're positively filthy. Let's get back and get you cleaned up. What possessed you to behave like this?" Joan started to move past her.

Laurel grabbed Joan's arm. "I said I need to talk to you! Or would you rather I sound the alarm now?"

"Alarm? What are you talking about?"

"Do you really want me to explain my suspicions now?" Laurel jerked her chin toward their growing audience.

Joan's eyes narrowed even further. "Okay, we'll talk." She turned onto a tiny path along the edge of someone's garden. Laurel felt sick. By agreeing to talk, Joan had as much as admitted her guilt. When the spectators started to follow, Joan shouted at them furiously. They hung back.

As soon as they were out of sight of the crowd, Laurel stopped. "No one can hear us now."

Joan kept walking. "I'll talk to you, but I choose the place. If you think no one is listening now, you're a fool. They'll follow us until we're off the Wilson. You want privacy, you come with me."

Joan's long strides seemed to eat the ground. They turned onto another path, and Laurel could see that Joan was right. The children were still following. Joan headed down a steep hill on a path Laurel had never seen. There were fewer and fewer gardens. She looked back to see that most of the children had gone. Joan turned onto a smaller path and walked on.

"No one can hear us now, please stop." Anger was growing in Laurel along with the certainty that this woman had just done something horrible.

Joan ignored her. Again Laurel looked back. No children were visible behind them. Laurel had enough. She grabbed Joan's arm. The tough, wiry woman shook her off and strode on. The path was in a narrow gully now. The air was hot and stifling down between the vegetation-tangled boulders.

Joan suddenly bent down, picked something up, and turned to wait. Laurel rushed up to her. "Did you contaminate their well with cholera germs?"

"Yes, I did, and good riddance too." Joan's hand

rose. At the last moment Laurel tried to dodge. Joan had a huge rock in her hand. There was a ringing crunch, and everything went black.

Darren had followed Laurel's tracks to the compound on Ndovu. Once there, he cut straight across to her banda.

"Laurel!" He leapt down and pounded on the door. "Laurel!" Only the sound of the mare breathing by his shoulder answered him. Without touching the stirrups, he vaulted into the saddle. He wasn't going to bother with looking for Ibrahim. Not when he could track Laurel directly.

Sensing Darren's agitation, the little mare danced sideways, obliterating a print he'd wanted to verify was Laurel's. He dismounted, undid the girth, and pulled off the bridle in two quick motions. The mare darted away. She'd go back to the other horses. Darren threw the tack over a nearby tree branch and focused on the ground. He picked up a fragment of a print, then another farther on.

She's heading for the airstrip. He began to jog down the path, watching the ground. Laurel had been running, stumbling. He saw a place where she'd fallen. This was the trail of someone desperate. Darren's throat was suddenly dry. He jogged along as fast as he could and still be sure of the trail. As he crossed onto the Wilson, the path was wider, pocked with other recent tracks, and he had to slow further. He wanted to roar, to hit something.

"*Na fanya nini?*" Two boys with impudent grins were staring at him.

"What am I doing? I'm looking for Laurel, the one who took the schoolchildren to Ndovu, have you seen her?"

"I have not seen, but it is said she was going to the well."

"The well?" Nothing made sense! "Thanks." As he spoke, he was already accelerating into a hard run.

"Wait!" The boy added something, but Darren wasn't listening. He could hear the boys following, calling out, both voices overlaying something about Joan and the well. He pushed himself harder, and the voices faded quickly behind him. Belting around a corner in the path, he nearly mowed down four women with big loads of firewood. He dodged and kept going, weaving around a whole group of people who suddenly poured in from a side path. Mud slid under his feet. He held a steady, hard run. Blasting into the open area around the well, he yelled Laurel's name.

There were always people at the well, mostly women, but now the area was crowded. A huge knot of arguing people surrounded someone he could not see. Those on the periphery of the group had swung toward him. "Laurel!" A woman's voice answered. *Not Laurel.* The crowd parted and Jede came toward him. She looked haggard.

"Jede, where is Laurel? What's happening?"

"I don't know. Look!" She shoved a note into his hand.

He read the words aloud: "Jede, please find a way to stop the people from using the well until we know the water is safe. I can't explain, but I ask you this in Christ's name. Laurel." He frowned and looked at Jede. "What?"

"I don't *know!*" Jede repeated the phrase on a raising wail. "I'm trying to stop them from using the well. I just stood on the cover and wouldn't move, but it's time for the evening meal, and I can't find Isaac and—look!" She pointed. Two women were filling five-gallon containers.

Darren grunted. *Laurel asked in the name of Christ.* This had to be serious. He took three strides forward, lifted both fists, and knocked the heavy containers of water flying. "No! There will be no water drawn here tonight."

The women squealed with dismay and dropped back. "But we must have water!" Other voices rose in agreement. Darren planted himself on the wellhead and crossed his arms.

Jede stood beside him. "They are right. We must have water."

"I know that!" He raised his voice so that it carried, speaking to them in their language. "You've been asked, in God's name, to refrain from drinking. If you comply, I promise you, somehow He will provide. For now, we must investigate this matter. All who know something of this, come close."

There were nods, and the air of antagonism decreased. People crowded around, and out of the babble, gradually he pieced together the story. Joan at the well, then Laurel sending the note to Jede. The two white women meeting.

"They went back to Ndovu by way of the ravine of the caves," the children called out. "Joan Doyle, she shouted at us like a crazy person. She told us to go home! Also we were near the place of the Somali, so we returned."

"I've got to go find her." Darren started to move.

Jede stood in his way. "If you go, they will use the well." Darren shut his eyes and fought for calm. Jede touched his arm. "Don't look like that, brother! Now that you are here, I can go and bring Isaac and the elders. I will pray for Laurel. Remember she is in God's hands. Don't fear."

"Go then, and quickly." He raised his voice. "Are there some here who will help Jede to find Isaac and the elders?"

Many children's voices answered eagerly. Like a hive of bees scattering after flowers, they sped off in many directions. The people who remained at the well sat, settling themselves for a long wait. Darren stayed on the wellhead. He felt like a dog, confined and lunging at the end of its chain.

Where was Laurel? The sun was beginning to sink, which meant he had precious little time to find her.

Each minute that passed was an agony to him.

25

CONSCIOUSNESS RETURNED TO LAUREL IN CONFUSING WAVES. Her head hurt. She was on her side, and someone was pulling her by the feet over an uneven surface. Her head banged on a rough spot. The pain intensified, flashing like strobe lights behind her eyes. Instinctively she tried to throw out her hands to stop the jarring. They seemed stuck together....

Her eyes flew open to see a dim earth ceiling not far above her. It was moving. *What?* She closed her eyes again, concentrating, trying to clear her fogged mind.

Joan! Joan Doyle had hit her with a rock. Laurel moaned, and then the realization hit her. She was moving. Someone had hold of her feet and was dragging her....

She opened her eyes and peered into the darkness, lifting her head, fighting the pain and a wave of nausea that followed it. Joan was dragging her by the feet. Twisting hard, Laurel kicked out. Joan staggered and let go.

Laurel tried to get up and failed. Her feet were tied. So were her hands. She tried again, pain pounding in her head. This time she managed to get to her knees. Nausea won. She threw up violently, then hung there, retching. The pain in her head was blinding. Joan jerked her down backward.

"Lie still or I'll hit you again!"

"You can't do this." Laurel's voice was a wheezing croak. In spite of the pain, she struggled to get up. "Let me go warn them. Please!"

Joan's foot swung at Laurel's head. She dodged, rolling half over, and the blow took her on the shoulder, knocking her onto her face. She lay still, fighting waves of nausea and waiting for more punishing blows. They didn't come. Instead, she could hear Joan moving. Her footsteps echoed oddly. Laurel tried to lift her head to see what was happening. The space seemed to spin around her. Laurel sank back and let her eyes fall shut. *Please, God, help me! Help Jede stop the people from using that well water.*

Joan suddenly gave what sounded like a grunt of satisfaction. "Perfect!" She came toward Laurel, grabbed her feet again, and dragged her a little ways. The pain and nausea triggered by the handling were almost too much for Laurel. She didn't even try to resist. Joan dropped her feet, then started pushing at her, trying to roll her across the rough ground.

In spite of herself, Laurel groaned. "No. Please."

Joan's hands bit into Laurel's side, rolling her over the gritty dust. Unable to protect herself, Laurel got a mouthful of the stuff. Now Joan's feet were on her, shoving until she rolled over again.

She heard Joan scramble to her feet and back away quickly. Laurel opened her eyes to find herself looking at…a snake! She flinched and froze. No, it wasn't a snake. It was shed snakeskin, a big one, twisted and translucent in the dim light. The shock cleared her mind. She blinked and tried to get a better idea of her surroundings. She was in a cave, a dry, dusty one. Her head was pounding with pain. She focused again on the shed skin.

Joan's voice was behind her. "A mamba den is perfect. You can't have my people, my troop! Nature itself can kill you. That will prove I'm right and you're wrong."

"What do you mean?" Laurel's voice was a croak.

"You are lying three feet from a mamba's den. See the shed skins, the excrement?" Joan spoke as if lecturing a room full of students. "A mamba is a venomous and highly irritable snake. This one is not going to be pleased to find you on its front step. One wrong move and it will strike. Their poison is a nerve toxin. You'll die with your eyes open."

"No!"

"Yes!" Joan crowed the word in a triumphant cackle. "You and your money, your soft-headed do-goodism. Did you really think I'd let you take over Ndovu? No, I'm going to sit here and wait for that snake to kill you."

Laurel could feel her heart beating, each rapid pulse thumping through her aching head. "I don't want to steal anything from you. You'll still direct the animal behavior study."

"So why does Farah want to go to this school of yours? You're taking over Ndovu! Corrupting my people with this God of yours. Let Him keep you safe."

Those words reminded her strongly of the story of Daniel in the lions' den. Suddenly her mind was crystal clear. "If God wants to keep the mamba from biting me, He can. Or He could take me home to Him. Either way, I serve God."

Joan snorted. "Don't spout religious nonsense at me!" She shoved Laurel hard in the back with her foot. Even closer to the den than before, Laurel froze. *I have to be still.* If she did nothing to irritate the mamba, why would it strike? No animal was intrinsically evil. Her breath caught in her throat as she willed herself to be calm. She could just see Joan out of the corner of her eye. The woman was crouched on her heels, leaning slightly forward in a way that reminded Laurel of a vulture. *Death bird! Waiting for me to die.*

"The snake will be out soon enough. That shed skin is fresh, and he'll need to hunt."

Laurel lifted her face slightly out of the dirt. "Joan, listen to me, please. You don't want to be a murderer. Let me go. We can warn the people about the well. God loves you too."

"I'm sure He does." Her smile was as full of mockery as her words. "I should have thought of this scheme years ago. After cholera kills a good percentage of the people on the Wilson, I will spread the rumor that the place is cursed. That should keep squatters out."

The dirt in Laurel's mouth felt gritty against her teeth. "They saw you at the well. Think about it. This won't work."

"No one saw me put anything into the well. Within a day, cholera will be everywhere. No one will be able to prove that it came from the well." Her voice was rising. "It will work, and I'll be free of your meddling. Lilith will probably even fund the project in your memory." She laughed almost hysterically. "Her beloved daughter bit by a snake while studying animals."

"But I'm here in a cave, not out with the troop. People saw me with you." Her mouth tasted of blood. Her neck shook as she fought to hold her head up.

"So? I'll say we walked to Ndovu, then you went back out with the troop. I'll get your body out there somehow, tonight on one of the horses maybe."

No longer able to hold her head up, Laurel let it sink

onto the dirt. She forced the words out, her jaw moving against the gritty rock. "You don't want to do this. You didn't keep kicking me after you pulled me down. You didn't beat me to death with the rock like you could have. You don't want to kill me. Please, let me go."

"Shut up! Shut up! Shut up! Shut up!" Joan was yelling over Laurel's words. "I'll kill you! I will! I'm not going to be too soft. Not anymore. I'll find a rock." The woman jumped up.

Laurel shut her eyes tightly and waited for the blow. *Help me! God, please help me!*

"Snake." Joan's voice was a startled breath. There was absolute silence for what seemed like ages. Laurel twisted unsuccessfully, trying to see what was happening. An odd *shushing* noise ended the silence. Joan's laughter echoed all around Laurel. "He's going to do it! The mamba didn't strike me, and now he's heading for you. So much for your God."

The mamba. The shushing of scales across dust got louder, closer. Laurel was afraid to even move her eyes to see. She didn't have to. The snake came into view. Broad head questing gracefully, he slid toward her. He paused, lifted his head, and tested the air with his tongue. Every tiny detail was clear. His eyes were cloudy. Crazy about animals, Laurel had kept a corn snake as a child. She knew well enough the cloudy, blue-eyed look of a snake about to shed. *This isn't the snake that had already shed.* There were two!

Her heart was thumping so hard, Laurel was afraid it was moving her body enough to irritate the snake. Half blind, snakes about to shed were cranky. This one reared up and sniffed at the strange scent of her, tasting the air with his tongue. He moved closer and closer until he was too near her face for her eyes to focus on him. She could feel herself shaking. Involuntary tears of fear began to trickle from her eyes.

Jesus...Jesus! It was the only prayer she could manage. The moment seemed to last forever as the snake hung there, just in front of her eyes. With a smooth movement he backed up three inches, tasted the air one last time, then turned and slid into the den. The breath came out of Laurel, and she went limp with relief. *Thank you, God!*

Joan swore loudly. "I'll kill you myself!"

There was a scrabbling noise. Joan came toward her but stopped. "No, I'm not going to risk my life again by getting close to that den. Not for a piece of trash like you. Let the snakes do it. You'll irritate them eventually." She moved away, but Laurel could hear her pacing.

The snake saved my life! She held the thought, trying to reassure herself. She failed. A venomous snake was within feet of her.

Joan was still pacing, muttering under her breath. The footsteps stopped somewhere behind Laurel. "No! I can't wait for the snakes to do the job. They are cold-blooded. They could sleep for days. People will look for you. Jede, Isaac, your darling Darren."

Darren! His name echoed in Laurel's mind like a cry in a canyon of loneliness and fear.

Joan's feet moved away and came back. "I've got to make them bite you." Laurel could hear her shuffling, as if she was trying to come forward yet couldn't make herself take the risk. Joan swore again. "Forget this! I'm going to get my rifle."

The footsteps receded rapidly, and silence enfolded Laurel. It seemed to stretch out like a rubber band until it hummed with tension. No sound at all came from the snake den. Something warm was trickling down her cheek and across the side of her nose. Gradually the dim light disappeared until Laurel was lying in total blackness. The rock against her cheekbone bit into her skin.

Through the pain, she forced herself to be still. Her arms, doubled up in front of her, ached in rhythmic, throbbing pulses. Something sharp was under her right shoulder. The ground bit into her hip. The tickling drip across her cheek and nose had become a tight, itchy area. Holding still was torture, but any movement that close to a mamba could mean death. If she didn't move, Joan would find her and kill her.

Jesus…help.

Her prayers were fractured, broken fragments. It was the best she could do. She couldn't seem to focus. Thoughts of Darren kept intruding. Prayers that Jede would stop the people from using the contaminated water got muddled together with trying to remember if mambas were nocturnal. The sharp spot under her hip seemed to have ground itself right into the bone.

Darren…where are you?

Helpless tears slid from her eyes into the dust. Here in the dark, nothing was left to her but her life, and even that could be gone any second. *Fear.* Her mouth was dry with it. It held her down, held her still. She felt as if she were floating on pain.

As the agony in her body increased, gradually something became clear to her. *I've been living on fear for years.* That's why she couldn't just logically do what Julie had said and stop pulling away from men. *That's why I have this precipice feeling about Darren now that there's no barrier of different beliefs, now that we've both learned something and think more alike.* She frowned. The answer seemed to echo in her mind. *I can trust God.*

Now? With this snake? She was up against a clear choice—take a risk and move away from the den or be killed when Joan returned. She swallowed again, but her mouth stayed dry as dust. *I can't afford to live on fear anymore. I can't. I won't!* But still she couldn't make herself move.

If I can't move, maybe I can pray aloud. That would be a start. Her voice came out in a choked whisper. "God, my life is in Your hands. I'm sick of being controlled by fear. Help me trust You. Help me move."

The clamping hand of panic loosened just a bit. Closing her eyes tightly, she pushed hard with her tied hands. With an aching jerk, her body rolled. Her breath came in gasps as she waited for the thump and sting of a snake strike. Nothing. She rolled over again, and then again. She had to be clear of striking range now. Flat on her back, she lay panting.

Gradually her breathing slowed. She listened hard. Only the faint sounds of the night insects filtered in from the distance. The pressure points—cheek, shoulder, and hip—burned fiercely as blood returned. *I'm alive!*

She sat up very slowly. It was awkward with tied hands and feet. As she came upright, pain knifed through her head. Clenching her jaw, she sat still. Gradually the pain leveled off into a pounding headache. She'd done it! She'd moved away from the snake in spite of her fear. Suddenly she was crying from released tension. *Thank you, Lord. Thank you....*

With her tied hands, she wiped at her face. God was faithful. How had she ever doubted that? He'd helped her just now.... He'd been helping her all her life.

And He'll help you with Darren, too.

She knew it was true. That was how any marriage survived, through both people trusting God rather than clutching to their "rights" or manipulating to feel safe.

But knowing it and doing it—those were vastly different things. Could she surrender herself to the trust a serious relationship—a marriage—required? It would be harder than rolling away from a snake.

Her right arm felt dead from the shoulder down. Was it permanently damaged? Her rough breaths threatened to turn to hysterical laughter. *Permanent damage!* She could die any second. *And here I am thinking about Darren Grant.* She took a quick breath as she realized just how much she wanted to be with him. The old bubble of fear, the precipice feeling, reared up with that thought. *Help me, Lord, please.*

After a long, slow breath, she bent her head and began to chew at the ties. They were tight and difficult to get between her teeth. The life began to flow back into her right arm in flaming waves. She gasped and chewed harder, biting down against the pain.

Flashes of fear slowed her. She would jerk her head up, listening for Joan's returning footsteps. Grimly she bent her head to chew. The verse Jede had quoted to her came back: *"Be strong and of good courage; be not afraid, neither be thou dismayed; for the LORD thy God is with thee whithersoever thou goest."* Whithersoever. The archaic word made her smile. A cave in Kenya, sharing space with a mamba or two was certainly whithersoever. "God, I guess if You can be with me here, You can help me not to panic about commitment. If You bring me out of here and don't take me home to You, I'll try not to run from Darren, but to trust You with him."

A warm flush washed over her body at that idea. *With Darren.* Would he still want her after how she'd refused to be near him, basically refused to listen to his apology? She bent to chew harder on the ties. If only she could get her hands and feet untied, she might be able to feel her way out along the cave wall.

Back at Ndovu, Farah shifted uneasily on his feet. He was part of a noisy circle of people around the supper fire. One of Ibrahim's cousins and three of that man's sons, with wives and smaller children, were there as well. Everyone talked at once as they tried to make sense of the strange afternoon. Even as they spoke, the last of the light turned golden, then indigo, as the quick, tropical dusk slid into full night. The more Farah heard, the more uneasy he became.

"Joan has been good to us!" Amina gestured emphatically. "She is the one who has shown us how to fight the cholera. Even now my sister recovers. Also, Joan has given us jobs. Because of her, my husband, your son, is at Nairobi in the great school there, and we have gained wealth."

Ibrahim made a chopping motion. "This is known to everyone. It is not questioned. But we must not be foolish. To plan wisely, the counselors must know the truth. Joan was seen walking from Ambaro's banda; she carried something. What was it? You were there with her."

Amina pressed her lips together stubbornly.

"We must not be ignorant! If we do not know this, how can we plan?"

"I will tell you then, but…" Amina wrinkled her face in disgust. "There were dirty rags on the floor. Ambaro was very sick. I had cleaned the sickness from her, and Joan took some of that filth into a glass jar. She left with it. Who can know the ways of the white people?"

Horror clutched at Farah. He must have made some small sound because Ibrahim turned to him. "What is it?"

He shook his head. "Perhaps I did not understand."

"Understand what? Speak!" All of them were staring at him.

Farah could feel the sweat start on his body. "The well. Laurel said something about the well, the borehole on the Wilson. I didn't understand. Not then. Perhaps I still do not understand, but could it be that Joan was going to put cholera into the well on the Wilson?"

There was a short silence, tight as a fiddle string. One of Ibrahim's cousin's sons spoke. "Can it be so? To kill an enemy in battle, that is a good and honorable thing, but to poison water?" He made a noise of disgust and spat on the ground.

"No! It cannot be!" Ibrahim gestured emphatically. "All of you know that sometimes Joan collects the dung of the baboon troop. It is sent away to be tested for this and that. She must have done the same with this."

Amina was shaking her head. "When she left, she walked down the path to the Wilson without stopping. I saw her go."

Again there was silence. Farah felt suddenly cold. No wonder Laurel had run. Had she been able to stop Joan Doyle? Why hadn't Joan returned?

The oldest of the visitors spoke. "If it is that Joan Doyle has done this thing, it has happened with none of our help. If those squatters drink and die, then it was fated to happen. They have been enemies since the time of our father's fathers. We should not question our good fortune. Let it be."

"No!" The word burst out of Farah. The others turned to look at him. He swallowed hard. These men were his close relatives. If he alienated them, he would be outcast, alone. They were the ones who would find him a bride, help him build his life. Carefully he weighed his words. "Does Allah care only for us? Is he not merciful to all men? If we do nothing, will we not be judged also? I say that we warn them and offer them water from our well here."

Everyone spoke at once. Farah knew they would go on talking and arguing into the night until there was a consensus. He was very junior. For him to speak at all had taken all the courage in him. He said what he had to say. Maybe if he went now, he could still prevent tragedy. He backed slowly away from the group. Ibrahim's gimlet eye caught the movement. "Stop! What is it that you do?"

Farah lifted his chin. "I go to find out what has happened."

The oldest of the visitors nodded. "Go with Allah, then return to bring news."

Farah turned and ran. First he would check that Joan was not back. As he came toward her banda, he saw her slip out. For a second she stood under the light on

the front of her banda. In her hand was the unmistak-
able shape of a rifle. Farah stopped in his tracks, holding
very still lest she see him. Normally he would have
called out to her, but even at that distance, something in
her face stopped him.

She strode away. Farah followed at a distance. A thin
quarter moon was dodging in and out of the clouds. The
ground was so muddy his feet made squishing noises.
He dropped back.

Joan used a flashlight when walking at night, an
odd-looking one that she wore on her head. He'd seen it
many times, and even asked about it. She'd said she
liked it because it kept her hands free, and it was water-
proof, a caving flashlight. When she was under the light,
he'd seen that she had the thing on her head. But she
wasn't using it now.

*She has a rifle. She hopes not to be seen. What is she
doing?* Dry mouthed, he glanced back over his shoulder.
It would be good to have help with him. *No! Not until I
know more.*

Joan's shape was only a flickering shadow far ahead
on the path. The moon went behind a cloud, and Farah
lost even that tenuous contact. Breathing quietly, listening with all his might, he kept following the path. A
rushing noise in the bushes made him lift his head. *Rain!*
The night got even darker, and the rain increased to a
steady roar.

Darren searched the moon-shadowed night, doing his
best to ignore the fear stabbing at him.

As soon as the elders arrived, he had borrowed a

flashlight from Isaac. The twilight had turned to darkness before he had reached the spot where the children had last seen Laurel and Joan. He'd never tracked at night. The artificial light made things look more flat, distorted. Initially, the tracks had been clear enough. A rumble of thunder made Darren look up. *No! Rain will erase the tracks.*

He froze. "Lord, please help me find her. Protect her. Keep her safe."

The thought of Laurel being hurt hit him like a sucker punch, and he sucked air through his teeth in a quick hiss. Moving the light from one footprint to the next in a steady zigzag, he jogged down the path. The first drops of rain hit the back of his neck. He moved faster. It was no use. A flash of lightning outlined each thornbush in odd blue light. With the boom came a deluge, as if the thunder had burst the cloud. In seconds his shirt was plastered to his body. Water trickled through his hair and dripped off his nose. Drops hitting his face made him blink. The path became a tiny creek. Raindrops flashed through the cone of brightness from the flashlight, then splashed down, making the water on the path dance.

Grimly, Darren kept going. He was on a path that Laurel had followed. All he could do was hope she hadn't turned off. The Meru children had told him this path was a back way onto Ndovu. His shoes were so full of water it squirted out around his ankles at every step. The flashlight flickered and died, shorting out. If he turned his head slightly and looked out of the corners of his eyes, the path was just barely visible.

The flash of lightning outlined everything garishly

for a second, then returned him to total blackness. It had destroyed his night vision and reduced him to feeling his way. He bent and stripped off his shoes so he could better sense the contours of the ground.

A close lightning flash painted the world blue-green. In that split second he'd seen something ahead of him. *A white person, thin and tall? Joan?* He couldn't be sure. The shape had been several hundred yards away. *Is Laurel with her?* He stood still, praying for another lightning strike.

It hit so close he heard it sizzle. The crack of thunder nearly lifted him off his feet, but it had shown him what he needed to know. *Definitely Joan.* The dark shape of bushes around her could have hidden Laurel's form. He called out, but the roaring rain covered any sound. A flashlight flicked on and wavered uphill, showing him tiny glimpses of thorn and rock. She'd turned off the path.

The dim light of Joan's flashlight was blocked by an obstruction between them. In spite of the pitch blackness, Darren ran. He'd just seen where Joan had gone, and he wanted to get there while it was solidly imprinted in his memory. He skidded and slipped in the slick mud. Something sharp rammed his foot, but he charged on. Miraculously, he stayed on the path and didn't fall.

Here! She turned off somewhere near here and went uphill through the bush. Darren stopped and stared into the blackness. He wasn't at all certain if he stood at the exact place Joan had turned. The ground around the path was rough and broken, full of thorns. He wouldn't have a chance barefoot.

Jittering with the need to hurry, Darren replaced his

boots, yanking the soaking laces tight. He began to move, crouched low, hands reaching out. A ledge of rock hit his shin. He stepped up and found himself up against a wait-a-bit thorn. Iron hard, fish hook shaped thorns grabbed skin and clothing. Wait-a-bit thorns were well named. Even in the light, moving carefully, it took time to get loose without damage. He didn't have that time. He gritted his teeth and threw himself backward. Skin and clothing tore.

Picking himself off the ground, he moved a few feet and tried again to find a way up the hill. Shaking the flashlight, he tried to get it to work. Nothing! He snarled and threw the thing into the bush. He'd find Laurel if it took all night.

26

LAUREL RAN HER TONGUE OVER THE TORN SURFACE OF HER LIP. Then bent to bite at the knots again. Rope sawed at her lips, doing more damage. She explored the rope with her tongue, then bit and pulled. *I can't even tell if I'm pulling on the right piece.* It moved slightly and she redoubled her efforts. The rope around her hands suddenly slackened. *Thank you, Lord.*

But her feet were still tied. Working with swollen hands in the dark, it took almost as long to untie those knots as it had using her teeth on the rope around her wrists. Finally that rope went slack. Laurel hung her head, gasping and gathering strength for the next move.

She was in the dark, in an unknown cave, with poisonous snakes around. *Moving is stupid. But Joan will kill me if she finds me.* "Lord, You got me this far. Please get me out of here."

Taking a deep breath, she stood up. Sick and dizzy, she swayed, nearly falling. She caught her balance and wobbled forward, hands outstretched. Her left hand hit something hard. Laurel stopped, leaning on it for support and gasping in relief. She'd found the cave wall, now she had to follow it to the entrance.

A shushing sound froze her in place. *The snake!* Hardly breathing she stood motionless. No, this sound was different. A gust of damp air touched her cheek. *The sound of rain?* She stood listening with all her might. A tiny swirl of wind brought the scent—wet earth. Her hand on the cave, she started to edge into the wind.

Her hand fumbled along the wall and then hit empty space. She groped in the darkness, but the cave wall had bent away from the direction the fresh air came from. Laurel hesitated. Should she follow the cave wall, or just move into the wind? *Lord, guide me. I need to get out of here soon.* She took a slow breath, tasting the fragrance of the rain. *The wind has to come from the cave mouth.*

Laurel stepped out blindly, keeping her face in the wind. One foot dropped into a dip in the floor. She stumbled and nearly fell. A hissing noise, very close to her, brought her heart in her mouth. *That was not the rain!*

The sound had come from just ahead of her to the left. Did she dare try to move backward? No, if the snake was hissing, he'd already been disturbed. Rigid with tension, she listened, her every sense tuned to any sound. Was he moving? The sound of the rain changed; other overtones joined the shushing sound. *The snake crawling?* She couldn't be sure.

Her knees began to quiver in earnest. Sounds in the cave mouth brought her head up. *Joan. She's back!* In the cave entrance, a dim light wavered back and forth, backlighting lumps and irregularities on the cave wall and floor. *She's got a flashlight.*

Her eyes adjusted to complete blackness, Laurel could see quite well. Frantically she scanned the ground. No snake in view. She took two running steps and dived behind a low ledge at the base of the cave wall. Joan's footsteps got closer. Laurel pressed herself backward, trying to melt into the ground. *A rifle! She did get her rifle.* Joan's shadow looked huge and ghostly on the wall of the cave. It danced, looming over Laurel as Joan swung the flashlight around the cave.

Joan swore when the cone of light touched the spot where she'd left Laurel tied. Pushed tightly against the base of the cave wall, Laurel stared mesmerized as Joan swung the flashlight wildly into all corners of the cave. The light swooped above her head, just missing her. It focused again on the place she'd been tied. Laurel could see the snakeskin gleaming dully. More than that, even from where she was across the cave, Laurel could see the marks of her movement in the deep, dry dust. Her mouth was paper dry as Joan took several steps forward. The flashlight was now focused on those marks. It began to zigzag slowly as Joan followed and came inexorably toward her.

I'm going to have to make a run for it. Slowly Laurel began to double up her legs and roll over, trying to get into a position from which she could leap and run. Her knee bumped a pebble that rolled. Instantly the flashlight shone full in her face. Laurel leapt up, but blinded by the light, stiff and dizzy, she fell.

There was a loud double click, and Joan pushed a round into the rifle. Laurel hung there on her hands and knees waiting for the impact of the bullet. She had a perverse desire to yell at Joan to get it over with. Her heart was pounding painfully.

"Move!"

Laurel began to crawl toward the entrance.

"Not that way." Joan's voice was high, brittle. "You have to go back to the snake den. A bullet wound won't work. They'd want to know how it happened."

Laurel didn't move. If Joan wanted the snake to kill

her, she would be reluctant to shoot.

"Oh no, you don't. I will shoot!" The crack of the rifle slammed though the cave, making Laurel's head ring. It took her a second to realize she wasn't hurt. Only a warning shot.

"You crawl." Joan shoved the rifle barrel against her neck. Cool and hard, it bit into her skin. "Get over there. Hurry up! I've got to get your body out by the troop by morning. I can't move it in the day. The stinking Meru might see."

A hard gust of rain slapped against the side of his face. Darren had no idea where he was or where Joan had gone. He'd slipped and scrambled in the mud, fighting rocks and thorn brush to climb the bank, and still there was no sign of either Laurel or Joan. He lifted his head and bellowed, "Laurel!"

A crash of thunder drowned him out. He sank onto his haunches. Scrabbling around in the dark was nuts. *I'm not accomplishing anything besides getting myself cut up by thorns and rocks.* When the storm blew over, maybe he'd be able to see enough to move intelligently. He lifted his head into the rain and let it pour down his face as if it could wash the frustration out of him. *Just give me another chance with Laurel, and please let her be okay, Lord.*

Another crash jerked his head around. That wasn't thunder! That was the crack of a high-powered rifle. It was close! Before he realized what he was doing, Darren was on his feet fighting his way toward the sound. *In the hill! Almost under me.* Joan had gone into a cave.

Through the tangled branches of a bush, he saw a

faint flush of yellow light dimly outlining a twisting hole in the hill. Not bothering to find an easy way, he bulled his way through the two-inch thorns of that bush. It slowed him enough to make him think. He came down the passage carefully, his feet silent in the deep dust.

The noise of the storm diminished. Joan's voice carried clearly in the still air. "The next bullet won't be in the roof. It will be straight into your head, Laurel Binet!"

She's attacking Laurel! He charged forward. The scene would be imprinted in his mind forever. Laurel was on her hands and knees. Joan stood with the rifle pressed into Laurel's neck.

The first thing Laurel knew of Darren's presence was a snarl, much like that of the leopard. His torn shirt showing a muscular torso, his mouth open in a threatening roar, Darren literally flew through the air at Joan.

Laurel's voice tore out of her throat, "Watch out! She has a rifle!"

It was too late. Joan brought the long shape up. The crack of it firing smacked through the confined space. Darren staggered but kept coming; his body slammed into Joan, the blur of his fist cracked her hard under the jaw. The light swung wildly at the cave roof. There was a sharp double thud, the smack of metal on rock, then silence.

"Darren!" He lay terrifyingly still in the dim light. Forgetting the snake...forgetting Joan...forgetting her own injuries, Laurel scrambled forward to kneel beside him. He was partly on his right side but twisted, laying almost face up. Her hands fluttered across his body.

"God, please help him to be okay!" She had to see more clearly. Laurel took two steps and yanked the flashlight off Joan's head. The woman moaned and moved slightly.

*If she wakes up...*Laurel sucked air through her teeth. She didn't have time for this! *But I can't leave her loose. She's already half conscious.* She shoved the flashlight onto her own head and yanked Joan's belt off. Pulling Joan's arms behind her back, she reached for Joan's feet with her other hand, wound the belt twice around her ankles and wrists, jerked it tight, and fastened the buckle. Not very secure, but she was in a hurry.

She shone the light on Darren. A glistening flash of red showed that blood slicked his upper torso. Her head spun as she moved to his side again. He was so bloody! Laurel put her hand on his neck. She felt his warm skin and found a pulse. His eyes were shut, long lashes over lean, brown cheeks.

She grabbed his shirt with both hands and tore it open. A button pinged off her forehead. The bullet hole looked so small. It was just above his left collarbone. *He won't die, not from that wound. Not unless he bleeds to death.* She had to get help.

Her eyes flew to his face—and her heart jumped. His eyes were open! "Darren?" Her voice was a cracked whisper.

He grinned crookedly. "You can rip up my clothes anytime."

That destroyed what little composure she had left, and she burst into tears. "I thought you were dead!"

He made a small noise in his throat and pulled her close with his good arm. The flashlight bumped his forehead, glaring in his eyes. His kiss landed all askew on her temple. "Give me that thing." His hand slid up the back of her head and pushed the flashlight to the ground.

His mouth came over hers. Discomfort, pain, fear, any awareness of her surroundings—all disappeared in the passion that poured through that kiss. Bonelessly, she sank down beside him, feeling the reassuring warmth of his solid strength all along her side. He rolled over so she was cradled in his arms, half under him. Something warm and sticky dripped on her face. With her whole body humming to his kisses, it took her a second to focus on that, then she struggled. He made hushing noises and rained quick kisses along her neck that threatened to melt her all over again. She fought for focus. "You're bleeding all over my face."

"So?" He bent to kiss her again, the stubble of his beard rough against her neck. "What's a little blood between friends?"

"But Joan, she—"

"Joan!" Darren went rigid and sat up abruptly. He fumbled for the flashlight, swept the light over the cave, and held it on Joan, focusing on her bound feet. "You did that?"

Caught in the light, Joan lay perfectly still. Laurel stared. *She's not in the same position and...* "Her hands are loose!"

Joan lunged toward the rifle. As she moved, something slid aside with a quick, fluid movement that caught Laurel's eye. She focused on that spot and saw the snake. It fled a few feet, then reared defensively, poised to strike. Darren was struggling to his feet, heading for

Joan. The mamba was between them.

"No! The snake!" Darren hesitated, and Laurel lunged forward to grab at him. "There. It's there! The mamba. She wanted it to kill me!"

The light from the flashlight made quick searching swings and stopped on the mamba. Dark olive, almost as black as the darkness behind, it gleamed dully, swaying. Completely oblivious, Joan continued to hitch her way closer to the rifle, and to the snake. Cursing them at the top of her lungs, she jerked forward, kicking at the belt around her feet.

"Joan. Hold still!" Darren's bellow made Laurel's head ring. Joan was only inches from the rifle. She grabbed at it and rolled to face them. Laurel felt Darren's body bend, then jerk as he threw something hard. Even while the rock he had thrown was in the air, the snake struck, hitting the stock of the rifle. Joan screamed, and Darren's rock smacked into the ground, driving an explosion of dust into the air.

A quick gleam of dark liquid movement fled from the dust. Darren kept the light on the snake until it disappeared in another puff of dust behind a rock fifteen yards away.

"Joan, are you hit? Did it strike twice?" Darren's voice was amazingly steady.

"I don't know!"

"Throw the rifle away so we can come help you."

Joan swore on a sobbing gasp, and the rifle flew out of the dust cloud, creating another of its own as it hit. Laurel could just see Joan, eyes shut and paper pale, lying flat on her back covered in dust. Laurel made a small noise of sympathy and rushed to Joan. Darren stood above her, feet planted, with the rifle firmly in hand. He'd put the flashlight on his head so she couldn't see his face. He loomed out of the dust fog, tall, solid…bloody.

"Darren, I don't know anything about snake bite. What do I do?"

"Check her eyes. If she's been bitten, they won't respond to light properly." He kept searching the area around them with the flashlight, then shone it on Joan's face. "There's not much we can do here if she is bitten. She'll be dead in less than five minutes. She knows that."

As gently as she could, Laurel pushed Joan's eyelid open. The pupil was huge, but it contracted quickly in the light. "It looked okay. But why…"

"Fear that you'll be dead in a few minutes can do that to a person." Darren raised his voice. "Joan, listen to me. We don't think you've been bitten. If you had, you could feel it. Is anyplace on you numb, burning, or hurting?"

Joan was still for a minute, then she shook her head. "I don't think so." Her chest rose and fell in a deep gasp, but she made no attempt to sit up. Darren switched the light's focus from Joan to Laurel.

"Hey!" She shielded her eyes with one hand.

"The blood on your face isn't only mine, is it? Let me see." He crouched beside her and turned her gently until the light shone on the place Joan had hit her with a rock. "That's ugly. We've got to get you help."

"Me? You're the one who just got shot." She'd put her hands over Darren's and held them tightly. "You've got to be hurting worse than I am."

"In that case, let's stagger out of here together." He chuckled. "And I thought you weren't tough enough for Africa."

Her whole body jerked as she suddenly remembered. "Darren! Joan put cholera in the well. Did Jede get the note and stop them from using the well?"

Shock registered in his narrowed eyes. "So that's what it was about." He shook his head. "I can't believe even Joan would go so far." Laurel wrung her hands together. "We've got to warn the people. You stay here with Joan and I'll go."

"I left Isaac guarding the well. Your note got to Jede."

The relief that swept her threatened to buckle Laurel's knees. "Oh, thank God. Then she stopped them."

"For now, but without knowing why, it won't be easy to keep people away from the water."

"Then we have to get back there!" Laurel's voice was close to a wail.

"Right." He jerked Joan to her feet none too gently. She didn't resist. Her face looked blank in the uncertain light.

"Are you sure she's not snake bit?"

"She'd be convulsing. Mamba poison is a neurotoxin."

Outside, fresh, cool wind met them. With the rough footing and dim light, it was all she could do to stay on her feet. The moon shone through ragged rents in the cloud cover. Prodding Joan down the slope ahead of him, Darren slipped in the mud and fell. The grunt of pain and the slowness with which he got to his feet spoke volumes, but he kept the rifle out of the mud and pointed at Joan. Laurel's head was pounding, and she felt as if her legs belonged to a different person.

Once on the path, the going was a bit better. Laurel's

head spun. *If Darren can do it, I can.* The path widened. There was an uneven ledge of rock on one side.

"Sit down." Darren waved the rifle at Joan. "You too, Laurel. You're weaving on your feet."

"But we have to hurry." She was seeing double.

"And having you pass out will help? Sit."

She sat and bent over waiting for the dizziness to recede. As soon as the worst of it passed, she looked up. Darren's torn shirt hung open to the waist. His chest was slicked with new blood. The fall had obviously restarted the bleeding. "Darren, let's put a pressure bandage on that. You're losing too much blood."

He grinned at her. "Feeling a bit better now?"

"Yes, and you need help. Sit down. Joan isn't going anywhere."

"And how do you know that?" He insisted on staying on his feet, focusing on Joan, but he did let Laurel rip up his shirt to make a bandage. Under her hands she could feel that he was shivering in long spasms.

Joan muttered something just as Laurel finished tying the pressure pad in place. Head and hands hanging limply, the woman sat there like a dropped puppet.

"What did you say?"

Joan lifted her head and looked at them tiredly. "I said, you should have let the snake kill me."

"Joan. No!" Laurel reached out to her.

"Why not? I tried to kill you." She made a chopping motion with her hand and raised her voice. "The mamba should have struck you. You're the one who is betraying Ndovu."

"She's not betraying anything." Darren kept his eyes on Joan, rifle ready in his good hand. Each word was carefully articulated with a pause between, as if he was finding it difficult to talk. "If any wild land is to be saved, we've got to do it God's way." He swayed on his feet, then sank down onto his heels, crouching like the Somali men.

"Darren!" *He must have lost more blood than I thought.* "I'll go get help." She turned to run.

If he passes out, Joan could get the rifle and— Laurel stopped herself with a jerk. The sound of running footsteps continued. Someone called Joan's name in the darkness, and Farah pelted into view.

He skidded to a stop, staring from one to the other. "Eeeeeh!"

"Farah! Go for help. Darren has lost too much blood, and tell Isaac we are sure the well has been contaminated with cholera."

Farah hissed through his teeth. "Then it is true. Joan Doyle, you have done this thing?"

She lifted her head and looked at him. Her eyes were very tired, and she said nothing.

He didn't move but watched them carefully, eyes questioning.

"Hurry, Farah! Tell them Darren is hurt. He needs a doctor." Still Farah hesitated. Laurel ran at him, making shooing movements with her hands. "Go. Hurry!"

Farah nodded, turned on his heel, and ran with an effortless floating stride. Laurel turned back to Darren. "You've got to lie down and get your head low. Quit moving. You're bleeding too much. Give me the rifle. I'll watch Joan."

"You know how to use one?"

"As if I'd study bears without knowing."

He gave her a tired smile and held out the rifle. "Here you go." Sighing, he lay down. She shifted the weight of the rifle from one hand to the other. She wanted desperately to put it down and see what she could do for Darren, but Joan was watching with a look Laurel didn't like at all. The woman started to stand.

"Sit still!" Laurel put every ounce of authority she could find into her voice, and still it shook.

Joan sat and stared at her. Laurel glanced at Darren. He was lying quietly. She looked back at Joan, who was still staring at her. The odd thing was that Joan didn't really look hostile. She stared as if she were trying to see into Laurel's soul. She stared back, almost mesmerized. Joan's voice made her jump.

"Do you intend to keep Ndovu wild?" Joan's eyes were intent.

"If I can, by God's grace, I will. But Joan—" She made a frustrated movement with her free hand. "Everything is going to be different now that you—"

"Yes." Joan's voice was flat. "It is." She stood up and turned to walk away.

"Stop!" With shaking hands, Laurel toggled the safety button and lifted the rifle.

Joan looked back over her shoulder. "Shoot me then. When the news of what happened tonight gets out, I'm finished anyway. Already I was barely welcome in Kenya. I have nothing else. This is my life." She kept going down the moon-silvered path.

Laurel held the sights on Joan's back. *I can't!* She pointed the barrel down and fired into the earth. Joan ran. Laurel dropped the rifle and ran after her. Within twenty feet, it was obvious that Joan was getting away.

Laurel's head swam, and she kept stumbling. She finally dropped to her knees, gasping for breath and nearly sobbing with frustration. Joan had gotten away. Darren was going to be upset. Her body jerked. He must have heard the gunshot. What if he tried to get up?

She forced herself onto her feet and started back. He met her halfway, rifle in hand, looming large in the moonlight. He dropped the rifle and hugged her tight against him. "You're okay?"

"I'm okay, but—"

"I love you." The words were a whisper. Darren's knees buckled, and suddenly his full weight was on her shoulders. She sank down with him.

"Darren?" He didn't answer. Frantically she felt for a pulse. It was there, but too fast. Using all her strength, she rolled him over. The wound was bleeding again. With both hands she put pressure on the opening. Tears streamed down her cheeks.

He loved her. Darren Grant…*loved* her! Her breath came in ragged sobs as waves of emotion washed over her—joy, gratitude, terror, uncertainty—each rolled over her, leaving her spent, uncertain.

She touched Darren's still face, traced his cheek with trembling fingers. He *loved* her…and now. She blinked back tears.

Now he was lying here, unconscious.

Oh, God, why did You let me come to Africa? Darren could die. And it would be my fault, Lord! The nearest doctor was probably in Nairobi, and it was too muddy for a plane to land. Laurel had never felt so alone in her life. The spinning in her head was getting worse. She swayed to one side, and her hands slipped off the wound.

Grimly she hauled herself upright. *I've got to keep the bleeding stopped. I won't let him die! I won't!* Her fists closed on the pad of cloth, and she pressed them down to maintain pressure on the wound. Her cheek dropped onto Darren's chest. The ground and sky seemed to tip and whirl drunkenly around them. Her last coherent thought was a prayer for Darren to live.

27

LAUREL STARED AT THE CEILING. IT WAS SMOOTH AND WHITE. The electric light in the center had one of those flat, frosted glass covers with flowers on it. *Where am I? A bedroom in someone's house?* Blearily she tried to bring things into focus…and she sat up with a jerk.

Darren! Did he bleed to death? Pain shot through her. She swayed but stayed upright, waiting for the dizziness to fade.

"Hello? Is anyone here?" No one answered. Shakily she climbed out of bed. She had on someone else's flannel nightgown. It was too big and trailed on the polished concrete floor. The room swam. Laurel clutched the bed, but the room kept spinning. Pain hammered her head. She sank down on the bed and shut her eyes until the pain began to recede.

She could remember people's hands picking her up. Being carried and then…*A helicopter? Can that be right?* But where was Darren? "Hello? Please, is anyone here?" This time there was the sound of footsteps. The door opened, and a gray-haired African man peered around the corner.

"Eeeeh, memsabu. Pole, pole." He said something else in Swahili about fetching someone. At least that's what she thought he said, but her numb brain wasn't translating very well. He went out, firmly closing the door behind him.

"Wait!" Tears sprang to her eyes. The door did not open again. She shut her eyes and took a deep breath, trying to calm herself. *Darren! What if he's dead?* Crying hurt, but she couldn't stop. The tears kept coming until she fell asleep again.

Laurel dreamed that it was time for school and Lilith was calling her. Lilith *was* calling her! Laurel blinked and tried to focus on the pale oval of her mother's face. A thin hand stroked her cheek. "I'm so sorry, honey."

Sorry? Is Darren dead then? "Lilith, how...? What...?"

"Reverend Grant called me at the hotel. He told me you had quite a bad concussion. To think that Joan Doyle would try to kill—" She groped for Laurel's hand. "You're going to be okay. We're at the Grants' house. They put you in the master bedroom. They're nice people, not at all what I would have expected missionaries to be like. They've dealt with this very well."

Dealt with what? Their son's death? Laurel's throat closed. *I have to know.* She tried to interrupt and frame the question, but the words wouldn't come. Lilith was talking fast, as if to prevent any questions.

"I've been doing some work for you. Before you woke up, I spoke on the phone to that man, the one who runs the primate research place. No way am I going to let one crazy woman stop my daughter's dreams. Anyway, the man wanted money for his research institute, said that will open doors for our foundation. When I sounded like I might do things his way, he got really friendly. He said if the elders from Ndovu and the Wilson agree, he thinks our foundation idea could still work."

"Could still work?"

Lilith nodded. "I just thought that might encourage

you. I'm not supposed to tire you, so I'll go."

"Wait!" Laurel grabbed Lilith's hand. "What happened? How did I get here? Is D—" Her throat tightened and choked off her question.

"They brought you here by helicopter. The one that came in with the cholera vaccine. When you're feeling better, you can hear the whole story. But for now, I won't trouble you with the harsher bits."

The harsher bits. Laurel's throat was as rigid as iron.

Lilith patted her hand, then reached for something on the bedside table. "I almost forgot. Dr. Grant gave me these pills for you."

Laurel put one in her mouth at her mother's insistence, but she couldn't swallow. Her throat was too tight. Water and pill stayed in her mouth. Lilith patted her hand and stood up. "Now you rest and get better. You and I may have a foundation to set up." Laurel watched the door shut behind her mother. *Darren said he loves me, but I never...I never got the chance to tell him how I feel. Oh, please, God, he can't be dead.*

Tears flowed, warm streaks that ran into her ears. *I can't do it. Not alone for the rest of my life, Lord. Let him be okay. I don't care if we don't agree on everything. I don't care if I get hurt sometimes. I love him.*

She hadn't deliberately swallowed it, but the pill in her mouth must have dissolved anyway. She slid into dark dreams. Laurel didn't wake until much later in the day when Lilith came in bringing soup. She was full of plans for the foundation. Twice Laurel started to speak, determined to ask about Darren. Both times, Lilith cut in, not allowing her to say anything. *She is. She's hiding it from me.* Laurel couldn't force herself to try again

Once more, the medicine put her to sleep. She woke in the still darkness before dawn. Her whole body ached. So did her heart. *Lord, the animals…the foundation…none of it matters if Darren is gone. Please, let him be okay.* She took a shaky breath and spoke aloud as if speech could hold off the darkness. "I don't actually know what happened. He might be okay."

She set her teeth and tried to stop the feeling of panic. She willed the words of the verse in Joshua through her head: *"Be strong and of good courage; be not afraid, neither be thou dismayed; for the LORD thy God is with thee, whithersoever thou goest."*

As clearly as though a steadying hand gripped her arm, she felt a calming presence. She took a deep breath and let it out slowly. God had kept her safe in that cave. He would be with her now. She laid her life in His hands. "If Darren is dead, I'm Yours. If he's alive and You want us together, I'm Yours. The foundation is Yours, too. I can't do any of this by myself. I need You, Father."

Her throat closed, and she had to wait a moment before she could go on. "I want so much to be with Darren, for us to find our way together. Help me not to be afraid. To trust You, with him or without him."

The hush of the night was full of comfort. Laurel lay still, in a kind of suspended peace, and waited for the dawn. Eventually, faint light flushed the window, then turned from pearl gray to gold. People began to move in the rest of the house. She could hear them talking. Laurel got out of bed. She felt as empty as a whistle with the wind blowing through and strangely light, but the room didn't spin around her.

Her reflection in the little mirror over the dresser

jerked her to a halt. Her hair stuck up in filthy clumps all around a bloodstained bandage. One eye was ringed with deep purple. Both were swollen from crying. Laurel touched her hair. It was stiff with old blood. She grimaced, and the effect of that on her amazingly altered face was bizarre.

Someone knocked at the door. *Lilith.* "Come in. Look at…"

Darren walked in, pale under his tan and with one arm in a sling. Laurel staggered backward and plopped on the bed.

"You're not dead?" Her voice came out in a squeak.

"Dead?" He stopped in his tracks, then shook his head, eyes twinkling. "Not so I'd noticed."

"But Lilith said—" She choked and burst into tears, covering her face with her hands.

The bed dipped as Darren sat beside her. His strong arm came around her. "Hey, take it easy. I'm fine. See?" He tried to turn her head toward him, but she resisted so that his kiss landed on her ear.

Her words came out in jerks. "You were losing so much blood, and then nobody talked about you, and your parents weren't here, and Lilith was hiding something, and I thought—" She gulped. Her nose was running, and she had no tissue. She twisted away from him and stumbled to grab the tissue box on the dresser. "Sorry. Sorry." She mopped at her face.

Darren followed and held her tight. This time she didn't resist. He stood like a rock, holding her. The weight of his arm around her, the feel of his strength surrounding her was wonderful. Gradually, the gasping sobs ceased. She turned her face into him, breathing in his warmth. For a long time they stood like that.

And there, sheltered in his arms, Laurel knew as she'd known little else in her life that this was the man she wanted to spend her life with. She leaned against him, very much at rest.

He lifted her face and kissed her lightly, then smiled and touched her hair. "You look amazing."

"I know. I'd just discovered my reflection in the mirror when you knocked. I'm so glad you're alive." She hesitated. "Darren, what was Lilith trying to hide from me?"

"Joan tried to kill herself." His eyes were gentle on hers.

"Tried?"

He nodded. "From what Dad told me, Ibrahim turned up all in a panic just as they were flying us out. He'd found her badly hurt. Apparently after Joan left us, she went back to the compound at Ndovu, left a note for Ibrahim, and took the stallion. Ibrahim followed when he found the note and saw the stallion coming back riderless. He backtracked and found Joan. She'd jumped off the cliff near the big fig tree."

"But is she going to be okay?"

"She should live, if that's what you mean. She's going to be flown out to Europe. Joan will have a long time healing and may be crippled. In the note, she turned the operation at Ndovu over to you."

"She what?"

He smiled. "I guess you made an impression. Joan is a very troubled woman."

"That's for sure, but can she even do that?"

"I don't know."

Laurel shook her head. "There's something I need to tell you. When I was tied up in that cave, I realized some things. I've been running on fear for years, trying to protect myself. Afraid I'd end up hurt and alone like Lilith. I've been using my work with animals and nature as a shield."

"Your shield opened some doors for me that had been shut tight way too long. I'd closed myself off from spending time in nature or with animals, had it down as a distracting but seductive waste of time. You opened my eyes, set me free to enjoy it again and work to save God's creatures as well as His people. I thank you. But more than that—" his hand closed tightly over hers—"Laurel Binet, I love you very much. I know you've been afraid, and I'm sorry I was so clumsy and made it harder for you."

"It wasn't your fault. That was only an excuse to run from you. I didn't want to love you, but…" She leaned against his shoulder. "I've changed my mind."

He made a small noise in his throat, and his arm tightened around her. "I'll do my best not to hurt you, Laurel. Not ever. And I'm going to do this right." In one swift movement he was on his knees in front of her. "Laurel, will you be my wife?"

Laurel sank onto the edge of the bed, her eyes on Darren who was still kneeling. "Yes." The word came out in a whisper, then louder, "Yes! I will. By God's grace." She laughed.

Then he was beside her, his lips on hers in a long kiss that made her dizzy in a way that had nothing to do with her head injury. They ended with his good arm around her and her head leaning on his chest. She suddenly laughed. "I know you must really love me, if you propose when I look like a war victim."

"We'll have to get engagement pictures and keep them on the mantle to show our kids." The dimples were back in his cheeks.

She touched one gently. "And to remind us that God can bring us through the tough times. Whatever comes, we'll be together."

He nodded, his eyes so tender she wanted to weep. "Together. You, me, and God." His smile warmed her like the African sun on a summer day. "Now *that* sounds like a team that can take on anything."

As he lowered his head to kiss her, Laurel couldn't have agreed more.

❧ Epilogue ❧

LAUREL WALKED AROUND THE CORNER OF THE PRIMARY SCHOOL building they'd built on the Wilson. She'd never worked as hard in her life as she had over the last two years. *We did it together, by God's grace.* Fire scars still showed on the cinder block, and she traced the outline of one with her finger.

The sound of the plane broke the stillness. *He's back!* She ran out into the open, waving with her whole body, unable to contain the joy that filled her at the thought of seeing him again.

Darren. Her love.

Her husband.

Darren swept low over Ndovu, the contour of the land as familiar as his own hand. *I'm home.* The little tourist lodge flashed under his wings. Figures ran out of the high school, waving. His eyes darted over them. Laurel's familiar figure wasn't there. He continued over the Wilson. *There she is.* A burst of gladness made his skin tingle. He wobbled the wings of the plane in response to her wild waving. Face creased in a huge smile, he circled to land.

Laurel dropped her hands and ran for the airstrip. She'd walked down to the Wilson, so she had no vehicle. The plane disappeared below the bush, wheels and flaps down. She pushed herself harder. Ibrahim would bring the Jeep to the hangar at the far end of the strip, and she wanted to be there first.

She burst out of the bush to see their two-year-old King Air plane taxiing toward her, not the hangar. Laurel smiled and stood, arms open wide, waiting in the wind. She blinked. *He's got passengers.*

The propellers stopped rotating. Darren leaped out and swept her into his arms, spinning her around. She twined her fingers behind the strong muscles of his neck and laughed, then his mouth came down on hers and time stopped.

"Now that's what I call a welcome home," an unfamiliar voice said, chuckling.

They broke apart, but Darren kept his arm around her waist. A bald man with a nice smile was watching them. Laurel tried to smooth her hair.

"Laurel, I'd like you to meet Dr. Victor Brown, the head of the department of biology at Livingstone College."

The man shook her hand. "It's a pleasure to meet the woman behind Livingstone College's newest affiliate."

"Affiliate?" She looked at Darren. "We're affiliated with Livingstone College?"

Both men were grinning, nodding. Laurel threw herself into Darren's arms. "You did it!"

Laughing, he spun her around once and put her down again. "God and the powers that be at Livingstone had something to do with it."

Laurel turned. "Dr. Brown, I'm so happy." She took both his hands. "I'm sorry if I'm acting crazy, but it's been so hard. Missions and churches didn't want affiliation because, with the animal study and wild land, we didn't fit into any of their categories. World Wildlife Fund and the secular universities didn't want links because of our openly Christian stance. We can't do this alone."

He squeezed her hands. "Call me Vic, and don't apologize. We're glad to be working with you too."

"I can't believe it. A school like Livingstone, known everywhere for academic excellence and Christian commitment is working with us." She threw out her arms. "Praise God!" Then she turned on Darren. "Why didn't you call or e-mail me?"

"I wanted to be with you when you heard." He touched her on the tip of the nose. "I couldn't miss that first hug, could I? And besides, I only knew yesterday, after the meeting they asked one of us to attend."

She took Darren's hand, his familiar, warm, callused fingers cradled hers. She held tightly and turned back to Vic Brown. "See, we need prayer support, help recruiting, academic accountability, and affiliation for the schools and for the study, and—"

"Hey, don't drown Vic all at once."

Vic laughed. "Don't worry. We'll have to talk through some ideas, maybe starting a summer science station here, providing opportunities to volunteer at the clinic for premed students interested in mission medicine."

"Yes!" Laurel laughed. "That sounds so good, and you decided to do it in spite of the trouble here. I was so scared you were going to back off."

"You mean the attacks from some of the more militant Somali?" Vic nodded. "Darren told us about it. We'll make it an urgent matter for prayer."

She looked up to meet Darren's gold-streaked and smiling eyes and gave a little hop of pure joy. *He's back.* He'd only been gone two weeks, but it had felt like forever. Darren kept her hand firmly in his as they showed Dr. Brown over the compound at Ndovu. The afternoon was warm across their shoulders as they came to the guest banda.

What is this man going to think of us? Laurel cleared her throat. "I didn't know when you were coming in, so people are busy. Is tomorrow soon enough to meet everyone? Not that there are that many, but—"

Vic held up a hand. "Don't apologize. I think you've done very well, considering how isolated you are. In fact, I'm impressed. Tomorrow is certainly soon enough for me. I'm just as happy to turn in for an afternoon siesta and leave you two alone." He looked from one to the other, his eyes twinkling. "Which I don't think will be a hardship for either of you."

Darren laughed and put his arm around her shoulders. "Have a good rest."

"I'll do that." He waved and went inside.

Darren bent and kissed her forehead gently. Together they walked the sun-baked path toward their own banda; the same one Laurel had stayed in her first season in Africa.

Darren looked down at her. "You know, we've been so busy with everything that I've never built you a better house."

She laughed and slid her arm around behind him. "I couldn't care less if we lived in a tree. Being with you is home to me."

They stepped out of the sunlight through the door

of the banda, and Darren swept her into his arms. "I love you, Laurel Grant, my very own animal woman."

She leaned her cheek against his chest and let out a long sigh of contentment. She was exactly where she belonged, with her man under God's African skies.

Dear Reader,

Kenya was my home from when I was four years old until I was eighteen. I've been back several times, but never for long. *African Skies* made me realize again just how much Kenya will always be a part of me.

Writing *African Skies* was a stretching experience, more so than I expected. Through Laurel and Darren, I revisited things I've struggled with and found out the issues weren't as settled for me as I'd thought. It's amazing how God keeps us learning. Like Laurel and Darren, I've struggled to find a way to spend my life effectively for God and His kingdom. It's not always easy. That's why writing their story was a joy to me. I could show the way they found to serve God together. I hope that you'll be encouraged to find the ways God has for you and those you love to serve Him.

As always, I love to hear from my readers. Feel free to write me at:

Karen Rispin
c/o Palisades
P.O. Box 1720
Sisters, OR 97759
E-mail: pkrispin@telusplanet.net
Web site: www.therispins.com

Thanks again for letting me share Laurel and Darren's story.
Sincerely,

Excitement, adventure, breathtaking romance—Linda Windsor has it all!

The Amazon wasn't at all what Jenna Marsten expected....

Jenna had come to this wild, exotic land of danger and wonder with one goal: to find the father she'd thought was dead. But the jungle has a mind of its own, and what she encounters there is a world beyond anything she imagined. For all its lush, tropical beauty, the rain forest is far from Eden—especially when it's inhabited by her father's partner, the ruggedly handsome Dr. Adam DeSanto. If ever there were a man in dire need of an attitude adjustment, it's Adam.

ISBN 1-57673-445-5

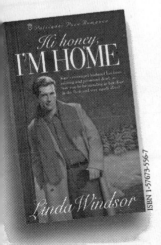

ISBN 1-57673-556-7

Kate's estranged husband has been missing and presumed dead....

Kate finds herself face-to-face with her supposedly deceased husband! An obsessive journalist, Nick was reportedly killed in a terrorist attack five years ago, but there he stands, ready to take up where they left off. Well, she's not interested. But Nick and their precocious boys are determined to prove to her that God has truly changed Nick's heart.

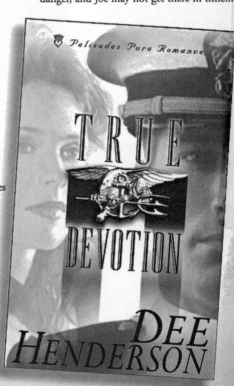